THE DESTINY MASK

Martin Sketchley

LONDON • SYDNEY • NEW YORK • TORONTO

First published in Great Britain by Simon & Schuster, 2005
This edition first published by Pocket Books, 2006
An imprint of Simon & Schuster UK Ltd
A CBS COMPANY

1 3 5 7 9 10 8 6 4 2

Simon & Schuster UK Ltd
Africa House
64–78 Kingsway
London WC2B 6AH

www.simonsays.co.uk

Simon & Schuster Australia
Sydney

A CIP catalogue record for this book is available from the British Library

ISBN 0 7434 6844 9
EAN 9780743468442

Printed and bound in Great Britain by
Cox & Wyman Ltd, Reading, Berks

Acknowledgements

A huge thank you, once again to:

John Parker and Joshua Bilmes, for hard work and guidance.

The entire cast at Simon & Schuster, particularly (in order of appearance): Ben Ball, Melissa Weatherill, Sue Stephens and Emma Noel.

Anne Glennon, for help with childcare while deadlining.

To all those friends who gave support and encouragement during difficult times.

And especially to Rosaleen, as ever.

To Daniel and Orla

more than a father could wish for

It could be said that what I am now is simply a purer form of what I have always been. That my current state is the culmination of all that has gone before. An affirmation of my worth and determination. A reward. And yet, although in one sense I have become all I ever wanted to be, attained the status I so fervently sought, still I feel incomplete.

Such harsh reality.

But I accepted the risks involved as I strove to achieve that which I so desperately desired. And thus I know that I can lay blame for my situation at the door of no other. Even if I were able to convince myself that my actions had not affected the course of my life, that this was a preordained conclusion, and that the struggles faced and decisions made were all a futile waste of time and effort, I am able to recall the events that brought me to this point with the absolute clarity my condition allows. It is a curse.

In truth, I know with certainty now that, despite all that has happened or will happen in times to come, I can change nothing. Whether to be comforted or dismayed by this, I cannot decide.

Translated from original Seriattic transcripts of the
conchey trinzig diasii

One

the stymphalian birds

Aboard the *Lex Talionis*, Atlantic Ocean

Alexander Delgado opened his eyes and remembered the day he died. Every time he woke he was transported back to that day twenty-two years before, back when the war – his war – was just beginning. Deep within the *Lex Talionis*, the memory of the all-consuming void opening before him was as real now as then. When he had opened his eyes the first thing he noticed was the layer of powder, covering the floor like grey velvet. His nostrils were clogged with bitter, metallic-smelling grit. Slowly, he had raised his head.

The chamber of General William Myson, Structure's Commander Supreme, had been a scene of devastation, filled with rubble, debris, toppled marble pillars, chunks of stone. The appalled silence that follows all such catastrophes was particularly vivid. The chaos of the scene was a stark contrast to the elegance and serenity of Myson's chamber on Delgado's last, formal visit.

He, Bucky and Ashala – back when they had known her only as Girl – had fought their way in, trying to reach the Seriattic *conosq* Vourniass Lycern, before she gave birth to Delgado's son. Lycern had been the assigned bearer to the Seriattic Royal Household, key to Myson's plans to obtain an heir to the position of Monosiell on Seriatt to enable his arms deals with the Sinz to continue. They were just components in Myson's political, greed-motivated machinations. He cared nothing for Lycern or the child; the child Myson believed was his own.

Desperate to rectify mistakes and save Lycern and the child from Myson's perverse grip, Delgado, Bucky and Ash had faced insurmountable odds. Delgado, shot by cyborgs within Myson's chamber, had managed to cling on to life until he heard his child's cries, only then allowing himself to slip into unconsciousness and apparent death.

Yet later, he had heard the conversation between Bucky and Ashala quite clearly: his child was safe. Believing Delgado dead, they had escaped with the infant in Myson's flier.

Despite his injuries, Delgado recovered quickly, and in the calm moments following the aircraft's departure he gingerly placed his left palm on the gritty floor, grimacing as he pushed himself up onto all fours. Slowly, carefully, Delgado stood. Sweating and slightly breathless, he looked down at his chest where there was little evidence of the wounds he knew he had sustained. His tunic was torn and bloodstained and appeared to be glistening slightly, but that was all. He probed his chest gently with the fingertips of his right hand. It seemed normal. He felt slightly sick and light-headed, and there was an occasional lance of heat and pain in his chest, but between these momentary shards of discomfort there was only a mild tingling sensation.

Then he had seen the cyborg lying around twenty metres away, apparently crushed against one of the marble pillars by the flier as it had crashed into the building. Around its shattered body was a sheet of dark blood that seemed to glisten like frost. The sparkling substance trailed across the floor to where Delgado had lain, its sheen becoming more evident where the cyborg's blood merged with his own. And then he had understood. Unable to repair the cyborg, in the face of their own death the very latest evolution had demonstrated the instinct of self-preservation, escaping their host and merging within Delgado's own nobics. Then they had set about repairing his body before it decayed, creating a new environment for themselves. The faint sensation of pins and needles he felt indicated that the nobics were still working within him, repairing and reorganising cells, regenerating fluids and membranes, giving him strength.

Then Delgado remembered discovering Lycern's body. Partially crushed by falling masonry, her face remained obscured by the marble column that had collapsed across one half of the bed on which she lay. But from the single wound to her abdomen it was clear that she had been killed before that, during the moments of his unconsciousness. The charred flesh around the wound still radiated heat. Overwhelmed by grief, frustration and anger, he had no one to blame but himself for what had happened. He had lost sight of or turned away from so much of importance. The *corniss* fur beneath her thighs was darkly stained following the birth of the child she had been carrying. His child.

There had been no sign of Myson, but whether this was because the general had left before the flier had crashed into the chamber, or because he was buried somewhere in the devastation, Delgado did not at that time know.

He turned, and through the window had seen the flier between the black shapes of the gigantic habitat towers, a speck climbing through turbulent layers of grey cloud on twin plumes of waste product. Bucky and Ashala were aboard it, he knew.

As was his newborn son.

His strength growing with every passing moment, Delgado had staggered to the huge, broken window, the wind coursing around him like warm breath. Looking down he had seen a flier platform on a lower level where a diplomatic vessel was being prepared for departure. As a hatch opened on the vessel's side to allow an automatic laden with water cells to enter,

Delgado had spotted his opportunity to escape, and chase Bucky, Ash and his son.

Now, so many years later he was in the heart of the *Lex Talionis*. He sat up on the bunk and swung his feet around. He leaned forward, resting his forearms on his thighs. He sighed and massaged his forehead and temples with his fingertips. This was another day, another raid, flying seat-of-the-pants escort to a small flock of lumbering bombers that would attempt to drop tiny bombs on insignificant Structure targets. Such gnat-bite attacks were all they were capable of. They did little harm to Structure, but gave the group some focus. At least that was the idea. Given that they had to use whatever ageing technology they could get their hands on or adapt to their purposes, they didn't do too badly.

Abruptly, the door to his left opened. Cascari entered the room and stood in the doorway. 'We'll be reaching the surface soon. You ready?'

Delgado nodded. 'Sure,' he said. 'Just give the old man a minute.' He looked at his son for a moment. Cascari seemed to have changed each time he saw him, becoming taller, stronger, his *mourst* characteristics increasingly pronounced, the ridges of ligament running along his jaw pulling the corners of his mouth down slightly. His skin seemed to be darkening, too, gaining the slightly scaly, reptilian-like qualities of a full-blooded *mourst*. This increased the intensity of his already striking blue eyes.

'You feeling OK?' Cascari asked.

Delgado nodded. 'Yeah, fine. What's the weather like up top?'

'Blue skies and sunshine. No cloud. Final briefing's in ten minutes.'

'Sure. Let me wash my face, then I'll be up.'

Cascari nodded once, then left the room.

Delgado sighed, and wished he could summon some enthusiasm. The remnants of the nobics lurking within him were a curse. Despite gradually failing due to their age, along with the odd useful attribute, they maintained the perfect memory of that time in Myson's chamber, automatically stimulating physical responses as he relived the events. Each time he experienced those final moments, his personal achievements seemed few, the regret and sadness overwhelming. They were feelings he found it increasingly difficult to shake off.

The Chamber of Visions, Oracles' Cloister, Seriattic Palace

Oracle Entuzo – the most senior of all Seriatt's seers – entered the chamber, accompanied by her six, young *vilume* attendants, the hem of her heavy outer robe trailing on the floor. The attendants lit lamps that cast pools of cream light across the brick walls, polished wood and brass, and candles beneath small glass bowls filled with scented oil. As the liquids warmed the air became rich and intoxicating.

Oracle Entuzo shed her robe and handed it to Coulieq, her senior attendant. Like all Oracles, Entuzo was taller than other *vilume*, and without her robe she looked brittle and fragile, her limbs and neck appearing a little too long, and slightly out of proportion.

She lay on the smooth black couch in the centre of the room, her movements slow and precise. Its sleek leather skin undulated gently as it changed shape to accommodate her.

'Are you certain you wish to do this?' asked Coulieq. 'The lack of a focal consciousness concerns me.'

'Calm yourself, faithful Coulieq,' said Entuzo, her voice soft and warm. 'There is no specific individual or event on which to focus, that is true, but perhaps this will make the visions easier to interpret, more accurate than the usual possibilities.'

'Or perhaps it is not possible at all and your individuality will be in danger. Can you afford to take such a risk? We should inform the Administrators.'

'Did the mask not predict the Great Plague? The Denessil Catastrophe?' Entuzo challenged, her tone gentle but firm. 'It is true that sometimes it cannot be relied upon, but given the current crisis we need some indication of what the future may give us. As for the Administrators, they need know only if I see anything of importance. If I see anything at all. Leave me now, Coulieq. I must open my mind to what may come.'

Coulieq nodded. From experience, the *vilume* knew that entering into an argument with Entuzo was futile. Prompted by a slight movement of Coulieq's right hand, the other attendants stepped back to take up designated positions near the circular room's wall.

As she lay, Entuzo glanced at the circle of plush seating overlooking the Chamber, where the Administrators and other Oracles would normally sit during important projections. She felt some uncertainty at using the mask without their approval, but knew her reasons were valid.

Entuzo relaxed, her pure black eyes reflecting the intricately carved wooden ceiling above her as she stared. Her breathing began to slow as she relaxed completely, but her eyes remained open. A few moments later, when Coulieq recognised that Oracle Entuzo had entered the dormant state of transcendence, on the cusp of departing the physical world and entering the spiritual environment beyond, accessible only to the Oracles, the senior attendant slowly turned to face the wall behind her. She touched a small square button and a panel slid to one side. It revealed Seriatt's most precious artefact – The Destiny Mask.

Ancient and of unknown origin, the mask had been discovered by archaeologists in one of Seriatt's most barren regions, but was believed by many to be non-Seriattic. Bearing the appearance of polished golden glass with a slightly metallic quality, it was delicately fashioned from a substance scientists had been unable to identify. Covering the front of the upper head when worn, the mask's features possessed androgynous characteristics similar to those of Seriattic *vilume*, yet there was something nonetheless different about it, a subtle *otherness* to the facial expression and distribution of the features, as if modelled on an ancestor of modern *vilume*. The wide, oval eyes conveyed innocence, wisdom, pity, and also great sorrow, as if continually dismayed by the ineptitude of those who wore it.

Coulieq picked up the soft black leather gloves that lay in front of the mask and put them on, then reached out and lifted the artefact carefully from its cradle. She turned, carried the mask towards the couch and carefully placed it on Oracle Entuzo's face.

Despite its apparently solid construction, as Coulieq backed away, the mask briefly emitted a very faint, high-pitched whine, then became slightly luminescent. Entuzo's lips parted, her fingers began to twitch slightly and her back arched a little as if she were anxious or aroused, the couch moving with her body. Oracle Entuzo licked her lips and swallowed. Her fingers gripped the sides of the couch. She seemed tense, disturbed, mumbling softly. The mask seemed to glow more brightly, and then its edges began to soften, losing definition and extending down the sides of Entuzo's face, until the strange substance started to merge with the Oracle's skin. As it hardened across her ears, eyes and the top of her nose the bond with her pale flesh was seamless.

Then, a few moments later, Oracle Entuzo began to see the future.

Some time later Entuzo seemed to relax. The mask darkened, and separated from the *vilume*'s skin, returning to its original, solid form. Coulieq stepped forward and gently removed it from the Oracle's face. It felt warm to the touch even through the leather gloves, and Entuzo's skin was slightly pink where it had made contact with her.

Coulieq placed the mask back in its cradle and closed the

panel. When she turned she saw that Entuzo was already awake, and had gratefully accepted a drink of iced water offered to her by one of the junior attendants.

As Coulieq walked towards her, Entuzo sat up on the couch. 'What did you see?' asked the senior attendant, recognizing the elated expression on the Oracle's face. 'The projections in the chamber were unclear.'

Entuzo reached out and touched Coulieq's wrist. Her fingertips were icy cold. 'I have some wonderful news, faithful Coulieq,' she said softly but with clear elation. 'I have seen something marvellous. I have seen the coming of Seriatt's Saviour.'

Aboard the *Lex Talionis*, Atlantic Ocean

The briefing was as relaxed – but as serious – as any other. Delgado stood in front of the other, seated pilots, a ragtag band, largely criminals and smugglers who had acquired their flying skills avoiding capture by various law enforcement agencies. They were making notes as he spoke.

'The weather is fine and clear today,' he said, 'so we'll stay fairly low. The escorts will fly in two loose formations of eight pairs, five hundred metres above the bombers. One group will be led by Bucky, the other by myself. Due to the weather conditions the bombers will fly in a tight formation to provide defensive cross-fire. The Mars Militia is to launch an angel sweep to disable the Structure Firedrakes before we take off, so we should have a clear run.' One of the pilots muttered something Delgado did not hear clearly, but which was apparently disparaging. A few others seemed to agree, but Delgado let it go. 'If we do run into trouble then you'll need to remember that your guns have been re-harmonised to one hundred metres, so make sure you get in close and hit 'em hard. It's difficult to bring a Firedrake down but a good burst in one of the turbines from that range should do it.

'The main targets are the research and comms facilities.' He indicated rectangular structures on the map, which shimmered slightly as the display zoomed in on the two buildings. 'There's no point going for the Firedrake bunker.' He ran a fingertip through one of the tabs and a larger building was also displayed. 'We simply don't have ordnance capable of penetrating it. However, if you find yourself trapped in a crippled aircraft over the target area and you can crash your machine into the bunker, then you'll be remembered for doing so. OK?' There was an uneasy silence, but a couple of the pilots nodded gently and quickly scribbled diagrams.

'Good. Are there any questions?' A hand appeared towards the back of the room. 'Yes, Blake.'

'I was just wondering if there's been any progress on the plans to attack Planetary Guidance Headquarters. There are rumours flying around that if we can get hold of a few more machines it's a go.'

'We have intelligence information on this,' said Delgado. 'Can you fill us in, please, Ash?'

Ashala was leaning against the wall at the back of the room, chewing gum. She had become more attractive as she aged, her slightly weathered appearance giving her an air of greater confidence and maturity. Occasionally she was disturbed by strange dreams that she believed to be fragments of memories of her past returning to her – it was one such dream that had led to her declaring that her name was Ashala, and that she should be called this rather than Girl – but the dreams' lack of clarity made them difficult to analyse satisfactorily, often casting her into depression. Whatever personal issues affected her, however, her skill as an intelligence analyst was unquestioned, and she commanded great respect within the group. As she stood upright and took a pace forward, the pilots turned in their seats to face her. 'Apart from the scarcity of fabric and wood with which to construct more Hornets,' she said, 'we have information indicating that due to the number of successful attacks we've made recently Structure has increased xip fighter patrols around PGHQ. Furthermore, some of the less essential landing platforms have been decommissioned and gun placements built on them. Given the increased risk this poses we're not going to be able to attack Structure at its heart in the short term.' There was a general expression of frustration and much chatter as the pilots turned to face the front of the room again.

Delgado held up a hand to quieten the pilots. 'I know it's a bitch,' he said, 'and that you're all keen to hit them where it hurts, but it's a measure of our success that Structure has been forced to take such steps. We have to congratulate ourselves on that. We are somewhat constrained by the primitive aircraft we are forced to fly, but rest assured if we can get our hands on better equipment, and if the right opportunity comes along, then we'll make the move. OK? Good. Anyone else?' Cascari raised a hand. 'Yes.'

'Have there been any developments between Seriatt and Earth? Last we heard there were rumours that Myson was preparing an invasion fleet.'

Delgado looked to his left. 'Bucky?'

'We think that was just speculation,' said Bucky. He seemed slightly embarrassed by this admission. 'Myson continues to challenge the Seriatts, but he also seems reluctant to engage in all-out war. He still believes he can somehow get Michael into position as Monosiell, so he's keen to keep his options open. There was recently a dust up in the vicinity of the M-4 wormhole, with the Seriatts preventing one of Myson's deals taking place, but although there was an exchange of fire no ships were lost. Reports are that a Sinz ship was damaged, then high-tailed it back to wherever it is they come from through the wormhole, without an exchange being made. It's unclear how much longer Myson's going to be prepared to put up with the standoff. I think if he was fitter then there'd be more action. As it is he seems prepared to continue playing wait and see.'

'We should go in there and scorch his ass for him,' called Blake. 'Then there'd be some action all right.' There were whoops of agreement from many of the other young pilots.

'You're the one needs his ass scorched, Blake,' called Fitzgerald, a blonde female pilot.

'Yeah?' Blake turned to face her. 'You wanna try it, Fitz?' Blake challenged. 'Bring it on, baby!' Fitzgerald's gesture indicated a reluctance to take him up on this offer.

'Well, maybe we'll eventually get a chance to deal with Myson at some point,' Delgado called above the hubbub. 'But for the moment we need to concentrate on the job in hand.' He looked at his watch. 'OK, everyone,' he said. 'The *Talionis* will be in position in twenty minutes. As ever, we'll need to be out of here ASAP, so let's get our ass in gear. OK? Good luck.'

The world blurred as Delgado thumbed the trigger, his Hornet shuddering violently as a stream of orange flame spewed from the guns packed into its wings. He muttered darkly to himself as he tried to keep the trembling, angular silhouette of the Structure Firedrake in his gun sight, sensing his aircraft's wooden frame flexing as he tightened the turn in pursuit of his technologically superior opponent. As the G-load increased, Delgado's peripheral vision began to fade, and he was forced to ease off slightly in order to remain conscious. Unlike their Structure adversaries, Delgado and his pilots did not have the benefit of G-suppression engines. He stopped firing a few seconds after he had first depressed the trigger, and clarity returned to his world.

Another Hornet suddenly attacked the Firedrake and the Structure pilot reversed his turn to avoid a collision. It was a clumsy move that reflected the Firedrake pilots' lack of close air-combat skills, and their inability to focus their weapons accurately at such close range. The aircraft's dark shape moved back across Delgado's gun sight, a glittering, grey triangle. When its nose reached the centre circle and the sight glowed soft orange, he fired again.

A rash of tiny explosions skittered along the Firedrake's nose, the upper surface of the fuselage and along one of the bulbous turbine housings. The turbine emitted a thick ball of dark smoke and flame and small pieces of the cowling fluttered gracefully away. The Firedrake's nose angled downwards a little, and then quite abruptly the Structure machine slipped sideways through the air, suddenly robbed of all lift. A moment later one of its short wings caressed the treetops, and the machine became a rolling ball of flame.

Delgado levelled out and scoured the sky, but there was no sign of the other Hornet that had attacked the Firedrake. Sudden isolation seemed to be an odd characteristic of dogfights.

The rest of the Hornet swarm was a long way off to his left, tangled up with the other Firedrakes. He wasn't sure how the Structure aircraft had managed to jump them so effectively. One moment the Hornet fighters and the Typhoons – the inadequately armoured twin-engined bombers that were to deliver the ordnance to the target – were all alone in the sky, the next they'd been ambushed by the Structure craft. He was sure the Firedrakes hadn't come out of the sun, but Structure did seem to be particularly good at predicting their targets these days. Almost suspiciously so. The ongoing fight ebbed and flowed, both sides suffering setbacks and making gains.

Delgado turned his aircraft and looked towards the rest of the swarm. They were in disarray, struggling to survive. Outnumbered at least two to one, the Typhoons and the rest of the Hornet fighter swarm had already suffered great losses. Black smoke rose from numerous sites where machines had crashed, their crews either mutilated by cannon shells or burned in the wreckage of their aircraft. None had hit the Firedrake bunker. All of this might have been acceptable had the mission been a success, but while they had definitely managed to destroy a few ground vehicles and some stores, the main targets were virtually untouched. Yet despite this, they were fighting hard, their zeal overcoming what they lacked in equipment.

Delgado pulled back on the stick and looked down behind the left wing as the aircraft climbed. The river shone like a trail of mercury drizzled through the forest. As Delgado turned his head again, light caught his eye, glinting off the silver hull of an orbiting dreadnought preparing to depart for the war zone; it was like a blade suspended overhead.

His eye was drawn from the ghostly shape of the huge vessel as one of the Hornets chased a Firedrake towards the ground, partly shrouded in the smoke pouring from the Structure craft's turbines. The Hornet stopped firing for a moment, then resumed and Delgado saw pieces fly off the Firedrake's fuselage. The Hornet stopped firing again and pulled out of the dive, but the Firedrake continued to descend, hitting part of the Structure installation. A few seconds later part of the facility exploded, a gout of flame and billowing smoke rising into the sky as if exhaled from the mouth of a sideshow fire-breather. Delgado exclaimed with satisfaction. Glittering embers cascaded to earth.

Bright sparks suddenly flashed past the nose of Delgado's aircraft and there was a guttural crackling sound interspersed by deafening pops and bangs. Delgado glanced to his left as he flicked the aircraft on to its side and pulled a gut-wrenching turn. His bladder emptied as he saw the aggressive silhouette of a Firedrake bearing down on him, its chunky muzzle spouting flame. Blood filled his head as he shoved his plane into a steep dive, yelling profanities.

After a few seconds, Delgado levelled off, then climbed briefly, his plane's wooden frame groaning and creaking around him as he flicked it on to one wingtip, searching the sky for his attacker. He ducked instinctively at a series of thuds just behind his head and screamed as intense pain filled his left hand. He heard the wail of his attacker's engine as the Structure machine passed behind him and he flipped the Hornet on to its back, then pulled the stick to his belly so that he was dropping vertically at full power. He raced towards the ground for perhaps six seconds before pulling out of the dive. He looked around quickly and found the other aircraft flying straight and level about five hundred metres above him, the enemy pilot having apparently lost sight of Delgado's machine against the chaos of the ground.

Delgado looked down at his hand, and for a moment stared blankly at the torn gauntlet and flap of skin. A brilliant white shard of bone was visible through the leather. A cannon shell seemed to have passed through the flesh between the thumb and index finger. It was painful and messy but probably looked worse than it actually was. He noticed that the side of the cockpit was spattered with a thin brown paste around the hole left by the unexploded shell as it had exited the aircraft.

Above, the Firedrake was turning gently, heading back towards the burning installation. With the fight continuing only a couple of miles away Delgado could only assume that the Structure aircraft was damaged, out of ammunition, or its pilot wounded. He deftly nudged the throttle, crying out as a sheet of white pain raged through his injured hand. The engine ahead of him growled sullenly and he felt a firm shove in the back.

He began to climb, calculating his trajectory and turning his aircraft so that he would stay in the other's machine's scanner blind spot – below and slightly to its left. Continually searching the sky for other Firedrakes that might jump him as he focused on his target, Delgado waited patiently as he gradually gained altitude. The Structure machine began to descend slowly and he caught a glimpse of turbine blades spinning as sunlight penetrated the port housing. Delgado adjusted his grip on the joystick and waited. At a distance of around two hundred metres the Structure pilot was still oblivious to his presence. Still slightly lower than the other machine Delgado allowed his Hornet to drift to the right until he was directly behind the Firedrake. He raised the nose of his own aircraft a little, aimed just ahead of the Firedrake's pointed nose, then fired.

It was a perfect shot. Tiny orange plumes smothered the underside of the fuselage, and ran the length of the port turbine housing. There was a surprisingly brief and contained explosion from the engine, and a comical puff of smoke sputtered from the exhaust vents before the machine began to trail a soiled streamer. Delgado allowed his Hornet to drift to the right and closed in slightly. At around fifty metres, with the starboard turbine outlet gaping like an erotic mouth in front of him, his Hornet bucking in the disturbed air behind the Structure craft, Delgado fired again until his ammunition was spent. The machine did not drop out of the sky or explode, but simply continued to descend towards the forest, as if this was the Structure pilot's intention. Then it brushed against the forest canopy, and was gradually absorbed by the trees. A few seconds later a dense fireball rose from the forest like a huge over-ripe fruit.

The moments immediately after an attack were notoriously dangerous, many pilots being jumped by the enemy as their concentration lapsed in the euphoria of a kill, so Delgado immediately dropped his aircraft's left wing and pulled back on the stick: it was time to go home before his own luck ran out.

★

Around an hour later, Delgado's head throbbed dully. He felt slightly queasy, his muscles ached and his body was clammy with sweat. He glanced at the fuel gauge, checked the position of the sun and looked down past the right wing. He saw familiar landmarks: the shell of the building next to the dirt track; the widening river; the still-smouldering wreck of the Structure scout flyer they had shot down the previous day. To the left the desert stretched away into the distance, a vast, bleached void. Ahead, the sea was like a beaten metal sheet.

He weaved the plane slightly and craned his neck to check behind him: Firedrake pilots were unlikely to chase them out this far, but he knew better than to make assumptions. Instead of Structure aircraft he saw the surviving Typhoons and Hornets, a ragged formation of damaged aircraft returning to the *Talionis*. Most were damaged, some trailing smoke.

Blake's Hornet was closest to his own, about two hundred metres away but at a slightly lower altitude. The machine was badly damaged, large chunks missing from the rudder and ailerons, the ground visible through a gash in the fuselage behind the cockpit that was easily five metres long. The aircraft was trailing a thin white stream of coolant and half the main undercarriage assembly was hanging limply beneath it; the single wheel turning slowly.

Within the cockpit Blake was just a silhouette, but he seemed to be sitting upright. Delgado tried to make contact but found his comms unit dead. He manoeuvred his aircraft closer to Blake's machine, but was unable to see through the canopy, many panes of which were starred or streaked with engine oil. Delgado waved his good hand vigorously, but Blake made no visible response.

Realising that he needed to lose some speed, Delgado swore softly as he looked at his left hand. Caked in congealed blood, the wrist throbbed with a dull, irregular rhythm that matched the droning of the engine in front of him. The hand was aching and stiff, his fingers reluctant to move. Carefully, he reached over with his right hand to try and pull back the throttle enough to slow the aircraft down without reducing the power so much that it stalled. With a deft movement he reduced the power to forty per cent, but the speed bled away more quickly than he had expected; instead of using the throttle again he lowered flaps to increase lift.

Delgado's aircraft was the first to cross the coast, the grey sea glistering below. He looked behind him again. One of the Typhoons was dropping towards the water, one prop windmilling. He checked the sky for Structure craft but saw only a couple of vapour trails high above. When he looked ahead again he saw a broad area of sea in the middle distance beginning to spiral, a shallow vortex rapidly increasing in speed to create foam-crested peaks and deep, smooth troughs. Four narrower but much deeper, faster vortices appeared around the spiralling central mass.

A gleaming silver dome began to emerge from the gunmetal water, the grey sea roiling and spitting as the shining surface emerged from the depths, the vortices deepening still further and increasing in speed. The circular lower half of the craft then began to emerge, numerous bulky protuberances rising from its substructure, long, jointed arms extending from various points around its circumference. Eventually the *Lex Talionis* was fully exposed, the highest point of the huge domed section standing some 30 metres above the water. With the *Talionis* on the surface the vortices disappeared, and the sea lapped ineffectively around it.

In the vessel's dark base a slit suddenly appeared as doors opened like some gigantic mechanical mouth. As a torrent of water immediately poured between the widening jaws, fountains of spray jetted into the air on either side of the craft as it was immediately pumped out again. When the jaws were at their gaping limit, a thick river of metaplas flowed like an iron tongue from a gland in the centre of the lower jaw to form a landing strip.

They were almost home.

Floodlights came on that illuminated the interior of the bay and revealed the extent of the *Talionis*' capacity. A former marine salvage vessel once used for the retrieval and processing of marine wrecks, the group had purchased it from a salvage merchant on the fringes of the Dead Zone with Mars Militia funding. Its submarine capabilities and huge internal space, coupled with the fact that it offered accommodation sufficient for twice the group's number and a sizeable inventory of everything from communications equipment to sticking plasters and analgesics, meant that it represented the perfect base from which to conduct their incursions.

Delgado looked over his shoulder; Blake's aircraft was very low now, and was obviously going too quickly. There was still around half a kilometre to go, but the shadow of Blake's plane was clearly defined on the sea below, expanding and contracting on the swell. Every couple of seconds either Blake or the autopilot – it was impossible for Delgado to know which – fed power into the engine and raised the aircraft's nose; but it was clear the plane was floundering. It was possible the autopilot had been damaged in some way.

More pieces of Blake's plane became detached, fluttering away from the machine like autumn leaves. The left wing dipped abruptly and the stray wheel smashed through the crest of a wave with an explosion of creamy foam. Then the aircraft lurched upward once more, as if some dormant system had been stirred into action by the brief contact and realised the danger.

The right wing dropped this time, levelled, then the left

wing dropped again. With the plane nose-high the undercarriage assembly hanging beneath it came into contact with the surf once more, and for a moment the aircraft looked like a bizarre, one-legged creature striding across the surface of the water. Then, just beyond the edge of the *Talionis*' metaplas tongue, a surge of swell enveloped the wheel, the nose tipped forward and the radiator intake plunged into the chop with sickening suddenness. The prop thrashed briefly, then the aircraft sank quickly into the gloomy depths.

With the smell of fuel and hot oil thick in the air, Delgado strode across the cavernous bay within the *Lex Talionis* towards Cascari, who was clambering from his own aircraft. One or two of the fitters running past him to rearm and refuel the returned aircraft called out congratulations, but Delgado ignored them.

Cascari turned to face him, slinging his harness over his left forearm. 'You OK?' Delgado asked.

'Fine. Got a little ventilation in the cockpit, but no injuries. You?'

Delgado held up his hand. It was caked in a dark brown crust of dried blood. Cascari winced. 'It's nothing,' said Delgado. 'Medic'll soon fix it. Guess your old man's getting sloppy.' His tone was casual, but he did not smile.

'Where'd they come from?'

Delgado shook his head. 'Don't ask me. They shouldn't have been there at all.' He glanced over his shoulder towards the bright slit. Aircraft were still making their approach and landing, others taxiing from the landing strip, their engines revving. 'Our friendly Mars Militia representative is going to have to come up with some answers, that's for sure.' Delgado called over the noise as they walked towards the locker room. 'Maybe Rodriguez isn't being exactly straight with us.'

'You think they didn't send the angels in at all? I never did trust him. You think he's trying to pull one over on us? Why would he want to do that?'

Delgado shook his head, pulling a stick of gum from his pocket and placing it into his mouth. 'I don't know, Cascari. But what I do know is that Blake's dead, and so are several other, equally good pilots. We have a high rate of loss as it is, but the angels were supposed to deal with the Structure systems and give us a fighting chance. I want to know what went wrong.'

'Hey, wait up.' It was Bucky, running to catch up with them. His expression was grim and he looked exhausted. 'Tough job, huh?' he said, slightly breathlessly. 'They jumped us good. Lost four from my flight. How 'bout you, Delgado?'

'Six,' Delgado replied sombrely.

'Shit.' Bucky shook his head. 'How many bombers did we lose?'

'Not sure. Haven't seen Marcus to ask him. But my guess is they were slaughtered. I only saw a handful following us in.'

An alarm suddenly began to sound, a piercing rasp accompanied by flashing red lights: the bay doors were about to close as the *Lex Talionis* prepared to submerge once again.

Almost immediately the metaplas landing strip softened, and slipped back into the bulbous gland in the middle of the bay entrance with a succulent sound. The light in the hangar faded as the massive, rigid lips of the bay doors began to close, and within two minutes the *Talionis* was sinking beneath the waves once again, seeking refuge in the deep.

As the *Talionis* vibrated, Delgado steadied himself on the doorframe as he, Bucky and Cascari walked into the locker room. Bucky and Cascari dumped their harnesses on a bench and unzipped their flying suits, but Delgado kept walking. 'Not changing?' Cascari called after him.

'No. I've got to talk to Rodriguez,' he called without turning. 'Then I'll go to the medic and get my hand patched up.'

'Ask him about those angels, man,' called Bucky. 'Reckon they must've had their wings cut off.'

'I intend to, don't worry.'

Just as Delgado was leaving the locker room Ashala appeared in the doorway. 'Hi,' she said. 'How'd it go?' The expression on her face indicated that she already had an idea.

'You don't want to know, Ash.'

'Not good, then.'

'Not particularly. We lost a lot of aircraft. Blake crashed right outside the *Talionis*.'

Ash's mouth twisted slightly, but she obviously did not know what to say. She saw his injured hand. 'You got hit. Let me see.' She touched Delgado's sleeve but he moved his hand behind his back.

'It's nothing,' he said, looking past her into the dark corridor beyond. 'Medic can treat it later for me. Right now I've got to go to Comms.'

Ashala turned sideways in the doorway to let Delgado past. As he walked away she called after him: 'You should go to the medic before you go to Comms. You don't want that hand getting infected.'

Delgado made no response.

A musty smell hit Delgado the moment he entered Comms – a dark, circular room at the heart of the *Lex Talionis* – and he suddenly remembered why he did his best to avoid the place as much as possible.

Although stuffed from floor to ceiling with all manner of communications machinery, most of the equipment was either massively out of date or inoperative due to lack of spares or incompatibility between systems. The pulse engines, energisers and signal boosters were antiquated and, despite being well maintained, their performance was declining. Although there was constant talk of a further injection of funding from the Mars Militia, nothing ever seemed to be forthcoming.

Throughout the room, plastic buckets were strategically positioned to collect the water that dripped constantly from the pipes suspended just below the ceiling; shining black patches on the floor indicated potential locations for more buckets.

Despite the conditions, the young lad with acne who had been given responsibility for the equipment was clearly immensely keen. His clothes were smartly pressed, his hair combed across his forehead in a shiny sweep. Numerous dark scabs and a certain redness of neck were evidence of inexperience in shaving. Although his appearance was somewhat at odds with the rest of the group, the young man's trim figure and exuberant demeanour were probably the main reasons behind his appointment.

The youth stood erect and pulled his tunic straight as Delgado entered the grim room. 'Ah, sir. How are you, sir?' he asked.

'Never mind that,' Delgado replied with a brusqueness that surprised even himself, 'let's just get on with things, shall we?'

'Yes of course, sir. Sorry, sir. If you'd like to walk this way then, sir.'

The young man strode into the depths of the room, escorting Delgado between the banks of dark equipment in his charge. One or two coloured lights flickered like signs of recognition as they passed, but overall the machinery seemed depressingly dormant.

At the far end of the room a tiny black screen was mounted on top of a slender black metal pedestal. A single black chair was positioned in front of it. Water dripped into a black bucket placed on the floor just in front of the black pedestal; the water it contained looked black. An almost imperceptible vibration produced thin concentric circles in the liquid.

'Please, sit down, sir,' said the young man, motioning towards the chair.

Delgado sat; the chair was hard and the back too upright. He frowned and glanced quickly around in search of alternative seating; none was available.

The youth went and stood behind a control panel to Delgado's right and appeared to make minute adjustments to something. Occasionally, he would glance anxiously at the small, seemingly inactive screen, then make further adjustments. 'Sorry about this, sir,' he said. 'The antennae array has reached the surface but something of a storm has developed since we descended again and it's distorting the signal. I'll have to give it a bit more juice.'

The young man frowned as he made more changes, then looked at the screen and smiled, apparently able to see something beyond Delgado's level of perception. 'There you go then, sir,' he said. 'I'll be outside if you need me.'

The youth left Delgado looking at an apparently inactive screen. Delgado waited. The lack of activity continued. He looked behind him towards the door wondering if he should fetch the keen young man, but when he turned to face the monitor again he saw faint lines of text fading in from the darkness.

SECURE TIGHTLINE ESTABLISHED: MARS-EARTH 61946
SOURCE/ROUTING: [UNIDENTIFIED]
FRAGMENTING PROTOCOL #333-059
CONFIRMED OPERATIONAL
ULTRABEAM COMMUNICATIONS START

The words were replaced by a man's face that phased in and out of focus before being engulfed by snow. After a few moments the blizzard eased, but the face skewed and split diagonally before joining again.

It was Rodriguez, their friendly Mars Militia representative.

Structure's occupation of Olympus Mons was at the root of

the Mars Militia's cause. The Militia's founder – an archaeologist named Louis Combelles – had been so awestruck, almost religiously overcome, by the apparent scale of the Martians' achievements when first experiencing the Olympus Mons remains, that he had immediately called for Mars to be declared a site of historical interest and demanded the cessation of all development, with the aim of preserving the planet's history more effectively than Earth's indigenous cultures had been. But although Combelles and his cohorts had barricaded themselves into the Olympus Mons base in protest, they were quickly – and brutally – evicted by Structure's PPD operatives. Combelles had been lucky to escape, and thereafter, the Martian cause dominated his life.

As time passed, his group gained power, attracting the support of wealthy businessmen who saw potential political value in his agenda. As a result, and despite the questionable motives of some of his new sympathisers, the Mars Militia was formed, subsequently becoming one of the most powerful political groups in history.

For a while, following Combelles' death in a flying accident, his small aircraft having mysteriously disintegrated over Tharsis, the Militia had concentrated on peaceful means of protest, occasionally striking purely military targets on Mars. With Combelles gone, however, the Militia's power fell into the hands of the proud, fourteenth-generation Latinos who provided much of its illicit funding and more extreme tactics were adopted. Many on the fringes claimed that the Mars issue was merely a smokescreen to obscure the group's real focus on increasing wealth. Fed by the spoils of piracy, illegal counter-production and graft within Earth's habitat towers, as time passed the Militia's wealth grew, and the group began to attack anything with even the remotest link to Structure. None of this had prevented Structure plundering Olympus Mars, or mercilessly converting the Martian installation to serve human requirements.

Rodriguez was a typical militiaman with tanned, unblemished skin over delicate high cheekbones and a pencil moustache on his thin upper lip. His shining black hair was smoothed across his skull in the customary militia style, and perfectly complemented the expensive suit he wore – a traditional black three-piece in heavy fabric. It might have had a faint pinstripe, but the reception wasn't good enough for Delgado to be certain.

One of the Latino's eyes was deep brown, a pool of intense emotion, the other a cybernetic replacement that looked soulless despite the engineers' best efforts. The red, sore lid blinked slowly and drooped, giving Rodriguez a slightly dozy appearance.

Externally a picture of clean-cut opulence, and perceived by many as little more than successful businessmen with contacts, the Militia's Latino core were activists without conscience, executing deadly operations from a safe distance, their main goal to achieve Mars' independence from Earth. Despite sympathising with some of the Militia's aims, Delgado disagreed with their methods: planting bombs on starliners or sending waves of angels to corrupt leisurestation life-support systems made no sense to him, and as far as he could see did little to attract more moderate supporters.

Yet Delgado knew that without Militia funding they would not have the *Talionis*, or the currency necessary to buy supplies and munitions on Earth. In return for this, the group attacked Structure on Earth, while the Militia concentrated on Structure's Martian facilities. And while it had crossed Delgado's mind several times that severing links with the Militia might be no bad thing, he well knew that without the Militia codes that prevented Structure from identifying the location of the *Talionis*, which were constantly updated and fed into the Structure system by the Militia's finest systems engineers, they would be finished.

On Mars the great prize the Militia sought was the extensive and ancient Martian facility within the gigantic dormant Olympus Mons volcano, which Structure had occupied since its discovery. Despite numerous attacks by the Militia, Olympus Mons had as yet proved an impenetrable fortress, protected by numerous gun turrets around its broad and ragged-edged crater, its internal expanse accessible only by a single shaft at the crater's centre.

It was Rodriguez – who seemed to have an ever-increasing influence on the course of the group's campaign against Structure – who had suggested bombing the facility they had so ineffectively attacked. A relatively easy target, he said he believed it would counter the group's low ebb in morale. Thus the bombers had lumbered into the sky like a flock of ungainly wading birds, while the fighter escort circled impatiently above.

So much for morale boosting.

So much for Rodriguez and his assurances.

So much for the Mars Militia.

On the screen, Rodriguez placed a closed fist to his lips and cleared his throat. Apparently unable to see Delgado, he appeared to look beyond the monitor in front of him as if seeking clearance to continue from someone out of shot. Delgado pictured a counterpart to the keen young man currently waiting in the corridor outside the Comms room, busily making adjustments to equipment somewhere on Mars.

Rodriguez looked directly at the screen and, as Delgado apparently appeared to him, the militiaman adopted a smile as artificial as his set of perfect white teeth. As he began to speak, the distinctive rolling lilt of his South American accent – an affectation adopted by all high-ranking militiamen in recognition of their Latino ancestry – was immediately grating.

'Ah, Alexander Delgado. How are you? How are all within your group?' His voice was slightly out of sync with the movement of his lips, giving the impression that the voice Delgado could hear was actually that of a translator. The Latino's cybernetic eye blinked lazily and wandered, as if already bored with the conversation.

'What happened, Rodriguez?' snapped Delgado. 'You and your cronies were supposed to take care of the Firedrakes.'

Rodriguez pursed his lips and nodded slowly. 'Ah, I thought I sensed anger in you, Alex. Now I understand why. Your mission was, um, unsuccessful, yes? And you are wounded, too, I see.' He pointed. 'Your hand. It is not too painful, I hope?'

Delgado let his injured hand drop to his side. 'Um, somewhat unsuccessful, yes. You could say that. We were slaughtered. Only a handful of us made it back and hardly any of the ordnance was delivered to the target. Some of my best pilots were killed. You said you'd make sure we had a clear run, Rodriguez. What went wrong?'

The militiaman raised his eyebrows and shook his head sadly. 'Really, Alex, I made no such assurance. I said we would endeavour—' he paused, frowned, looked upward for a moment somewhat theatrically. 'Yes, I believe that was the exact word I used – *endeavour* – to take care of the Firedrakes. And we did try. However, for some reason as yet unclear to us I am afraid the angels failed to do their job effectively. Your losses are unfortunate, but not our fault.' He smiled broadly as if this was some kind of achievement.

'You let us down again, Rodriguez.'

Rodriguez shook his head. 'I think that in truth, Alex, you feel as though you let yourself down. It was not I who led that mission.' The militiaman adopted a sincere expression. 'Men died under your command, Alex. That is a terrible, terrible thing.' He paused for effect, looking down as if seeking inspiration, or reading from a script. He looked up again and clasped his hands in front of his face as if praying, his head cocked slightly to one side. His wayward eye seemed to be searching for something in the corner of the room. 'But it is the nature of war. Acceptable losses, Alex. It is the reality. What you are experiencing now is called survivor guilt. As leader, you are wondering why you should have survived the mission when those under your command did not.'

Delgado held his breath, barely containing his temper. He briefly wondered what effects the assassination of a key militiaman might have. It would be expensive and risky, but it could be done.

'It is of no matter now, Alex,' Rodriguez was saying. 'We must move on.' Delgado wasn't sure he was prepared to move on just yet. But what choice did he have? Rodriguez was right. 'We have intercepted some interesting messages,' the militiaman was saying. 'The Seriatts have announced that the Monosiell has died suddenly. Apparently the victim of disease.'

Delgado blinked. 'What kind of disease?'

'We do not know. In truth it is not important. What *is* important is that Myson will see this as an opportunity, and seek to get his son into a position of power on Seriatt.' Delgado's mind raced as numerous possibilities opened up before him. 'That would not be a great problem in itself,' said Rodriguez. 'I believe that Myson fails to appreciate the problems he would face entering into such a close union with Seriatt. Their society is thick with bureaucracy and hierarchy. However, there is an additional factor about which we are gravely concerned. We understand that the Seriatts are on the verge of making a breakthrough in time travel.'

Delgado sat more upright. 'Myson getting Michael into a position of power on Seriatt would be bad enough, but time travel . . . Do you know any details?'

'Few, Alex. The messages we have intercepted are somewhat ambiguous and occasionally difficult to translate, but from what we can gather the Seriatts have extrapolated the properties of their Destiny Mask to produce some kind of time portal. More than that we do not know. Whatever it is, the Seriatts appear confident of its successful application. And Myson wants it.'

'We have to stop him,' said Delgado flatly. 'If Myson gets into power on Seriatt through Michael and gets his hands on this time machine or whatever it is God alone knows what he'll do.'

Rodriguez looked grave. 'Indeed, Alex, indeed. From what we have been able to establish, Myson is to send Michael to Seriatt with a trusted operative to stake his claim within the Royal Household. A Commander Osephius, we believe.'

Delgado's eyes narrowed. He felt his heart rate quicken slightly. 'That name rings a bell,' he said quietly. 'I take it Myson isn't going himself for health reasons.'

Rodriguez nodded. 'His health is failing. He is simply unable to make the journey. The members of the Planetary Council are apparently already squabbling over who will succeed him.'

'He's close to death?'

'He is gravely unwell, of that there is no doubt.'

Delgado looked thoughtful. 'Perhaps that's why he's so interested in time travel.'

Rodriguez chuckled insincerely. 'Indeed, my friend, indeed.'

Delgado looked directly at Rodriguez again. 'We have to make sure Michael doesn't get to Seriatt, and stop Myson getting his hands on that time-travel device. Whatever the cost.'

Rodriguez nodded slowly. 'I agree, Alex. There is one possibility. Michael is currently taking part in a Structure exercise in Brazil, and is due to leave for Seriatt when it finishes in two days' time. Some time ago we acquired an old Structure snubship. It is one of the first examples of such a vessel, and although we have only a small amount of the necessary fuel, as these vessels are currently taking part in the exercise, it would perhaps be possible to get to Michael this way, before he even leaves Earth. This could make things much simpler. What do you think?'

'The snubship would have to be re-coded so Structure controllers think it's something commonplace. A Class Four transport would do it. There'll be plenty of those around.' Delgado spoke quietly as he thought the plan through. 'These exercises take place over such a wide area visual identification's not likely to be a problem. If we're quick enough they might not even realise what's really happened.'

Rodriguez smiled broadly. 'Sneak in, kill him, sneak out again. I like your style, Alex. Who knows, if we're careful we may be able to send our own representative to Seriatt and acquire their time-travel device for ourselves, no?'

Delgado said nothing: there were too many things for him to consider. One of them was that very possibility.

'I'm not sure this is such a good idea, man,' said Bucky, pulling meat from a roasted chicken leg. 'I can understand where you're coming from, but going after Michael's a big risk.'

Ashala sat on the tattered sofa to Delgado's left, arms folded. Images on the muted TV screen next to the sofa flickered brightly on the side of her face. Cascari was sitting cross-legged on the floor. So far neither of them had said anything. Delgado wasn't sure what Cascari was thinking, but he could almost see Ashala's mind working. 'What do you think, Ash?' he asked her. 'What would you do?'

She shrugged. 'You know me, Delgado. I kinda like to play safe these days. Especially when the intelligence is from a source we're not entirely sure about. Like Bucky says, I can see where you're coming from. But . . .' She hesitated.

'What?'

'I just don't know if you're doing this for the right reasons.'

Delgado looked slightly taken aback. 'What do you mean?'

'Well, are you sure this isn't more about you, rather than Cascari.'

Delgado leaned forward, resting his elbows on his thighs, hands together in front of his face. 'Look, this is Cascari's opportunity. The one we've waited so long for. Besides, even without him we still couldn't let Myson get hold of whatever time-travel technology the Seriatts might have developed. There's no arguing with that, right?'

'No, there isn't,' confirmed Bucky, tearing off more chicken.

'No,' said Ash.

'So whatever happens we have to stop Myson getting into a position of leverage on Seriatt through Michael. Now the Monosiell's dead he's going to get Michael to Seriatt as quickly as possible, not waste time approaching the Andamour Council to try and challenge the legality of the Seriatts' objections again. I think what he'll do is get Michael to Seriatt and bank on them being so grateful for an apparent heir that they'll give him a hearing. I know how Myson's mind works. There's been no new Monosiell born in the last twenty years. The one they stuck in place just after Cascari was born was a stop-gap.' He spoke more quietly. 'But if we can kill Michael before he leaves, all we have to do then is get Cascari to Seriatt in one piece, and he's in with a real chance. *He's* the real heir after all.'

'That's all, huh?' said Bucky.

'But if Michael's human anyway,' said Ash, 'the Seriatts aren't going to let him become Monosiell are they? No matter how desperate they are, and no matter what Myson says. If he's not a Seriatt, he's not a Seriatt, period.'

Delgado's mouth twisted and he shook his head. 'I don't think we can count on something like that. Myson's biotechs are the best. Always have been. I reckon they'll have found a way of altering Michael's physiology so he appears at least half Seriatt, which is what he's supposed to be: gene manipulation, a batch of highly advanced nobics. Something to conceal his real origins. Apart from Myson, only *we* know Michael's really human. When you two got Cascari out of that chamber that day, Myson had no choice but to use a human infant to claim his link to Seriatt and save face. Michael even *looks* completely human for pity's sake. Any idiot can see Cascari's a *mourst*. He's even got a Seriattic name. Not that that would count for much, I guess.'

'OK. Say we deal with Michael,' said Ashala. 'What if the Seriatts dispute Cascari's claim, too?'

'I don't see how they can,' said Delgado. 'If there's a dispute then maybe they can use this Destiny Mask of theirs. I don't know how it works, but perhaps it could be used to establish the truth of his identity. Somehow, I don't think that'll be a problem, though.'

Bucky looked at Cascari. 'What do you think, man? You want to kill the charlatan and high-tail it to Seriatt to stake your claim?'

Cascari toyed with the food in his bowl. 'It's important for me to go to Seriatt,' he said.

'You see?' said Delgado. 'He recognises the opportunity here.'

Cascari looked at Delgado. 'But I'm not so sure you should come with me.'

Delgado looked slightly shocked. 'Why not? You're not going to be able to do this on your own, you know.'

'Your presence might just lead to more problems. The Seriatts might resent it.'

'But you know how they value family units. I'm your father. How can they resent that?'

Cascari looked down at his food. 'I don't know.'

Delgado paused for a moment. 'Perhaps it's you who resents me, huh.'

Cascari looked up and shook his head. 'That's not true and you know it.'

'Come on guys,' said Ashala. 'Delgado's right, Cascari: you couldn't do this on your own. Even if Michael was out of the equation you'd still need some backup approaching the Seriatts.'

Cascari looked frustrated. Although he seemed to want to argue with them, either he felt he couldn't or he was unable to express his feelings well enough.

'Right, that's it then,' said Delgado. 'We'll head for Brazil in Rodriguez's snubship, remove Michael from the equation and then make a dash for Seriatt before they can inaugurate another puppet Monosiell.'

'It's an admirable plan, but rubbing Michael out might not be that easy, man,' said Bucky, picking meat from between his teeth. 'Myson's bound to have his son well protected, you know? Xip fighter escorts, all kinds of shit. He's kept him well wrapped until now, after all.'

'It's worth a shot, though, Bucky. If we can kill Michael before he leaves for Seriatt then the battle's half won.'

There were a few moments of silence as they contemplated the situation.

'Maybe we should send someone else with Cascari,' Ashala ventured quietly. She looked at Delgado in a way that made him feel uncomfortable; the way she did when situations were potentially dangerous. Bucky remained ignorant of the brief affair they had had some years ago and there was an unspoken agreement between them that Bucky must never find out. But sometimes Delgado wondered whether she would tell Bucky just to see what happened, or as a way of getting back at him for ending it.

'Yeah,' said Cascari, 'you should let someone else take this one. You're too emotionally involved. It might not be the best thing for you to go for it yourself, given the circumstances.'

Delgado shook his head. 'No way,' he said emphatically. 'If

someone's going with you it's going to be me. Besides, who else would we send? No one's got the necessary experience for one thing.'

'I'll come with you,' said Ash suddenly.

The others all looked at her.

'I'm not sure that's a good idea,' said Bucky.

'Why not?'

'Well . . . we need you here. You're our intelligence expert. Our collator of information.'

'Shit, Bucky,' she said angrily, 'get someone else to collate the frigging information for Christ's sake. I'm sick to death of collating information.'

Bucky looked at Delgado. 'You don't want her along, though, do you, Delgado?'

Delgado looked Ash in the eye. 'I have no objections,' he said. 'Who knows, maybe we'll need some information collated along the way.' Ash half-smiled.

Bucky looked from one to the other of them as if he felt he was missing something. 'You're sure?' he asked. 'What about you, Cascari?'

'Look, Bucky, you know what Ash is like. If I can't talk him out of going,' he pointed to Delgado, 'I'm sure not going to be able to talk *her* out of going.'

'So we're going to go to Brazil first?' asked Ash.

Delgado nodded. 'Yeah. We can head straight for Seriatt after the job's done. We'll need some backup, though. Some ground troops in case it comes to a fist fight. Some weapons, grenades, personnel armour. Maybe a few liftpacs. That OK with you, Bucky? We've got all that stuff in the inventory, right?'

Bucky snorted and shook his head. 'You're really going to go through with this, aren't you, Delgado?'

'You bet.'

'Whatever the consequences?'

'Whatever the consequences.'

'Do you really think you can succeed?'

'Positive,' he said.

'Then I guess you better have all the personnel and gear you need,' said Bucky.

'Great. Let's arrange to get hold of this snubship from Rodriguez. Then we'll really be in the game.'

Two

amphion's net

Structure military exercise, Brazil

The wyverns' multi-jointed legs clattered as the trio of machines strode through the forest. Huge hydraulic joints wheezed as the powerful limbs forced them through the trees, snapping branches and completely uprooting younger specimens.

The lead unit unexpectedly entered a large clearing and halted so abruptly that the two following wyverns almost collided with it. Unprepared for the glade, which did not appear on their maps, the first machine's three crewmen scanned frantically for interneural patterns indicating the presence of enemy hardware.

As the three units wavered unsteadily on the soft ground, a squad of imps emerged silently from a camouflaged pit. Small and muscular, their unclothed bodies were covered in a thick, dark pelt. Ammo belts rattled and tackbomb clusters bounced joyfully as they scurried, chimp-like, towards the machines.

Imps' lack of complex cognitive processes, coupled with modern cloning techniques, made their replication quick, easy and – most importantly – cheap. As a result they were used as cannon fodder in most campaigns, deployed whenever overwhelming numbers were considered likely to be the most effective strategy. For particularly bloody or prolonged campaigns basic imp replication equipment could be transported to the field to enable the immediate replacement of losses – a cloned cell group could be transformed into a ready-to-go imp in less than eight hours, although this was up to four times their expected combat survival time.

Each troop of twenty-four imps had a 'chief' that was more intelligent than the rest. However, due to the erratic nature of all imps and their inability to fully comprehend the concept of discipline, let alone appreciate its benefits, even chiefs could sometimes prove wayward. As a result, chiefs were 'influenced' by specialist Structure officers in aerial control vehicles, who manipulated the signals sent to the chiefs' decision-making synapses via the very basic nobic evolution with which they were imbued. While this made chiefs considerably more expensive to produce than their standard counterparts, there was no argument that without them imps would be simply uncontrollable. Influencing the imps from ACVs also meant that the Structure officers themselves were safe from attack by the imps – something which had happened all too frequently in the early days of ground-based control units.

In this case, however, an angel attack of unknown origin had led to a malfunction aboard an ACV that had caused the craft to crash in the forest six kilometres south of the wyverns' current position. As a result, this particular imp troop had for a number of days been without external guidance, reliant upon the chief's basal instincts alone.

After unsuccessful attempts by one or two young and particularly ambitious imps to depose the troop's chief, a certain basic battle strategy had been followed, culminating in the digging of the pit. There the imp squad had waited, without knowing for what. Fights and squabbles broke out as they became increasingly bored, hungry and fatigued, defecating, masturbating and fornicating with each other. But the chief had maintained control – just.

The pit's position, slightly behind and almost directly below the angular, sealed command modules a hundred metres above, was in a scanner blind spot. This was not down to luck, but the imp chief's innate awareness of the route by which approach to this clearing was most likely.

When they reached the wyverns the imps set about their task quickly and efficiently, acting in an organised manner that belied their primeval nature. Within a few minutes several tackbombs were attached to each machine. The majority were positioned around the ankles of each powerful leg, as these were the easiest to place, but one or two particularly enthusiastic imps managed to scale the wyverns' long, segmented tails to attach bombs behind the knees or just below the command module, where the wide metal legs entered the gear housing. Explosives in place, the imps scampered quietly back to the dark confines of their pit, snarling and spitting enthusiastically as the camouflage cover was hastily drawn across above them.

A few moments later the three wyverns began to move forward once more. They had taken barely half a dozen steps when the first of the small bombs detonated, followed by a rapid succession of other explosions. The wyverns dropped heavily on to shattered legs, the heavy command modules toppling either forwards or to the side, raising clouds of dust as they crashed to the ground.

The imps erupted from the pit and charged towards the fallen units, pulling the fat-bore HiMag subrifles strapped across their backs to bear as they ran. They howled in anticipation, shrill cries of arousal and delight.

The first wyvern had fallen forwards, and the command module remained upright. A dozen imps leaped up on to the thick lip that ran around the outside of the module while the rest took up guard positions on this narrow ledge. The imps looked down into the machine, snarling lips trembling.

Although the crew was still inside the command module,

for some reason – probably as a result of the severity of the impact with the ground – the metaplas hatch that formed most of its upper surface had melted back into its gland. The imps cast a ragged shadow across the wyvern's crewmembers, two of whom were attending to a third, who was sobbing gently.

'What the hell d'you think you're doing?' yelled one of the men, without looking up. 'Who told you to use live ordnance for Christ's sake? This man's back is broken.' When there was no response he raised his head. He paled upon seeing the imps staring down at him and began muttering prayers.

The imp chief made a guttural sound, and the imps unleashed the full power of their weapons into the module. When they stopped, the wyvern's three-man crew was lost in a pit of flame and acrid smoke. The chief threw back his head and released a long, triumphant roar, thick strands of saliva trailing from his putrid mouth. Then he turned and jumped to the ground, leading his troop in search of more targets.

By this time the other wyvern crews had seen the imps and were running for the trees. They were all young and inexperienced. Being chased by a hoard of Structure's most terrifying constructs in what was supposed to be a safe, simulated combat environment, they failed to see the second camouflaged pit. The forest was filled with a sickening song as all but one of the Structure operatives fell, and became impaled on the sharpened wooden spikes embedded in the pit floor.

Many of the imps fired rounds into the air in excitement. The sole wyvern crewman who had not fallen onto one of the spikes whimpered as he looked up at the imps standing at the pit's edge. He begged weakly for mercy. But the imps could not understand the language in which he spoke.

Six of them jumped down into the pit, and the man was stripped and buggered by each before being inexpertly decapitated using the imps' standard-issue knives. In a state of frenzy they paraded his bloody head before the rest of their troop like a trophy, vociferous in their exhilaration. The rest of the imps watched in silence. Many of them were masturbating.

The imps then returned to the fallen wyverns and smothered the machines in tackbombs. As they scampered back towards the edge of the clearing an ageing snubship passed overhead, just a few metres above the treetops. Foliage caught in its powerful containment fields shuddered violently. One or two of the imps turned and screamed briefly at the craft before following their brethren into the darkness beneath the trees, where they vanished like apparitions.

The snubship's distinctive shape cast a cool shadow over the glade. As it slowed, the sound of its engines dropped from a high-pitched whine to a deep and resonant drone. In the dimly lit, armoured safety of the command suite, Delgado, Cascari and Ash sat in large padded seats looking at the displays hanging in the air in front of them. Delgado didn't like it. Although the entire command suite could be ejected from the snubship in the event of an emergency, it isolated them from both the pilot and the operatives in the large bay beneath them, which accounted for most of the snubship's interior.

Used by Structure primarily as assault craft to convey troops directly to the scene of a skirmish, or to transport munitions or supplies, this particular vessel contained fifty of the group's finest, fittest combatants, wearing the best assault gear available. They had given it their best shot. Yet here was Delgado, locked away in an armoured cupboard.

'What do you think is happening down there?' asked Cascari as he watched the display.

Delgado shook his head, frustrated. 'Don't know. Looks like three wyverns. They don't seem to have collided, though. Can't make it out.' He reached forward and switched between views. A rapid succession of patterns scrolled up the screen as the ship's core collated and analysed the available information. The screen switched back to realview and zoomed in on a much smaller area, panning from the clearing towards the trees. Individual traces were spot-lined by the enhancers, stat blocks overlaid on to each.

'It's a bunch of imps,' stated Ash. 'Out of control by the looks of it.'

Delgado snorted. 'You're right. They're a liability, those things. I remember them well. Never do what you want. Always screwing each other.'

Cascari looked at him. 'We going to go down? Might capture some wyvern crew.'

Delgado shook his head. 'Not what we're here for. No point putting ourselves at unnecessary risk for small fry. We've come for Michael. And Michael we'll get.' He opened a link to the pilot's bubble on the underside of the craft, just below the gaping, rectangular mouth to the bay. 'Ryan. Take us east. According to our information the target's supposed to be aboard a cerberus. Keep your eye on tracks from other aerial units, though. There's supposed to be a hydra in the area. If that gets a sniff of us and realises this ship's not what it's meant to be we're done for.'

'Understood.'

They felt firm pressure against their backs as Ryan increased power, the ship climbing away from the clearing.

Cascari gazed at the huge number of glowing plots moving smoothly across the display. 'There are two cerberus squadrons in this little party,' he said quietly. 'How are we going to find an individual craft among that lot?'

'I got Dogstar on the *Talionis* to hack into the biocomp in PGHQ,' said Ash placing a stick of gum in her mouth. 'Left him ploughing through the files trying to find out which ship

Michael's allocated to. Once he has it he'll let us know. It's an exercise in collating information. It'll do him good.'

Delgado smiled. 'Then we identify his ship, force it down, board it with our mercenary hoards and take him captive,' he said. 'Simple.'

A message icon blinked momentarily and then Dogstar's rugged face appeared on the screen, an ageing neural interface spread across one side of his face like burnt tissue.

'Well, speak of the Devil,' said Delgado humourlessly.

'Say what?' said Dogstar with a frown.

'Nothing, doesn't matter,' said Ash. 'What've you got for us, Dogstar?'

'Cyclops identifier code hash seven oh four seven oh four stroke six. Not old, not new, nothing special. Just a cerberus.'

'Great. Thanks, Dogstar.'

'No problem. You take it easy, OK? Keep those guys in line.'

As Dogstar's face faded, Ash linked to the snubship's pilot. 'You get that, Ryan?'

'Sure. The core's searching for the code now. OK. Got him. He's only a few klicks away.'

The snubship banked to starboard and Ryan applied more power. Delgado switched views. They were passing over minor skirmishes in clearings: dragons spouting flame as they advanced on enemy placements; wyverns striding through undergrowth and rivers.

Ryan's voice came to his ears once more. 'OK. We have a positive track. There's a lot of traffic, though. And I mean a lot. Shit.' The snubship lurched to port and descended abruptly. The engines seemed to groan in protest.

'What's the matter, Ryan?' asked Delgado.

'Xip fighter nearly hit us.'

'Collision detection must be shot,' said Cascari.

'Ours or theirs?' asked Ash.

Cascari shrugged. 'Well, if it happens again I guess we'll know it's ours.'

'I'll have to go to manual,' called Ryan.

Both Cascari and Ash looked at Delgado, who rapped his fingertips on the arm of his chair with one hand and scratched his nose briefly with the other. 'You're the pilot,' he said eventually.

The snubship rolled, turning hard. There was a muffled bang from somewhere towards the rear of the ship. Cascari looked at Delgado, his expression communicating concern. Delgado tried to get a realview outside the vessel but for some reason no image was now available.

'What was that noise, Ryan?'

'Just a surge in one of the generators. I'm lining up for an attack.' They could hear the pilot breathing heavily and muttering to himself as he struggled with the controls. They felt the snubship accelerate, heard a sudden wailing noise like engines passing close by. The displays in front of them flickered and briefly showed garbled information before returning to their former state. The snubship bucked and rocked momentarily, but whether this was due to turbulence or some other force acting upon the vessel, the three occupants of the command suite could not know.

As Delgado opened his mouth to speak to Ryan again the pilot's voice cut through the clamour. 'OK, here we go. Just a little bit more and we'll have him . . .'

The snubship steadied and the sound of the engines smoothed. Then they heard the resonant zing of the plasma canons – three groups of three pulses, then a pause as the weapons recharged.

The snubship veered as Ryan broke off his attack. There was a pause, then came three loud explosions somewhere behind their heads. The vessel shuddered violently. A locker door burst open, and at the rear of the command suite a pipe in the ceiling split open, spraying dark liquid.

'What's going on, Ryan?' shouted Delgado. 'We're all but blind up here.'

'Missed the target, sir. Sorry. They returned fire and got lucky. I'll go round again. But I think they might've got wind of the fact that we're not part of the exercise.'

Delgado laughed bitterly, shook his head. 'You don't say.' He closed the comms link for a moment, then opened it again. 'Is this ship healthy enough for the objective to still be achievable?'

No answer.

'Ryan?'

'Think he's been hit?' asked Ash.

'This ship's flying pretty good if the pilot's dead,' said Cascari flatly. Ash looked across at him with a stony expression, but said nothing.

'We're losing coolant,' Ryan came back. 'Lots of it.' They could hear panic in the pilot's voice. He was losing control. 'The cerberus is turning hard, coming after us. Xips too. Shit . . .'

There was another tremendous bang and the snubship suddenly listed to port, nose down. An alarm began to sound. A calm, automated voice began to report compromised hull integrity.

'I can't keep her up, sir.' Ryan sounded desperate, scared. Delgado was aware that Cascari was looking at him. 'We're at fifteen hundred feet but she won't respond. Shit. Eject! Eject!'

'Eject my ass, Ryan,' Delgado growled. 'Get this thing's nose up and bring her in as soft as you can.'

'If he engages the ground effect system it might cushion the impact,' suggested Ash. She spat her gum clean across the command suite in frustration.

'Since when were you an expert on snubships?' demanded Cascari.

'Ryan,' called Delgado, 'apply the ground effect system. If we hit, Ash says it might help.'

'No ifs about it, sir,' came the response. 'Ground effect system's on now. It's no good. Engine's too hot. We're going in. I'm sorry, sir. Oh my God! The trees!'

The combination of the trees and the limited power of the ground effect system had softened the snubship's impact to the extent that most of the troops in the bay were unharmed, as were Delgado, Cascari and Ash. They had been lucky. Luckier than Ryan. Due to the pilot's position on the underside of the craft, he was now spread across several hundred metres of forest.

They had evacuated the craft quickly and hidden among the trees as Structure aircraft passed overhead. The forest possessed a rich scent, a combination of moist earth, singed foliage and impure air. The snubship lay like a slain dinosaur, intact but somehow distorted, its fuselage buckled as if slowly melting. Many of the panels from which it was constructed had peeled away like reptilian scales.

Despite the rounded edges of the vessel's long, rectangular hull and its short, almost vestigial tail, its geometric form was a stark contrast to the natural surroundings. With the front of the craft buried in the soil and its rear end slightly higher than the nose, it appeared as though the earth was in the process of expelling a foreign body.

A surprisingly short gash in the trees indicated the steep angle of the snubship's descent. The energy shield normally in force across the ship's mouth, which protected the grunts prior to disembarkation in a drop-zone, had become disengaged as a result of the impact. This had allowed branches and a huge amount of soil to enter the vessel as it slid along the ground, covering much of the bay floor and rising almost level to the ceiling on the port side. Some of the troops had sustained injuries – mainly minor cuts and grazes – but none could be considered serious. In the few moments following the crash, medics had quickly applied copious amounts of frozone to stem blood loss and seal gashes.

Now, as they crouched in the undergrowth, Delgado assessed their situation and considered the options. The troops that surrounded him were anonymous, their faces covered with glossy black enmask and datastream goggle combinations, their skulls protected by helmets looted from some or other Structure storage depot. Numerous pits and scars in the matte black ultralite blastplate were evidence of previous combat use. Most also wore chameleon ground assault ensuits with bodywaste recykitz and full-point armour integration within a flexible, lightweight overskin. The garments rendered them virtually invisible against the foliage. All had close-reaction Jayman sidearms strapped to their left thighs, and apart from the four snipers – who had Xenon Longshot rifles and AG liftpacs – all had short-range Ghost disseminators. There was a popular phrase associated with these basic, high-power blast weapons: 'Hit 'em with a Ghost, turn 'em to toast.'

Delgado pressed his fingertips against the mike at his throat and spoke quietly, 'If we keep our heads we can still get out of here in one piece. Might be a fight but that's what we're used to. If we can get to the river, then there's a chance of a pickup from a sub if the *Talionis* knows where we've gone down. We'll spread out and move in a line, outriders above. Keep your eyes open. You see or hear anything, call in. OK. Let's go.'

Delgado indicated where the group should split with a movement of his right hand, and the operatives separated, their chameleon suits constantly rephrasing to match the surroundings as they moved. As the line was forming, the outriders charged their lifters and rose in eerie silence until just above the tree line. Their chameleon suits took a few seconds to adjust to the bright blue sky that was such a contrast to the gloom beneath the canopy, but when the adjustment was complete they could not be seen, and Delgado gave the signal for the group to move.

A few minutes later a red and white Structure medivac ship extended spindly legs to land just behind the crashed snubship, its turbines raising clouds of dust. It was five hundred metres or so behind them, he estimated, but Delgado knew that, although they would not easily be seen, their traces would show up on any scan. He indicated to those on either side of him that the line should spread out further to weaken the concentration. There was no point making Structure's task easy, after all.

Delgado looked up and tried to discern the outriders; he briefly perceived a faint shimmering above the trees, a momentary distortion of cirrus cloud, but it did not last long enough for him to be sure it was one of the men. He stopped moving and crouched. The rest of the group did the same. He looked around: something did not seem right. He opened a comms link. 'Delgado to outriders,' he whispered. 'You guys see anything up there?'

'There's a clearing ahead, sir,' came a soft reply. 'But air activity seems to be concentrated behind us, around the snubship.'

'Maybe they think it was an accident,' suggested Cascari, who was crouching a few metres to Delgado's left. 'Maybe they're not looking for a bunch of escaping guerrillas.'

'So why did they return fire? Why make an accident worse?'

'Trigger happy? Overenthusiastic?' suggested Ash with a thin smile.

Delgado peered grimly into the gloom. There seemed to be less aircraft overhead now. He wasn't sure what this meant. 'I don't like this,' he whispered. 'We'll wait here . . .'

A series of brilliant orange flashes appeared ahead and to his right, and a wave of heat and the sound of weapons fire – a crackling fizzing like the tearing of wet fabric – hit him a moment later.

There were screams. Fireballs bloomed. Trees began to burn.

Imps.

Delgado ordered return fire. One of the outriders was hit. With his chameleon suit damaged, the sniper's body reappeared as it fell, and by the time he hit the ground, numerous impacts with tree branches had given his limbs several additional joints.

The forest was consumed by a firestorm as the fighting became increasingly intense. Lines of light sliced the environment like strobes. The discharge of closely focused, high-intensity weapons was thick and fetid. Delgado glanced around and saw Cascari and Ash firing at targets they could not see.

He extended his nobics but they were weak and he could not focus on a single imp. All he seemed to be able to identify were human traces: lots of anger, bitterness, sexual arousal. But more striking than the human patterns were faint Seriattic streams; weak, beneath the surface – but evident nonetheless. He looked at Cascari again, but the traces he felt were different to those that normally characterised his son, and seemed to emanate from a different source.

As Delgado was thinking about their chances of reaching the river, he heard a slightly muffled voice: 'Outrider four to Commander Delgado. Structure transport heading this way, sir. Ten kilometres and closing. ETA two minutes. Looks like a cyclops.'

Delgado looked up. 'Good. Do nothing unless I say so. Understood?'

'Yes, sir.'

The battle died down abruptly, a sudden lull in which there were only sporadic bursts of fire. Delgado checked in with his operatives; some failed to reply, indicating casualties; none could confirm a single imp kill or even a positive sighting of the enemy.

Delgado saw bracken ahead of him tremble slightly and

sprayed it with ammunition. The trembling ceased and the rest of the forest remained still, as if deserted. He looked towards Cascari and Ash. Cascari was sweating and dirty and looked scared as hell, his shoulders rising and falling as he breathed. Ash seemed more composed, her expression revealing that she appreciated the gravity of the situation, and wasn't sure how they were going to get out of it.

'You OK?' Delgado asked.

Ash nodded unconvincingly, then looked away.

Cascari also nodded. 'I'd rather be in the air, though,' he said quietly. 'It's a lot less . . .'

'Flier closing, sir,' interjected the outrider. 'Positive ID: it's a cyclops.'

Delgado peered up at the light flickering through the canopy of leaves above. He heard an odd combination of sounds as the vessel's engines became audible both directly and through the comms link. Suddenly the vessel passed overhead, a triangular silhouette casting shadow, its three huge weapons glowing brightly. Its engines thudded dully like a series of loud yet muffled explosions as they propelled it slowly through the air. Delgado felt a surge of nobic activity that made his skin tingle, as if they were acting independently of him. The noise faded as the ship moved away.

A few moments later the outrider's voice returned. 'It's turning, sir,' he said. 'Heading back this way. I have a clear shot. I think I can bring it down, sir. What are your orders?'

'Do nothing yet,' whispered Delgado. He was unsure what motivated him to give this instruction, but for some reason it felt right. He looked around for those under his command, but the chameleon suits and natural camouflage obscured them completely. He could almost be alone.

'It's moving this way again, sir. Very slow. I'd say it's scanning. Descending. Barely above the trees now.' The slow rhythm of the vessel's engines increased in volume again, a concussive dissonance that shook the ground beneath them. 'There's a hatch opening on the side of the craft, sir. Ropes being dropped. Enemy operatives descending.'

Delgado stared through the trees. He was sweating heavily, could feel his heart beating. In the distance he saw flickering lines like silken threads, down which drops of black liquid appeared to flow.

Structure agents.

'All outriders, open fire,' instructed Delgado. 'Take them out! Take them out!'

The outriders opened fire from their vantage points above the trees, but the shots from the long-range sniping weapons they carried revealed their locations immediately and they did not last long. The body of one fell through the trees and landed just a few metres in front of Delgado. The man had a dark, smouldering hole in his abdomen. He stank of shit and charred wood.

An eerie silence returned after a few minutes of intense activity. Delgado could feel the tension, fear and uncertainty in his own operatives. He hunkered down, tightly clutching his weapon. With the slightest of movements, he signalled to Cascari and Ash: keep low, watch yourself.

The forest was a puzzle of light and dark segments that blurred definition and distance. There were insects wherever he looked – tiny, hovering specks. Cascari suddenly fell forward on his face. Ash was gone. Delgado looked behind him and saw a silhouette looming over him. He saw nothing, but heard the unmistakable fizzing of a primed sizzler. Then he lost consciousness.

In the vicinity of the M-4 wormhole

As the Structure Standard Patrol Vessel *Absolute Zero* made its way to the Dasslios system, it passed near the M-4 wormhole. Captain Canoba was aware of tensions in the region, with Seriattic vessels continuously challenging any craft passing close to the wormhole in an effort stop Sinz and Structure ships coming into contact with each other, and so had raised the level of alert to maximum.

As the *Absolute Zero* neared it, the mouth of the wormhole began to shudder, regular gravitational shock waves pulsing into space for hundreds of thousands of kilometres. Gradually, the pulses increased in frequency and strength, and Canoba ordered the vessel to be moved to a safe distance for observation. Spaceborne particles were pushed away from the wormhole mouth at increasing speed; gravity wells deepened and merged, creating ever-greater gravitational vortices. The *Absolute Zero* wanted to move despite the crew's efforts to maintain its new position and the ship's systems began to demonstrate unusual characteristics, the core reporting phantom anomalies.

The wormhole mouth began to increase in size, dilating like a cervix. Its black core suddenly began to glow, brightening from deep brown through luminescent orange to a brilliant yellow. The wormhole suddenly expanded rapidly, and the area of space around it momentarily became super-heated as an ellipse of orange light burst from it.

The wormhole contracted back to its original size almost instantaneously. Gravity wells ebbed, flowed and coiled as the glowing bulb of light decelerated from immeasurable velocity to a near standstill in just a few moments. The alien object enveloped the *Absolute Zero* as it decelerated. As it was momentarily consumed, the Structure vessel's hull warped and split, its crew evaporated by the immense heat.

The matter that had emerged so dramatically from the mouth of the wormhole hung in space, a lozenge of orange light like a half-blown glass bottle. Ripples and ridges generated in its soft surface by the enormous pressures of the huge deceleration began to settle again. As the outer shell cooled rapidly, hexagonal flakes began to peel away, thin and brittle detritus floating into space like dead skin, and within a few hours the object had metamorphosed from a soft malleable mass to a large oval structure.

Gradually, long tentacular extrusions of varying lengths emerged from it. They narrowed slightly towards the tip, and moved slowly, as if stirred by flowing water. The core of the vessel glowed, alternating through every vibrant colour imaginable, casting light along each tube; different parts of the craft glowed different colours, the colours changing at varying speeds.

The Sinz warship *nDegio Vahal* had arrived.

The wormhole began shuddering once more as another vessel approached. As the *nDegio Vahal* manoeuvred to a safe distance away from the wormhole, it began to release its payload, small boulder-like structures emerging from each of its tentacles, and accelerating rapidly as they dispersed towards their preordained destinations.

Structure's Olympus Mons base, Mars

'Remove their hoods.'

Delgado winced at the light as the cloth was removed from his head. Squinting, as his eyes became accustomed to the brightness, he looked around the room. It was too large to be the brig of a cyclops, and there was something odd about it he was unable to pinpoint. There seemed to be faint lines in the walls, but their irregular pattern made Delgado uncertain whether they were simply an optical illusion arising from his period of unconsciousness. His eyes ached like hell and a dense fug permeated his head. The combination of feelings reminded him of a time long ago when he had emerged from a deepsleep pod.

He twisted his hands, but his wrists were bound tightly behind him to the red plastic chair upon which he was sitting. He looked at Cascari who was sitting to his left. Cascari was similarly bound to a chair. His eyes were slightly bloodshot and puffy, but otherwise he looked OK. Ash was sitting next to

Cascari. She looked as determined and stubborn as ever, and was clearly struggling to contain her anger; Delgado had seen it released enough times to recognise the signs.

He looked up at the two men in front of them; one was a smart young Structure officer with blond hair and a crisp, clean uniform. Although the uniform itself had changed since Delgado's day, the Military Intelligence insignia on the collar was the traditional silver spiral. He looked the Military Intelligence type: self-centred, cruel, clinical. Despite his confidence he was clearly uneasy in the presence of his superior, and it was the latter who held Delgado's attention.

Michael was not wearing a uniform, but tailored clothes fashioned from black leather. He was a striking, fiercely handsome young man who looked confident, arrogant and relaxed in the familiarity and safety of his surroundings. His leather garments creaked softly as he moved.

'A father and son team,' he said, smiling thinly. 'Appropriate adversaries for my father and I. And a damsel in distress as a bonus. How nice.' His voice was warmer and softer than Delgado had expected, but he spoke with all the strength of character appropriate for General Myson's son. And although he looked wholly human, upon seeing Michael in the flesh for the first time, Delgado realised there was something slightly disturbing in his appearance, an intensity of expression – and a certain familiarity he could not quite isolate. Despite being unafraid, Delgado found himself trembling slightly. He was unsure why this was. 'I have to say that your audacity impresses me,' Michael continued, beginning to pace slowly. 'You attempted to put an outdated snubship into one of the largest military exercises ever to take place, attack my ship and *escape*?' Michael shook his head and snorted. 'Your group has been a thorn in my father's side for too long, Delgado. You have clearly become much too sure of yourselves. No more. Now we have you, and we will have some answers. We want to know details of the Mars Militia, details of their bases, contacts, safe locations.'

'Don't waste your time,' spat Cascari defiantly. 'You might as well kill us now.'

Delgado and Ash both looked at Cascari but said nothing.

Michael stepped closer to Cascari and leaned forward until their faces were separated by only a few centimetres. 'Oh dear,' he said quietly. 'Is your Seriattic *mourst* blood boiling, my friend? You need to learn to control it. Believe me, I know about that all too well.'

Delgado expected violence, but none came. Instead Michael stood and looked down at Ashala. He tipped his head to one side. 'And what are you?' he asked her quietly. 'Filling for the father and son sandwich?' He looked at his colleague and smiled broadly.

'Better that than an impotent puppet for William Myson.'

Michael struck Ash across the face with the back of one leather-gloved hand. Her face snapped to the right, spittle flew from her mouth and her nose began to bleed.

'I think perhaps we should speak to each of you in private,' Michael said in a louder voice. 'Here in Olympus Mons we have many interesting ways of extracting information. Indeed,' he glanced at his young colleague, who quickly flashed a broad but uncertain smile in return, 'many of them remain untested. Perhaps we should give you the privilege of trying them out for us.' He smiled benevolently.

Delgado blinked: he must have been unconscious for longer than he had thought. Olympus Mons was Structure's prestigious base on Mars within the ancient Martian labyrinth that lay beneath the dormant volcano. Details of the base were few, but there were plenty of rumours. Structure used the huge open space the Martians had apparently excavated immediately beneath the surface of the volcano as a giant hangar; but that was only the beginning. The base was immense, the lower levels extending for hundreds of kilometres in every direction beyond the volcano's edge. There were also rumours that Structure had stumbled upon an ancient Martian installation deep beneath the planet's crust, and that they had as yet managed to harness only a fraction of its apparent potential. There were also reports of mysterious disappearances and paranormal occurrences, visions and voices, which, despite the careful analysis of statements made by several extremely reliable witnesses, could not be explained.

Delgado looked at Cascari; he had a slightly split lip; his left cheek was bright red.

'You take this one,' Michael said to his colleague, indicating Cascari, while staring intently at Delgado. 'Officers Jones and Leyland can interrogate the female. This one I shall deal with myself.'

The expression Michael wore made Delgado uncomfortable.

Delgado's right cheekbone and head throbbed. His head hung forward. His hands were taped so tightly to the back of the chair they felt hot, the blood flow restricted.

'I hope your little boy's tough,' said Michael with a slight, affected snigger. 'Andersen likes a little rough and tumble. Especially with the feisty ones.' He walked to the wall and pressed his ear against it. 'Hmm. Can't hear anything,' he said quietly. 'That's not a good sign. Your female looks as though she can handle herself. But Jones may well loosen her tongue.' He turned and took a few steps towards Delgado, who braced himself for another blow. Instead Michael turned again, and began to pace, looking at the floor. 'You know, we could strike a bargain here,' suggested Michael. 'If you tell me the location of the Militia's base on Mars, give us a few names, a few locations to search, there's not really a problem. We could see to it that the Judgemaster is lenient. Lead us directly to Rodriguez and his cronies and we'll perhaps be able to make sure that you're . . . well catered for. Money, a new start on a colony. You were once part of the establishment, Delgado. It's a long time ago now – well before my time – but that still counts for something despite all the trouble you've caused.' Michael seemed sincere, but Delgado knew better than that. Myson had wanted him dead for a long time.

He glanced up; Michael's blue eyes were as striking as Cascari's. He looked down again. 'I don't know where the Militia's Martian base is,' Delgado uttered. Swollen lips distorted his words slightly. 'We've never seen Rodriguez in the flesh. We don't have any other contacts or information to give you. You're wasting your time.'

Michael struck Delgado on the side of the head with something blunt plucked from a nearby table. It was a sickening blow that made Delgado cry out. He found himself embarrassed by this. 'We're sick of you,' Michael sneered. Delgado blinked and closed his eyes, assigning another batch of nobics to physical repair. 'But my father's too wrapped up in other things to deal with you himself, so it's down to me.'

Delgado coughed and spat a gob of blood on to the smooth floor. 'I hear Myson's on his last legs,' he said hoarsely. 'That the members of the Planetary Council are just waiting for him to die and are already fighting among themselves for his position.' As Michael walked behind him, Delgado decided to take a gamble. He sat up a little straighter. 'I reckon you're just trying to get him to pay you some attention. Must be difficult, being the son of General William Myson. Groomed your whole life for the role he's had planned for you since before you were born. It's not like he's ever wanted you for yourself. You're just the key to something he wants. That must be tough.'

Michael turned, hooked his foot under the chair and tipped it over. Delgado grunted as he hit the ground and felt something in the back of the chair give way. The floor was cold against his cheek. It reminded him of the marble floor in Myson's chamber.

Michael walked a few steps, so that his feet were directly in front of Delgado's face. Delgado could see a distorted reflection of the room in the toes of the young man's polished leather boots. 'Maybe I should just take him your head,' Michael said quietly, as if thinking aloud. 'I think he'd be rather touched by such an old-fashioned gesture.'

Delgado looked up. Michael was gazing down at him with his head on one side, like an artist appraising a piece of work.

There was a gentle chime. Michael cursed softly and walked to the phone on the wall. He reached out and touched the screen. 'Yes, what it is?'

'Message for you, sir. From General Myson.'

'OK. Thank you.' A change in Michael's tone was evident. 'Put him through.'

Although he could not see the display, Delgado's skin tingled as he heard Myson's distinctive, wheezing rasp. He perceived Michael bowing slightly, presumably as Myson's face appeared on the screen.

'Michael,' he heard the general say, 'I am told you are on Mars.' Clearly angry, Myson was forced to pause as he was made even more breathless than usual. 'What are you doing there? This is not a time for games.' He coughed and hawked. 'You should be taking part in the exercise, as instructed, before your trip to Seriatt. It is important.'

'Sire,' replied Michael. 'I have captured Alexander Delgado, and other leading members of his terrorist group. We are trying to extract intelligence from them regarding the Mars Militia. I had intended to contact you when I had some concrete information.'

Delgado heard Myson cough again. 'I see. I appreciate your enthusiasm, Michael, but unfortunately I must ask you to curtail your activities. We have received further news of the device.'

Delgado blinked. Instinctively he knew this was the time-travel machine Rodriguez had mentioned.

'Has it been tested?' Michael asked.

'Not yet, but the Seriatts appear confident it will work. I must have access to it, Michael. Only through you can this be achieved.' Myson was forced to pause. 'I need you to go to Seriatt, Michael. Immediately. Forget the rest of the exercise, forget your captives. The diplomats have already wasted too much time engaging in negotiations with the Seriatts. You must go there now and take the place that is rightfully yours. Commander Osephius is waiting for you on *Zavanchia*. You must meet him there and he will ensure that you reach Seriatt safely.'

Michael bowed again. 'I will depart immediately, sire.'

'Very good. You must be careful, though, Michael. Your journey is dangerous, but the rewards for success are great.'

'I will not let you down.'

Michael disconnected, then walked back across the room and looked down at Delgado. 'I guess you've got a few days' grace,' he said warmly. 'I'll ask someone to keep you fresh until I return.'

'It's sad you're so desperate to please him,' whispered Delgado. 'It stifles your potential.'

Michael said nothing. He simply kicked Delgado's head until he lost consciousness.

When Delgado woke he was still lying on the floor. In front of him a stocky man was using the phone, but he was wearing the earpiece so Delgado could only hear one side of the conversation. He was clearly agitated, but spoke in hushed tones. He kept glancing nervously at the door.

'I know, I know. He just comes over and tells me he's got a "special assignment" for me. Then he brings me to this room and leaves. I don't know how long he'll be gone. Yeah. You think I don't know that? I can hardly argue with him, though, can I?'

Delgado twisted his hands around behind him; although the tape was tight he found he could move them a little. He felt a jag of plastic against his fingertips where the strut across the chair back had broken.

'Look, I don't like it either,' the man was saying, 'but what can I do? When General Myson's son tells you to do something, you do it.'

Delgado twisted his hands as much as he could, and managed to bring the tape into contact with the sharp points. As the man continued to complain, Delgado carefully tried to separate his wrists, applying pressure to the tape while simultaneously pressing it against the plastic shards. As the stocky man's conversation became more heated, Delgado felt the tape give way. There was a faint snapping sound as he pulled his hands apart, but due to the earpiece and the ongoing conversation the man did not hear it.

'Well, when he comes back I'll tell him to call you, shall I?' he was saying. 'Then you can express your views to him in person. See how he likes that, huh? Maybe he'll give you some of what he was obviously giving this guy before he left.' Delgado froze as the man jerked a thumb over one shoulder, but he did not turn.

While staring at the man's back, Delgado slowly drew his arms from behind him. His hands throbbed warmly as blood flowed rapidly back into them. Slowly he began pushing himself along the floor. When he reached the wall he silently got into a crouching position. He could now see the person to whom the stocky man was talking – an intimidating square-jawed woman who appeared to have a faint moustache. Although certain he was currently beyond the camera's field of view, he would have to ensure she didn't see him.

'That's all I've got to say,' the stocky man asserted. 'No, I don't. Why?' The woman's head moved somewhat jerkily as she asserted her apparently indignant viewpoint.

Delgado straightened his legs, moving from a crouch to a stoop. Slowly, his eyes still fixed on the man, he reached out and gripped one chair leg firmly in his right hand. The woman continued her tirade. Carefully, Delgado lifted the chair a few inches from the floor and drew it close to him.

'Well maybe it's best if we do, Ursula,' the man said. 'I've seen this coming for a while.' The woman responded with folded arms and a bitter expression. 'Yeah? Well, that's just how I feel too.' She wagged an apparently accusatory index finger. 'Oh, I knew you'd have to bring that up. She was nothing to me. It was just sex. But damn good sex, I'll tell you that. Yeah, yeah. I'll call you later to arrange collection of my things. Yeah. Right. Fine.' The stocky man reached out, touched the menu and the screen darkened. 'I'm better rid of you anyway,' he muttered as he snatched his ID card from the phone terminal.

Delgado crept a little closer and saw himself appear on the darkened screen, stooping slightly, chair leg visible over his right shoulder. The stocky man looked up and froze momentarily upon seeing Delgado's ghostly shape. He turned, open-mouthed, his card still clutched between the tips of his fat fingers. For a few seconds they simply looked at each other.

Then Delgado hit him with the chair leg.

The plastic creaked and flexed as it made contact with the side of the man's head. The man cried out and dropped to his knees, his left hand clutched to his ear. He took his hand from the side of his head and looked at his palm. His ear was very red but there was no blood. He looked up at Delgado with an expression of anger rather than fear. Delgado blinked and frowned: this wasn't how it was supposed to go.

He kicked the stocky man under the chin. The man's jaw clamped shut and his teeth severed the tip of his tongue. Blood blossomed from the man's mouth, but he was still far from disabled. Delgado looked at the flimsy plastic chair leg in his hand and decided that in its current state it was of limited use as a weapon. He hit it against the floor several times until it broke, then took one of the long, pointed strips and plunged it deep into the man's chest. The stocky man gasped as if in excitement and reached out with both arms, his eyes wide. His back arched, then a moment later he relaxed and fell forward.

Delgado looked down at the corpse. A dark slick was spreading slowly across the smooth floor. The feelings that stirred in Delgado were reminiscent of times long past – back when he was someone else. He rolled the body over and yanked the plastic shard from the man's chest, then bent down to wipe it clean on his clothing. It occurred to him that red plastic chairs concealed blood very well.

He stood, turned and checked his reflection in the phonescreen. He was pleased to see that the nobics were already having a marked effect, and that his bruising and swelling were already considerably less noticeable.

He stooped to pick up the man's ID card, then walked across the room to the door. He placed the card in the slot and heard the door click as it unlocked. He opened it slightly. Satisfied there was no one in the immediate vicinity, he stepped cautiously into the empty corridor outside. With the piece of broken chair concealed up his tunic sleeve, Delgado walked with confidence to the next room, where Cascari was being held. He paused at the door, glanced in both directions along the corridor, listened for anyone approaching, then pressed his ear against the door seal.

He could hear little. Certainly nothing that sounded like an interrogation. Nonetheless, strong emotional traces were clear: hatred, desire, greed; a basal combination that disturbed him. He glanced at the lock to the side of the door. It was different to the one on the door to the room in which he had been held, far more advanced, lacking an ID card slot.

Suddenly he heard footsteps, conversation and laughter along the corridor, but the hard, bare walls and floor caused reverberation that made it difficult to tell from which direction the people were approaching. Faced with a limited number of options, he knocked on the door.

Delgado looked past the man who opened the door and took in the scene in a moment.

Cascari was standing, tied by the wrists to a blue plastic chair in front of him. His trousers were pulled down to the knees, the rest of his clothes tugged and twisted out of shape. His shoulders were low, his head lolling forward as if he were completely exhausted or utterly defeated. He was sweating to an extent that seemed disproportionate to the temperature in the room, beads of perspiration visible at his temples. There was a thick, slightly foul odour.

There were three other men in the room. One was the young, blond-haired officer Delgado had seen earlier. He had removed his tunic and rolled up his shirt sleeves. The other two were of a similar age, possibly of equal rank to the first. They were looking at Cascari.

As the people he had heard in the corridor passed behind him, Delgado looked directly at the man who had opened the door for the first time. His face was jowly, the skin somewhat flushed, as if he had just performed a task requiring a level of exertion to which he was unused. The whites of his eyes were slightly bloodshot; he had a creamy glob of spittle at one corner of his mouth and uneven, discoloured teeth. He seemed to be trembling slightly. He swept a limp strand of thin, greasy hair from across his face and back into position on top of his head. He tried to paste it down with one podgy palm, but it seemed reluctant to remain in place. An embroidered badge on his breast pocket revealed his name to be Simmons.

'What the hell do you want, for Christ's sake?' Simmons

demanded. A faint snort was audible at the end of the sentence. 'We're busy here.'

Delgado smiled warmly, and assigned a small batch of nobics to physical-strength enhancement. He glanced to his left to check that the other people were out of sight, then punched the flabby man in the face. Simmons cried out and staggered backwards across the room, arms windmilling. He crashed into the chair Cascari was tied to, his weight and momentum pushing it across the smooth floor and Cascari staggering sideways with it. The chair broke when it hit the wall and the tape binding his wrists came away, freeing his hands.

As Delgado strode into the room he allowed the shard of plastic to slide down his sleeve and into his hand. The two other men were moving towards him. The first immediately fell to the ground as Delgado plunged the shard of plastic into the side of his neck. Delgado then grabbed the blond officer by the front of his tunic and lifted him from the floor, pushing him across the room. The young man gasped and paled at the severity of the impact of his body and head against the wall. Delgado pushed the makeshift blade into the blond officer's abdomen in a slow, almost considerate movement.

His victim's colour drained and he weakened quickly. As Delgado gripped him around the neck with his left hand and watched him die, he heard a dull thud behind him, followed by a muffled shot.

Delgado turned, allowing the now unconscious blond officer fall to his feet, and saw Cascari trying to wrest a sidearm from the other officer's grip. As Delgado stepped forward there was another shot, and a spray of dark paste that coated an area of the ceiling like paint.

Delgado walked over to the two men and rolled the corpse now pinning Cascari to the floor over with the toe of his boot. The dead man's expression was like that of a lotto winner. One side of his neck was missing, the rest a mass of burnt flesh.

Delgado extended a hand to help Cascari to his feet. 'You OK?' he asked.

Cascari nodded, but did not look Delgado in the face. He busied himself by straightening his clothes and buckling his belt. 'Sure, fine,' he replied stiffly. 'You?'

Delgado looked at him with uncertainty. 'Sure. No problem.' He stooped and picked up the sidearm, looking the weapon over. It was a nice, compact unit and he held it loosely in his fingers. It seemed fairly heavy for such a small gun but its weight distribution was perfect. Judging from the small FCT screen on top of its chunky barrel and the row of mini-SGN jacks along each side it was also relatively advanced. Delgado hoped it did not posses any personal recognition capabilities that could prevent him from using it. He looked at Cascari again. 'You sure you're OK?'

Cascari looked at him and forced a smile. 'Never better,' he said.

Delgado nodded doubtfully. He looked around the room. Built into the wall to the left was a large screen of some kind, beneath which there was another, smaller screen. There was also a phone like that in the room in which he had been held. Opposite these was a two-seater sofa next to a low table. The wall to the right of the door was covered in shelving that contained a variety of storage media: hundred of microdiscs and smartcarts, a few books. On the table lay an empty confectionery wrapper, a passcard, a glass half-filled with colourless liquid. Delgado picked up the glass and sniffed at its contents, but there was no odour. He replaced it, took the passcard, glanced at both blank sides, then placed it in his pocket.

'Come on,' said Delgado. 'We've got to find Ash. And quickly.'

'She's in the room next to this one.'

'You're certain?'

'I heard her shouting,' explained Cascari.

'Shouting? You mean screaming?'

'No, I mean shouting. Giving whoever's in there with her a hard time.'

Delgado smiled.

They walked to the door and peered into the corridor.

'All clear,' Delgado whispered. 'Come on.' He and Cascari stepped into the corridor and carefully closed the door to the room behind them. They walked the few paces along the corridor to the next door. They didn't have to listen too closely to hear Ash's voice, as she advised her interrogator about the likelihood of getting any information from her. There was the sound of an impact, a momentary silence, followed by profanities from Ash.

Delgado looked at Cascari. 'I reckon she's on the other side of the room. What do you think?'

Cascari listened for a moment, then nodded. 'Yeah. Far corner on the left. Sounds like there're just the two people in there with her.'

'OK. Good. Well, knocking politely worked last time. Let's give it another go, shall we?'

Cascari shrugged. 'Your call,' he said.

Delgado rapped on the door. They heard muffled voices and footsteps.

'What is it?' a woman demanded from the other side of the closed door.

'Maintenance,' stated Delgado. 'We've come to fix the phone.' He felt Ash's emotional shift as she recognised his voice.

There was a pause, then a few more muffled words. 'There's nothing wrong with the phone. Get lost. We're interrogating a prisoner.'

'But we've been told to fix the phone. Could you just let us in to inspect it?'

'No. The phone's not broken and we're busy.'

Delgado looked at Cascari and rolled his eyes. 'If we don't fix the phone we'll be docked pay,' he said.

'Not my problem, buddy,' came the terse reply. 'Come back some other time. Preferably when the phone's broken.'

Delgado looked at the door and the wall surrounding it, then produced the sidearm and examined it. 'Think this thing's powerful enough to blow a hole in the wall?' he asked quietly.

'Let's try it and see, huh?'

Delgado opened menus and scrolled through options. The weapon was basic and had few settings. He selected that which seemed the most powerful – high-intensity projectile ordnance – then armed the gun. 'Better back off,' he said, walking across the corridor. 'We don't know how big the bang's going to be.'

They stood in the recess to a storage-cupboard door in the wall opposite the interrogation-room door. Delgado briefly checked that no one was approaching, then aimed at the wall to one side of the cell door and fired three times, the small handgun recoiling far more violently with each shot than when firing plasma. The blast echoed around the corridor, which filled with a dense cloud of pale dust. They heard rubble falling. Delgado and Cascari began to cough.

'Jesus,' said Delgado. 'What's this place made of?'

As the dust began to clear they saw that the shots had made a hole in the wall about a metre in diameter, around waist-height. They stepped towards it and peered through the dust into the room.

Ash was where they had suspected, bound to a chair with her hands behind her back. She was looking in their direction, and appeared simultaneously angry and relieved.

There were two women in the room with her. One was lying on the floor with a dark, wet patch of hair on the back of her head where she had been hit by either a hunk of rubble or one of the rounds. The other woman was to the right, fumbling to get an ID card into the phone on the wall. The screen brightened.

'This is a security alert,' she yelled, 'area six, interrogation suite . . .'

Delgado reached through the ragged hole in the wall and fired another three shots. One entered the woman's abdomen just below the ribcage and punched a large exit hole. She dropped to her knees then fell forwards, landing heavily, face down. The other two shots smashed the phone she had been using, shattering the screen and destroying the casing.

'You get in there and free Ash,' Delgado instructed. 'I'll stay here, just in case they managed to work out where she was calling from. Quickly.'

Cascari stooped and squeezed through the hole. It was a surprisingly tight fit. A few moments later Ash's head appeared in the hole made by the blast.

'Never been so glad to see you, Delgado,' she said as she clambered into the corridor. 'They were nasty pieces of work. Fortunately for me, they kept arguing about who was going to do what to me.'

'So what was all your shouting about?' Delgado asked.

'What? You think I was going to let them touch me?' She began dusting herself down. 'No way. They came near me, I kicked out. I kinda threw my weight around. I bit one on the hand. Drew blood,' she said with some pride.

Delgado and Ash both looked down at Cascari as he emerged through the wall.

'You know what they need in here,' he said

'No, what?'

'Someone to fix the phone.' The others laughed briefly.

'So what do we do now?' asked Ash. 'We're stuck in the middle of a Structure facility and we don't know where Michael is.'

'Michael's gone.'

'Where? How do you know?'

'A call from Myson himself came in while I was there. Michael's meeting Osephius on *Zavanchia*, then they're going to Seriatt.'

'Shit,' said Ash. 'We need to get out of here. Get a ship.'

'You bet.' Delgado looked at the bodies in the room. 'Ash, you take her clothes,' he said indicating one of the dead women. 'She looks about the same height and build as you. You come with me.' Delgado and Cascari left Ash to change and returned to the room where Cascari had been held. 'I'll wear this,' he said, indicating the blond officer's tunic, which was lying on a nearby table. 'You take his.' He pointed at the man Cascari had killed. Cascari looked at Delgado with a doubtful expression. 'Well, OK, I admit it might be a bit short in the sleeves and legs but you'll be fine. Stick your hands in your pockets. No one will notice.'

The Olympus Mons facility was maze-like. The three of them spent the next half hour walking stealthily along mostly empty corridors only to find they were dead ends. The one or two people they did pass paid them little attention, although Cascari's short sleeves and trousers did lead to the odd second glance. Delgado listened intently at a few doors, but those they could open turned out to be to vast warehouses or small storage rooms which seemed to contain more than the vast warehouses.

'Where do you think everyone is?' asked Cascari quietly.

They turned a corner and walked along a corridor lined with lockers; Delgado tried to open one or two, but they were all secure. 'Beats me,' he replied.

'Gone home for Thanksgiving?' Ash suggested.

'Hang on.' Delgado held up one hand and stopped walking. 'Listen.' They could hear singing. The voice was very high-pitched and faint, the tune unrecognisable.

They continued walking slowly along the corridor, then turned another corner into a shower and latrine area. To the left was a communal shower block, opposite which were a dozen toilet cubicles. Next to these were empty clothing racks. There was a strong smell of disinfectant.

They continued to follow the singing. It was coming from within one of the cubicles. Delgado gently pushed open each door and peered in. The fourth door was already open. Kneeling in front of the toilet was a waif, a creation of Myson's biotechs to perform menial duties for which automatics were too cumbersome or clumsy, or which the Artificial Intelligence Rights Institute – a body comprised solely of AI devices – said were beneath semi-sentient automatons.

Roughly the size of a slim eight-year-old boy, the waif wore pale blue cotton shorts and a grubby white vest that was slightly too small for him. He was busily cleaning the toilet bowl with a small sponge. A bottle of disinfectant stood next to the pedestal. The singing faded abruptly and the waif stopped scrubbing. Then the tiny creature slowly turned his head to look over his right shoulder.

The waif stood and turned to face the three people silhouetted against the glare, the backs of his legs pressed against the aluminium bowl he had been cleaning. He passed the sponge from one hand to the other nervously.

The waif stared at them, large, dark eyes set in a dirt-smeared face. His pale, bony limbs trembled slightly. Delgado looked down at the creature's white singlet and blue shorts, both of which were stained various shades of grey. There was a small pool of urine at his bare feet.

Delgado turned his head and whispered to Cascari. 'Go back there and keep watch while we talk to our little friend here, will you?'

Cascari nodded and walked away. Delgado knelt. The waif gazed at him, clearly terrified. Delgado smiled with as much warmth as he could summon, but the expression felt unusual and fake. 'I'm not going to hurt you,' he said, speaking softly and slowly. 'Can you tell me which way we need to go to get to the hangar?'

The waif frowned and tilted his head to one side a little.

Delgado cleared his throat and the waif started as if electrocuted. Delgado uttered soft assurances and reached out to touch the waif on the forearm. The creature flinched. 'Jesus Christ,' he said softly. 'What the hell do they do to you?'

Although the waif's expression remained unchanged, tears began to run down his delicate cheeks.

'Look,' said Delgado calmly. 'We're looking for the hangar. You know, where the spacecraft are kept.' The waif simply moved backwards until he was crouching on the toilet seat. Delgado held his hand out in front of him, thumbs at right-angles to the rest of his hands, their tips touching. 'Spaceships,' he said, raising his eyebrows and nodding. 'Spaceships. Yes?'

The waif edged nervously off the seat, turned to face the toilet, pushed down his damp shorts, then leaned forward and stuck out his pale buttocks.

'Jesus, no, no.' Flushed and feeling slightly sick, Delgado turned his head away and quickly pulled up the waif's shorts. The waif stared at him, clearly bewildered.

'Here,' said Ash. 'Let me try.' Delgado stepped out of the cubicle and she took his place. As she crouched, she pulled a stick of gum from her pocket. She broke it in two, popped one half into her own mouth and offered the other to the waif. He looked at the small grey square for a moment, then placed it in his mouth and began to chew. He smiled and his eyes widened as the flavour spread across his tongue. Ashala looked into the waif's eyes. He flinched only slightly as she took his small, cold hands in her own. 'You know where the spaceships are, little fella?' She let go of the waif's hands and held her right hand out in front of her, fingertips pointing upward, palm facing the waif. Raising her hand in the air she tried to make a sound like a pulse engine.

'You sound like a frustrated horse,' Delgado observed.

'Spaceships,' Ash repeated, ignoring him. 'Stars. Earth. Space?' She thrust her hands in the air several times, continuing to make the same strange, equestrian sounds.

Suddenly the waif became excited, nodding vigorously. The tiny creature pushed past her out of the cubicle and past Delgado, skipping towards the door at the end of the room where Cascari was standing guard. Cascari turned when he heard the faint slapping sound of the waif's bare soles on the smooth floor, and simply watched as the creature skipped past him into the corridor beyond.

Delgado and Ash followed. 'Come on,' she said. 'Our little friend here's either taking us to the hangar or the stables.'

Cascari frowned, glanced from one to the other of them, then opened his mouth to ask a question but thought better of it.

Fifteen or so minutes later they emerged from the corridor to find themselves on a platform overlooking the interior of the immense Olympus Mons hangar. Row upon row of space-ships, aircraft and ground vehicles were housed within the enormous cavern, which was dissected at regular intervals by thick, square pillars. These had an internal luminescence that appeared to be the only source of light. People were working on vessels of various sizes, while spare parts, tools and diagnostic equipment was ferried to technicians by couriers speeding along a grid of smooth, wide tracks. The shrill sound of drills, pneumatic hammers, and the roar of engines created a deafening cacophony.

Delgado pointed towards the centre of the hangar where a ship was emerging slowly from a large dark circle in the rock ceiling. Several other vessels hovered or circled slowly nearby like predators. 'Looks like that's the way in and out,' he called above the noise. He looked around and saw a stairway to their right that zigzagged down to the hangar floor. 'Reckon we can steal a ship from under their noses?'

'Do you?' asked Cascari.

'Well, I'd say that they're not going to miss one ship from among this lot, and even if they realise what we're up to before we get out, I reckon they'll be reluctant to start a fight in here. It's just too enclosed.'

'They might have vessels outside, though,' said Ash. 'Shoot us down as soon as we emerge from the other end of shaft.' She pointed towards the hole.

'Yeah, well, that's more than a possibility,' Delgado admitted. 'Guess we'll just have to find out, won't we?' He scanned the hangar floor, looking at the various craft, then pointed towards one particularly distinctive vessel nearby. It looked like a flat triangular dart with a short tail and wings. 'There,' he said. 'That's the one. A Colonial Armouries Strapher unless I'm very much mistaken.' A tiny cascade of brilliant white sparks danced briefly beneath the craft's nose as a technician welded part of the forward landing assembly. Mid-way along the Strapher's fuselage the ship's hatch was open, a wash of yellow light spilling onto the hangar floor.

'You think we can fly it?' asked Cascari. 'It looks pretty old.'

'That's *why* we can fly it. Tough as old boots, those things. Built to fly fast, hit hard and take plenty of incoming fire without coming down, with simple systems a couple of people can control and a core that doesn't give backchat. Just what we need.'

Delgado turned to Ash. 'Better say goodbye to your little friend,' he said.

Ash nodded. The waif was peering in wonderment through the railings at the incredible scene in the hangar. She walked over to him and placed one hand on his right shoulder. Ash crouched as the waif turned to face her. 'Here,' she said, and plucked a few more sticks of gum from her pocket, placing them in the waif's right hand and closing his tiny fingers around them. The waif smiled broadly, his eyes bright and vibrant. 'You take care, OK?' The waif simply gazed at her for a moment, then skipped away.

The double-doors leading off the platform flew open as the

waif reached them, and he was flung backwards through the air, skidding along the ground on his backside. Two leather-clad Structure security officers strode from the corridor beyond, their sidearms already drawn, apparently confident of the identities of those in front of them. They gave no warning, but simply raised their weapons and started firing, killing the waif instantaneously.

In a single movement Delgado shoved Cascari and Ash towards the stairs, yelling at them to run, and threw himself behind a nearby control desk. He fired the weapon he carried twice, hitting one of the security officers in the chest. He fell as if his feet had been kicked from under him. The second security officer was a woman, and clearly more alert than the first. Even before her colleague had hit the ground she had activated a microshield – a protective, bell-shaped blister that enveloped her, its surface swirling like a soap bubble. In Delgado's Structure days microshields were for use only on large vehicles such as wyverns, and required huge generators to produce them. It seemed the art of miniaturisation meant they were now available for personal protection. While the shield allowed her to fire out, it would absorb the energy of any shots fired at it.

Delgado glanced towards the stairs as the Structure officer advanced. Unarmed, Cascari and Ash were powerless to help him. 'Get out of here,' he shouted. 'Go on. See you at the bottom in five.' Although clearly uncertain, they did as they were told and ran down the metal stairs.

Delgado peered over the top of the control panel. The officer was almost upon him. He fired three shots in rapid succession that were all perfect hits. The microshield blister shimmered and became like frosted glass, the officer's shape obscured by the distortions in its surface. She stopped walking for a moment, firing a few shots blindly as she waited for the blister to clear. Two missed completely, while the third disembowelled the control panel that was providing Delgado with cover.

Delgado glanced over his shoulder at the metal railings, then scampered towards them, keeping low. He poked his head through the railings and looked down. It was a good eight or ten metres to the hangar floor, but he could see the foot of the stairs to his right. He turned, stood and fired again – five shots that hit in exactly the same place; the blister frosted and deformed. A rapid calculation: he reckoned it would take five or six seconds for the shield to clarify again, another five or six for the officer to realise what Delgado had done and deactivate the shield to enable her to get down the narrow staircase. No problem.

Delgado shoved the sidearm in the back of his waistband, clambered quickly through the railings, then lowered himself down until he was hanging from the edge of the platform. He glanced over his shoulder; it occurred to him that this would not be a good time to suffer two broken ankles. But what choice did he have?

He let go of the railing.

Delgado landed heavily on a courier that appeared from beneath the platform. He was fortunate as it was carrying sacks of grain, and although the impact took the wind from him he was otherwise unharmed. As he rolled off the sacks in search of cover before the security officer appeared, the courier trundled on, spilling its load.

Delgado ran to Cascari and Ash who were near the foot of the stairs. 'Come on,' he yelled, 'let's get out of here before she can follow us down here.' He grabbed Cascari by the sleeve and dragged him forward, running towards the parked ships.

As they crossed the open space of some twenty metres, a small airborne surveillance drone – a ten centimetre diametre sphere covered in dimples – suddenly appeared, hovering in front of them. Delgado hardly aimed before firing but destroyed the drone with a single round, fragments of its plastek casing scattering widely. Delgado looked around quickly, but, despite his fears, their activities attracted little attention in the hubbub of the hangar, the noise level drowning out the sound of the shot.

Delgado glanced over his shoulder towards the stairs while they were still in sight. The security officer was looking around her, scowling, having lost her prey among the crowds and machinery.

They ran around the side of a toilet block, slowing to a quick walk as they came to an area swarming with people standing in queues waiting to be served at a food vending hut. The aroma of hot meat and warm bread was thick, and Delgado's stomach grumbled fiercely.

He leaned close to Cascari and Ash as he led them through the crowd. 'Keep behind me,' he hissed. 'Don't make eye contact with anyone and keep your hands in your pockets so no one notices your uniforms. And don't slouch. This is a Structure base, remember. Structure operatives don't slouch. Walk as though you're proud as hell just to have the opportunity to shit here.' He paused as they passed close to the tail end of one of the queues. 'We'll need to be quick,' he continued a moment later. He glanced up, looking for more drones. There seemed to be some, high up in the hangar, but they hadn't yet identified them. 'When we get to the Strapher,' said Delgado, 'we walk straight up the ramp. If we're challenged at any point, or if we meet anyone on board, just leave things to me. Got it? Good. You two pilot the thing and I'll man one of the guns.'

They turned along a much narrower, almost deserted pedestrian walkway that ran alongside one of the tracks used by the couriers, and into the shadow cast by a large freighter, dwarfed by its gigantic, smooth-edged rhomboid shape. Through the viewports towards the front of the craft, low down on the hull, several technicians could be seen working on the vessel's flight deck, their heads just visible through the thick window as they knelt to work on circuits beneath the instrument panel. One of them glanced up as the three of them passed, but immediately returned to his work.

On the other side of the freighter, cargo was being loaded. Three long conveyor ramps on gigantic bogies were positioned against open hatches about twenty metres above the hangar floor, carrying large transport cases from parked couriers up to the freighter's cargo holds. Ahead, Delgado saw a scattering of sparks appear from beyond the next ship: they had almost reached the Strapher. He looked up, searching for drones, which might be able to get a fix on them more easily now they were among fewer people. He could see none.

A young man in a dark uniform suddenly stepped from between the freighter and the shuttle next to it. A shiny black rectangular badge on his chest stated in clear white lettering that his name was Ormerod, P. The name carried an unwelcome resonance for Delgado, and he unconsciously increased his pace.

Ormerod blinked rapidly and frowned as he saw Delgado and his two companions approaching. He straightened his posture and looked as if he were about to salute, unsure whether Delgado was someone of rank he should know about. Ormerod glanced with uncertainty at Cascari and Ashala, his frown deepening.

As the two men met, Delgado saluted. When Ormerod automatically reciprocated, Delgado grabbed him and spun him round so that he was facing the freighter. He placed his right arm around Ormerod's neck and across his chest, gripping his tunic firmly. Delgado felt confusion sweep through Ormerod as he began to struggle, gripping Delgado's forearm and attempting to throw him. Had Delgado not placed the sidearm against Ormerod's temple the Structure officer might have been more resistant.

'Keep your mouth shut and your hands by your sides and there's little chance of this thing going off,' sneered Delgado, shoving the barrel of the gun against the side of Ormerod's head. 'Now, we're going to move backwards, towards the Strapher.' Ormerod tried to look over his shoulder to see the ship Delgado was referring to, but Delgado yanked at his tunic. A drone suddenly appeared in front of them, the small sphere bobbing up and down on the air. Delgado fired once and missed, but hit it with a second shot. He looked up and saw two more drones spiralling down towards them, attracted to the weapon like flies to a corpse.

With Cascari and Ash walking between himself and Ormerod and the nearby courier track, Delgado had one arm locked around his captive's neck, and began to move towards the Strapher.

Abruptly a klaxon began to sound, its shrill tone cutting through the hangar's clamour. High above Delgado saw a snap of light reflected off the barrel of a weapon as the person carrying it ran along a gantry.

With Delgado's attention momentarily diverted, Ormerod managed to get one leg behind one of Delgado's and the two men fell into a sprawling heap, the gun sliding along the floor. Ormerod elbowed Delgado in the stomach and leaped to his feet. As he ran towards the nearby courier track Ash lunged for the gun and brought it quickly to bear.

'Leave it,' yelled Delgado before she had an opportunity to fire. 'He's not a threat. Let's just get out of here. We'll need to move fast now they're on to us.' Delgado looked towards the track where Ormerod was trying to dodge the rapid flow of traffic he had so willingly run into. He failed. A bulky, rectangular courier caught him a glancing blow that sent him spinning into the path of another automatic, the leading edge of which broke his thigh. Ormerod yelled in agony and fell, lost from sight among the multitude of speeding drones. The machines lurched and bounced as they ineffectively tried to avoid the man.

As they neared the Strapher, Cascari pointed at the technician who was still welding part of the landing skid, a dark visor clamped firmly over his face. 'What about him?' he called.

'Forget him,' responded Delgado. 'Not a problem.'

As they neared the hatch Delgado heard a loud, brief fizzing sound behind him and turned to look. The security personnel on the high gantry had apparently mistaken Ormerod as one of those they were chasing. The gunman was no sniper, however, and instead of Ormerod the shot had hit one of the couriers – a medium-sized low-loader carrying several large containers. The initial shot had destroyed part of the sensor array at the front of the vehicle and the unit immediately veered off course, crossing the path of several vehicles travelling in the opposite direction. Unable to relay information to the central controlling computer quickly enough, they collided.

In an instant the traffic was thrown into chaos. One unit overturned, spilling its cargo of pre-packed meals; others trundled leisurely off the track, hitting parked vehicles, control desks or each other. A further shot from the security operatives was as poorly aimed as the first and another large courier left the track, disappearing from sight between the freighter and the shuttle. A few moments later one of the bogies carrying a conveyor ramp emerged sedately from between the two craft, a man dangling by one hand from halfway up it, clinging desperately to the metal framework as it moved slowly towards the courier track.

The security operatives on the gantry were running towards a lift tube leading down to the hangar floor. Delgado destroyed two more drones but saw half a dozen others approaching rapidly. As the three of them ran towards the Strapher the welder stopped what he was doing and looked up, pushing up his visor.

Delgado, Cascari and Ash ran up the ramp into the vessel's belly. As they entered the craft all sound seemed to be absorbed by its armour. Even with the hatch door still open the environment within was a stark, muffled contrast to the tumult outside.

Delgado briefly examined a small control panel next to the door and thumbed one of the tabs. The thick hatch door slid shut with a rumble they could feel through the soles of their feet. When it was closed Delgado thumbed a combination of other tabs, and there were several loud clunks and a hiss of compressed air as the hatch sealed.

'Right,' he said, turning and grinning brightly at Cascari and Ash in the gloom. 'Up to the flight deck.' He rubbed his hands together eagerly. 'Let's get this show on the road.'

Three

the embrace of salmacis

The Chamber of Visions, Seriatt

Arbiter Messinat stood in front of the Oracles' couch in the centre of the Chamber of Visions. Oracle Entuzo sat to her left, near the door, her head bowed as if she were sleeping. Entuzo's fellow Administrators looked down at her from the circular room's auditorium. Proctors Coortien and Rümini were in the front row, looking as stern-faced and conspiratorial as ever, while Arbiters Shorial and Alovia were among those seated further up the tiers. These were the most powerful of the Administrators, and Messinat knew how great their influence was over the opinions of the others. As well as Seriatt's interests, they also had their own agendas to consider, and the two were not always compatible. She knew she would have to be wary of them.

A few other Oracles were also present, standing at the rear of the auditorium, apart from the Administrators. The relationships that existed between these mysterious, secretive *vilume* and other Seriatts were impossible to analyse, and Messinat was unable to guess at the Oracles' motives or moods.

When the Administrators seemed settled, Messinat addressed them. 'Thank you for convening at such short notice,' said the Arbiter warmly. She looked down, loosely linking her fingers before her to indicate gratitude and respect. 'I have exciting news. A short while ago, Oracle Entuzo adorned the Destiny Mask.' As she gestured towards Entuzo, there were murmurs among the Administrators: no projection was scheduled, no one had been informed that the Mask was to be used; this was an irregularity, and the Administrators almost always looked unfavourably upon irregularities. Messinat continued, disregarding the slight hubbub. 'The Oracle has seen many things in the past,' she said, 'but this latest projection is particularly important. Oracle Entuzo believes the mask has shown her something of great potential.' There was more chatter. When the Administrators quietened in anticipation, Messinat continued, 'The Oracle believes she has seen something wonderful: the coming of a Saviour.'

There was a shocked silence. The Administrators looked at each other, their former suspicion replaced with quiet excitement; but there was also some uncertainty regarding the implications of this statement.

Proctor Coortien – a particularly surly-looking *mourst* – stood. 'Explain yourself, Arbiter Messinat,' he demanded. 'I'm sure that, like myself, the other Administrators would be interested to know what kind of "Saviour" we are to expect, and when.' He looked at those around him, seeking support. 'How will this Saviour be manifest,' he continued, 'and, more importantly, from what do we need saving?'

There were a few quiet noises of agreement, led by Proctor Rümini and Arbiter Alovia. Arbiter Messinat glanced at Oracle Entuzo, whose head remained bowed. 'Given Seriatt's current turmoil, with the sudden and tragic loss of the Monosiell, the impositions of the Andamour Council and the continued friction with Earth, Seriatt is particularly vulnerable at this time. Unfortunately, the Oracle cannot provide more details,' the *vilume* admitted, 'but is nonetheless confident of the accuracy of the prediction. A Saviour will come to us.'

Coortien did not seem convinced. 'The Oracles' visions are a guide at best, Arbiter Messinat. This is a fact of which we are all aware. Many such predictions have been inaccurate in the past. Why does the Oracle feel that this one is so different?'

Messinat tried to remain patient. 'The Oracle believes there was . . .'

To Arbiter Messinat's left, Oracle Entuzo suddenly looked directly at the Administrators in the auditorium. She stared at Proctor Coortien, her completely black, oval eyes shining like polished stone, startling and eerie. 'The clarity of the visualisation cannot be questioned,' Entuzo stated, her voice surprisingly strong and clear given her fragile frame. 'I cannot accurately describe the Saviour's form, but I assure you there is no doubt that we are to be visited by one who can help us greatly. How or when, I am unable to specify, but it is a certainty. I would also remind the Proctor that the *conchey trinzig diasii* predicts the arrival of a Saviour "in times of dire need". Given the circumstances on our world I would suggest that, without the guidance of a Monosiell, Seriatt's need has never been greater.'

Proctor Coortien sat down again, clearly frustrated. Despite his disliking for Arbiter Messinat, even he did not feel able to directly challenge an Oracle. 'I am not convinced, Arbiter Messinat,' the *mourst* stated quietly. His addressing her while seated was indicative of his feelings. 'The *conchey trinzig diasii* is a speculative document, and its origins are unknown. Those who follow its teachings in modern times do so at risk, in my opinion. Should this so-called Saviour reveal itself to us in due course then I will of course review my position. In the meantime, however, I will remain sceptical.' He glanced at those around him again, but this time they remained silent.

'You are entitled to your opinions, of course, Proctor Coortien,' said Messinat. 'However, this is not the only announcement I have to make. I am pleased to be able to inform the Administrators that our Continuity Scientists believe they have made an important breakthrough in their development of the time portal. They believe they have managed to achieve the conditions necessary to create a temporal gate at the destination, the existence of which will enable travellers to return to us.' There was more excited chatter. Arbiter Messinat raised a hand in a request for quiet. 'This is not all,' she continued. 'A brave *mourst* has volunteered to test the gate soon. Due to its nature and dynamic state, we cannot know where he will go, what he will experience, or indeed whether he will survive to return to us. But the time is near. He will depart soon.'

'Perhaps he will come face to face with our Saviour, Arbiter Messinat,' blustered Proctor Coortien.

Arbiter Messinat stared hard at the Proctor. 'Who knows, Proctor Coortien?' said the *vilume*. 'Perhaps he will.'

Structure's Olympus Mons base, Mars

Built by Colonial Armouries and used by at least six of the ten most powerful military forces in the galaxy, Straphers were designed to deliver ordnance to concealed, fortified targets such as underground bunkers or the Olympus Mons facility, or to interdict convoys of ground vehicles, troops, encampments or supply trains. Turrets on the top, the leading edge and each side of the craft were crewed by gunners to fend off attacks, as the efficiency of the auto-targetting systems of the day was unreliable.

At the time of the Strapher's design, low-level attacks on ground targets were consigned to the distant past. Instead, high-precision strikes were conducted from orbit, reducing risk and increasing efficiency. However, as the spaceborne platforms proved to be at the mercy of ground-based defence systems with increasing range and accuracy, Colonial Armouries saw a potential gap in demand.

Specifically, Straphers were designed to be dropped from high-speed transit vessels on the opposite side of the target planet, entering the atmosphere rapidly. They would then fly low and fast to the target zone to attack and withdraw quickly, to be picked up by the waiting deployment vessel when their mission was complete.

Due to their low-level approaches, Straphers were forced to carry a great deal of physical armour. But what Straphers benefitted from in terms of inherent physical strength was offset by a lack of agility. Moreover, while automatic targeting systems could in theory be used to deliver ordnance, this was generally unsuccessful due to the low operating altitude. So, as well as the pilot and navigator, Straphers also carried three additional crew members, who were responsible for bomb targeting, weapons' control and fending off attacks by interceptors.

Straphers were extremely basic, brute force tools that lacked refinement. Yet they were revered by those who had crewed them in anger as being able to remain airborne even when they had sustained a level of damage that would have finished a lesser vehicle. Delgado had even heard of a Strapher making it back to the rendezvous with half the fuselage missing. And so, since his childhood he had longed to skim a planet's surface in one of these ageing dinosaurs at combat speeds. Now it seemed that his opportunity had arrived.

The flight deck was larger than Delgado had expected, but the technology was very basic. He attempted to extend his nobics to communicate with a core of some kind, but either there was none or it was dormant.

He looked at the instruments and controls. A couple of the screens were cracked. Dust motes drifted through the beams cast by small, round spotlights in the ceiling. At the front of the flight deck blastplate shields covered the viewports. At the rear were five lockers, presumably one for each of the Strapher's crewmembers. Delgado opened one. It contained a two-piece flight suit suitable for an average-height human male and a few personal effects.

Cascari and Ash sat at the master console. Ash fired up the primary power feed like a veteran Strapher pilot. A series of clicks followed, and motors began to hum softly as fans cooled circuitry and circulated air around the vessel. Screens flashed and flickered; characters, graphs and warnings began to appear through layers of dust.

Cascari removed the visuals strip from its sleeve in the console, then placed it over his eyes and rubbed the strip's upper edge with the tip of his right index finger. The glossy purple visor shimmered gently as the thin film merged with his face to become a single, violet eye.

Cascari became quiet and still as visuals and maps appeared to him. Then control panels became illuminated and more screens became active as he began powering up various systems. The craft's narrow corridors were suddenly warmed by functioning heaters and a glow of ambient lighting. Within a few moments of their entry, the Strapher had become a living entity, a roused beast.

'Think you can handle it?' asked Delgado.

'Sure. No problem,' said Cascari after a few moments' pause. 'The interfaces are clumsy but it's simple enough.'

Ash looked over her left shoulder. 'Go on, old-timer,' she said. 'Go play with your guns.'

Delgado pulled a face; he was glad Cascari could not see the way Ash smiled back at him.

The upper turret was a fat blister on the Strapher's back, constructed from panels of lightweight transparent blastplate in a high-density melocor frame. The six guns the turret controlled – Maurann 507s, basic hi-charge plasma units very popular in their day – were mounted on a cradle. Triggers on short stems rose from the end of each arm of the gunner's seat.

Delgado strapped himself into the seat and found that the triggers and turret controls fell easily to hand. While these would enable him to fire as and when he was ready, their presence illustrated the age of the Strapher's technology: at the time of its construction nobic evolutions were unable to handle targeting and firing information delivered by interneural systems, hence the manual controls. Besides, in an environment as contained as the interior of Olympus Mons, autotracking would be of little use to him.

He reached for the headset and put it on. It sat uncomfortably on his skull like an odd, technologically advanced tiara whose gems had been removed from their settings. The unit seemed inoperative. He was about to remove it when three very basic visuals opened in his mind. The interface was so old that for a moment the layout confused him. He sighed heavily and opened the comms link to the flight deck as he searched through the visuals maps.

'How's it going down there?' he asked.

There was a burst of white noise, then Cascari's voice. 'Fine. Soon have all systems powered up. How about you?'

'Nice turret. Lots of pretty lights. Great view.' He looked out at the drones now swarming around the Strapher. 'How long before we can go?'

There was a momentary pause. 'Ash says about two minutes. Are the guns live?'

'I'll give them a try.'

The turret wheezed as Delgado rotated it to the right. Apart from the chaos on the nearby automatic track and the hubbub on the gantry high above – the lift had still not arrived, apparently – life seemed to be continuing pretty much as normal in the hangar.

He searched for a suitable target. Unsure of the guns' capabilities, or indeed his own ability as a gunner, he decided to play safe, and chose something large.

He turned the turret towards the freighter.

Delgado looked down at the small instrument panel just above his left thigh and touched the PREP GUNS tab. There was a sudden, loud buzzing sound and a strong vibration through his ass that was not entirely unpleasant. Four small columns appeared on the screen next to the ARM tab. They rose slowly, indicating the guns' charge level. Eventually they reached their limit and the words GUNS ARMED blinked encouragingly.

Delgado looked up and licked his lips. He realised he felt safe within the turret: no one could get him here; he was unreachable. He checked his target, checked the screen and adjusted his grip on the stalks. Then he depressed the triggers.

There was a series of huge explosions as each Maurann spat fat slabs of golden light, the whole turret shuddering violently with each discharge. He released the triggers again after a few seconds and looked at the results of his assault.

The side of the freighter was severely damaged. Part of its superstructure had disintegrated, there was massive damage within the craft, and a fierce fire raged across two decks. One of the cargo gantries had been destroyed. People around the base of the craft were running in different directions. Further away, people were staring at the turret, open-mouthed.

The intercom came to life. Cascari's voice was warm and close. 'I take it the guns are operational?' he said.

'They sure appear to be.'

'Well that's good because there's a small aircraft approaching.'

'That'll be security.' As Delgado looked around, searching for the approaching craft, the noise of the engines rose quickly, the sound of the strong, uneven vibrations running through the vessel increasing in frequency until they merged to become a continuous drone. He perceived buoyancy in the Strapher: they were airborne.

Delgado saw the incoming vessel several thousand metres to his right, an indistinct shape against the rock wall in the distance. It was within range of the Mauranns, but he decided to wait until it represented a clearer target. The Strapher pitched and rolled slightly as Cascari and Ash wrestled with the ageing ship. Delgado looked down and to his right. He estimated that the Strapher was now around twenty metres off the ground. Almost everyone below was looking up at the vessel; some were pointing.

He looked up again and saw that the other ship was getting into position to attack. He turned the turret slightly, his fingers resting lightly on the trigger stalks.

As the vessel closed on the Strapher its shape became clearer, like two equilateral triangles joined at the point opposite the base: it was a Scimitar light transport/heavy fighter, first used by Structure during the Buhatt Rebellion. One fat end was packed with engines, the other with plasma generators for the guns: Scimitars were known to pack a powerful punch. Delgado moved the target information visual to secondary-peripheral and put the remaining weapons and enemy craft status visuals to prime. He relaxed, breathed slowly, waited.

What looked like a bunch of blue orbs emerged from the front of the Scimitar, moving seemingly slowly at first, then suddenly accelerating and swelling as they flashed past him. Several pulses came extremely close, bathing Delgado in cold blue light and emitting a buzzing sound so loud the turret shook. But the confined space and mass of machinery and electronic systems within the Olympus Mons facility confused the targeting systems and none of the shots hit home.

He felt Cascari feed more power into the engines and the Strapher accelerated slightly. As the vessels continued to close on each other the Scimitar released more bolts, but again they missed. As it rapidly approached the Strapher the Scimitar began to turn away. Delgado turned the turret slightly and raised the angle of the guns. As the Scimitar's profile increased, Delgado aimed just ahead of its nose and fired.

The turret shuddered as each of the six powerful Mauranns lurched back and forth on the cradle, the thick cable connecting the weapons to the turret flexing like a muscle. He fired for around three seconds, then stopped. The first bolt to hit the Scimitar seemed to do little other than knock the already steeply turning vessel to an even steeper angle. But as the remaining bolts hit home there was an explosion from the Scimitar's rear end and the craft's nose dropped abruptly. A thick jet of white gas spouted from its underside and there were further explosions and a scattering of debris. The Scimitar continued to roll until almost inverted. The vessel manoeuvred erratically for a moment, then plunged towards the hangar floor.

As Delgado watched he clearly sensed the traces of the men within the craft: fear, anger, elation, guilt. Then the ship hit the ground with an abruptness that made Delgado blink. There was a large but short-lived explosion, a plume of dense smoke; then the traces he had sensed so clearly a few seconds earlier were gone.

The Strapher continued to fly slowly towards the wide, dark circle of the shaft's mouth. As it occurred to Delgado that this was an absurd speed at which to be making any kind of escape he saw three specks emerge from a distant slit in the hangar wall – presumably the entrance to another, smaller hangar – flying in a tight echelon formation. He opened an enhancement visual: more Scimitars, moving more quickly than the last. 'Cascari,' he said, 'see if you can find any information about this shaft we're about to enter, will you? It's going to be sealed somehow and we need details.'

'Sure,' Cascari replied. 'I mean, I'm sitting down here with my feet up.'

Delgado was about to retort, but the three Scimitars were suddenly swarming all over the Strapher. Their weapons were clearly subject to the same problems as those of the first, but, with the added disadvantage that with so many bolts of plasma flying around a stray shot would result in the deaths of their own operatives.

Due to the number of Scimitars, Delgado was unable to move the turret quickly enough or aim at all the targets, and the Strapher quickly began to sustain damage: a stream of compressed gas began jetting from the vessel just in front of the turret; several areas of the hull were compromised; numerous alarms began to sound while announcements were made about systems and environmental statistics.

The three Scimitars shifted into a triangular formation as they turned and headed back towards the Strapher. Delgado opened fire but hit none of the three vessels. At the same moment as he stopped firing the three Scimitars fired simultaneously, and Delgado saw nine bright blue bolts of plasma speeding towards him.

There was no impact. Delgado glanced around him, turning the turret through one hundred and eighty degrees. He saw the three craft turning in different directions and the aftermath of an explosion on the far side of the hangar where the plasma bolts had hit. He realised that the Strapher was now listing to port at an angle of around thirty degrees, with a slight yaw. The angle of roll increased slowly until it was around forty-five degrees. With the straps digging into his shoulders, Delgado reached out with his left arm and pressed his palm against the side of the turret to support himself. Still the angle of roll increased, but now the Strapher was beginning to slip sideways through the air as well, the tip of its stubby, port wing dangerously close to the craft on the ground. He could see people running, automatics trundling along their tracks.

Delgado opened the intercom. 'What the hell's going on, Cascari?' he yelled. There was no answer. The Strapher's nose began to angle towards the ground and it lost more of its already limited altitude. 'Cascari?' He called again. 'Can you hear me?' There was a slight fracture in his voice as raw panic welled in him, faced with the sudden possibility that his son could be dead.

Delgado frantically removed the harness and was about to open the hatch below him when the craft began to roll the opposite way, its nose rising slightly. The engines roared. Delgado looked towards the rear of the craft and saw arcs of energy leaping from one side of the vessel to the tail.

Cascari's voice came through the intercom. 'You there?'

'What's going on?' asked Delgado, somewhat breathlessly.

It was Ash who replied. 'One of the containment field generators is damaged,' she said. 'Must've been a lucky shot. Had to be shut down pronto, power routed through the other generators.'

'But they're stable now, right?' No answer. 'Are they stable?'

'Yeah, he thinks so.'

'What do you mean, he thinks so? Either they are or they aren't.' Delgado strapped himself back into the seat and looked ahead at the gaping mouth of the shaft, which was now only a few hundred metres away, then turned in search of the Scimitars.

'He just says things might get a bit hot,' Ash responded calmly. 'The other generators are running at one hundred and forty per cent. If another one goes we're screwed.'

Delgado swore as he turned the turret and fired a prolonged burst at the Scimitars, which had resumed their triangular formation and were approaching again. When he stopped firing he saw another group of specks emerge from a second slit in the hangar wall. 'Better get your skates on down there,' he muttered grimly. 'Reinforcements are on the way.'

He turned the turret again and fired at the first group of Scimitars as they closed in for a further attack. The bolts missed the two nearest to him but hit the third. The rear quarter of the vessel was seriously damaged and the craft plunged towards the hangar floor trailing flames and intestines. The other two Scimitars opened fire. One bolt hit the Strapher's underside, but the others struck the hangar ceiling, sending large, hot boulders raining down on top of the Strapher and bouncing off the turret.

The second batch of Scimitars was closing rapidly, but by the time they were in a position to fire their weapons the Strapher was already rising into the darkness of the shaft, albeit with agonising slowness. One of the plasma bolts fired by the Scimitars hit the Strapher on the port side, another passed so close to the turret Delgado felt its heat on the side of his face and a wash of charge. It hit the shaft wall, dislodging chunks of rock that fell into the hangar or became lodged around the rim of the shaft opening.

As the Strapher rose further into the shaft, Delgado undid the harness and leaned forward, looking down into the brightness below. Momentarily, he saw the grey shape of one of the Scimitars passing beneath the opening, moving much more slowly than before. As the uneasy throb of the Strapher's two remaining containment-field generators deepened in tone, becoming increasingly off-beat, Delgado realised that in the confines of the shaft they were denied evasive manoeuvres of any kind. All the Structure ships had to do was get into position to fire up into the shaft and the Strapher would be hit.

He peered at the shaft walls, occasionally illuminated by small red lights. The surface was uneven and jagged and hunks of rock protruded. He brought the turret around until the guns were facing a large fissure in the rock, and then fired. He continued to do so until the rock split, and gigantic pieces began to fall from the side of the shaft towards the opening. While much of the rock fell through, larger boulders became wedged in the opening and eventually the mouth of the shaft was blocked completely, only narrow beams of light penetrating the tiny gaps highlighting motes of dust drifting in the darkness.

'There,' Delgado said to himself. 'That should keep them out of our hair for a while.'

As he peered into the darkness outside the turret, which was broken only by the small red lights set into the shaft wall and the faint glow emitted from the flight deck and the turret itself, Cascari's voice issued from the speakers again. 'You OK up there, old timer?'

'Yeah, no problem. I've blocked the mouth of this shaft so

they can't get at us. At least not yet. Did you find out anything about the shaft?'

'Yup. Two big hatches near the top, installed by Structure years ago. They act as an air lock, so human operatives in the hangar below can work without breathers or environment suits. Presumably the Martians didn't need that sort of thing. They're opened using codes unique to each ship, assigned on arrival or departure.'

Delgado nodded. 'Yeah, I bet. You reckon they'll assign a code to us if we ask them? Let us out nice and easy?'

'I doubt it.'

'Me too.' He looked up, but the lights in the turret caused his face to be reflected off the blastplate. He looked sick, older and heavier than he felt, his skin washed the pale green of the screen in front of him. He looked like a person whose past was rapidly catching up with him. 'Guess we'll just have to try brute force. Blast our way out. Any information on the composition of these hatches?'

'Hang on.' There was a pause. 'Apparently they are constructed from high-density blastplate. Tough as hell, in other words.'

'Great.'

'And there's more. Defences around the crater rim. Heavy guns.'

'Heavy enough to bring down a Colonial Armouries Strapher?'

'Most definitely.'

'OK. Cut the power to the screens in here, would you? Just leave power to the turret.'

'And the guns, right?'

'And the guns.'

Delgado was cast into utter darkness as the screens closed down. 'How far to the first hatch?' he asked.

'Just under five thousand metres.'

'Do we know the distance between the two hatches?'

'Around two thousand metres.'

'Right. OK, here's the plan. When we're about a thousand metres from the first hatch I'm going to start firing. There'll be a lot of debris so you better keep those shields closed. Let me know when we're about fifteen hundred metres from the first hatch. Ash, you hold the Strapher in position.'

'I'll try, Delgado,' she said, 'but, while I may be able to slow our rate of ascent, hovering in such an enclosed space isn't possible.'

Delgado closed his eyes for a few moments. 'OK then,' he said eventually. 'Slow us down as much as you can. But when the hatches are blown we'll need to get out of here fast if we're going to take the guns on the crater rim by surprise. Think you can do that?'

There was apparent consultation. 'Yeah, we think we can do that.'

'Is there any sign of vessels trying to break through and follow us up through the shaft?'

'No, nothing.'

'No. My guess is that they're sitting it out, expecting us to be unable to get through the hatches. They'll probably have craft waiting outside for us, though. Just in case'

'You're really selling this to me, Delgado,' came Ash's reply. 'Can you remind me why we decided to do this?'

'No other choice, dear Ashala, no other choice.'

'One thousand five hundred metres,' interjected Cascari.

Delgado looked up into the darkness; it wasn't a lot of room.

'Might I make a suggestion?' said Ash.

'Fire away.'

'Why not change flight modes now, within the shaft? We use the forward guns to blow the hatches, use the main engines for greater acceleration, and the Strapher's lower profile will give us a greater chance of getting out in one piece.'

'You're a genius,' replied Delgado. 'I'll come straight down.'

*

As Delgado strapped himself into the seat, Cascari opened the blastplate panels shielding the flight-deck viewports.

'I'm not sure that's wise,' said Delgado, 'considering the huge amount of rock that's likely to fall this way. Last thing we need is depressurisation.'

'Well, if this ship is hit we may lose visuals, but if we still have control of the vessel I might just be able to fly it – if I can see where we're going.'

Cascari cycled through visuals maps, and the Strapher's nose began to rise until the vessel was vertical in the shaft, pointing towards the hatch, which was now visible as a small grey disc ahead.

'OK,' said Delgado. 'Give me control of the forward guns.' A small control panel in the arm of his chair became illuminated.

'They're yours,' Ash replied.

Delgado activated the menu that appeared in the air in front of his lap and worked his way quickly to targeting menus. He focused the forward Mauranns on the first hatch, then fired.

The weapons' huge power brought a golden brilliance to the interior of the shaft, releasing the rough rock walls from dark confinement. Huge chunks of stone and molten metal fell towards the Strapher, the sound of the impacts audible even above the noise of the Mauranns. There was a sudden snapping sound and a crack appeared in one of the blastplate panels.

Ash looked at Cascari. 'You sure it wouldn't be better to close the shields,' she yelled above the noise. 'If we're going to go vertical it doesn't make much difference.'

'We're not going to *keep* going vertical,' Cascari yelled. 'They'll be expecting that. We'll turn hard and run close to the ground, see if we can't lose them, so I need to be able to see where we're going. Release a couple of ether ghosts as soon as we're clear, then if they've got ships out there waiting for us it might send them on the wrong path for a while. It won't give us long, but it might be enough.'

Ash's expression was doubtful. 'You just say the word,' she said.

Delgado stopped firing and comparative quiet returned. 'Well?'

'The inner hatch is completely destroyed, the outer hatch and the rock surrounding it are damaged, but still in place. Pressure in here is stable.'

'OK. Good.' Delgado changed the display and fired again for several seconds. When he ceased, all that remained of the outer hatch were two spikes opposite each other, like teeth in the jaws of a gigantic beast. Beyond them was the Martian sky.

'We're rising more quickly,' said Cascari. 'The hangar below is depressurising and the escaping air is pushing us up.'

'We've nearly got it. When I give the word, apply full thrust, OK?'

'Got it.'

Delgado fired the Mauranns again. More fragments of metal and rock cascaded on to the Strapher, thundering down the shaft. Delgado stopped firing and saw that one of the blastplate shards had been destroyed, leaving a single, protruding spike. 'OK, let's go!'

'We won't get through that gap,' Cascari protested.

Delgado began firing again. 'Just go!' he shouted.

Cascari powered up the engines, and their tone shifted from a bassy background hum to an immense roar. The Strapher's three passengers were pushed into their seats as the vessel accelerated, the tiny red lights in the shaft wall becoming an unbroken, blood-red line.

Delgado continued to fire as the Strapher raced upwards. As the remaining obstruction disintegrated, hot rock and blast-plate rained on to the Strapher's nose. Cascari applied more power and the faint grey circle of light increased in diameter as they sped towards it. Then the three occupants' pupils contracted rapidly as they exploded from the depths of the underworld and were bathed in the bleak light of the Martian afternoon.

Long lines of light and bright pulse streams streaked past the craft's nose as the weapons on the rim of the Olympus Mons crater opened fire. They climbed vertically for a few seconds, the Strapher juddering as a result of both its speed and the incoming fire.

'Ether ghosts activated,' said Ash. 'Two blocks. Diverse patterns. Shields up. Tracking scrambler online.'

'Any sign of Structure ships on our tail?' asked Delgado.

'Just two.'

There was a loud yet muffled thud at the rear of the craft. Delgado looked at Cascari but the young man was concentrating on maintaining control of the speeding vessel. As Cascari reached out to one of the control panels there was another much louder bang, followed immediately by a slight but nonetheless perceptible shift in the engines' tone. An alarm shrieked, but Cascari silenced it quickly. They heard a series of thuds, two loud explosions, then felt the Strapher's speed bleeding away quickly.

'We're taking a lot of hits,' called Ash as she sifted through displays.

'You don't say,' retorted Delgado.

'Shield strength, drives, weapons systems, hull integrity. All either compromised or malfunctioning.'

'Those ships buying the ether ghosts?'

Ash consulted her displays. 'Yeah, they seem to be. They're certainly not coming right after us anyway. I reckon we've got five, maybe six minutes before they realise they're chasing thin air.'

Loud popping and banging sounds indicated plasma bolts fired by the guns on the crater rim hitting the hull, most of their energy absorbed as they passed through the shields. Another faint explosion was followed by a screaming whine that faded abruptly. Alarms too numerous for Cascari to silence began to sound. The Strapher seemed to be having the equivalent of a *grand mal* epileptic seizure, shuddering and lurching violently. One of the lockers at the rear of the flight deck burst open.

G-loads acting upon the Strapher seemed to change and it became more unsettled, jolting the three passengers around in their seats. There was another thud and a grinding sound.

'What was that?' Delgado called above the noise.

'We just lost another generator.'

'The core is acting erratically,' said Ash. 'Some of its cells seem to be corrupt.'

'Can you rectify it?'

'I don't know. I'll try.'

Delgado looked at Cascari. The *mourst* ligaments on his neck were pink and swollen in arousal. 'You think we're going to make it?' he called.

Cascari shrugged. 'Depends on what "it" is,' he replied. 'Out of the atmosphere? Probably. All the way to *Zavanchia*? Possibly. All the way to Seriatt? Your guess is as good as mine.'

'Structure ships are in pursuit,' Ash stated calmly.

'OK,' said Cascari, rapidly manipulating visuals, 'hang on to your bootstraps. We're about to see how fast this thing can really go.' He pushed the Strapher's nose forward, and the heavy craft lunged enthusiastically towards the ground.

Having lost the Structure ships, Cascari had applied full power and taken the Strapher out of the Martian atmosphere with a course set for *Zavanchia*, a tax-free business centre in freespace. It was a prestigious place from which to operate, where space was expensive. *Zavanchia*'s security force was comprised of personnel from a number of different worlds, which rendered it ineffective due to difficulties of coordination and communications: despite the official adoption of Counian as a standard language, its implementation was sporadic and occasionally reluctant. As a result, the port was also popular with criminals.

The station consisted of numerous wheels linked at the hub, with the hubs in turn joined to the main areas of the spaceport by cylindrical structures like fat spokes. The station glistened like a jewel as the wheels rotated, the different speeds of revolution reflecting the gravitational requirements of Zavanchia's customers. The lower levels of gravity compared to Earth in some of the more slowly spinning wheels made them made them highly popular among humans who could not afford cellular obesity treatment, due to the greater freedom of movement they enjoyed within the low-G environment.

'So what's the plan, Delgado?' asked Cascari as they sat waiting for the ship to be allowed to enter *Zavanchia*. 'I mean, Michael may be here, but how do we find him? The words needle and haystack spring to mind.'

'While you were asleep I checked out a few things,' said Delgado. 'The station's core links with every ship arriving or departing, accessing the ID code of each one, automatically logging its point of origin, the course it took to get here and its ultimate destination if this is just a stopover. It's all recorded. I traced his route by accessing the traffic log for this area and downloaded it on to this.' He held up a Universal Interface wafer. 'If we can gain access to *Zavanchia*'s systems, then we'll be able to find him. If we can kill him here then go on to Seriatt with him out of the picture, then that would be ideal. Here, you better have one of these.' He threw Cascari a small sidearm. Although compact it was obviously powerful. 'I found a small armoury back there.' Delgado jerked a thumb over his right shoulder. 'These are new units. Light, fast plasma charge, built-in concealers to make them invisible to scanning devices. Got a few canisters of frozone and some grenades, some electroflash, some standard detonators. There was even this.' He held up a small black, elongated object. He moved his thumb slightly and a double-edged blade shot from one end. 'It's a switchblade,' he said. 'I reckon the Strapher must've been on course for a special mission of some kind before we came along. I don't see why it would be carrying this stuff otherwise.'

Ash, who had been sleeping in her reclined chair, began to stir. She yawned and stretched her limbs, screwing up her face as she did so.

'Hey,' said Cascari. 'Welcome back.'

'Thanks.' She yawned again as she put her seat back into its upright position. 'Where are we?'

'Almost there. We'll be landing soon. Then we have the task of finding Michael, son of General William Myson, among who knows how many hundreds of thousands of guests, and killing him despite whatever security he's got around him. Dear old dad here thinks it's going to be a cinch.'

'That's not exactly what I said. What's up, Ash?'

Ash rubbed her eyes, pulled a face. 'Nothing. Well, I had this weird dream. There was this archway in a wall. I went through and there was, like, a weird garden on the other side. I mean, beautiful, right, but weird.'

'Weird how?' asked Cascari.

She shook her head, wrinkled her nose. 'Can't say. Just wrong somehow. Like, the leaves on the trees were just *too* big, or the wrong colour, or something. You know what dreams are like. Oh yeah, and Delgado was with me, but it didn't look like him although I knew it was him. He was being real mean. And he kept calling me Alannah. Or maybe it was Anna . . .' Her voice tailed off and she frowned, as if saying this had triggered something she didn't want to talk about or wasn't certain of. She looked up. 'Anyway,' she said more brightly, 'you think we can find Michael, or is this a wild goose chase?'

Cascari jerked his head towards Delgado. 'He's got it all worked out. Haven't you?'

Delgado shrugged. 'If we can just find an official with access to the registration system then we should be able to identify his ship no problem. All we have to do then is find out where it is.'

'There you go, that's all there is to it. I mean, we're just going to walk right up to the son of General William Myson and assassinate him in front of his personal bodyguard and whatever the hell else other security measures are in place to protect him, right?'

'You're half Seriattic *mourst*, Cascari. I would have thought you would savour the challenge.'

'Hey look, you just show me where he is and I'll show you how much I savour the challenge. He won't know what's hit him.'

'Oh well,' said Ash, yawning again, 'it sounds as though you have it sewn up. I may as well get some more sleep while I can. Before all the excitement begins!' And with that she let her seat recline, and closed her eyes once more.

Thursemiol, Fahoun system

A fat, grey *raltat* pup suckled at the belly of its mother as it lay on its side on the iceberg. The mother flapped one fin lazily as she slumbered, absorbing what heat it could from the weak sun, which was a milky disc low on the horizon to the north. All around, the rest of the *raltat* herd looked like dashes of rock protruding from the snow. In the cold grey Arctic sea, *yariaks* surfaced briefly to gulp at the cold air before becoming submerged once more, sweeping through the icy waters in search of food. It was a desolate place.

Abruptly, the dozing adult *raltat* thrashed and rolled its body upright, its small ears twitching. Suddenly deprived of its milk, the pup began to shriek. Spines linked by thin sheets of grey skin rose on the adult's back, and the creature became agitated, hurrying towards the edge of the iceberg and sniffing at the air. All around it, other adult *raltat* became similarly disturbed, and began to emit throaty wails of distress.

A shape appeared among the clouds to the east, and within a few seconds it had become a dark gash in the sky. A sonic boom startled the *raltat* herd as the object passed overhead, causing them to become even more vocal. When it hit the turbulent sea a few moments later, the adult *raltat* threw back her head and emitted an immense, bassy wail, the spines on her back rising and falling in agitation.

The sea seethed and foamed, and a huge wave rode out from the point of impact a kilometre or so distant. Salt water rose high up the sides of the iceberg and washed over the *raltat* at the herd's extremities, but within a few minutes quiet had returned, and the pup was once again suckling hungrily and gratefully at its mother's fat belly.

Beneath the surging waves, as the meteorite sank towards the sea bed, trailing a constellation of bubbles, a crack appeared in its rapidly cooling surface. The split widened to reveal the interior, the surface of which shifted between a range of different colours. As it continued to plunge into the ocean's bitter depths a million tiny spores emerged from the long tendrils that extended from the core, and instinctively dispersed to seek dark crannies in the deep, where they would take refuge, rest and grow.

Zavanchia Freeport

Systems Overseer Benton was a human male little more than one metre high, and not far short of that in diameter. His thinning hair was lank and greasy. Grey stubble gave the lower half of his face a silvery, metallic sheen. The armpits of his stretched, short-sleeved khaki shirt were darkened by sweat, and the back of the chafed collar was also damp. Occasionally he would poke his right index finger deep into the back of his mouth as if searching for a morsel of food either trapped or deliberately stored. When he wasn't doing this, one index finger was probing one or other nostril.

'Look, man,' said Systems Overseer Benton, shaking his head, his mouth twisting and one eye partially closing, 'far be it from me to stand in the way of Structure, but Christ, I can't just let you guys walk in here and go rifling through the data willy-nilly. Hell no. A lot of people come to *Zavanchia* for the sole reason that they know their identity is safe here. Jeez, you might be Structure but if I let you guys get access to the database, who knows what could happen?'

Cascari looked down at Overseer Benton. 'Well, what could happen?' he said stiffly.

Benton pulled his finger from his mouth and shrugged so deeply that his short neck disappeared for a moment. 'Well, for Christ's sake, who the hell knows? That's just what I'm saying, buddy. No one knows. Are you stupid or something?' He looked at Delgado and jerked his head in Cascari's direction. 'Is he stupid or something?' Delgado looked away, as if trying to disassociate himself from the whole affair.

Cascari clenched his fists and his neck throbbed angrily. 'Look,' he said, 'all we want is . . .'

'Just to locate one little ship,' Ash interjected. She took a step forward and took one of Overseer Benton's fat, clammy hands in hers. 'Just one ship,' she said softly, looking into his eyes. 'It's a recent arrival, so it must still be on record. What possible harm could it do, Systems Overseer Benton? We won't damage the system. Not with you helping us out. This is very important Structure business, after all.'

Benton stared at Ashala for a moment, as if entranced by her. Abruptly he seemed to snap out of his reverie. 'No, I'm sorry, miss.' Benton shook his head, stood and hitched up the waistband of his trousers. 'You just don't get it, do you? This isn't about damaging the system. I *know* you won't damage the system because I'm not letting you anywhere near the goddamn system. That's why you won't damage the system. Hell, yes.'

Ash stood, placed one hand on each of Benton's shoulders, and tilted her head to one side, pouting. 'Aw, come on, Benty,' she said. 'It'll take five minutes. Less, I bet.' She faked suppressing a smile.

Benton frowned hard for several moments. 'Are we

speaking a different language here, miss, or are you as stupid as him?' Benton nodded towards Cascari.

Delgado decided it was time to step in. 'Look,' he said, 'we appreciate this is a free zone . . .'

'You're damn right it's a free zone.'

'. . . but this is part of a secret and ongoing operation.' He took a step forward and stood next to Benton. Delgado looked over one shoulder as if to check that no one was listening, then put his left arm around Benton's shoulders. As Benton looked at the hand hanging over his shoulder, Delgado leaned close to him and breathed in one ear, 'Your help would be well rewarded.' He patted Benton's chest with his other hand and stepped away.

Benton glanced from Delgado to Cascari to Ash, head cocked to one side, eye partially closed. 'Rewarded in what way?' he asked slowly.

Delgado walked away from the short man as if he hadn't heard the question. 'I can see you're a man of integrity, Systems Overseer Benton,' he said. 'And I must say it's refreshing to come across someone with such an honourable trait in times like these, when self-interest comes above all else as far as most people are concerned. I respect you for it, I really do. Come on,' he said to Cascari and Ash. 'We're clearly wasting our time here. We must leave the Overseer to his duties. We have failed in our mission. It's a shame. I had expected our bribery fund to be almost spent by now, yet it's hardly touched. It's both heartening and frustrating.' He motioned towards the door. 'Come, we'll leave.'

'Hey now, hey, come on. Let's not be too hasty. Hell no.' Delgado smiled as he, Cascari and Ash stopped and turned: the lure of money never failed to turn even the most ethical of people. Benton was walking after them. He briefly rose on to his tip-toes as he grasped the waistband of his trousers with both hands and hitched them us as far as he could. He appeared to half wink and half nod as he did this. 'You know,' he said, 'you have to understand that a guy in my position has to be, well, careful.' He laughed briefly and shook his head in a false, slightly nervous manner. 'I can't allow just all and sundry to go poking through the register information. Hell no. There's some sensitive stuff in there. Yes indeedy.' He frowned and gave a curt nod as if to emphasise the truth of this. 'You said something about a UI wafer when you arrived.'

Delgado smiled and held out the small sliver of dark material. 'Do you know, Overseer Benton,' he said as he walked towards him, 'I recognised your integrity as soon as I saw you? I said to my colleague here, I said, there's a man with integrity, Commander. But he's sensible, too. You can see it in him. I said to you, didn't I, Commander?' Cascari pursed his lips and gave a slow, sombre nod.

Benton smiled and nodded rapidly, looking from one to the other of them. 'Well, I lived on Earth for a long time, you know. In *Gratuity* habitat.' Delgado nodded his recognition of the name. 'It's good to be able to, um, give something back to Structure, I guess.' He stopped at a desk, a relatively small workstation with an interface screen in its horizontal surface and three multilevel ISO displays in the vertical section. This was clearly where Benton spent most of his time. He sat down in the large, well-padded cream leather seat positioned in front of the desk. The shape of his body perfectly matched the deep back and buttock impressions in the somewhat worn upholstery.

He swung the chair round and rested his feet on the luxurious and obviously non-standard footstool positioned beneath the desk, and immediately seemed to become more confident. The chair creaked gently as he leaned back, adopting what was almost certainly his preferred posture. Judging from the round, slightly off-centre impression in the chair's high back, he often fell asleep here. He swept aside a multitude of sandwich and confectionery wrappers, moved half a cup of what looked like black coffee from one place to another, and spent a few moments rubbing a smudge from the glass surface of the interface screen. The desk was scratched and heavily branded with cup-rings. Delgado noticed a small picture of a naked woman, inexpertly scrawled on the desk in biro, near the corner of the screen Benton was now touching.

The central screen in front of Benton flickered. Displays updated. Columns of figures – some white, some dark green, others a dark orange – began to scroll downwards. Occasionally Benton would stop the list in a particular place, and a quiet female voice would issue from a speaker, only to be cut short as the Systems Overseer continued his search. Eventually he followed a path through to another display. He entered a password, and something like a two-dimensional representation of a visuals map opened up, albeit very basic. He half turned in his seat.

'OK. The wafer.' Delgado handed it to him. Benton placed it into a slot in the desk and it was pulled within. The Overseer leaned across the desk and picked up a small package, then popped a tablet of gum in his mouth.

Ash leaned forward. 'Could I . . . ?'

Benton made a poor attempt at discretion, glancing at her chest several times as she took some gum from the packet. 'Right,' he said. 'So we're looking for the ship which has this reference.' He indicated a string of characters in the top right of the display. 'Which arrived from Mars within the last eight hours, having travelled via these coordinates.' He switched displays and a column of waypoints began to scroll up the screen; it seemed a long list. 'Am I right?'

Cascari nodded. 'That's correct.'

Delgado could hear tension in his voice, could see it in his stance.

'Well, this shouldn't take too long,' said Benton. He jabbed the screen with his right index finger and sat back in his chair, arms folded. He looked at his audience of three, wearing the smug expression of someone in an unfamiliar position of power. Cascari was staring hard at the screen; Delgado rocked on his heels, eyebrows raised, his hands clasped behind his back. Ash smiled brightly at Benton and held his gaze. When the Systems Overseer looked away, she looked at Delgado and rolled her eyes.

As they waited, a door behind them opened. All turned. Benton appeared startled. A middle-aged woman entered the room. She was of medium build and wore a uniform in the same khaki colour as Benton's. Its shapeless design stripped her of all femininity. Her tightly curled hair was mousy, cropped too short, its style obviously a natural, life-long burden about which she could do nothing. The embroidered eye on her epaulettes indicated that she was also a Systems Overseer. She looked at the three strangers as she walked across the room, her gait slow and lazy, arms hanging by her sides. Her eyes rested longer on Ash than they did on Delgado and Cascari; she was either attracted to her, or saw her as a threat. Finally she looked at Benton, who was clearly somewhat disturbed by his colleague's apparently untimely arrival.

'Hey, Steve,' she called casually.

Benton nodded once but did not look at her. 'Judy,' he said curtly.

'What's going on here, buddy?' she asked with a smile. 'Who are these guys?' She looked at each of the visitors in turn.

Benton glanced at Delgado, Cascari and Ashala, then looked back at the still-scrolling text and figures. 'I can't say too much, Judy, but they're, um, they're S—'

'Systems Analysts,' interjected Delgado. 'Overseer Benton is kindly performing some tests for us. We'll be through in a few minutes.' He smiled broadly.

'It's time for me to log on, though, Steve. I gotta start my shift.'

'We'll be finished here in just a few moments,' repeated Delgado. 'The final test is almost complete.'

'Well that may be,' said Judy stiffly, 'but I gotta tell ya, handsome, that if I don't log on slap-bang on 23:00,' she clapped her hands, 'then I'm docked pay. Pay I can't afford to lose.'

'We appreciate that, Judy,' said Delgado softly, 'but these are essential tests to check the configuration and integrity of the information retrieval files. We'll be through in just a few more minutes.'

'Well, hey, I'm sure you will, but who's gonna make up my lost pay? That's what I want to know. And anyway, I've worked here for three standard years and there's never been any tests like this carried out before. Did you check their ID, Steve?'

Cascari took a step forward. 'Look, just shut your mouth for a few minutes until we're out of here, OK?'

Judy stiffened, took a step towards Cascari. 'Now you just hang on there, buddy,' she said. 'Who the hell do you think you are? You can't just . . .'

Delgado stepped between them, put one arm around Judy's shoulders and began steering her towards the door. 'I'm sorry about that, Judy,' he said. 'My colleague's had a very tiring few days. We've been halfway across the galaxy performing tests such as this and, well, I'm afraid it's taken its toll on his morale. He's young, you know. He gets homesick easily.'

'Yeah, well, he needs to learn some manners, that's clear enough. Good manners cost nothing, that's what my ma used to say.'

'I know, I know. Please accept my apologies on his behalf. I think it's the *mourst* in him, you know.'

'Yeah, well, I never did trust them Seriatts. A funny-lookin' bunch altogether in my opinion.'

'Listen, while we're waiting, would you be an absolute angel and fetch us some coffee? While you're gone I'll contact a few people and make sure you get a bonus for being so inconvenienced. How does that sound?'

Judy seemed to brighten. 'Sure. OK. That sounds just swell.'

Her face suddenly became serious again. 'I don't make a habit of fetching guys coffee, mind.'

'I'm sure you don't.' He grinned and glanced back towards the desk as she walked away. There was some activity indicating that the information they required had been found. 'Why don't you bring something to munch on, too?' he called after her. Judy raised one hand in acknowledgement as she left the room.

When she had gone, Delgado walked quickly back to the desk. 'Get it?'

'Yeah, we got it,' said Cascari, waving a small printout in the air. 'But we need to move fast. He's leaving for Seriatt within the hour.' Cascari looked at Benton and tapped the piece of paper with one fingertip. 'Where is this bay?' he demanded. 'How long will it take us to get there?'

Benton pushed himself out of his excessively, padded chair, hoisted up his trousers and took the paper from him. He examined it for a few moments, head angled to one side, fishing around at the back of his mouth with one fat finger. He wrinkled his nose, pursed his lips, clearly savouring his moments of power. 'This ship is in a bay over in wheel four. It's hard to say how long it'll take you to get there, though. Depends if you're lucky and get good monorail connections.'

'How do we find it?'

Benton shrugged. 'Piece of cake,' he said. 'It's all signed. Just follow this path and you'll end up in the right place. See this?' He pointed at the top line on the paper. 'It's basically an address, broken down into hub section, deck, casting and bay number. You can't go wrong unless you're a complete idiot. Just make sure you don't give it to this guy.' He nodded towards Cascari.

'Great. Come on, let's get out of here.' They began to walk away.

'Hey, just a minute. What about my money?'

Cascari spun around, but continued to walk backwards. 'We find our ship, you get your money,' he called, waving the printout above his head. He turned again and whispered to Delgado: 'I thought telling him we were Structure was supposed to avoid all this nonsense.'

Behind them, Benton took a step forward. 'Now you wait right there . . .'

'And don't think of calling security,' Cascari called back. 'We're Structure officers, remember? Try to cross us and the PPD will come and slit your throat while you're asleep.'

Benton's face reddened. 'Goddamn. God*damn*.'

The other door opened and in walked Judy carrying a tray set with mugs of steaming coffee and a small pile of sugary doughnuts on a plate. Her broad smile faded when she saw that Benton was alone. 'I brought coffee and doughnuts, Steve,' she said. 'Where'd they go?'

'Blah. Who the hell knows?' He waved one hand in the air dismissively. 'Who the hell cares? Goddamn.'

'But I brought coffee and doughnuts.'

Benton walked over to her, took one of the doughnuts and began chewing on it in an almost aggressive manner, before turning abruptly and walking away.

'I brought coffee and doughnuts,' Judy repeated flatly. 'He seemed like such a nice man.'

Benton kicked his chair. 'God*damn*.'

Benton was right: they found the bay easily. What the Systems Overseer had failed to tell them was that it was reached via a corridor swarming with faeries, and with a Gorgon Class cyborg standing guard. As they peered through the door into the corridor, Delgado increased the strength of the concealers on the guns to make sure they were not detected.

The faeries were blurred points of brilliance drifting around like energised dust particles, their minute systems constantly scanning for potential threats. Their size was deceptive: although they looked insubstantial, the tiny weapons they carried were powerful indeed.

The Gorgon Class cyborg was a lithe woman with bright green skin covered with elaborate, swirling tattoos in maroon and gold. She wore only bands of black leather around her breasts and waist. Every muscle was well defined. Upon her head a clutch of semi-sentient blast weapons writhed on flexible stems like agitated vipers. A faerie drifted in front of the gorgon's face. She swiped angrily and glared at it as it moved away, her irises golden ovals that shone like precious metal.

Delgado turned to Cascari and Ash. 'We're going to need those grenades,' he whispered. 'The faeries can be destroyed by a basic blast weapon but they're so small it's not easy to do. We'll divert their attention, then try to take them all out with a couple of the electroflash grenades. If a couple survive then we might be able to deal with them individually, but as it stands there are just too many of them. The gorgon's going to be the real challenge. They're fast and strong, and those weapons on her head can just about think for themselves.'

'Can't you just cut them off with the switchblade?' asked Cascari.

Delgado shook his head. 'They're controlled by systems implanted below the cerebellum. You see that lump at the top of her neck? That's it. Cutting the weapons from her head won't stop them working. They'll still be able to find and shoot at targets. You've got to disable the controller in her skull to deactivate the weapons.'

'So, what's the plan?'

'You take out the faeries, Ash distracts the gorgon, I deal with her weapons.'

Ash looked at him. 'I'm no coward, Delgado, but why do I have to be the one to distract the gorgon?'

He shrugged. 'I'm banking on her feeling some empathy towards a fellow female. She might just give you a fraction more time than she'd give either of us. That could make all the difference. Here.' He handed Cascari a couple of the grenades. 'You'll need these.'

But Ashala wasn't finished. 'Besides, just how am I supposed to distract . . . her?' she said. 'I don't reckon conversation's going to be her thing somehow. Military personnel are bad conversationalists as it is, but cyborgs are the worst.'

'I'm sure you'll think of something. I mean, you're both women, right?'

'Oh, screw you, Delgado.'

'Here, you better give me your gun. I know it's got a concealer but it might still be detected at such close range.'

She handed him her weapon. 'So I go in there unarmed, too, huh? That's just great.'

'How do these things work?' Cascari was examining the tiny grenades, spheres just a few centimetres in diameter.

'See that slightly rough area around the centre? Push it until it clicks. They're preset to a five-second delay from activation to detonation and will frazzle all insufficiently protected systems in a hundred-metre radius. Don't activate them by mistake.' Delgado peered through the glass panel in the door into the corridor again and watched closely for a minute or so. He then edged away from the window. 'Right. The faeries are obviously flying regular patterns. It looks random but it's not. The entire corridor is always covered. The gorgon *might* be linked to the faeries, autotargeting on whatever they perceive as a threat, but as this is such a temporary arrangement I don't think that's likely to have been set up.'

'Delgado, why don't we just high-tail it out of here before Michael does?' asked Ash. 'Why do we have to take such a risk now? What if Cascari is killed here?'

'They have a fast ship, so they'll probably get there before us anyway. If we can deal with Michael here it takes him out of the equation when we get to Seriatt ourselves, giving us one less obstacle to overcome. We have to go for it.'

Cascari looked into the corridor. 'And what if all the fuss attracts more attention than we can deal with?'

'Then we'll take it as it comes,' Delgado replied. 'There's an air lock between the corridor and the bay itself, so we should be OK, especially if they're on board the ship performing pre-flights.' He looked at each of them in turn. 'So, are we ready?'

Ash smiled warmly at him. 'I guess so,' she said. 'Just like old times, huh, Delgado?'

Delgado looked at Cascari. He saw unusual vibrancy and alertness in his son, whose neck was slightly swollen at either side, the skin tender and slightly flushed. 'How about you?'

'Sure,' he said. 'You bet.'

'OK.' Delgado placed his right hand on Ashala's left shoulder. 'It's all yours, Ash,' he said. 'Break a leg.'

She smiled sweetly. 'Gee, thanks, Delgado.'

Ash stepped into the corridor with a confidence she didn't feel. The moment she walked through the door every one of the faeries immediately altered direction, drifting quickly towards her like tiny, illuminated dandelion-heads.

'Stop. This is a restricted area.' The gorgon's voice was strong, husky and assertive. As she turned to face Ashala the stalks on the cyborg's head flexed, each of the shiny alloy blast heads widening as Ash was targeted.

Ash walked quickly, even running a couple of steps, trying to ignore the faeries now dancing all around her. Adrenalin surged; she felt light-headed and slightly sick. 'There's been an accident,' she said. 'I'm a medic. I need to get to the other bays.' She pointed at the door in the bulkhead further along the corridor. The faeries moved closer to her until they were just centimetres away from her skin. She could feel the prickle of their sensors upon her. Delgado had been wise to take her gun. She glanced to her left as she passed the window into the bay and caught a brief glimpse of the ship. There was no sign of anyone within the bay.

The gorgon took a few steps towards her but seemed reluctant to stray too far from the door she was guarding. 'This area is off limits. You must find another route.'

'But it's just on the other side of that door,' Ash protested, pointing towards the opposite end of the corridor. 'Someone's been hurt. If I don't treat them quickly they may die.'

'That is not my concern. You must leave immediately.' The gorgon tried to block Ash's way, the faeries swarming around her like a sparkling aura. Ash looked up into the gorgon's golden eyes and was overwhelmed by the cyborg's beauty. She suddenly felt incredibly safe and calm. She could hear only the dull sound of her own blood rushing through her veins.

As Ash opened her mouth to speak the faeries darted away from her as one, moving like a shoal of fish, and the gorgon's weapon stems moved to one side like reeds in a fast stream as something attracted their attention.

Ash saw two of the grenades rolling quickly along the smooth corridor floor. Time seemed to slow. She heard a shout, turned and caught the gun Delgado threw to her. The faeries began firing their weapons at the grenades, trying unsuccessfully to destroy them. Ash looked at Delgado as he yelled at her to get down, then threw herself to the floor.

There was a brilliant flash and a loud, brief crackling sound.

When Ash looked up she saw most of the faeries scattered across the floor, many of them smouldering. There was an odd aroma in the air. Cascari was firing his sidearm at one of the two faeries unaffected by the electroflash grenades. He seemed to have been hit in one leg and was unable to stand.

Delgado had leaped on to the gorgon's back, wrapping his legs around her waist and gripping the slimy gun stems on the cyborg's head tightly in one fist. The gorgon flailed, trying to reach behind her, grabbing at Delgado as her weapons fired at the ceiling.

Ash fired at one of the faeries and it exploded, releasing a cloud of grey smoke and showering Cascari with far more matter than it seemed possible for its tiny shell to contain. The other surviving faerie immediately shot a needle of blue light at Ash that hit her upper arm. She looked at the wound but saw only a rip in her sleeve. She turned back to the gorgon and saw the cyborg convulsing wildly as she tried to throw Delgado from her back.

As Delgado struggled to maintain his hold on the gun stems with one hand the switchblade slipped from his grip and slid along the floor. Ash stooped, picked it up and ran towards them, then plunged the blade deep into the base of the gorgon's skull, twisting it several times.

As the gorgon flexed her body and managed to fling Delgado over her head, the limp, lifeless stems fell in front of her face like long strands of pale, wet hair. The cyborg reached down, gripped Delgado's clothes at the waist and chest and lifted him with ease. As she raised him above her head to throw him against the wall, Ash and Cascari fired their weapons simultaneously. The blasts tore into the cyborg's back, waist and head. Her back arched, her muscles weakened, and she fell to the floor with Delgado landing on top of her.

Ash ran forward and crouched next to him. 'You OK?'

'Sure. Thanks. I owe you one.'

'You owe me plenty. It's not the first time I've saved your ass, after all, Delgado.'

'I guess not. How's Cascari?'

She stood and ran over to the younger man, who was sitting towards the end of the corridor with his injured leg outstretched in front of him. 'He's OK,' she said. 'A good dose of frozone will fix him real quick.' She produced a canister from one of her pockets and began spraying it on to Cascari's wound.

'Ow, sheesh, that stuff stings, man.'

Ash stuck out her bottom lip. 'Aw, poor little boy grazed himself, has he?'

Delgado stood slowly and rubbed his aching limbs. He began hobbling towards them, looking at the contorted cyborg corpse and stepping over the charred faeries that now littered the corridor floor like flakes of burned paper. He was careful to make sure that he kept out of sight of anyone within the bay. 'Boy, she was tough,' he said.

'Yeah. I was worried she'd start reforming again,' said Ash.

'Only Hostility Class have that capability. The nobics are just too expensive to load them into every model. She had plenty going for her, though. Hey, you took a hit.' He pointed at Ash's sleeve. 'You OK?'

She looked down at her arm. The sleeve was wet with blood. 'Yeah, fine. It's nothing. Just a graze.'

'Yeah, but you're losing blood,' said Delgado. 'Here, give me that frozone.' He took the canister, opened up the tear in the fabric and sprayed a liberal amount of the chemical directly on to the wound.

'Ow! Shit!'

'See,' said Cascari. 'Who's laughing now?'

They stood on either side of a window peering through at the vessel in the bay. Standing on four short struts that looked too thin and weak to support its weight, it was a relatively small, modern craft. It was like a flattened cone in shape, its exterior smooth and grey. Above the vessel's sharp nose were two heavily tinted viewports, beneath which its name was painted in italic script: *Maquiladora*.

A hatch mid-way along the *Maquiladora*'s fuselage was open, its curved shape raised above the section of hull of which it otherwise formed part. A smooth ramp on a wheeled framework led from the ship to the bay floor. Just behind this a thick, ribbed pipe leading from the bay wall was connected by metal couplings to the *Maquiladora*'s fuselage. Gas emerged in vaporous clouds from vents towards the rear of the vessel's hull. Behind the ship the huge containment fields surrounding the bay's portal glowed around the craft like a golden aura. To the right of the window through which they were looking was the door to the bay.

'Never seen a Structure ship like that,' Delgado whispered.

'They must be playing this real cagey. See those bulges towards the rear?' He indicated minor swellings between the craft's open hatch and its tail. 'They seem to merge with the power plant. I'll bet it's a slipspacer.'

'Seems big for that. They'll want to get to Seriatt as quick as possible, though, that's for sure,' said Ash. 'Before the Seriatts can instate another Monosiell.'

'Yeah. Well, the Seriatts will want to keep on the right side of the Andamour Council, so they won't rush into anything,' said Delgado. 'Whatever happens, we need to get there before *they* do.'

'Where do you think he is?' asked Cascari.

'Just because there's a ramp leading down from an open hatch, don't assume he's not on board.' Delgado looked intently at the *Maquiladora*'s viewports, but could not see through them.

To their right, the door in the bulkhead in the corridor opened suddenly. All three of them turned and pressed themselves against the wall, drawing and priming their sidearms. A few moments later a small automatic appeared, trundling slowly through the bulkhead. The door closed as the automatic moved towards them, constantly correcting its course with minute pauses of one of the two tracks driving it. Abruptly, the machine stopped, turned itself through ninety degrees by turning its tracks in opposite directions, then disappeared through the door to the bay. It seemed to be carrying small packets of dehydrated food, compressed water cells and other miscellaneous supplies. They looked through the window and saw the second door into the bay open. The dissonant throb of the containment fields suddenly became louder.

As the automatic crossed the open space towards the *Maquiladora* it corrected its course with a jolt that scattered several food packages across the bay's white floor. The courier then ascended the ramp, to be absorbed by the brilliant light within the ship.

As a man appeared at the top of the ramp the three of them moved back to ensure they wouldn't be seen. Delgado recognised him immediately: it was Osephius. He was twenty years older, but otherwise the same man who had informed Delgado of his mission to fetch Lycern from the Affinity Group so long ago. Delgado felt bitterness and hatred rise like a riptide, threatening to overwhelm his usual calmness.

'This is probably our best chance,' whispered Delgado as Osephius walked down the ramp. 'Michael's on that ship. I'd bet on it. Especially now we know Osephius is here.' Osephius began to gather the spilled food parcels.

Ash turned her head slightly towards Delgado. 'What say we deal with these two then take their fast ship to Seriatt ourselves, huh?'

Delgado nodded slowly and re-set his weapon to micro-plasma. 'That would be very convenient,' he said. 'You two wait here. I'll take care of him.' He moved cautiously towards the door to the bay and peered into the small room connecting it to the outside corridor. It was not lit. He stepped further in to the room and stood deep in the shadow cast by one of the two doors into the bay. He looked around the door. The *Maquiladora*'s shape was somehow more elegant from the side elevation, its sharp nose widening to a muscular rump. He could hear Osephius muttering complaints to himself as he collected the food packs.

Delgado noticed the flow of cool air out of the bay. He sucked on one index finger then held it in the air, confirming the direction of the draught. He looked up at the ship's open hatch and squinted. Within the vessel he could see someone transferring the courier's cargo into storage compartments. Although he could not be certain, he assumed it was Michael.

Delgado took a few deep breaths and assigned clutches of nobics to combat streams. His alertness and energy levels increased immediately. He stepped from behind the door, but remained hidden in shadow, hidden from Osephius' view. He was heavier and more weathered than when Delgado had last encountered him so long ago, his skin aged, his eyes tired. In truth he bore little physical resemblance to the man Delgado had once known – if he had indeed known him. But the person behind the face was still there: cold, calculating, selfish.

The Structure officer represented a difficult target: he was constantly turning, moving, bending down and standing up again. While he would be relatively easy to hit, Delgado did not feel that a kill was guaranteed, especially using a weapon with which he had no relationship. And although he could see no obvious weapons on Osephius, he was almost certainly armed.

Delgado reached into a pocket and found one of the small tokens used in the drinks vending machines within the *Lex Talionis*. He looked at it briefly, turning it over in his fingers; he could not remember when he had acquired it. He looked up again, assessed the distance, then casually flicked the coin into the bay.

The token hit the smooth bay floor, bounced once, hit the floor again, then rolled in smooth, ever-decreasing circles. The ridges on its edge produced a thrumming sound that seemed disproportionately loud for the coin's small size. It finally fell on to one side directly in front of Osephius' face as he reached for the final package.

Delgado smiled. Osephius remained in a stoop, staring at the token for a few moments before reaching out and picking it up. He stood upright, turning the token over in his fingers the way Delgado had. He patted his tunic's chest pockets and checked that they were still zipped shut. He then looked towards the door. Delgado saw that Osephius had a deep scar running down the side of his nose, across his left cheek almost to his left ear. It looked as though he had tried to perform DIY cosmetic surgery to make him look like a Seriattic *mourst*. But the scar was old and pale, the result of some event that had occurred in the intervening years since that day in Myson's chamber.

Osephius frowned, an off-centre crease forming on his forehead. Delgado grinned at the confusion in his face. The now empty automatic began to make its way slowly down the ramp again.

Delgado took a few steps forward. As he moved from shadow into light, he appeared to Osephius like a phantasm. The two men made eye contact. Delgado felt his opponent slide to what he would have to admit was a useful combination of caution and aggression.

'Remember me?' Delgado knew he should kill Osephius without putting anything at risk, but couldn't resist it.

'Delgado?' His voice was deeper, more mature. 'Alexander Delgado? What the hell . . . ?'

Delgado saw movement of the silhouette in the *Maquiladora*'s hatch and threw himself bodily to the right, rolling across the smooth bay floor towards some containers. He narrowly avoided the shot that had been aimed at him, which instead destroyed one half of the door and part of the wall. Delgado fired at Osephius and then at Michael's slightly diffused outline in the *Maquiladora*'s hatch. Both were poor shots that missed their targets.

Osephius scurried behind the lower part of the ramp and began firing back, but soon realised he was exposed to fire from Ash and Cascari, who had also entered the bay. He stood, fired several shots at both Delgado and Cascari, then leaped up on to the ramp and ran up into the *Maquiladora*.

As Osephius sprinted up the slope, Delgado fired a volley of shots, the microplasma bolts peppering the *Maquiladora*'s hull around the hatch with tiny explosions that caused marginal damage to the vessel. Michael's silhouette was still visible. Delgado's nobics tingled with a feeling of identification he could not rationalise. There seemed to be a distinct flavour to Michael's traces that Delgado had only previously experienced in Seriatts, but that made no sense. Perhaps Cascari was so excited his own traces were overwhelming Delgado's perception of Michael.

Shots from Cascari and Ash damaged the ramp's framework, and the structure began to buckle. As fire was exchanged between those aboard the *Maquiladora* and those within the bay, one side of the ramp began to tilt towards the bay floor due to the intensity of the heat being generated in its frame. As the angle became increasingly steep the automatic tried to stop itself from falling off the edge. In an effort to steer itself back towards the centre of the ramp the machine's left track stopped turning. The front of the automatic pointed towards the centre of the slope, but as the ramp leaned still further the courier began to slide sideways, until eventually it fell off, landing on one side on the bay floor. The track against the floor continued to turn, and the disabled machine began to describe circles beneath the *Maquiladora's* nose.

Osephius and Michael disappeared from sight as the *Maquiladora*'s hatch began to close. Delgado, Ash and Cascari stepped from their positions of cover now that the incoming fire had ceased, but their continued efforts were futile. On the floor of the bay the courier was still turning slowly. The *Maquiladora*'s hatch was now fully closed, liquiform seals smoothing away the edges so that it was impossible to identify its exact location in the hull.

Delgado looked along the side of the *Maquiladora* and, despite the tint of the viewports, was just able to distinguish either Michael or Osephius putting on a visuals visor and reaching up to an overhead panel.

He ran to Cascari and Ash. 'We've got to get out of here,' he said. An alarm began to sound and a distant, aloof female voice warned of imminent vacuum conditions. Delgado could feel the air pressure and temperature dropping. The bay doors were beginning to close, despite the damage caused by the earlier shots.

'But we're so close. He's right *there*.' Cascari jabbed a finger towards the *Maquiladora*.

Delgado shook his head. 'It's no good. They're about to

upship. We've got to get out of here or we'll be dead meat, frozen, vacuum packed.' He grabbed Cascari's sleeve and pulled him towards the door, but Cascari resisted. With the bay doors almost completely closed and the rush of air increasing, both Delgado and Ash had to try to persuade Cascari to leave the bay. Their eyes were streaming from the rush of cold air. 'Come on,' cried Delgado above the noise of the wind and the *Maquiladora*'s engines. 'We're not going to get him here. We have to get out of this bay.'

Cascari stood firm for a moment, then screamed as loudly as he could. The ridges in his neck stiffened with rage, but the noise in the bay was so great the others were unable to hear him. Delgado could feel the intensity of the young man's hatred quite clearly. It was one of the most intense and pure emotions he had ever encountered.

Eventually Cascari was forced to concede that there was nothing they could do and they edged sideways out of the bay as the doors closed the last few centimetres. With no way for them to stop Michael leaving, they walked around to the window into the bay and watched as the amber glow of the containment fields around the bay mouth faded.

A few moments later the *Maquiladora* was hovering a few metres off the floor. Its ugly landing struts retracted into the fuselage, giving the vessel an even sleeker look, and tiny thrusters in the nose pushed the vessel back out of the bay. As it moved backwards, the thick pipe connected to the wall rose into the air, became taut, stretched, then broke, spewing a viscous brown liquid. As the ship moved away from them, the umbilical remnants hanging from its side, Delgado thought he saw Michael and Osephius waving from the flight deck. When it was finally outside the bay in the central channel of *Zavanchia*'s port, the *Maquiladora* turned slowly and gracefully through ninety degrees, then moved forwards, and out of sight.

Delgado looked at Cascari. The young man was staring into

the space the *Maquiladora* had occupied just a few moments earlier. Delgado placed a consolatory hand on the young man's shoulder. 'Nothing we could do,' he said quietly. 'We had to cut our losses.'

'We were so close,' said Cascari. 'So close.'

'So what do we do now, Delgado?' asked Ash.

'We go to Seriatt, as planned. We can't beat them now. We just have to hope we can get there before anything's set in stone, so we can prove Cascari's the rightful heir.'

'Well, we won't be able to go in the Strapher,' remarked Cascari. 'It won't make it.' He looked at Delgado. 'Look, you head back to the *Talionis*. I'll find a ship and make my own way. I'm sure the Seriatts will be more receptive to me if I'm on my own.'

'No way,' said Delgado, shaking his head emphatically. 'We'll find someone who'll buy the Strapher off us or trade her. It *is* a Strapher, after all. Apart from anything else, I'm sure the Seriatt's wouldn't exactly welcome us with open arms if we turned up in that. When we've got a new ship then we'll get out of here, double-time.'

High troposphere, Seriatt

Panels rattled and shook as their newly acquired craft – *The Lost Cause*, obtained from a gummy, stooping smuggler called Mereweth, in exchange for the Strapher on a no-questions-asked basis – was buffeted by the rapidly thickening Seriattic atmosphere.

'She's registered as an Open Trader, so you'll get landing permits for most any port you care to go to, so long as you behave yourself. She's got a no-nonsense core that's got me outta many a scrape, too, young feller,' Mereweth had enthused fondly, 'so you look after her, y'hear? One o' the finest ships as ever there was. God bless 'er. I always wan'ed me a Strapher, though. Fast an' furious. You come under some fire, sonny?'

Delgado had assured Mereweth that, despite the obviously recent damage, the Strapher was in overall good order. A little bit of TLC, he had said, would soon put her straight. He was about to say something along the lines of spaceships being like women, but realised Ash was looking at him and thought better of it. After Mereweth had been linked into the Strapher's core for half an hour, he was happy to trade.

Following one particularly sharp jolt, Delgado, who was sitting at the rear of the flight deck, found himself covered in soiled clothing when a locker above his head burst open. He threw the stinking laundry into a corner, muttering profanities.

At the master console, Cascari was becoming increasingly frustrated with the craft, which seemed quite temperamental. He swore bitterly.

'What is it?' Delgado asked.

'It's this core, that's what it is,' he answered grimly. 'I reckon it's corrupt somehow and our friend Mereweth decided to keep that little nugget of information from us.'

'Every time he tries to check the heat-shield efficiency,' said Ash patiently, 'the visual opens then shuts down immediately, then there's a list of what look like currency conversion rates. It's beginning to annoy him.'

'Too right it's beginning to annoy me,' Cascari blustered, becoming even more agitated.

'But you don't need to check the heat-shield efficiency, Cascari,' said Ash, placing one hand on his shoulder. 'If it gets very warm in here we'll know there's a problem we can't do anything about. If it doesn't get very warm in here there's not a problem. Stop worrying.'

'Will you shut up?'

'I can't promise to do that, no.'

'How long until we land?' asked Delgado.

'About twenty minutes,' Ash replied.

'Any signs that the Seriatts have seen through our disguise?'

'No. Assignment of Open Trader status continues to be

accepted. At least Mereweth seems to have been straight with us about that.'

'OK. Let's open the blastplates.'

After Ash had briefly checked the craft's speed and the external temperature, the shields began to withdraw.

The view was breathtaking. Thin strips of cloud across the rich turquoise sky cast dark slivers of shadow across the glistering ocean. A chain of atolls formed a delicate coral archipelago that looked like a discarded necklace. From this altitude three continents were discernible, upon which population centres looked like patches of grey and brown lichen. There was also rich vegetation, dense forests watered by wide, meandering rivers. The whole planet exuded health. It was a vibrant, colourful world, exuberant in the very fact of its existence.

The Lost Cause reduced its rate of descent, and began to slip through the highest layers of cloud. Gradually the horizon flattened, and the grey landmass ahead filled the viewports. The huge city that was their destination seemed to flow like liquid from the snow-peaked mountains in the distance to the right. While this was a massive urban area, a technologically advanced metropolis, it was also infused with many lush green areas that appeared to sprout through the buildings, randomising the sprawl. There was a definite sense of openness and space.

The buildings were predominantly low rise, white-painted with rounded corners and flat roofs. There were certainly no structures to compare to the habitat towers on Earth or Planetary Guidance Headquarters. They were dissected at right angles by wide, straight canals that reflected light as *The Lost Cause* passed over them. The canals were vivid arteries that provided an extensive transportation and leisure infrastructure. The wide main channels were intersected by narrower canals, and those by even narrower channels. Some of these waterways fed warehouses and factories, while others ended in circular marinas in residential areas, where numerous craft of varying sizes were moored at jetties.

As the ship descended, it was possible to discern a variety of waterborne vessels on the canals, and ground vehicles on the tree-lined roads. The heavy craft banked as it turned and the mountains drifted across the viewports. Two gigantic skyships hung in the air above the city, fat, round-edged discs with elegant gondolas slung from metal frameworks beneath them. Each driven by four huge propellers, two pairs of engines on each side, both ponderous vehicles appeared to be making their way slowly towards the mountains, or whatever lay beyond.

Cascari pointed at a flat, grey area in the distance. 'Looks like a port,' he said. 'Lots of ships.'

Delgado looked at Ashala. 'They still not on to us?'

She shook her head as she cycled through visuals. 'Doesn't look like it. Glideslope is set, and it's a clear run to an assigned landing slot. We've actually been sent an Acceptable Open Trading Policy Statement, so they must think we're genuine. Estimated remaining flight time is five minutes.'

'Do we know if Michael's ship has arrived yet?'

'It arrived this morning and landed near the port's eastern perimiter. They don't seem to have disembarked yet. I'll keep an eye on it.'

'I would have expected them to get things moving immediately. Interesting.'

'Not as interesting as this.' Ash removed her visuals visor and touched a tab on a panel in front of her. A display appeared above her lap. It showed a group of people standing around a small aircraft constructed from an aluminium-like material. Like the *Maquiladora*, the forward half of its fuselage was smooth and curvaceous, while the rear was more angular. A group of *mourst* was standing beside it; despite their fearsome appearance they were all extremely beautiful creatures, their facial features strong but delicately structured, their stance conveying personal pride and confidence. A picture of Michael appeared on the screen, followed by shots of Earth and the Planetary Guidance Headquarters. Delgado sat more upright. 'I intercepted it while you were asleep,' she explained. 'It's a news feed from Seriatt. Cascari translated some of it. He says it's some kind of race due to take place soon.'

'Play it again from the beginning,' said Delgado. 'Cascari, translate it, will you? My Seriattic's not too hot.'

Cascari took off his visor and looked at the images. 'Yeah, its a race,' he said, translating the Seriattic words now drifting from the speaker in front of them. 'Some of it I didn't understand but I can give you the gist.' The image cut from Michael to a rotating example of the svelte craft, various parts of which were highlighted as the commentator described it. 'An air race,' said Cascari. 'Very dangerous. He's giving lots of technical information about the craft. It's very powerful, but basic. There are . . . he's using lots of words I'm not familiar with now . . . there is no help, I think that was. No technological aids, that's it.'

The image changed again, now showing a landscape. The sun was shining; colourful triangular banners billowed and snapped in a strong breeze. The camera panned down towards huge pale grey tubes conjoined in groups of three, emerging from the ground and curving towards the sky like amputated mammoths' tusks. The surface of each was stippled and rutted, covered with vein-like distensions that resembled tree roots. The sea was a sparkling backdrop. The Seriatt voiceover stopped, and a moment later one small craft was launched from each of the three tubes with a dull thud. Cones of blue flame appeared behind them as engines fired, powering the craft towards the mountains' snowy peaks.

The camera followed the craft as they jostled for position, undulating gently. Two of them drifted closer together, then collided. One machine disintegrated immediately, and the frail body of its pilot was briefly visible as the Seriatt was torn from the shattered cockpit into the cold air. Having lost one of its short wings the other machine spun towards the ground with the grace of an autumn leaf. The camera followed the vessel down. No parachute or ejection cell deployed.

The view then switched back to the remaining aircraft. They were heading towards a huge metal hoop hanging in mid-air above the mountains. Its edges glowed orange and a bright pulse of light circled its outer edge.

Delgado leaned forwards, his eyes narrowed. 'What's this?' he said.

Cascari listened. 'He's calling it a buoy. It acts as a . . . catapult, I think that was.'

Delgado frowned. 'To where.'

'The next one. That's the race.' He listened some more, then continued. 'There are several of these buoys at various waypoints. The first pilot to successfully pass through them all and complete the course is the winner.'

The commentator was becoming increasingly excited as the small craft jinked and dodged as they sped towards the gigantic hoop ahead of them. As they closed on the buoy it became clear that only two or three craft at most would be able to pass through at one time and there were now ten machines in the race. As the distance between the aircraft and the hoop decreased, all but the few machines at the rear got into a line-astern formation, apparently happy – or forced to accept – their respective positions. In contrast, those at the back became frantic in their efforts to get ahead of each other, their trajectories increasingly erratic as they fought to reach the buoy before their competitors.

'Oh, I see,' said Cascari, nodding and smiling as the commentator continued to talk. 'That's a nice touch. Very nice.'

Delgado and Ash looked at him. 'What?'

'Each buoy has a limited amount of power, so the energy level in each one, and therefore its ability to act as a catapult, declines as the race progresses. The aircraft are flung from the launch tubes but carry a very small amount of fuel. Basically they have to glide most of the time, using the slingshot provided by each buoy to get them to the next one. They keep some fuel in reserve to give them a boost if they need it, but there's not much, and when it's gone, it's gone.' Cascari paused, listening to the Seriattic voice for a moment. 'He's saying something about G-forces. Not all of them can get through successfully as the power of the buoy diminishes with each slingshot. And if you don't get through, there's nowhere to land.'

'So what happens?'

'Crash and burn. It's entertainment sport, Seriattic style.' He said this with a combination of satisfaction and pride.

The first craft reached the buoy. As the aircraft passed through, the orange pulse circling the buoy's edge intensified momentarily. The craft shimmered, became somewhat indistinct, and then vanished. Although nothing obscured the view beyond the buoy, with distant cloud formations visible on either side of its rim, the craft could not be seen in the sky beyond.

As the excited commentary resumed, Delgado noticed that the brilliance of the pulse circling the buoy had diminished slightly. It lost more of its luminescence as each subsequent aircraft passed through, disappearing like the first. The rate of the pulse's revolution also began to slow.

As they fought for airspace two aircraft at the rear of the pack touched gently, and spun away from each other with a ferocity that was seemingly disproportionate to the slight impact. One of them hit the glowing edge of the buoy and vaporised, becoming a spectacular blue-white fireball; the other passed by the outside of the gigantic hoop. The camera followed the latter machine as its pilot pulled a hard turn, the small aircraft skidding on the air as its short wings struggled to grip the thin atmosphere. By the time it had turned and was aligned to make a second attempt on the buoy, all the other aircraft had passed through, and the rim was no longer a vibrant orange but a slow-moving, lacklustre smudge of brown.

The *mourst* commentator seemed to be laughing as he spoke, a series of throaty cough-like sounds interspersing his words.

'What's he saying?' asked Delgado.

'Something like, "this guy's got no chance but he's going to try anyway." He admires his courage.'

Suddenly a plume of blue flame erupted from the rear of the small aircraft and it accelerated towards the buoy. But when it passed through it did not disappear like those that had preceded it, but simply continued on, a solitary craft in the open air. The flame faltered, then ceased. The silvery machine flew level for a few more moments, then plunged towards the mountains.

'Game over,' said Cascari.

'So what's Michael's connection to all this?' Delgado asked.

'Apparently the Seriatts have insisted on him racing,' said Ash, 'and Myson's agreed. Michael has to prove himself somehow, the Seriatts say. The race is a rite of passage for high-ranking *mourst* or those of noble birth.'

Delgado nodded. 'Yeah. I bet the Seriatts are trying to keep on the right side of the Andamour Council by appearing to offer this as a possibility. But secretly they'll be expecting – or at least hoping – that Michael will get killed during the race anyway. I'm not sure they're going to be that lucky.'

'What makes you say that?' asked Cascari, a tone of indignation evident in his voice.

'I've heard he's a pretty good pilot. He's young and fit, got a lot to prove. No, he's quite capable of getting to the end. Then everyone's in trouble. Except Myson. He's probably dreaming about that time machine of theirs right now. We've got to get into that race. Make *sure* he doesn't finish. Then when we approach the Seriatts we'll already have performed their rite of passage.'

'What if we don't survive the race ourselves?' asked Cascari. 'We won't be the only ones in the sky.'

Delgado shrugged. 'It's a risk we have to take,' he said.

As *The Lost Cause* sank lower and the tone of the engines deepened, their rapid pulse slowing to a slightly offbeat throb, Cascari placed the visor back over his eyes and returned to monitoring the systems. The vessel descended until it was so low, that through the viewport to his right, Delgado could see people walking along sidewalks and playing ball games in open spaces. A Seriattic child looked up at the sound of their passing, and waved one hand; the child's arm seemed disproportionately long.

The Lost Cause slowed even more, bobbing and rolling very slightly as Cascari guided the craft in. It drifted across the perimetre of the spaceport at an altitude of around three hundred metres, and the beauty and space of the residential areas was replaced by a stark grey expanse. The vessel followed a path marked on either side by long flashing strips. To either side of this broad channel huge circles were marked on the ground, many of which contained landed vessels and the services required for their turnaround: fuel tankers, supply trucks, bulk cargo couriers. In one particularly large circle was a sleek spaceliner from which hundreds of passengers were disembarking along transparent tunnels that led into a waiting articulated coach. In the distance, Delgado could see a cluster of tall, fragile towers, to which more of the skyships were moored. The vessels hung like vast, airborne fungus, casting elliptical shadows across the ground.

The braking engines became briefly active, and *The Lost Cause* turned off the main strip towards the landing slot assigned to it. When above the designated zone, the vessel slowly descended vertically, a faint wheeze audible as the landing skids extended from its underside, followed by a slight bump as the craft finally touched the ground.

Ash removed her visuals strip, unbuckled her harness, stood

and stretched. Delgado and Cascari remained seated, looking at the mountains, the clouds, the large, lilac-tinted crescent moon that hung in the sky like a cynical smile. Albeit for different reasons, both men were trying to comprehend the fact that they were, at last, on Seriatt.

Four

the thirteenth labour of herakles

The Laboratory of Continuity Studies, Seriatt

Long, narrow spikes and short, thorn-like hooks protruded from the otherwise smooth substance from which the portal's glowing golden frame was made. Tiny points of light danced within it, circling the perimeter. The *vilume* and *conosq* scientists looked at the field within the frame; it was like a membrane of skin, glistering gently as it surged and boiled. Behind the field, the frame was a bulbous, solid mass the same colour as the delicate frame, a shell-like object covered with hard nodules and blisters.

'A strong channel has been established and stabilised,' stated one of the *vilume*, who was standing behind a small control panel and monitoring the readings on the small dials set into it. He checked the slender needles and looked towards his colleagues. 'Conditions are optimal,' he said. 'I believe it is time.'

'I agree,' said a *conosq*. 'I do not feel that we can make any further improvements to the device without testing it. We have established certain facts and have certain expectations, but if these prove inaccurate we may have to begin afresh. So, test it we must.' She looked towards the *mourst* who was standing nearby. He was dressed in close-fitting garments of black leather, adorned with brown leather panels engraved with images from the *cursilac*, the great stories depicted in the ancient texts of the *conchey trinzig diasii*. 'Do you feel ready, Hescar?' asked the *conosq*.

The *mourst* inhaled, and held his head high. 'I am ready, *Conosq* Sherlaq.' he confirmed.

'You have eaten? Made peace with yourself?'

'I have.'

'Very well.' Sherlaq turned to face the Oracles, who were standing at the far end of the room observing impassively. She bowed low, showing them the palms of her hands. 'It is with great respect that I ask the Oracles' permission to perform the first test.'

'You may proceed,' said Oracle Entuzo.

Sherlaq and the other *conosq* and *vilume* scientists gathered around the *mourst*, taking turns to embrace him. Although this was a formal gesture, the *conosqs*' *assissius* glands, visible above their clothes at the neck, became slightly swollen and moist as they did so, their arousal automatic and inevitable in the close physical contact. Even the *vilume* were stirred sexually by the intensity of the moment. All the scientists were moved by the fact that Hescar was prepared to put his life at risk to test the device they had spent so long developing.

Hescar took a few paces forward and stood in front of the portal. The *mourst* took several deep breaths. Despite being a former warrior, and having experienced many wonderful and terrible things, he was nervous: this was the territory of the Oracles, who saw possibilities through their analysis of the visualisations generated by the Destiny Mask. He was a mere *mourst*. How could he consider himself worthy of the Oracles' trust?

'It is time,' said Sherlaq. 'The channel is at its most stable.'

Hescar stared at the beautiful, silvery field within the portal and thought he could see shapes moving within it, but they were too indistinct for him to be certain. He took another deep breath, and muttered some words from the *conchey trinzig diasii*: 'I am not complete without those that surround me. I must give myself up for the good of others.' Then he strode towards the portal.

As Hescar stepped into the field, a sudden warm wind coursed through the laboratory, blowing documents from one of the tables on to the floor. When stillness returned, the *mourst* had vanished.

Capital Port, Seriatt

Ash's fingers danced across touchtabs and through projected icons. 'Delgado.'

'Yeah. What's up?'

'There's a vehicle approaching *The Lost Cause*.'

Delgado leaned close to her as she brought up a display showing the small, four-wheeled vehicle approaching the ship. A tail of dust was drawn into the air behind it. 'Guess this is a welcoming committee,' said Delgado. 'Although the ship checks out they probably want to give us the once-over face to face, too.' He looked out through one of the flight-deck viewports and saw the vehicle pull up next to the ship. It was a small, rounded, bubble-like vehicle with heavily tinted windows covered in a layer of brown grit. As he watched, gull-wing doors opened on either side of the vehicle. Two *mourst* stepped from the rear of the car and one from the driving position in the front. The doors closed again as the three *mourst* walked towards the ship. Delgado watched them until they were too close to the craft to be seen, then activated one of the cameras on the underside of the vessel. One of the *mourst* drew a length of cable from a coil at his waist and plugged the card on the end of it into the universal comms slot on one of the forward landing struts. The Seriatt's voice suddenly boomed through the flight deck.

'*Cour, driecfod marrce*.'

'What did he say?' Delgado asked, looking at Cascari.

'Immigration. Let us in. More or less, anyway.'

Delgado looked at Ash. 'Better let them in,' he said.

'Is that wise?'

'We don't have much choice, do we? Besides, we could do with their car. Extend the ramp and release the seals.'

She reached out and touched a sequence of tabs, and a few minutes later the heavy footfalls and gruff voices of the *mourst* could be heard within *The Lost Cause* as they approached the flight deck.

'Ash,' whispered Delgado, 'you hide in here.' He indicated the lower portion of the locker at the rear of the flight deck. 'Quickly. We'll distract them, try to split them up. You'll be able to see through these slits. If you see an opportunity to strike, then take it.'

'You sure do put me in some positions, Delgado,' she said as he bundled her into the confined space.

'Consider it a sign of respect,' he said, as he quietly shut the locker door.

'Respect? Gee, thanks, Delgado.'

Delgado moved towards the front of the flight deck just as the three Seriatts stepped through the door. They had a hard, scaly, almost reptilian appearance but were as strikingly handsome as any *mourst*. Small metal plates on their chests indicated that their names were Maghme, Groutenay and Coluum. Delgado instinctively knew that Groutenay was of higher rank than his two colleagues.

These pure *mourst* were considerably taller than Cascari, who was himself tall by human standards. While clearly muscular, they also appeared agile despite their cumbersome uniforms and equipment. Their long forearms rested on top of the chunky weapons slung across their chests. The narrow muzzles of their guns protruded from beneath their left armpits like the snouts of timid animals. Their long fingers appeared to have at least one more joint than humans', and there were also ridges on the backs of their hands that ran out of sight under their sleeves. The sinewy ridges at their necks were much more pronounced than Cascari's: hard, well-defined lines ran from their chins, along their necks and rose up to the back of the ears. Delgado had not been in the company of pure *mourst* since the Buhatt Rebellion, and had forgotten just how imposing and powerful they were. Compared to these creatures, Cascari was an overweight pup and Delgado could sense his son's discomfort in their presence quite clearly.

For several seconds not a word was spoken as the tall *mourst* officials looked down at the two men. Their deep-set, thick-lidded eyes were cold and threatening.

Delgado's perception that Groutenay was the leader appeared to be confirmed – and reciprocated – when the Seriatt addressed Delgado directly. The *mourst* uttered a string of Seriattic words Delgado did not understand.

'Can you ask him if he speaks Counian?' said Delgado. 'We have some hope of conversation if he does.'

'*Goggheg iidiyec mettonar Counian,*' said Cascari.

The three Seriatts looked at Cascari. One of them stepped closer to him, and looked him up and down. Groutenay turned his attention back to Delgado. 'We need to know your origin and reason for visiting Seriatt,' the *mourst* said, in what was not only Counian, but very good Counian. His words were thick with the throaty tone particular to his species. Delgado saw rows of serrated, razor-sharp teeth lining the Seriatt's mouth. His warm breath carried a thick, pungent odour that was a combination of stale sweat and rotting meat.

'We've come from *Zavanchia*, replied Delgado. 'We're Open Traders. We're visiting Seriatt to trade goods.'

Groutenay gently caressed his weapon with his long, hard fingers, stroking the gun like a pet. Delgado noticed that his fingernails were long and chipped, the colour of dried blood.

'Goods of what kind?' Groutenay growled.

'Fabrics, spices, minerals, delicacies. Whatever offers a reasonable profit.' He smiled, but was uncertain whether the Seriatt would appreciate what the expression indicated.

Groutenay looked at Coluum, who said a few short, thick Seriattic words, then looked back at Delgado. 'My colleague says the records indicate that there should be three of you aboard this vessel. Where is the other?'

'Asleep,' Delgado replied. 'She's in her cabin.' He gestured towards the door.

Groutenay looked at Coluum and Maghme, snarled something brief, and jerked his head towards the door. 'You will show my colleagues,' he said to Cascari. 'I will stay here with your captain. Bring this third passenger to me.'

Cascari looked at Delgado, then left the flight deck followed by the two Seriatts. The door closed automatically behind them.

As Groutenay pulled some kind of electronic notepad from one of his pockets and began to write on it, Delgado glanced at the locker in which Ashala was hiding. He raised his eyebrows and nodded briefly.

Groutenay looked at Delgado. 'You say you have come from *Zavanchia*,' he said.

'That's right.'

'But you are human.'

Delgado shrugged, nodded. 'Sure. Haven't been there for a long time, though.'

Groutenay made a few notes. 'Your ship has Open Trader status. I need to verify your trading licence. Fetch me your card.'

'That could be a problem.'

Groutenay looked up. 'Why? What is the problem?'

Delgado tried not to look towards the locker at the rear of the flight deck, from which Ashala was slowly emerging. 'I'm afraid it's been mislaid.'

Groutenay blinked, milky inner lids rolling over his eyes.

Delgado was unable to read the Seriatt's expression. 'Mislaid where? How?'

As Delgado was about to point out that if he knew where it had been mislaid, there was a good chance it wouldn't be mislaid, Ash put the barrel of her gun against the back of Groutenay's head. The Seriatt moved his eyes, but did not turn.

'OK,' said Delgado. 'Slowly give me the pad, then remove the gun. Otherwise she'll blow your head off.' Delgado nodded in Ash's direction. 'She's funny like that sometimes.' Groutenay stared at Delgado for a moment, then did as he was instructed. 'Now put your hands on top of your head and link your fingers.'

Delgado took the *mourst*'s gun and turned it over in his hands. It was fat, angular and heavy, the greater size of *mourst* hands compared to human hands evident in the proportions of the weapon's grip and trigger. It looked like a simple but powerful projectile weapon, with few settings to change and little in the way of enhancements. Just how Delgado liked them.

'My colleagues will return soon,' said Groutenay. 'Then you will be outnumbered, overpowered and killed.'

'Not necessarily,' said Delgado. 'Turn around.'

The Seriatt turned and faced Ashala for the first time. 'So,' he said, 'a human female. Your appearance is as I had heard.'

'Yeah? The feeling's mutual, buddy, so just zip it.'

As Groutenay opened his mouth to speak Delgado took a step forward, reached around the Seriatt's neck, gripped a handful of his greasy hair and pulled back his head, cleanly slitting the *mourst*'s throat with a swift movement of his knife.

The *mourst* fell to the floor, coughing as dark jets emerged from his neck in a steady rhythm. He seemed to lose blood surprisingly quickly, and was motionless within a few moments.

Ash looked at Delgado. 'This is a take-no-prisoners mission, huh?' she said.

'No time, too dangerous,' he said as he opened the flight-deck door. 'Get behind this console.' He indicated the control desk at the front of the flight deck. The others will be back in a minute.' He turned the chairs on their pedestals so he and Ash would be at least partially obscured from view.

They squeezed into the small gap between the rear of the master console and the flight deck's forward bulkhead, just below the blastplate viewports. Delgado crouched, resting his left elbow on the desk's upper edge, and cradling the barrel of the Seriattic weapon in his left hand. Ash knelt next to him, the sidearm gripped in both hands, her forearms resting on top of the console, aiming between the two chairs.

Suddenly they heard throaty *mourst* utterances in Seriatt, an apparent argument as if they feared returning to Groutenay empty handed.

Delgado waited.

'You know how to use that thing, Delgado?' Ash whispered, nodding towards the Seriattic weapon he was holding. 'It kinda looks like you need to grow into it.'

'Don't you worry about me,' he said quietly. 'Just keep your pretty little eyes peeled on that door, and when I say shoot, you shoot.'

'When you say "shoot", shoot. OK. I think I've got that.' She looked at him. 'You've never said I've got pretty eyes before.'

Delgado shrugged slightly. 'Well, you know, it just never came up in conversation, I guess. Now, will you please shut up?'

Delgado adjusted his grip on the weapon as he saw the two *mourst,* followed by Cascari, turn into the corridor. The Seriatts were talking as they walked, and failed to notice that the door to the flight deck was now open. Delgado aimed along the barrel.

'You ready?' he asked.

'Aren't I always?'

As the Seriatt's argument became more intense, Cascari was passing the door to the latrine. 'Fire in the hole!' Delgado shouted.

Cascari dived through the latrine door. The two *mourst* looked behind them then back towards the flight deck. Coluum took a few steps forward until he was in the doorway. He looked down at Groutenay's body and the pool of blood in which he lay, but before he could react Delgado opened fire.

The Seriattic weapon was incredibly powerful, and Delgado struggled to keep it under control as it released a stream of high-power bullets that smashed through the Seriatts, the bulkhead and the door, and tore through the corridor beyond, shattering plastic and piercing metal. The sharp whistling of the high-velocity bullets was accompanied by an irregular percussion of pops and bangs and the deep thrum of the gun's magazine as bullets were pushed up into the breech.

When Delgado stopped firing the return of quiet was abrupt.

'So when are you going to say "shoot", Delgado?'

He patted Ash's right forearm. 'Not to worry,' he said. 'I think I've managed to take care of it by myself.'

Delgado put down the gun as they extricated themselves from the confines of their hiding place and walked towards the flight-deck door.

'Cascari,' he called. 'Are you OK?'

'Jesus, these guys stink,' muttered Ash as they stepped over the dead Seriatts' bodies. 'They were bad enough when they were alive, but now . . . sheesh.'

'Cascari!'

The latrine door opened slowly and Cascari leaned forward, peering out into the corridor. 'Have you two finished?' he asked.

Delgado looked down at the dead *mourst*. 'I think so,' he

said. 'Come on. We need to get out of here before anyone comes looking for them. Ash, get the location of Michael's ship.' He looked through the viewport nearest to him. 'We'll take that vehicle of theirs.'

The vehicle's gull-wing doors opened automatically as they approached it. The car was divided in two by a partition. The driver's compartment at the front contained a red leather bench seat, a steering wheel and gearshift lever the colour of ivory. There were two pedals in the footwell, but there did not appear to be a visuals interface or AI core to take over routine functions. In the louvred metal dash were three dials with slender needles and fine Seriattic characters. The central dial was larger than those to either side of it. The rear passenger compartment contained two bench seats facing each other.

'OK, you two get in the back. I'll drive,' said Cascari as he got into the driver's seat. He peered at the controls and dials then stretched his legs towards the pedals.

Delgado and Ash clambered into the rear compartment.

'How come you get to drive?' asked Ash. 'I suppose you think you're best qualified, being half Seriatt or something.'

'Better qualified, maybe. Being half Seriatt's got nothing to do with it, though. Where're we headed?'

'He's near the eastern side of the port,' she said. 'There's a Lyugg freighter next to Michael's vessel. If we drive towards that we'll pass the *Maquiladora* and can have a reasonable look at it without appearing suspicious.'

Cascari craned his neck, looking through the windscreen and side window. 'OK. East is that way. How do I get this thing started?' He stabbed at the controls in front of him and pushed a black button beneath the central dial but nothing happened. There was a short stem protruding from the steering column which he twisted to no avail. He tried to push it, but it obviously wasn't meant to be pushed. When he pulled it, however, the engine coughed momentarily then sprang into life. The vehicle shuddered and a cloud of dark grey fumes wafted from the exhaust at the rear, blowing forwards over the car in the slight breeze. Judging from the sound of the power plant it was very basic – possibly a two-stroke fossil-fuel unit. 'Fantastic,' he said. 'Now which of these pedals is the accelerator and which is the brake?'

Delgado leaned forward to speak through the gap in the partition. 'I tell you what . . .'

As Cascari gunned the engine and the small vehicle surged forward, Delgado fell back on to the bench seat at the rear of the passenger compartment. Cascari threw the car into a tight one-hundred-and-eighty-degree turn, and the car's small tyres squealed loudly on the hot surface of the apron. Delgado slid across the seat and was pressed against Ash, who was herself pressed against the door next to her. Cascari straightened the car up and accelerated across the expanse of the apron, ignoring the routes marked out on the grey surface.

The vehicle was difficult to control due to its very narrow wheelbase and high centre of gravity. Cascari swore bitterly, fighting the car as it lurched over potholes and shuddered across the markings on the ground. As Cascari cut corners and made rapid course corrections across active landing zones, the two passengers in the rear were forced to cling to the grab handles above the doors. The already unstable vehicle became increasingly light as Cascari swerved it around obstacles and made rapid changes of direction.

At one point he took the car directly beneath a sub-orbital shuttle completing the final few metres of its descent. The vessel was so low when the car passed directly through the tight vortices of dust and dirt whirling beneath the ship that the occupants felt the entire vehicle shake, and a sudden rise in temperature.

After around ten minutes of this white-knuckle ride, Ash pointed. 'There it is,' she called out. 'The *Maquiladora*.'

Delgado leaned forward, but continued to cling to the grab-handle. 'Head for the Lyugg ship,' he called to Cascari, 'and we'll see how the land lies.'

As the vehicle passed through the shadow cast by the *Maquiladora*'s long nose, Ash pressed her face against the window and looked up at the craft. It possessed the same dark, sinister qualitites as a building left abandoned for many years. 'It looks deserted,' she said.

'You think he's gone?' Cascari called over his left shoulder.

'That might be the impression he's trying to give, although I doubt very much that he's expecting *us* to turn up here and knock on his door.'

'You think that's what we should do?' asked Ash.

'No. The hatch is too far off the ground. We'd never reach it.'

'Oh, very good. Well done.'

The vehicle's tyres squealed again and both Ash and Delgado slid across the bench seat as Cascari turned sharply, passing into the shadow of the Lyugg freighter. On the side of the vessel farthest from the *Maquiladora*, large containers were being transferred from a long, articulated transporter on to a ramp up to one of the vessel's cargo decks. Numerous Lyugg crewmembers were on gantries around the ramp, with many more on the ground, standing at temporary control panels set up on the apron, chatting in groups, guiding crates from transporter to crane or from the top of the ramp into the freighter itself.

Cascari braked hard, the car's rear wheels locked and it skidded to a halt. Ash and Delgado looked at each other as the gull-wing doors hissed open. Several of the Lyugg freighter's crewmembers were staring at them.

'Cascari,' said Delgado, 'you come with me. Ash, you stay here. Get in the driver's seat. If there's any trouble we'll need to get out of here fast.'

'Sure, Delgado,' she said. 'Whatever happens, I'll be glad to take over the driving for a while, believe me.'

'Yeah, I know what you mean. Keep the doors closed, the engine running and your eyes open. OK?'

'Whatever you say, Delgado, whatever you say.'

Delgado touched her arm and looked at her seriously. 'I mean it.'

Ashala looked at him for a moment. 'Yeah,' she said more quietly. 'I know.'

Delgado got out of the car, and the doors closed as he and Cascari walked away. Delgado glanced briefly towards the Lyugg freighter. The ship's crew were obviously suspicious of the two men, and many had stopped work to watch them. Light reflected off the elaborate, garish jewellery most of them wore, which on Lyugg, reflected social status or aspiration. Despite their appearance to the contrary, with their jewellery, fondness for soft fabrics – particularly white silk – and somewhat portly physique, both males and females were known to be ferocious fighters.

'Look ahead,' said Delgado. 'We'll walk casually towards the forward landing skid as if we're heading towards the *Maquiladora*. Once we're out of sight they might assume we've gone.'

They walked into the shadow cast by the bulbous nose of the rotund Lyugg vessel, where the air was noticeably cooler. The underside of the craft was around fifty metres above them, its bloated shape darkening the ground for five hundred metres or so ahead. The front landing skid was a thick metal plate around ten metres wide by thirty metres long, beneath a rugged carriage mechanism. Two gigantic metal springs, smothered in old, black grease, angled away from a vertical hydraulic rod at forty-five degrees, disappearing at either end into huge pivot housings. Delgado looked up as they walked beneath the landing-skid bay. The space above the two thick open doors was illuminated by small, bright lights.

Delgado and Cascari leaned against the landing skid's raised leading edge and studied the *Maquiladora*. Delgado glanced at the Lyugg crew. Most were simply watching them, but a couple were walking purposefully towards them and another appeared to be talking on a communications device of some kind.

'No sign of life,' Cascari observed of Michael's ship. 'No lights, no movement, nothing.'

'We'd only be able to see that if they were on the flight deck, which they won't be by now. They'll be in the back of the ship, preparing to leave. Assuming that Ash was right and they haven't already left.'

'True. Maybe we should go take a closer look.' Cascari turned and looked over his shoulder. 'Our Lyugg friends aren't too happy about our presence.'

Delgado turned to look and saw more of the Lyugg crew heading towards them. Of greater concern was the fact that four more were striding towards the car. 'You can hardly blame them for being irked,' said Delgado absently. 'Serves them right for not having better security.'

'They don't seemed to be armed. Although they could be calling for back up.'

'Yeah. Let's just walk towards the *Maquiladora*. If we're challenged we'll just say we made a mistake and are leaving. You think they'll buy that?'

Cascari looked at him.

'No, me neither. Come on, anyway.'

They had walked only a few steps when they heard the shrill, high-pitched cry of one of the Lyugg males. Delgado calmly turned so that he was walking backwards, drew his right hand from his pocket, waved briefly, then turned again and continued to walk across the apron towards the *Maquiladora*. There was another shout, a different voice this time.

Cascari turned his head briefly so that he could just see the podgy figures of the Lyugg in his peripheral vision. 'They don't like us one bit,' he said.

'Hardly surprising. They probably think we're rival traders. They following us?'

Cascari looked. 'Only slowly. More are approaching the car, though. A few others are walking down the ramp. I think they have guns.'

'Shit. We're sitting ducks in the open if they decide to start taking pot-shots.' Although they did not run, the two men began to walk more quickly. Suddenly Delgado pointed. 'Looks like we've got company.' In the distance a plume of dust, rose high into the air behind a small speeding vehicle and spread across the apron on the breeze. When Delgado and Cascari were still around half a kilometre from the *Maquiladora*, the car changed direction towards the vessel. The vehicle was partially obscured from view by the *Maquiladora*'s forward landing assembly, but they saw a figure – a *vilume*, it appeared to be – get out and approach the ship, from which a ramp could be seen descending slowly on the far side.

Delgado and Cascari immediately drew their weapons and began running.

They were still a long way from the ship when they saw two figures walking down the ramp towards the *vilume*. Delgado kept running but Cascari stopped and dropped to one knee. He raised his gun, arms outstretched, but was too far away to get a clear shot. Cascari cursed as Michael and Osephius ducked under the car's door, which closed behind them. The *Maquiladora*'s ramp retracted automatically as the vehicle accelerated away.

Delgado had also stopped running by now, and turned and began walking back towards Cascari. He was quite breathless; both of them were sweating. The bitterness and frustration in Cascari's expression heightened the Seriatt in his appearance.

'Too late,' said Delgado. 'We could've had him there.'

'Not much of a welcoming committee considering who he is,' observed Cascari. 'They must be keeping this well under wraps.'

'Yeah. They'll be keeping the Andamour Council happy, but won't do any more than they have to.'

The fading roar of Michael's car was replaced by the sound of distant shouts. They saw that their own car was now surrounded by a mob of apparently angry Lyugg, who were shouting and hammering on its roof and windows with clenched fists. They could hear the car's engine being revved.

'At least we know she's still alive in there,' said Cascari.

'Yeah, but for how long? Come on.'

They began to run back towards the car and Ashala. They had gone only a short distance when they saw the group of Lyugg in front of the vehicle separate as the car surged forward a little then stopped. There were more shouts. Then the vehicle forced its way through the crowd once more, only this time one of the Lyugg crewmembers slipped and fell in front of the vehicle. They saw the car rise briefly as it passed over the Lyugg crewman's waist. There was an audible, high-pitched scream. As the Lyugg crew's attention was drawn towards their fallen colleague, Ash saw her opportunity and broke free; the car accelerated quickly. A mob of angry, shouting Lyugg began to run after her.

Ash careered across the dusty apron and came to a skidding stop just a few metres in front of Delgado and Cascari.

The door clicked and then wheezed as it began to rise. Ash was sitting in the driver's seat, looking back at them wearing an unnerving smile. 'You better get a move on,' she said. She looked over her right shoulder towards the Lyugg. 'They're getting pretty close now.'

'Thanks, Ash,' said Delgado. 'You're as timely as ever.' He and Cascari threw themselves into the car and on to the rear bench seat. The car's doors closed. There was a thump at the rear of the car as the first angry Lyugg reached it, followed by an irregular rhythm of thuds and bangs as the rest of the mob began pounding on the vehicle. The sound of the large rings worn by the crew impacting the car's bodywork added a brittle, staccato clatter.

'OK. Let's get out of here,' said Delgado calmly. 'There are a lot of them now. They seem rather angry.'

'You'd be angry if some human had just run over one of your colleagues,' observed Cascari.

'True, very true.'

'Well, he was blocking my way,' said Ash. 'What was I supposed to do? Ask him if he would excuse me please?' She revved the car angrily. 'I suppose if it had been one of you, you'd expect a medal or something. Jesus.' She floored the accelerator and the car sped away. Although they seemed less keen to stand in front of the vehicle to block its path than they had before, one or two Lyugg were still knocked aside in the process.

'So where are we going now, Delgado?' Ash yelled back at them.

'Get after Michael's car. It's at the head of that plume of dust over there.' As he pointed to the left. Ash yanked hard on the steering wheel, sending both Delgado and Cascari sliding to one side of the bench seat.

Delgado looked at Cascari as they pushed themselves up again. 'I think I preferred it when you were driving,' he said.

'I heard that, Delgado,' Ash called back to him.

Ashala drove hard, swerving around other vehicles, landing ships and buildings, and they caught the car carrying Michael and Osephius quickly. A brilliant point of light reflected off its slightly convex windows as they closed on it.

She steered the car across the path of a tug towing a train of luggage wagons. The *mourst* tug driver made a sudden, sharp turn to avoid a collision and the train gradually toppled over, carriage by carriage, small wheels racing as cases and containers spilled across the hot surface of the apron.

Ash weaved between a cluster of small buildings, brief moments of contact scarring the sides of the vehicle. The car suddenly descended into a short subway, and was briefly immersed in cool dark air before bottoming out with a crunch and rising into the heat of the sun again. The vehicle's engine began to make a particularly unhealthy rattling sound.

With the sun behind them and the ground apparently less dusty in this area of the port, the vehicle ahead was clearly defined now that they were closer to it, its form and colour perfectly balanced against the light of the Seriattic day.

They sped towards a building near the port's eastern perimeter. It looked like a garage, containing lifting gear, metal frames, vehicles on elevated platforms and fuel dispensers. Michael's car continued past this building towards another, a fantastic assemblage of dark glass and sweeping silver arcs.

It became evident, however, that Michael's car was not heading towards the terminal, but a vehicle checkpoint to its right. A high wire fence leading away from this marked the port's boundary. A short distance beyond the fence was one of the wide main canals they had seen from the air. Gentle ripples glistered as vessels cut through the water, plying thick, foaming wakes. The long, elegant fronds dangling from the branches of tall, slender trees lining the bank fluttered in the breeze.

A wide, dusty road, currently devoid of traffic, led away from the checkpoint to a bridge over the canal around one kilometre away. It consisted of two huge, metal arcs that crossed over the waterway, with what appeared to be an observation or control room suspended between them at their apex. Numerous tension wires fanned out from the highest points of the gigantic arcs to points along either side of the bridge itself. On the far side of the canal were Seriattic buildings, roads and a railway line. An airship overhead cast a large shadow over part of the scene.

As Michael's vehicle stopped at the checkpoint, a black-clad *mourst* guard stepped from the small hut. The Seriatt leaned into one of the car's windows. Then, after a few moments, he stood upright again, and appeared to insert something linked to his waist by wire into a slot just above one of the car's front wheels. The barrier rose, the *mourst* stepped back, and the car passed through. As the barrier closed again, Michael's car accelerated quickly towards the bridge.

Delgado leaned forward. 'You won't be able to crash through that barrier,' he said. 'It looks pretty solid.'

Ash was breathing hard and sweat was visible on her brow. 'Yeah,' she said, revving the engine, 'but that fence looks a bit flimsy.' She turned and grinned at him. 'You better sit down.'

Delgado smiled and sat back. 'Better tighten that lap strap of yours,' he said to Cascari.

Ash accelerated rapidly and turned the small car towards the fence. As they gained speed Delgado saw the *mourst* guard step from his hut, his arms folded across his weapon. Delgado could sense the Seriatt's puzzlement. The guard took another step forward until he was standing on the edge of the kerb. Clearly unsettled, aware that something was amiss, he unfolded his arms and gripped his gun uneasily, but did not bring the weapon to bear.

A few seconds later the vehicle reached a speed at which it would be impossible to avoid crashing into the wire fence. Apparently realising this, the guard ran back into his hut. Through the dusty windows Delgado could see him talking heatedly into something.

Delgado looked ahead again. The fence loomed.

There was a loud thud and a thin clattering sound as sheets of wire wrapped around the small vehicle like a lover's limbs.

The resistance slowed the car, which bumped and jarred over the rough ground beyond the fence. Ash struggled to maintain control of the vehicle, desperately trying to guide the shuddering, groaning car around large boulders set into the baked earth.

Abruptly the car tilted forward as it began to go down the embankment towards the canal. As Delgado looked towards the bridge, part of which was now to his right, he saw fountains of dirt and stone exploding into the air. He looked through the car's rear window and saw the *mourst* guard kneeling beside his hut, firing short bursts from his weapon. But his aim was poor and Delgado recognised inexperience in his handling of the gun. He hoped the Seriatt did not enjoy a lucky shot before the car was further down the slope and out of sight.

There was a sudden lurch, a raucous metallic din, and the car came to an abrupt stop, throwing its three occupants forward. For a moment Delgado thought the guard had been lucky after all, but when he looked ahead he saw that the vehicle had collided with a particularly large boulder, and that steam was now rising from the car's slightly crumpled bonnet.

As Ash wrestled with the gear stick, trying to engage reverse, a loud grinding sound issued from somewhere beneath the vehicle. Delgado looked towards the canal and saw the helmsman of a long barge shade his eyes and point towards their car as a colleague joined him from below deck. As the Seriatts stood together, watching intently, their vessel began to drift slowly off course towards another craft approaching from the opposite direction. Movement to Delgado's right caught his eye and when he looked towards the bridge he saw Michael's car beginning to cross it.

The car lurched and shuddered, and Ashala made enthusiastic noises as it began to move backwards away from the boulder. The car stopped again, and there was more grinding and cursing as Ash fought to engage a forward gear. The car's engine raced briefly, then the vehicle leaped forward, veered around the gigantic hunk of rock, and angled steeply towards the wide path running alongside the canal at the foot of the embankment.

Many Seriatts were walking along the path. Some of them were looking at the approaching car. Delgado saw Ash look towards the bridge. Looking in the same direction, Delgado saw a walled, zigzag path leading up to the bridge from the canal-side. He assessed the size of this path in relation to the car and knew what she was planning; but was uncertain how long they would remain dry given the car's speed, the angle of the slope and the narrowness of the path ahead of them.

Loud thuds and bangs filled the car as it careered towards the water, scraping against boulders, the rear wheels locking as Ash jabbed alternately at brake and accelerator. The vehicle seemed to be under only partial control.

Then, with an immense bang and a gut-jarring bump, the now battered car lunged on to the smooth, flat path, and slewed slightly to one side as it skidded to a halt in a cloud of dust. The car completely blocked the path, its front wheels only centimetres from the edge. The engine raced and dense plumes of steam billowed from the bonnet, obscuring their view of the canal immediately ahead. There was a distinctly unhealthy smell of hot metal.

To either side of the car, curious Seriatts attempted to peer through the tinted windows. Austere, asexual *vilume* were dressed predominantly in straight, ankle-length garments in shades of brown or green, with a few wearing maroon. While some of these garments had delicate gold braiding at the neck, down the front and at the hem, most lacked decoration of any kind. The way the garments hung indicated the quality of cut, and the weight of the cloth. Seeing a *vilume* up close, Delgado was reminded of their fragility, and demure, detached expressions. He noticed their long fingers, the uniformly black hair, which was either cropped very short or swept back across the head and cut straight at the shoulder, and their striking golden irises. Although he knew they were asexual, Delgado tended to perceive most of them as feminine.

There were a few *conosq*, too, voluptuous and imposing, wearing clothes carefully crafted to accentuate their sexuality. These creatures stirred something in Delgado, something he had learned – with difficulty – to control over the years. But, feeling queasy and light-headed, he was forced to consider that perhaps its strength was as great as ever, and that he remained at its mercy. Briefly, he was transported back to the time that had changed his life so completely – his time with Lycern. There were also some *mourst*, too – tall, muscular, athletic creatures whose appearance was more like wild animals than that of a technologically advanced race. Yet despite their clear physical strength, the *mourst* seemed dominated by the two other sexes.

Ash bullied the car into reverse gear and backed away from the water. The onlookers jumped back as she repeatedly drove backwards and forwards in an effort to turn the car on the narrow path, it's engine wailing, until eventually she was able to accelerate towards the bridge.

The path in front of the vehicle cleared quickly as strolling Seriatts were forced to leap to one side or the other to avoid being hit by the car; Delgado saw at least two of them jump into the canal.

The zigzag ramp was narrower than it had appeared from a distance, and the car acquired more new body styling as it impacted the walls of the confined space. Seriatts jumped on to walls out of the way as the car lurched up the slope, paint and brickwork generously exchanged as the vehicle bumped and banged its way around the deceptively tight corners.

When the car reached the top, Ash, who was by now becoming used to the vehicle's characteristics, skilfully turned it through use of the accelerator, then sped towards the bridge leaving a bemused group of Seriattic onlookers shrouded in brown dust.

Michael's car had by this time passed the apex of the bridge and was rapidly disappearing from view. As Ash gave chase, Delgado looked past Cascari through the window to his left. The people on the canal bank had resumed their strolls, although a small crowd had gathered around one Seriatt who was struggling to clamber from the water. On the canal itself, the long barge had collided with the larger vessel, and was now perpendicular to it. Crewmembers were running around on both craft, gesticulating frantically and wielding long poles in an attempt to separate them.

Delgado looked to his right and saw a magnificent white ship approaching the bridge, huge sails billowing from tall masts, its sharp prow cutting a clean wake. He looked at the vessel for several moments as the car continued to scream towards the bridge's apex, assessing the height of its masts and comparing this to the bridge itself: the ship's central mast was simply too high to pass underneath. On one of the higher decks towards the huge vessel's stern, sunlight reflected off a window. A figure was looking towards the bridge through binoculars. Delgado looked up at the room suspended between the bridge's metal arches, but there was no sign of activity.

He looked ahead again as the car crossed the bridge's apex and Michael's car came back into view. He noticed a narrow black line in the road ahead. It appeared to be widening. He looked from the widening black strip, to the ship, back up at the tower. He turned and looked back through the car's rear window, and saw another black band. And then it came to him: this was a swing bridge.

He unbuckled his lap strap and leaned forward to speak to Ash. 'Look at the . . .'

'I know, I know. I've seen it.'

The gap was rapidly growing wider but Ash showed no sign of slowing down. Instead, she was accelerating.

'You're not going to stop, are you?'

'You bet your sweet ass I'm not going to stop, Delgado. We've got plenty of speed and there's a ramp formed by part of the bridge's superstructure – look.' Delgado looked. There were metal triangles on either side of the bridge, rising from the road at regular intervals. The bridge had split one such triangle in two, forming a wedge shape. 'We can jump it, no problem,' Ash called back to him.

Delgado looked at the gap, which was growing still wider as the bridge continued to turn. He admired Ash's courage, but had some misgivings about her judgement of speed and distance. He opened his mouth to say something, then decided that perhaps there wasn't much point and sat back down again.

The car increased speed as it headed down the slope. Ash steered it gradually to the left until the ramp was almost directly ahead.

The bridge's suspension wires dissected the passage of time into flickering fragments. To Delgado's right, the sailing ship continued to close on the bridge. The water looked deep and cool and clear, every detail and colour perfectly enhanced by the wonderful quality of the Seriattic light.

Delgado looked ahead again. At that exact moment the car hit the ramp.

There was an agonised scraping sound as the vehicle's underside panned against the ground and was launched into the air. With the bassy thrum of the road beneath the wheels suddenly lost, the unhealthy screaming of the engine was highlighted.

The bridge continued to open, the shaded water beneath it visibly lapping against the dark metal and concrete supports as the gap increased. The car began to yaw, one battered corner dipping slightly as it flew. Delgado looked at the hard edge of the static section of the bridge ahead. He wasn't sure the car would reach the other side. It would either make it or strike the edge with force.

The engine wailed, the angle of yaw increased, the ground ahead rushed up.

The car hit the other side of the bridge with a violent impact, the right front wing crunching against the ground. Tyres screeched as they fought to gain purchase on the dusty road and the side of the vehicle slapped hard against the bridge wall immediately to the left. One side of the car scraped along the metal structure, and then the vehicle slewed towards the centre of the road, fish-tailing wildly. When Delgado turned and looked through the car's rear window he saw the top of the ship's masts and sails passing smoothly through the fully open bridge like a mirage above the road.

Ash regained control of the car and accelerated rapidly down the hill, quickly gaining on Michael's car, which had stopped at railway crossing barriers; a long train, with large, silver, double-deck passenger cars at the front and windowless freight carriages at the rear was passing through. When the train had passed, the barriers rose again and Michael's car crossed the tracks, then turned out of sight on to another road running perpendicular to the one they were on.

Ash demonstrated no sign of slowing as the car rumbled across the tracks, forcing the unwilling machine to turn sharply on to the same road at high speed.

And suddenly they were in the heart of the Seriattic city.

They were on a busy highway several lanes wide, surrounded by large passenger cars, buses, taxis and trucks. Brightly coloured, lozenge-shaped trams with shining chrome railings and varnished wooden seats clattered across points, sparks flashing from overhead wires. All the vehicles Delgado could see appeared to be either new, or very well cared for. They also possessed what Delgado had come to perceive as a distinctly Seriattic style: clean, elegant lines, a certain delicate and stylish design. The architecture possessed an Art Deco feel. The buildings were geometric, predominantly cream-coloured, with flat roofs and tall, multi-paned windows, taller than the residential areas on the other side of the port.

On the wide sidewalks to either side of the road were a broad mix of *mourst*, *conosq* and *vilume*. The flagstones were grey in colour, with partial shade afforded by voluminous bushes set in large planters and tall, palm-like trees. The shiny, heart-shaped leaves of the latter were the colour of rust, and a stark contrast to the bright green fruit they bore. Fat and juicy-looking, the size of small apples, the fruit hung in bunches of five or six that weighed heavily on the slender branches.

At its new low speed the taxi sounded even less healthy than it had before, and, judging from the sound emanating from somewhere towards the rear of the vehicle, it was now also trailing part of its bodywork along the road. With the rest of the traffic in immaculate condition without exception, they were beginning to attract attention.

Ash craned her neck in an effort to see Michael's car, but it was lost among the traffic. Suddenly a gap appeared between the vehicles as a passenger car turned off the main road, and she jabbed at the accelerator and steered the car into the space. Other vehicles sounded horns and flashed lights of warning and anger. Delgado looked up as he heard a loud thudding sound, and against the dark clouds forming overhead caught a glimpse of two bulbous copters heading in the direction of the port. Perhaps the alarm had been raised.

In front of him, Ash swore, and thumped the steering wheel.

'Looks like we've lost him,' said Cascari. 'Nice one. Well done.'

'Screw you,' Ash retorted.

'No thanks, you're not my type.'

'Come on, now,' said Delgado. 'This isn't going to get us anywhere.'

'Not in this traffic,' Ash observed.

Delgado looked ahead, peering between vehicles, but he could not see Michael's car. The air was growing darker and noticeably cooler. He pressed his face against the window next to him and looked up again; dark storm clouds were gathering rapidly, sucking in the light.

Suddenly the car accelerated and Ash steered it into another gap, to the irritation of more Seriattic drivers. 'There he is,' she cried. 'I've got him. Just over there.' Delgado and Cascari looked in the direction she indicated, but neither of them could distinguish the other vehicle.

'Are you sure?' Delgado asked, frowning.

'Of course I'm sure.' She frantically tried to force the car through almost non-existent gaps and across lanes of traffic, intent on keeping track of a vehicle neither Cascari nor Delgado could see. The first drops of rain began to fall and within a few moments they were in the middle of a rainstorm, the sky as dark as slate, the rain falling in thick, cascading sheets that smudged away detail. A large blade automatically began to sweep across the car's windshield, pushing off sheets of water. All around, lights on vehicles, in buildings and set into the sidewalks became illuminated as Seriatts scurried into buildings and under awnings in search of cover.

By the time Ash had manoeuvred their car into the next lane, raindrops were bouncing knee-high off the road's dark surface. Lightning momentarily bleached the sky, followed by thunder like distant drums. A sudden wind flung fallen palm leaves in tight whorls.

It was like a portent. Delgado felt increasingly uncomfortable with the situation.

'Can you still see him?' Cascari asked.

'Yeah, I think so.'

'What do you mean, you think so? Can you or can't you?'

She leaned to one side, peering ahead. 'I can,' she said. 'I think. Hang on, they're turning.'

Cursing with frustration at the speed of the traffic, Ash turned their own car left, on to the same road as that taken by Michael and Osephius. It was much narrower, only one lane in either direction, leading away from the city. The road and sidewalks were less crowded and the buildings became less densely packed until, just a few kilometres away, they could see that the city gave way to a barren scrubland. More of the mountain range was visible, with roads snaking up through the foothills and into valleys between the peaks. They could all see the car carrying Michael and Osephius now, around half a kilometre ahead, with only a few other vehicles between the two cars.

'They're going to the other side of the mountains,' said Delgado.

'What makes you so sure?' Cascari asked.

'Two things: first, there aren't many places *to* go out here by the looks of it, secondly, we saw the race taking place with mountains in the background. We also passed over the coast on our way into the port. They're heading to the race. All we have to do is follow them.'

Cascari nodded slowly and looked at the mountain range ahead. 'Oh, is that all?' he said grimly. 'That's all right then. And there was me thinking we had a difficult job on our hands.'

Delgado looked through the window to his right, and said nothing.

Five

agamemnon's legion

The Koss-Miet racing facility, Astragarda, Seriatt

Delgado woke with a dry mouth and a craving for chocolate. He had slept with his cheek pressed against the cold window next to him, his head lolling back, and now his cheek felt numb and his neck stiff. Immediately outside the window to his right was a sheer wall of rock, the narrow road having been hewn into the mountainside. In front of him, Cascari was driving, having swapped with Ashala when she became tired. She now slept next to Delgado on the bench seat, arms folded across her chest, legs drawn up against her body, knees tucked under her chin. She wore a stern frown. Her eyelids moved rapidly beneath their lids as she dreamed.

He looked past her and out of the window on the opposite side of the vehicle and saw Michael's car some way ahead on the same road, which doubled back on itself as it snaked down the mountainside. It was the only other vehicle in sight, but other similar roads leading from distant valleys were packed with cars heading towards the coast. In the sky, numerous copters and airships moved like giant, ungainly insects. When he looked down again Michael's car had disappeared around an outcrop of rock.

Cascari glanced over one shoulder. 'Sleep well?' he asked.

Delgado yawned and shrugged, which gave him a twinge in

his neck. 'Well enough. I guess we passed through a tunnel, right?'

'Right. Some way back. A long one, too. You'll be able to see the racing facilities when we get around that corner. I don't think we have too much further to go now, but progress might get slower. These roads are tight.' He steered the car left as the road turned back on itself, angling downwards. A few minutes later, as the road curved sharply to the right, Delgado sat more upright as the scene was revealed to him.

The road snaked down to a plain, which was covered in small fields separated by hedges or dry-stone walls. There were numerous shacks with thatched roofs, a variety of grazing animals, the occasional copse of tall, slender trees. Delgado saw in one field a *mourst* guiding a plough through the ground as it was pulled by a dark and hefty beast of burden. A bland grey sheet of slightly luminescent cloud hung above the land.

Beyond the fields the sea was a grey-green texture almost as sombre and lifeless as the sky. Pale seabirds wheeled above it like feeding fleas, while others bobbed gently on the crests of waves. The coastline itself formed a large crescent, the horns of which were several kilometres to either side of the bay. Along the bay's inner edge ran a narrow strip of golden sand.

Around a kilometre out to sea a dozen towers rose from the waves, the purpose of which Delgado was unable to ascertain. A multitude of landing platforms sprouted from angular accommodation blocks, and from the top of these structures antennae reached for the sky like fleshless fingers.

A cable car joined buildings on one side of the mountain to others on the plain. As two large gondolas moved in opposite directions, passing a metal gantry, the thick wires from which the cars were suspended seemed to vibrate like the strings of an over-sized bass instrument.

There was an aerodrome near the coast. By Delgado's

estimation it was capable of handling most normal aircraft, perhaps even a few space-going vessels if they had vertical landing capabilities.

A small delta-winged aircraft crossed the coast. It looked like an expensive private machine, probably seating no more than a dozen people. It turned sharply, and approached one of the aerodrome's short runways. As the landing gear extended beneath it, an apparent off-shore breeze caused the aircraft's tail to drift, and a deft rudder correction was required prior to landing. The machine straightened, kissed the ground, and a parachute immediately deployed from beneath its tail. It slowed abruptly, then turned on to one of the narrower taxiways trailing the now limp parachute as if disembowelled. Small clots of creamy light over the sea indicated more aircraft approaching.

As Cascari drove the car around another long bend on the mountainside, the launch tubes came into view.

The newscast they had seen aboard *The Lost Cause* had failed to convey the true magnitude of these incredible structures. They were architectural wonders, seemingly requiring no external support despite their huge size and curving shape. They seemed to defy the laws of physics, arcing upwards from the ground.

'Wow,' said Cascari. 'They're pretty impressive.'

'Yeah,' said Delgado, leaning forward. 'You reckon they've been built or grown?'

'It's hard to tell what they're made of. They look pretty solid.'

Ash stirred next to Delgado. She yawned and stretched, then sat up a little and rubbed her eyes with her knuckles.

'You OK?' asked Delgado.

She pulled a face. 'My arm's stiff.' She rubbed it where the faerie had hit her. 'Got a headache, too,' she said, frowning. 'Bad dream.' She pushed herself up a little and looked out of the window. 'Wow. I take it those are the launch tubes we saw?'

'Yeah. Impressive, aren't they? What was it about?'

'What?'

'Your dream.'

'Oh. I'm not sure exactly.' She shook her head as she dredged her mind for the already fading memory. 'I was being smothered by something. It was warm, but hard, like glass or stone, which didn't seem right somehow. I couldn't pull it off because I couldn't move. I don't know why. That was it, really. How long till we get there?'

'A couple of hours, I reckon,' Cascari called from the front. 'The road should straighten out as we get lower down, then we'll be able to speed up a bit.'

They heard a faint pop and looked to their left. One of the small aircraft had emerged from each of the launch tubes. From the end of each tube hung a long cone of wet tissue like a prolapse, trailing viscous slime. The lengths of skin hung outside the tubes for a few moments, then withdrew smoothly inside again.

The aircraft that had launched from the tubes approached the cloud base at an extremely steep angle and high speed, powered by smooth plumes of blue flame. They rolled and pitched as they climbed, their raw power apparently difficult to control. A few seconds after they had first been launched the machines penetrated the cloud and were lost from sight, the thin vapour trails they had produced dissipating rapidly.

'Some ride,' said Cascari. 'How far underground do you reckon those tubes go?'

Delgado shook his head. 'It's hard to say. But you saw the speed of those aircraft. They were already going quickly when they left the tubes. They must go pretty deep to achieve that kind of velocity. The newscast said something about those machines utilising basic technology, though, right? Well, if the technology's that basic those things won't be fitted with any kind of G-suppression, so the acceleration can't be so high the pilots lose consciousness.'

'Are you sure you're fit enough for that kind of stress?' Cascari asked.

'Don't you worry about me. Your old dad can look after himself despite being an old-timer.'

'You really think you can fly one of those things, Delgado?' asked Ash. 'I mean, I know you're used to flying very basic aircraft, but at least you usually have plenty of fuel.'

'We'll be fine. In an aircraft like that, which is basically a projectile, you just need to maximise lift. Because the pilots have to use as little fuel as possible it's more of a glider when racing. You need to make use of warm air pockets to maintain speed, as warm air is less dense than cold. If it was a ramjet, say, then the opposite would be true because colder air would enable the engines to function more effectively. The other thing to watch out for would be turbulent air flowing off other aircraft, as that'll unsettle your own machine.'

Ash looked concerned. 'Sure, you know the principles, Delgado, but you can't just expect to go up there and do much more than maintain control of the thing. And even if you can do that you still have to get through the buoy before most of the others or you're dead meat. What if Michael's first through and you're last? What if you don't get through at all? Your slingshot might be weaker than his, or non-existent. Or you could find yourself in a different piece of sky altogether.'

'Or exactly the same piece of sky,' suggested Cascari.

'Precisely.'

Delgado looked at Ash for a moment, then past her through the window towards the launch tubes. In the distance, above the torrid sea, a dozen rays of sunshine burst through broken cloud, serene and vibrant shafts linking turbulent elements.

'I understand your concerns, Ash,' he said. 'But I really don't see that we have a choice. If the Seriatts are going to demand such a display of bravery or skill or whatever other motivation is behind this race, then that's what we're going to have to give them. If we can kill Michael in the process, all the better. We don't have much to bargain with, let's face it. We need some validation, something to strengthen our position, especially if Michael stays in the frame. I think this might just be the answer.'

They followed the vehicle in which Michael and Osephius were travelling on to a narrow lane with hedges and fields on either side and dirt tracks worn in the grass by the passage of vehicles. There was a lot of traffic, with most of the other main roads to the coast apparently converging on to a few such lanes.

The sea was to their right, with what appeared to be grandstands to their left. There were three, possibly four of these, but only the grey back of the one closest to them could be seen, with lines of spectators visible climbing metal stairs towards the stands on the other side, to face the launch tubes. The size of the tubes meant they were truly intimidating at such close range. They looked like vast, solidified arteries entwined with many smaller veins and muscle-like fibres, with sinews of ligament spiralling around the outside.

It was difficult for Cascari to keep track of Michael's car in the traffic, but gradually the number of other vehicles on the road decreased as they turned off to park in fields and eventually there were no other vehicles between the two cars.

Michael's car pulled up at a checkpoint at gates set into a very high wire fence. On the other side of the fence row upon row of large vehicles were parked. White or silver or black, they were large corporate vehicles, expensive and luxurious. On top of many were compact relay dishes and ultrabeam compressors, with masses of thick cabling snaking through the grass in heavy clusters.

'That'll be the paddock area,' said Delgado, leaning forward on the seat. He peered through the windshield, trying to see beyond the fence, but the vehicles on the other side were parked too closely for much to be visible between them. Only the dirt track beyond the gate could be seen clearly. 'We'll need to get in there to gain access to the launch tubes,' he said.

They watched as the *mourst* guards at the checkpoint approached Michael's car. One of the vehicle's doors rose slowly and the *vilume* stepped out. Although some distance away, there was something in the way the Seriatt stood and walked that caused Delgado to perceive the *vilume* as female. The dark braiding of the long fawn-coloured gown she wore dragged in the dust. She spoke to the *mourst* guards for a few moments and handed something to one of them. The other guard stepped towards the car and stooped to look beneath the open door. Apparently satisfied, he stepped back to his colleague. After speaking to the *mourst* for a few moments longer, the *vilume* returned to the vehicle, the car's door closed, and the gates were opened.

As the car passed through the gate one of the *mourst* looked directly towards their own car, shielding his dark eyes from the sun.

Delgado reached through the partition and tapped Cascari on the shoulder. 'Come on,' he said. 'Let's turn this thing around before they come asking questions.'

Cascari parked in one of the fields along with the other spectators. The few Seriatts that were in the field were some distance away, up a slight incline, walking through an archway on to a wide path of earth baked hard by the sun; the path was separated from the field by a low wire fence. *Vilume* in uniforms of grey and maroon were checking tickets as the Seriatts filed slowly and calmly through the archway, watched over by bulky *mourst* enforcers.

Delgado, Cascari and Ash got out of the car and convened in front of its battered hood.

'So, what's your plan now, Delgado?' Ash asked.

Delgado folded his arms and leaned against the car. 'Well, we need to get into a position where we have access to those aircraft.' He looked up at the launch tubes, back over his shoulder at an aircraft making its final approach to the airport, then towards the mountains, and up at the airships and copters in the sky. Then he looked at the ground, staring for several moments as if trying to see through the earth to whatever might lie beneath it. 'Somehow, we're going to have to get underground.'

'I know,' said Ash. 'Why don't I go in first and secure the area? Then you two can waltz in as you please. That seems to be the way things usually work out.'

Delgado looked at her and pulled a face. 'Don't put ideas into my head,' he said. He looked around again. 'Something tells me there might be gaps in security we can take advantage of here, though.'

'Like what?' asked Cascari.

'Like the fact that this is obviously some kind of temporary setup. The land in the immediate vicinity is distinctly agricultural, the infrastructure is inadequate.' He looked at the grass around them. 'And judging by the short grass and the amount of dried shit around here this place is usually used for grazing animals. No. This race occurs infrequently, or perhaps only at certain times of the year, meaning that any security measures have to be set up and dismantled each time. Staff probably change, too, so they're never completely on top of who's who and what's going on.'

'Yeah. It might also mean that they're *extra* vigilant because of those same factors,' Ash pointed out. 'If this was an ongoing thing then the staff might become complacent due to routine. It happens all the time in Structure, right?'

Delgado nodded and shrugged slightly. 'Yeah. It could

mean that as well,' he conceded. 'But that doesn't make me feel so good.'

'So, what are we going to do?' asked Cascari. 'Despite what you say, from what we've seen so far security seems pretty tight.'

'Right,' Delgado admitted. He looked towards the Seriatts. They were talking and laughing as they made their way towards the grandstands. He noticed that the crowd consisted almost entirely of *conosq* and *vilume*. Other than the security staff there were only one or two *mourst* that he could see. Perhaps this race was more important than just some kind of *mourst* rite of passage; perhaps it was something that touched the core of Seriattic society.

Although he knew their power was fading and that the perceptions they gave him were increasingly inaccurate, Delgado opened a batch of cognition nobics. There were huge gaps in the information they fed to him, but a sea of emotional tension surged. There were traces of what would in human terms be considered greed, envy and lust. Although these were extremely pure, he sensed no direct threat.

To the left, more Seriatts were approaching from other fields, but the path was less crowded, and beyond the fence on the other side of the path, there were more vehicles like those they had seen earlier. Beyond them, rising above the vehicles around a kilometre away was a large silver arch.

He squinted. 'What's that?' The others turned to see what he was looking at.

'Can't tell,' said Ash. 'Looks like some kind of gateway.'

'Whatever it is it looks important. Come on, this way,' said Delgado, walking away from the car. 'I think this is where the answer lies.'

They walked between the cars and up the slope to the low wire fence. Delgado and Cascari managed to clamber over it, but although nothing was said Ash was clearly pissed that she couldn't get over without Delgado holding the wire down for her. A few passing Seriatts looked at them with expressions Delgado took to be incredulity, although he could not be certain that was what they truly represented – in human terms they were more like dismay or wonderment. Whether this was because he and Ashala were human and they saw the human blood in Cascari despite his distinctly Seriattic features, or simply because they had stepped over the fence, which stood out as a rebellious act in a society that seemed particularly compliant, he did not know. What he did know was that they didn't particularly want to draw attention to themselves.

Delgado looked down and spoke in hushed tones. 'Walk quickly and confidently, but don't rush. Avoid making eye contact. We'll stop by that white trailer up ahead and see if we can get through the fence.'

Two tall *mourst* suddenly loomed in front of Delgado; one placed his large, dark hand against Delgado's chest and stopped him dead in his tracks. Ash and Cascari also stopped walking. Although one looked slightly older than the other, the *mourst* were younger than Cascari. They were also taller and leaner, and recognised their own physical superiority. They did not appear to be officials of any kind – they were not wearing uniforms and did not possess a particularly high level of confidence or exude discipline.

They looked from Delgado to Cascari and Ash in turn. White secondary eyelids flashed across their eyes. Delgado could smell the fetid breath of the one standing directly in front of him. He was also aware that other Seriatts, while continuing to walk by, were staring.

'*Degasso mediag nour fa*,' barked the taller of the two gruffly. The language appeared to be pure Seriatt. Perhaps they were political extremists of some kind. When Delgado gave no answer the *mourst* repeated his apparent question, this time addressing Cascari.

'*Conosog tretios mg do*,' said the younger *mourst*. He seemed to be speaking to his companion.

Delgado smiled briefly – an odd reflex action the Seriatts probably wouldn't appreciate – and tried to simply step past the two *mourst*, but the older one grasped the front of Delgado's tunic with his long, gnarled fingers and stopped him from passing. The *mourst* leaned close to Delgado's face and uttered a quick string of Seriattic words Delgado did not understand. He glanced to one side and saw that the laughter and chatter among the nearby Seriatts had stopped as they watched the sudden altercation. Delgado sensed a combination of concern and abject distaste among them. He also noticed that while *vilume* shielded young eyes or turned heads away, they themselves continued to watch.

Cascari said something, reached out and gripped the *mourst*'s sleeve, but the younger *mourst* hit him across the side of the face with the back of his hand, the impact so hard that Cascari staggered backwards then stumbled to the floor. Ash protested and stepped forward, but the older *mourst* grabbed her with his free hand and threw her to the ground. Several *vilume* and *conosq* gasped, but whether this was because of the violence perpetrated against Ash in particular, or all three of them, Delgado did not know.

He looked down at Cascari who had a slight cut to his lower lip and watering eyes. 'Stay calm,' Delgado said firmly. 'We can't afford for this to turn into anything.' The *mourst* in front of him exclaimed angrily and shook Delgado. Thick, yellowish drool trailed from the Seriatt's mouth. When Delgado looked down at Cascari again he caught sudden movement in his peripheral vision and glanced over his right shoulder. He saw a *mourst* enforcer some distance along the path, heading towards the disturbance at a pace.

The young Seriatt stepped forward and punched Delgado across the side of the face. The impact was strong and Delgado's head spun; images jarred; there was a distinct ringing in his ears. *We're in too deep. We need to start looking for a way out or we're not going to get out. I can't let you go through with this you can't stop me I won't give up.* He wasn't sure whether he'd said, heard or imagined the words. He blinked and shook his head, trying to clear the sudden fug. Maybe somebody else had said it for him. Perhaps his errant nobics had developed some kind of autonomy. He didn't know. It didn't matter.

He was aware that Cascari had stood, drawn his gun and placed it against the younger *mourst*'s throat. There was excited chatter among the Seriatts.

Cascari was saying something, speaking Seriattic words Delgado could not understand, but the gravity of which was clear in his tone. The older *mourst* looked at him with a bizarre expression, and let go of Delgado's tunic.

Abruptly he heard a loud pop and the full volume of excitement around him became evident, the sound bursting on to him. He felt Cascari's hand grip the back of his tunic and push him towards the high wire fence. The watching Seriatts parted without resistance. They seemed placid creatures, like a herd of docile animals.

Delgado, his head still spinning, walked a few steps then stumbled. There were exclamations from *conosq* – strange, high-pitched, throaty ululations. He could hear the voices of the two *mourst* behind him and heard what he took to be the *mourst* enforcer. He looked to his right and saw that the Seriatt was now nearby, and was being followed by two others further along the track.

Delgado saw Ash look at him. She was saying something he didn't understand. *We have no time, there is no point. You shouldn't have come here.*

They reached the fence. Cascari stooped, gripped the wire at the bottom and heaved at it. The fencing was stretched taut and the thin wire cut into his hands, but he managed to pull it from the metal posts and out of the dry soil. Most of the Seriatts were paying more attention to the enforcer's argument with the two other *mourst* than to Delgado, Cascari and Ashala. There were raised voices, protestations and accusations.

Cascari pulled hard at the wire until their was sufficient room for them to get beneath it, and bundled Delgado down on all fours, pushing him through to the other side, where the long grass was cool and trapped moisture. He then followed Ash underneath the fence.

As they ran between the parked vehicles, the sound of their own breath and soft footfalls audible against the sides of the nearby trailers, Delgado's sense of reality began to return to him. He was aware that the *mourst*'s blow had stunned him slightly, but there seemed to be more to the confusion he had felt. He could not rationalise why this was.

He glanced over his shoulder, looking back through the fence. Many more Seriatts were now watching them. The three *mourst* were pushing their way to the front of the crowd as if the enforcer had finally been convinced of something.

There was a shout, a hoarse, *mourst* cry, followed by the discordant wail of a weapon firing. Part of a nearby trailer exploded, showering them with fragments. Plastic material melted in the heat and dripped on to partially grass-covered cables in globs. The cables began to burn slowly, releasing thin, dark smoke. As fire began to take hold on the trailer, shouts and an alarm could be heard within it.

The three of them turned down a narrower trail between the backs of trailers; the grass was longer and greener due to the shade afforded by the vehicles on either side and the fact that this route was obviously less used. Occasionally they had to jump over mounds of thick cabling.

They paused at an intersection. 'Which way now?' asked Cascari.

Delgado glanced around. There were far more trailers than he had thought. It was a maze in which they could be confronted at any corner. Although this made it more difficult for the Seriatts to follow them, it was also difficult to keep track of their own position. Delgado looked up at the arch they had seen, the top of which was just visible above the vehicles in front of them. The launch tubes were some distance to their right. Within the trailer they were standing next to they could hear *mourst* and *vilume* voices.

Delgado turned. 'Listen,' he said. He looked towards the sky, his head cocked slightly. A dissonant drone could be heard, faint but growing louder. 'It's an aircraft of some kind,' he said. 'Moving slowly. They're looking for us.' He walked a few steps, looked around and down at the sides of the trailers. Around the base of each was a wooden lattice skirt. He crouched and kicked a sizeable hole in the one nearest to him. 'Quick.' He motioned to the other two. 'Get under here out of sight.'

'You don't think they'll have sensors on board that'll pick us up?' Ash asked as Cascari clambered through the ragged hole Delgado had made in the trailer's skirt.

'I don't know,' said Delgado. 'I'm banking on there being enough bodies and equipment in the trailer that they won't be able to distinguish us from the white noise.'

'But what if they pick us up because we're not Seriatt?'

'I don't know! We really don't have time to stand around arguing about this, Ash. Get underneath this goddamn trailer before we get our asses singed, will you?'

Ashala shrugged, crouched and followed Cascari into the darkness. Just as Delgado followed them, the shadows cast by the copter's fat blades flickered on the ground.

The three of them lay face down on the cold, damp floor. There was little room beneath the trailer, only around sixty centimetres between the ground and the trailer's dark underside. The thick musty smell reminded Delgado of something, but he couldn't pinpoint what. They could hear footsteps on the trailer floor above them, muffled voices in conversation. There were several shallow puddles, grit, droppings left by small creatures and a hundred different types of bug. Cascari squirmed and shuffled backwards as a large, spider-like creature scurried across the floor in front of his face, long antennae waving, hairy back a-bristle.

'Say, Delgado,' said Ash. 'You sure know how to show a girl a good time, you know that?'

'Well it's either this or be fried. Take it or leave it.'

'And you have a way with words, too.'

Delgado was right next to the hole in the wooden skirt. He moved his head slightly and caught a glimpse of the bulbous shape of the copter silhouetted against the brightness of the sky. It seemed to be moving away, but it was still too soon for them to move. He noticed a few Seriattic coins lying in a nearby tuft of grass. He reached out, grabbed them and put them in one of his pockets.

Delgado looked towards Cascari and frowned. The young man had pulled away part of the skirt on the opposite side of the trailer and was sliding through the gap. 'What the hell are you doing?' Delgado hissed.

Cascari wore an odd expression a combination of fear and sadness. He looked out from underneath the trailer, then back at Delgado. 'It's time I made my own way,' he said. 'I need to do this myself. I can't let you be involved.'

'What? Don't be . . .'

'Sorry. I just think this is something I have to do on my own. It's too risky. I should have done something about it sooner. I'm sorry.'

Delgado began to protest further, but another flier appeared overhead. It was a different kind of machine to the previous aircraft, and the deafening noise of its engines drowned out his words. There was an aroma like singed wood and a fierce, hot wind that tore around them, flattening the grass at the sides of the trailer. Delgado pressed his cheek against the ground and looked up. He could see part of the aircraft's smooth, silvery rear end. It appeared to be a modern VTOL craft rather than one of the copters, driven by the Seriattic equivalent of K-fans judging from their sound.

Delgado looked back towards his son; instead of waiting for the flier to move away Cascari's continued to edge back on his belly, moving from beneath the trailer into the sunlight. Delgado called out to him in desperation, but could not even hear his own voice due to the sound of the arcraft's engines. Ash reached out to Cascari and managed to grab his sleeve, but he yanked it away, smiled thinly at her and shook his head. As he edged from beneath the trailer he looked up at the sky, then glanced at Delgado and Ash one final time. Delgado called to him again, begging him to stay. But his son just stood upright and ran.

When the flier had gone, Delgado and Ash edged out from beneath the trailer themselves. The sky was now cloudless, the sun high and the temperature rising rapidly.

Delgado looked in both directions along the deserted, narrow lane. 'What the *hell* is he thinking?' he said bitterly. 'What does he think he's going to do?'

'Maybe he's done us a favour. Maybe he thinks he's better off without us. Maybe he's just plain greedy. What do you want to do?'

Delgado was pacing back and forth and didn't seem to have heard Ashala's words. 'What's he planning? Where's he gone? We have to find him.' He shook his head.

'Look, Delgado, he's been talking like this for a while. Maybe it's for the best, you know? Perhaps he doesn't want to let you down, or doesn't want to put you in danger. Maybe this is the time you just have to let your son go.'

He wasn't listening. 'They must have a good idea where we are. Our only chance is if the Seriattic authorities are as secretive and proud as we've always believed, then they won't broadcast the fact that they're looking for us. Come on. We'll try to get to the paddock. Whatever he's thinking, he's going to try and get into that race because it's the *mourst* thing to do and I think he needs to validate that part of himself now more than ever.' He strode along the track in the direction of the silver arch.

'Delgado,' Ash called as she began to follow him. 'Delgado. I'm not sure this is such a good idea.'

Delgado ignored her, and kept on walking.

Delgado and Ashala stood in the shadows at the edge of a wide, low arch that separated the trailers behind them from the more open space of the paddock area. Directly in front of them was a wide thoroughfare of dry, hard earth, riddled with cracks. The grass had been worn away by the volume of people and automatics moving in both directions along it, and only the hardiest of bleached grass blades protruded from the soil.

'This seems to be where the action is,' Ash stated. 'What do you make of that thing?' Slightly to their left, on the opposite side of the thoroughfare, they could see the huge arch in its entirety. The arch itself seemed to be constructed from tubular metal, with the back enclosed by a sloping, curved sheet of matte silver aluminium-like material.

'I don't know,' replied Delgado. 'It looks like a huge gateway.'

Within the structure were a dozen or so Seriatts – they were mainly *mourst*, but there were also a couple of *vilume*. Most wore uniforms. They were standing in groups of three or four, engaged in conversation. In front of them, towards the rear of the space, was a large metal partition that divided the interior of the structure. Around four metres high and chrome-like in appearance, it separated the main part of the vestibule from a smaller area immediately behind it. Set into the partition, slightly towards the right of the vestibule from their perspective, was a tall, rotary turnstile.

'It looks like some kind of security gate,' he said. 'See those Seriatts? There's an informal rank system in play in there. The focus of each group is a *mourst*, see?' Ashala nodded. 'I would guess they're the pilots.' Delgado squinted, peering into the shadows within the arch. Beyond the chrome partition he could just about discern six silver rectangles, their metallic surfaces dully reflective in the subdued light. 'Those rectangular shapes at the back look like elevator doors.'

'Yeah. And they sure as hell aren't going up. They must go down to the start of the launch tubes. Access for official personnel only.'

'There seems to be a distinct disparity in wealth distribution here, too.' He indicated the dozens of freighters to the left of the arch. Many were old, with antifriction coatings peeling away in large flakes like crisp autumn leaves. Once bright detailing was stippled with rust. 'You compare those to those.' On the opposite side of the thoroughfare, to their right, was a long line of large and obviously luxurious trailers – Delgado estimated sixty or so. Each was dressed in its own distinctive, colourful livery. The smooth, curvaceous lines of these vehicles was the antithesis of the utilitarian units behind them and the freighters to the left. Separating the luxury machines from the broad thoroughfare was a low fence, consisting of a single wire stretched taut between white posts around half a metre high.

'Opulent accommodation for important Seriatts, no doubt,' Ash suggested. She looked around. 'You think Cascari's around here somewhere?'

'He won't be far away. He'll want to get down to those launch tubes and won't waste time about it. He's not stupid either. It wouldn't surprise me if he's down there already.'

Delgado looked back towards the elevators and saw that some of the Seriatts were stepping through the turnstile. 'Come on,' he said. 'Let's take a closer look at this, see if we can work out what's what. Be confident, but avoid making eye contact.'

'That's your standard advice in situations like this, huh?'

'Well it makes sense, doesn't it?'

'I guess so.'

They stepped from the shade and walked across the thoroughfare, avoiding speeding automatics and groups of

Seriatts. As they walked casually past the entrance to the gateway and looked in, one of the elevator doors opened. Some of those waiting at the turnstile stepped forward. One of them – a *mourst* – pulled a small card from a holster at his waist and placed it into a slot in the pedestal next to the turnstile. The Seriatt waited for a few moments, then when two small lights above the slot became illuminated he retrieved the card and pushed at the gate. Each one did the same, making their way through the turnstile until the elevator was full.

As they passed the edge of the vestibule entrance, Delgado could see only two *mourst* guards, and they were paying little attention to either the turnstile or the elevators.

'Back over there,' said Delgado. He pointed to the opposite side of the thoroughfare, and steered Ash towards a small stand with a green canopy sunshade, from which a vendor was selling hot food. 'Hungry?' he asked.

'You bet. I can't remember when I last ate properly.'

They looked at the wares on offer. All the food was deep-fried, coated in thick, glossy batter, floating in small cauldrons of bubbling oil. Prices and descriptions were chalked on a board in front of the trailer, but neither of them was able to read the Seriattic text.

Delgado reached into his pocket and fished out the coins he had found earlier. There was no way for him to know which were of the greatest denomination, so he simply selected four that looked as if they held the most value.

The vendor was a skinny *vilume* with a sallow complexion and wholly miserable appearance who bore none of the usual superiority of her kind. Wearing a grubby brown tabard spattered with questionable stains, she seemed to be doing her best to pretend that Delgado and Ashala were not there, busying herself needlessly at the back of her stand.

Eventually she grudgingly turned to face them. Delgado pointed to one of the seething vats and held up two fingers. The *vilume* pulled a sour expression and Delgado was uncertain whether to be insulted or grateful. With little enthusiasm the *vilume* took a knife with a long, serrated blade and slit open two cakes of unleavened bread taken from a pile to her left. Using long tongs she pulled two fat, dripping cylinders of batter from the hot oil and jammed them into the bread. She handed the food to Delgado seemingly unwillingly. He placed the coins heavily on the counter and turned away.

He handed one of the snacks to Ash, and took a bite. The food was still very hot and burned his lips and tongue, but was firm and succulent and tasted better than he had expected. Behind him he heard the *vilume* speaking rapidly, and could tell from her tone that something was not right. He turned. The Seriatt was holding out the coins he had given her in one hand and was gesticulating wildly with the other. *Vilume* were normally such placid creatures. Delgado had never before seen one in such an agitated state.

He reached into his pocket again and pulled out the few remaining coins, then offered them to her. She calmed somewhat, and took all but the two smallest coins, glancing at him as if expecting him to challenge this. Delgado suspected that he had paid dearly for the food.

He turned away from her again and took another bite. 'Over there,' he said quietly through a mouth full of food, indicating an area cast in deep shadow where they would be relatively unobserved.

As he and Ash ate, obscured by shadow, Delgado looked from the arch in front of them to the launch tubes, although the point at which the tubes emerged from the ground was out of sight beyond the line of luxury trailers and small buildings beyond.

'So you think Cascari's already down there?' Ash asked, picking at a bit of meat stuck between her teeth.

'I'm not necessarily convinced of it. But if he's not down there now he'll be trying to get down there. The question is how. There's more security here than elsewhere. You obviously need one of those cards to get past that turnstile, yet the only way to obtain one would be to steal one from someone. I'm not sure Cascari would be able to do that.'

'Why not? He's used to killing if that's what you mean. He's a Hornet pilot, after all.'

Delgado shook his head briefly. 'Yeah, but that's different. Sure, you're killing whoever's flying the other machine, but you don't really come into contact with them, or even see them. This would have to be done by hand, at very close quarters. That's a different ball game. Takes considerable guts.'

'You don't think Cascari's got guts?'

He shrugged. 'I never said that.'

Ashala finished her food, picked another morsel from her teeth and belched loudly. 'Excuse me,' she said.

'Filled the gap, has it?'

'Indeed. Just right. I didn't realise how hungry I was.' She passed wind softly as if to validate this statement.

As Delgado ate the last of his own food a number of raised voices some distance to their right attracted his attention. He looked past the line of luxury trailers and saw a couple of Seriatts running. A *vilume* was walking round in circles with her hands clasped to her face. A *conosq* was pointing between two trailers while looking towards a *mourst* enforcer who was running towards her. Seriatts from all around were gravitating towards the *conosq*. Delgado stuffed the last of his food into his mouth and tugged at one of Ashala's sleeves.

'Gub ob,' he said, spitting crumbs. He swallowed hard. 'Let's go see what's going on.'

They walked quickly, crossing the busy thoroughfare towards the commotion. By the time they reached the scene a sizeable crowd had gathered, and there were many people in front of them.

'Wait here,' he whispered. 'I'll go take a look.'

Delgado pushed his way through the jostling, chattering crowd, past *mourst* and *conosq*. The musky scent of one of the latter made his head spin momentarily. He could see another *conosq*. She appeared to be sobbing. The *mourst* enforcer was looking impassively at something on the floor, his expression grim even for a *mourst*. Delgado edged his way through the crowd until the reason for the disturbance was clear.

A *vilume* lay face down in the grass.

The Seriatt was wearing a one-piece suit in the same colours as the nearest trailer. A *conosq* kneeling next to the body said something to the *mourst*, a soft, mellifluous utterance. Delgado was unable to translate the words, but their meaning was clear, and there was perceptible shock among the crowd: the *vilume* was dead.

Conosq in the crowd began to make strange, throaty warbling noises that Delgado perceived to be expressions of grief or shock. As the *conosq* stood, the *mourst* enforcer hooked a booted toe under one of the *vilume*'s shoulders and rolled the body over. The corpse's head lolled. Unseeing eyes reflected the silhouettes of those looking down. The tip of the *vilume*'s swollen, slightly pointed tongue protruded between purple lips. The Seriatt looked like a beautiful male human youth, fragile, delicate, on the cusp of manhood. There was a further surge of collective sorrow and the cries of the *conosq* became an increasingly loud and discordant ululation. To Delgado's right one of them collapsed in apparent grief.

Growling words Delgado could not hear clearly, the enforcer crouched and reached out to open the *vilume*'s already loose collar. His neck bore fresh bruises, purple smudges that were clear evidence of cause of death: the Seriatt had been strangled.

At this the crowd erupted. The *conosq* seemed far more affected by events than their *mourst* or *vilume* counterparts, and those not already vocalising their grief began to do so. Some even fell to their knees and began pounding the ground with the palms of their hands. Delgado heard a nearby *vilume* mutter one of the few Seriattic phrases he recognised: *di-fio na'atu*: the ultimate crime.

Delgado glanced around. All eyes were on the corpse and widespread distress and grief was evident in all of the Seriatts, even on the hard faces of the *mourst*. More *conosq* fell to their knees, alternately clasping their hands before them and patting the ground. There came a point at which, apart from a couple of *mourst*, Delgado was one of the few still standing. Beginning to feel somewhat conspicuous, he took in as much information as he could, and slipped away.

As he walked back towards Ash, two copters appeared overhead, slowing to a hover over the scene of the murder. Delgado glanced up at them: their long blades shimmered against the blue sky, their fat bodies casting dark shadows across the nearby vehicles.

As Delgado reached Ashala one of the copters landed on the far side of the trailers. He reached out, turned her around, and they began to walk back in the direction of the elevator arch. As word of the murder spread most other people were going in the opposite direction.

'What happened?' Ash whispered as they walked.

'Cascari killed a *vilume*.'

'What? You're sure?'

He nodded grimly. 'Certain. The bruises on her neck and their positioning indicated that she was strangled by someone with hands smaller than those of a *mourst*, yet stronger than either a *conosq* or *vilume*. And she had one of those key-card holders.'

'And it was empty, right?'

'You got it in one. I guess it shows how much I know, huh.'

They walked in silence for a few moments, then Delgado glanced over his shoulder. The crowd had swollen to around twice its previous size. He estimated that around two hundred Seriatts were now kneeling in the vicinity of the corpse. Although faint, the tremulous cries of the *conosq* could still be heard above the sound of the copter flying in wide circles over the scene.

The area immediately around and ahead of them was now virtually devoid of Seriatts. Only the automatics continued to work, moving steadily along the wide thoroughfare. Delgado reached into one of his pockets for his sidearm. He withdrew it slightly, checked its status, gently touching on-screen tabs with his right thumb, then set the weapon live and placed it back inside his pocket.

'What we have to do now,' he said, 'is obtain one of those cards ourselves and follow him underground.'

'Excellent,' said Ash brightly. 'Can I be the one to draw the enemy fire?'

'Well,' said Delgado, not looking at her, 'it's funny you should say that . . .'

The Chamber of Visions, Oracles' Cloister, Seriattic Palace

Oracle Taquorta lay on the couch. The young *vilume* seemed nervous as its leather surface altered to accommodate the shape of his body.

'You must try to relax, Taquorta,' Oracle Entuzo advised gently.

'I am nervous, Oracle,' said the young *vilume*. 'It is my first time using the Mask.'

'Tension and doubt cloud your sight, Taquorta. You must allow yourself to see if we are to establish Hescar's location, and ascertain his condition. The scientists are worried that they have sent him to his death. We must do our best to try and alleviate their concerns, as they have requested. It is an excellent opportunity for you to gain experience. But if you cannot see anything of help, you must not reproach yourself. Do you understand?'

'I do, Oracle Entuzo.'

'Good. Relax now, Taquorta. I will fetch the mask.' Entuzo walked across to the wall and opened the panel. She then removed the Destiny Mask from its stand and took it to him.

'Remember,' said Entuzo as she placed the mask on the young Oracle's face, 'you must allow yourself to become a conduit for the visualisations if they are to appear. They must flow through you. Do not try to resist, do not try to force them to appear. Merely accept them. I know you are ready. You will do well.'

As Entuzo stepped away from the couch there was a faint, high-pitched whine, and the mask began to glow. As it appeared to melt down the sides of Taquorta's face, merging with his skin, the young Oracle gripped the sides of the couch.

Taquorta began to moan gently, as if experiencing a vivid, disturbing dream and a vague distortion appeared in the air above him, strange apparitions moving within a thin grey mist. They appeared to be marine creatures, or slowly moving floral organisms. These images were followed by others of a meteor shower, large objects lighting the sky as they fell to earth, smashing into a turbulent sea, devastating forests, razing cities.

The visualisation ended after only a few minutes, leaving Oracle Taquorta physically drained and emotional. Entuzo walked over to the couch and looked down at Taquorta as the mask reformed back into its original, dormant state. She could see him trembling. 'How do you feel?' she asked when she finally took the mask from him. She handed him a glass of cold water.

'I did not see Hescar,' he replied between gulps as he sought to quench his raging thirst.

Entuzo could see his disappointment. 'I know,' she said. 'But you did well. Much was revealed.'

'But it made no sense, Oracle. I fear I am too weak to be a good Oracle.'

'Nonsense, Taquorta. You are strong and will improve with time. It takes experience to channel the images with clarity. Nothing comes without effort. Now you must rest yourself. We can discuss your experience later, when you are stronger.'

'Thank you, Oracle.'

Oracle Entuzo turned and walked away. As she placed the Mask back on its stand she considered what she had seen in Taquorta's visions. Despite the fact that an Oracle wearing the Destiny Mask usually experienced far more detailed mental visions than those who were merely observing, she believed that in this case Taquorta had seen little more than those in the Chamber. But he was a novice; it was to be expected.

Oracle Entuzo was certain, however, that Taquorta was correct in his assertion that the visualisations were not related to Hescar. There were other indications of the true meaning of Taquorta's visions. Yet Entuzo did not want to entertain them, for if they were accurate, the Saviour she had herself predicted needed to arrive soon.

The Koss-Miet racing facility, Astragarda, Seriatt

Delgado and Ashala loitered in the shadows opposite the lifts. There was now only one *mourst* guarding the turnstile and he was leaning against the right side of the arch, head back and eyes closed, enjoying the sun's warmth on his face. One leg was crossed over the other and his arms were folded across the top of the short stem weapon hanging over his shoulder by a thin leather strap.

Delgado extended his hyperconsciousness, trying to penetrate the *mourst*'s mind. Although he found Seriattic patterns difficult to analyse, he perceived tranquillity, an almost numb resonance indicating that the *mourst* was extremely relaxed, possibly bordering on sleep.

Abruptly, a clutch of random visuals opened in his brain, a series of seemingly unrelated sheets that overlaid rapidly across each other. Some were blank, others contained information of which he caught only a glimpse, but seemed to make little sense. Other sheets merged, mutated and split within a moment. The surge lasted only a few seconds, but was sufficient to disorient Delgado somewhat. His age, and the clutter of remnants of long defunct nobics and incomplete threads, were increasingly working against him.

When the rogue visuals seemed to have reached their natural conclusion he backtracked and closed down each one individually, but even when this process was complete a certain hollow feeling remained at the back of his skull long after the visuals had gone.

He looked at Ash to his left. 'OK,' he said. 'This is the plan. We walk a short distance that way.' He indicated the ageing freighters and trailers to the left. 'Then we circle around between them to the back of that structure. Got it?'

Ash looked in the direction Delgado had pointed. 'I think I understand that, Delgado,' she said. 'Although maybe you better run it by me one more time, just in case.'

Delgado snorted at her sarcasm. 'Then you cause a diversion . . .'

'Well thank the stars for consistency.'

'You cause a diversion,' he repeated, 'and attract the attention of our friend there. Try to draw him towards you. I'll deal with him after that.'

She looked across at the half-dozing *mourst*. 'That's a big gun he's got there, Delgado. A very big gun.'

'Good,' he said with a grin. 'I knew you'd be excited. Is there anything you want to ask before we proceed? Anything that's unclear?'

'Well . . .'

'Wonderful,' he said. 'Now let's get on with it, shall we?' He strode from the cool darkness of the shadows and across the thoroughfare.

They walked past the line of trailers and dilapidated aircraft once more. At what seemed like an opportune moment Delgado glanced back towards the arch. The *mourst* had not moved. He put his left arm around Ash's shoulders and they turned into the narrow gap between two vehicles, then began to jog in the quiet and cool confines of the shadowy space.

They turned right behind a trailer. They were to the rear of the silver structure housing the elevators. It rose into the sky like the fin of a huge beached marine creature, casting a thick, dark shadow. Delgado looked between trailers towards the main thoroughfare. Apart from the automatics and couriers, he could see a *vilume* – another food vendor judging from her attire – walking on the far side, but otherwise the area remained quiet. He extended his hyperconsciousness again in an attempt to ascertain whether there had been any change in the *mourst*'s mental state. If anything he seemed even more relaxed than before. Delgado turned to face Ashala.

'This is our chance,' he said. 'It's perfect. No one about, only one guard. Couldn't be easier.'

Ash raised her eyebrows. 'I shall resist the urge to say something about famous last words,' she said. 'What do you want me to do?'

'All you've got to do is walk out into the open and call him.'

'And say what, exactly? "Hey there, we're the human fugitives you might have heard about and our friend's just murdered one of your *vilume*."'

'Well, you can say that if you want to. Frankly it doesn't matter what you say, because if you say it in human the likelihood is that he won't understand you anyway. Just make it clear that it's something urgent that he has to see *right now*. Then beckon to him and run back round here. You must make it look important. If you're in a panic he's bound to follow you to see what's up.'

'What if he doesn't?'

'He will. Now get a move on.'

Ash turned and began walking towards the main thoroughfare. After a few moments she stopped and turned again. 'Say,

Delgado. Why the hell can't you be the one to go attract his attention, anyway? How come I'm always the stooge?'

'Hard as it may be for you to believe, he's less likely to perceive you as dangerous. If I go out there and cause a stir he'll be wary. But he won't see you as a potential threat. At least, that's the idea. Now will you please get a move on?'

'All right, OK, take it easy.' She turned and continued walking.

Delgado watched as she walked on to the sunlit thoroughfare. She would be visible to the *mourst* now – assuming he was awake. For a moment Ash simply stood, looking in the *mourst*'s direction; then she cupped her hands around her mouth, and Delgado saw her body move as she shouted. There was a pause, then she shouted again. With her change of posture he knew she had successfully attracted the *mourst*'s attention. Delgado smiled at her performance as she became agitated, shouting again and pointing back in his direction. Then she began to run back towards him.

Calmly, Delgado stepped back out of sight and took the small sidearm from his pocket to check it again. After a few moments he paused and closed his eyes: his heart was beating too rapidly; his breathing was too fast and shallow. Another rash of rogue visuals blossomed, fluttering briefly through his mind, and for a moment he was forced to concentrate on quashing them. Yet, despite his best efforts and the implementation of the best techniques, he knew he remained nervous.

Ash ran around the corner, breathing heavily. Despite the grass the *mourst*'s heavy footfalls could clearly be heard as he chased after her.

Delgado looked at Ash. 'You just pretend you found me here.' She looked puzzled.

But there was no time left for explanations. Delgado lay on his back on the grass, one arm at a right angle to his body, his other hand – in which he clutched the sidearm – tucked inside one of his tunic pockets. Blood pounded dully at his temples.

His palms were slick with sweat. Beneath the back of his head he could feel the cool dampness of the thick grass. It was a contrast to the hot numbness growing in his skull.

Delgado heard the *mourst* stop running and felt the Seriatt's strength of presence quite clearly; he was suspicious, wary. There was a moment's silence before, speaking in Counian, his voice like the sound of cloth tearing, the enforcer demanded information: 'What is going on here? Who is this?'

'I just found him,' Ash said in human. 'I think he needs medical help.'

Clearly failing to understand what Ash was saying, the Seriatt demanded to know who she was and what she was doing here. Ash did not reply. She was probably pretending to not understand the questions. The *mourst* grunted, and Delgado sensed the enforcer kneeling beside him. He even heard the sound of the grass being crushed, the creak of leather and the sound of the metal links on his weapon's strap. The enforcer mumbled something quietly, then Delgado felt a heavy hand on his chest. The *mourst* opened one of Delgado's eyes and peered down at the human. His eyes unmoving, Delgado saw the Seriatt as a blurred silhouette against the glare of the sky. A few white cumulus clouds formed a rough halo.

When Delgado felt the *mourst* begin to search his pockets he judged that it was safe to assume he was no longer looking at his face. He half opened one eye, then opened both eyes fully. When the *mourst* moved to search another of his pockets, Delgado yanked his right hand from his tunic to raise the sidearm and kill the *mourst* in a single, swift movement.

The butt of the gun caught on the flap of his pocket and stuck there.

The *mourst* made a wet growling sound and fell back, sitting on his haunches for a moment before losing his balance and falling on to his backside. Delgado rolled and tried to get to his feet, desperately trying to retrieve the sidearm.

The *mourst* tried to push himself up while simultaneously attempting to pull his rifle around in front of him. Delgado kicked the weapon so hard its thin strap snapped, and the gun flew from the enforcer's hands, landing on a patch of sunlit grass several metres away. The *mourst* gave a roar that Delgado recognised from his experience with *mourst* during the Buhatt rebellion as a battle cry, and lunged towards him.

The impact knocked the air from Delgado's lungs but he rolled with the blow, grasping the *mourst*'s leather tunic and taking the Seriatt with him. Using both feet and a surge of nobics, Delgado launched the enforcer into the air. Before landing heavily against the side of a nearby trailer, the *mourst*'s feet caught Ashala's head and she fell to the ground. When Delgado raised his sidearm to fire the weapon he found that the small screen was blank.

The *mourst* charged again as Delgado tried to reactivate his sidearm, but as the weapon's screen became illuminated once more the enforcer smashed into him. He groaned at the impact; the weight and momentum of the Seriatt pushed him back to smash against a large metal container.

Delgado was pinned in place, his left arm trapped by the weight of the *mourst*'s body, his right arm forced upwards so that the sidearm was pointing towards the sky. The enforcer's right forearm was pressed firmly against Delgado's throat, forcing his head back. Delgado struggled in an effort to free himself, but the *mourst*'s weight and strength were simply too great.

Delgado looked down at the *mourst* and saw the creature's face contorted into a sour grimace as he wore what seemed to represent a victorious smile. The Seriatt's breath stank and his impressive incisors were stained brown. The enforcer muttered some words Delgado failed to catch, but which appeared to be self-congratulatory.

The *mourst* pressed harder against Delgado's throat and uttered more barely audible words, increasing the pressure with each syllable. Delgado felt himself beginning to lose consciousness. His eyelids fluttered. The *mourst*'s face became increasingly blurred. A tingling sensation prickled Delgado's fingertips and face, and he felt a slight numbness in his limbs. A sudden and intense wave of sexual euphoria washed over him as the grip of unconsciousness tightened. The *mourst* enforcer spoke softly to Delgado. He seemed to be referring to Seriattic culinary techniques.

In the final few moments of consciousness, disconnected and dreamlike images blurred into a surreal stream of interconnected thoughts. The *mourst* was an odd, distorted shape in front of him. Somewhere in his fading mind Delgado saw the enforcer turn his head. Then he heard a noise, a combination of rippling, resonant base notes stippled with piercing squeals.

Delgado lay on the ground and gently rubbed his throat, then pushed himself up so that he was resting on one elbow. He looked around. A few metres away lay the enforcer's motionless body. Most of the Seriatt's head was missing. What little remained – the lower part of the rear of the skull, in a diagonal line from the lower jaw up behind the ears – gave the impression that the front of his head had been cleanly removed using a gigantic ice-cream scoop. And a hot one, at that: most of the tissue was blackened, melted together in misshapen globs like pus-filled blisters. Ash was standing over the body, looking down at it. She was holding the *mourst*'s weapon in her hands.

Delgado stood and walked over to her. The Seriatt's face was gone, although one or two odd details remained: two of the lower incisors, some jawbone – both of which were startlingly white – the hard and elaborate curls of skin that formed the lower part of the ears. But all else was distorted, new shapes formed where other definition had once been. The general stench of death – a unique and particularly distinctive odour in Delgado's experience – was strengthened by the equally distinctive smell of burned flesh.

'Saving my skin's getting to be a habit,' he said.

'Yeah, well, someone's got to look out for you, Delgado. I learned that a *long* time ago.'

'Whatever. I owe you my life. Again.'

'It's a good job he didn't have a Seriattic weapon. Otherwise I might not have been much use.'

'What do you mean?'

She looked down at the *mourst* gun. 'This is a Gabangch ES4,' she said. 'Originally developed on Earth for use by Structure. It utilises relatively standard technologies similar to the fundamentals on which Jutt and Hi-Mag weapons are based, but it also has some particularly impressive capabilities that make it highly adaptable. It can be customised by individual users to suit their personal taste.'

'Very impressive,' said Delgado. 'I don't know why he has it but it might sure come in handy. He stooped and pulled the key-card from the holster at the *mourst*'s waist. 'This should get us through that turnstile. After that, we'll just have to see what happens. Come on.'

They walked back to the main thoroughfare and paused at the edge of the vestibule.

Delgado looked to the left. The crowd around the scene of the *vilume*'s murder had swollen still further. In contrast to similar situations he had experienced in the company of humans, he perceived among them a genuine sense of collective grief rather than a morbid curiosity. He wasn't sure how this squared with the fundamental bloodlust the air race seemed to satisfy. Perhaps the reason was that in this case a *vilume* had died; maybe *mourst* held a different status in their society. Remnants of an infocram file he'd once had stored in his nobics flickered briefly as they automatically tried to offer answers, but the information was too old and fragmented to be of any use to him now.

The thoroughfare was becoming busier as some people began to return to their normal businesses. Graceful *vilume* passed by, the hems of their long, heavy robes brushing the ground as they walked with their customary serenity. They seemed to have become subdued and contemplative as a result of their counterpart's death. *Conosq*, passing in supportive groups of three or four, were a stark contrast, many of them mourning in an almost theatrical manner, wailing shrill cries of grief. Some of them even seemed unable to stand without help, so great was their distress. *Mourst* were either extremely angry, gesticulating wildly and vocalising aggressively, or – as seemed more common – completely unmoved by the incident. Delgado perceived a combination of confusion and fear, underpinned by a faint but definite sense of satisfaction or pleasure. The latter was a trace it was rare to identify with any level of purity. It was as if the *mourst* were grateful for the opportunity for such emotional release; the *vilume* were frightened of the potential such release held, while the *conosq* were on the verge of such release throughout their existence.

'You wait here,' he said to Ash. Delgado waited for a group of *conosq* who were grieving particularly enthusiastically to pass, then took a few cautious steps into the sunlight so that he could see the turnstile and the elevators: the vestibule was deserted. He stepped back into the cover of deep shadow.

'No guard, no queue, no nothing,' he said. 'Hide that thing inside your tunic.' He indicated the *mourst*'s weapon. 'And stick with me.'

'Should I walk with confidence and avoid making eye contact with anyone?'

Delgado looked at her for a moment, then checked his sidearm and walked purposefully on to the thoroughfare.

Brilliant sunshine warmed them briefly as they passed from the cool shadow then turned quickly into the vestibule. They approached the turnstile. The movable part of the gate was sturdy, short horizontal bars around a thick central pillar fixed firmly into the ground at the bottom, and into a thick metal bar running the width of the vestibule about six metres above Delgado's head. The slot for the security card was in a stumpy column that formed an integral part of the turnstile. The lights above the slot were both dark.

'Keep watch,' he said. 'Let me know if we get company. Make sure you keep the gun hidden.'

'What's the point?' she asked. 'Anyone who comes in here won't see it straight away anyway because of the transition from light to dark.'

'Just keep it out of sight. For now, at least.'

As Ash watched the entrance, Delgado took the card and placed it into the slot's mouth. With a faint wheezing sound it was pulled smoothly from his fingers by the internal mechanisms.

Delgado waited, but nothing happened.

Ash glanced over her shoulder. 'What's the hold-up?'

'Damned if I know.'

Ash looked towards the entrance again. 'Hello,' she said quietly. 'Look who's come to tea.'

Delgado half turned. Two *mourst* wearing race team uniforms had entered. They were deep in serious conversation and did not look at the two people standing in front of the turnstile.

'Be cool,' Delgado said. 'Turn this way, and keep that thing hidden.'

'You forgot the bit about walking confidently and not looking anyone in the eye.'

'Very good. You are an extremely funny person.'

Ash and Delgado stopped talking as the Seriatts joined what they must have assumed was a queue, paying little attention to the two figures in front of them.

Delgado looked at the column; the lights remained off. The card emerged from the slot, but still the lights did not become illuminated. Delgado frowned and pushed the turnstile gate, but it did not move. Deciding not to force it in case it was alarmed, he looked closely at the card, turning it over in his fingers; it seemed completely featureless on both sides, no datastrips or encoding of any kind. He realised that the two *mourst* had stopped talking and, while he did not sense suspicion in them, some impatience was becoming evident. Despite assigning nobics to maintenance of calm, Delgado was sweating. When he looked down at the card again he noticed that his hands were trembling.

He began to formulate combat and attack strategies, but when he turned the card over and inserted it into the slot again the lights became illuminated after a few seconds, and a faint click was heard within the turnstile. Delgado pressed against one of the bars in the gate, and felt a surge of elation as it gave way.

He stepped through into the smaller area in front of the elevator doors, holding the turnstile open for Ash, but the heavy metal gate slipped from his grip and closed with a firm, mechanical clunk.

Ashala stepped forward and pushed at the gate with one hand, trying to ensure that she did not drop the rifle concealed up her tunic with the other. But the gate was not about to open. Delgado saw that the two *mourst* were looking intently at her; it was hard to judge their expressions, but Delgado sensed in them generic blends of confusion and suspicion, slightly flavoured by a range of uniquely Seriattic traces he was unable to analyse satisfactorily.

One of the *mourst* challenged them in Seriatt. They ignored him. The *mourst* repeated his words and placed one of his long, dark hands on one of Ashala's shoulders.

Ash looked at Delgado, eyebrows raised. 'Should I look him in the eye now, do you think?' she whispered.

The *mourst* looked from Ashala to Delgado to his colleague and back again, then spoke in Counian. 'You I do not recognise,' he said. 'Which team are you with?'

'We're tech,' said Delgado with a brusqueness he hoped the Seriatts would recognise and respect despite its human flavour. He reached back through the gate and pushed the card into the turnstile slot from the other side.

'Tech ops occur at night,' said the other *mourst* evenly. 'You are not authorised to be in the launch area during periods of pre-race testing. Name your overseer, human.'

Delgado stood his ground but felt unconvincing. 'There's a system failure,' he said. There seemed an interminable pause in the card's verification. 'We've got to check it out. Rectify the problem as soon as possible.' Beyond the vestibule entrance, movement caught Delgado's attention: Seriattic *mourst* were running towards the side of the structure: the enforcer's body had been discovered.

'What is the nature of this failure?' asked the other *mourst*.

Still the gate refused to open. Ash was gradually lowering the gun from the bottom of her tunic.

'We don't have the details as yet,' Delgado replied. 'Something to do with the heating system in tube three.' He shrugged as if he found such trivia tedious, but sensed an immediate shift in the mental patterns and general demeanour of the two *mourst* that suggested that, in all probability, there was no tube three. And even if there was it probably had no heating system. The Seriatts muttered between themselves. Delgado sensed increased anxiety and suspicion, as well as some threads of sexual arousal – they were often the most dangerous of all.

Suddenly the turnstile gate clicked and Ash pushed open the gate with her free hand, while the other cradled the butt of the gun. As she stepped through, the two *mourst* also stepped forward. As one of them tried unsuccessfully to stop the gate from closing the other reached out and grabbed at Ash, but failed to get a firm grip and only caught one sleeve. The *mourst* yanked at the fabric. As Ash spun around and fell backwards the gun dropped from beneath her tunic and landed heavily on its butt, releasing a dozen high velocity projectile rounds within a fraction of a second.

There were three explosions high above, and a cascade of thin, sharp-edged metal sheets a metre wide fell as sections of the structure shattered. Smaller flakes fluttered slowly to the ground like butterflies. Slabs of sunlight burst through the new holes in the ceiling, forming hot white pools on the grass. The other rounds, released as the gun fell to the ground, hit the *mourst*.

Two hit the one standing nearest to the gate, the first bursting through his shoulder, the second entering at the collar bone on the left side and passing up through the neck and out again behind his right ear. He fell backwards and hit the ground with a muffled thud.

One round caught the other *mourst* in the face, entering on one side of his mouth and exiting on the opposite side, at the rear of the Seriatt's heavy jawbone. The shot destroyed the soft tissues – his lips, tongue and cheek – and shattered bone and teeth. A second round hit him in the right side of the chest, throwing him backwards. For a few moments he lay where he landed, his chest rising and falling rapidly as blood fizzed and bubbled through the ragged rent of skin and bone.

The *mourst* managed to roll on to one side and push himself up on one elbow, leaning forward slightly. Drool and blood and snot and glistening white shards of bone and tooth trailed from the side of his face. His tongue was a glistening flap of muscle that hung loosely by a thin sliver of tissue from the side of his head, one cheek and much of the muscle inside his mouth having been completely destroyed.

The *mourst* managed to turn his head to look at Delgado and Ash as they stood by the elevator. He appeared confused, bewildered. Then he appeared to try to speak, as if unaware of the extent of his injuries, but managed only a few dull, wet sounds, his tongue squirming uncontrollably, before he fell back to the ground.

'Where's that goddamn elevator, Delgado?'

'Somewhere between here and hell,' he said grimly.

'Well, it needs to get its hot ass up here double quick. We're beginning to attract attention.' Two *conosq* had stopped outside and were peering into the darkness, squinting and shading their eyes as they tried to see into the gloom. Delgado hit the elevator call button again but there was no indication of whether it was on its way. He looked back towards the *conosq*. Judging from their stance and the patterns he could perceive in them, they had not seen what had happened but were aware that all was not well. For a moment they seemed uncertain. Then one of them looked directly at Delgado, stood more upright, pointed and called to someone out of sight. A moment later a *mourst* enforcer appeared at her side.

Delgado swore. 'Over here,' he whispered. 'Get down, make yourself as small as possible.'

The enforcer stepped slowly but confidently into the comparative darkness. The moment he saw his two fallen counterparts he crouched, simultaneously bringing his gun to bear and thumbing a comms unit at his throat. He raised his weapon to his face and searched the gloom for a target, but Delgado and Ash were obscured by the shining chrome of the turnstile. The enforcer's right thumb moved rapidly as he changed his weapon's settings, but still he did not see them, the metal frame apparently interfering with his gun's perception settings.

Delgado reached out and gently touched Ash's right elbow. 'Give me the rifle,' he whispered. '*Slowly*. It'll recharge much more rapidly than my sidearm.'

As the *mourst* glanced between the two fallen Seriatts and the holes in the roof, as if wondering whether these might represent the source of danger, Ash slowly extended one arm and pointed. The weapon lay in the grass around four metres away, mid-way between the gate and the elevators.

Delgado glanced between the *mourst* and the stranded weapon. He hesitated, momentarily uncertain. Increasing his nobic flow he watched as the enforcer continued to move slowly towards his two counterparts. Delgado was not certain, but he seemed to be speaking to one of them. Delgado waited until the enforcer had reached the *mourst* nearest to him, then launched himself towards the gun.

He rolled across the grass, picking up the weapon on the way. Not practised in such acrobatics, aching, tired, and with the bulk of his useful nobics already assigned to other tasks, his efforts were clumsy and he fell against the turnstile framework as he tried to bring the weapon around in front of him. The enforcer's attention was drawn to the movement and, as Delgado tried to stand, the *mourst* also stood.

They brought their weapons to bear at almost the same moment, and there was a fraction of a second during which each had his gun trained on the other. A copter passed low over the vestibule, powering upwards away from the scene of the *vilume*'s murder. The downdraft from its huge rotor caused the weakened metal of the structure to shudder, loose edges buzzing as they vibrated. The enforcer looked up, and raised his right arm to protect his face as sharp metal shards rained down on him.

Seeing his opportunity, Delgado fired.

Despite squeezing the trigger only briefly the vestibule was sprayed with ammunition. He had no time to absorb detail, but was aware that some ordnance passed through the entrance and destroyed one of the couriers on the thoroughfare outside, littering the track with its cargo. Only two rounds hit the enforcer, but these were sufficient. Both impacted him on the right side, one severing at the elbow the arm with which he had been holding his own weapon, the other hitting him square in the shoulder. The *mourst* yelled, spun around as a result of the hits and fell to the ground. Despite the Seriatt's injuries Delgado sensed the *mourst* was full of anger and frustration rather than fear.

The *mourst* rolled on to his stomach, blood squirting from his upper arm. He clutched at the blades of grass with his remaining hand and pushed with his legs in an effort to reach his weapon, grunting with the effort. To Delgado it seemed futile, and he let his own weapon drop to his side. When the *mourst* was almost within fingertip reach of his own gun, he was forced to pause, breathless and weak. His life was draining away rapidly, as Delgado's once had, a long time ago in Myson's chamber. Exhausted, the *mourst* turned his head and looked at Delgado, his dark eyes full of bitterness and fear. Delgado met the Seriatt's gaze and realised that he was uncertain of his feelings. He knew what the *mourst* wanted and it seemed dishonourable not to give it to him given the circumstances. He trained his weapon on the enforcer once more, and fired again. The *mourst* shuddered, then lay motionless.

With the return of relative quiet Delgado could hear the shrill warbling of the grieving *conosq* in the distance, and the fading sound of the climbing copter. Within the vestibule itself, all was still.

'Delgado,' called Ash. 'Our elevator's finally arrived.'

He turned and saw that the silver doors were now open. Outside, the sound of copter engines was growing louder again, apparently heralding the arrival of the assistance summoned by the *mourst*. The noise swelled, and in the thoroughfare in front of the vestibule the few short blades of grass were pressed flat as the aircraft landed.

As Ash called to him from the elevator, Delgado realised that they would not pass through this turnstile a second time. He was uncertain what events were likely to transpire in the coming hours, but was confident in the integrity of his instincts. As dozens of *mourst* enforcers stormed into the vestibule, he turned and stepped into the elevator and a few moments later he and Ashala were plummeting into the Seriattic crust.

Six

in pursuit of zetheus

The Koss-Miet racing facility, Astragarda, Seriatt
Although rapid, their descent beneath the surface of Seriatt took several minutes. It was longer than Delgado had expected, and he was unable to estimate how far beneath the ground they might have travelled given the elevator's speed.

When the elevator doors opened they saw a low, black semi-circular tunnel leading away from them. A single luminescent strip running the entire length of the tunnel's roof cast thin grey light. The floor was laid with dark, hard-wearing carpet. There was a distinct smell of damp. There was also an oppressive sensation, as if the weight of the earth above the tunnel was tangible.

'Better conceal these guns again,' said Delgado. 'No need causing unnecessary alarm if those down here aren't aware of what's going on up top. Here, you have the rifle back. And remember, walk confidently and . . .'

'. . . don't look anyone in the eye. Thanks, Delgado. I'd forgotten about that.'

They stepped from the elevator and saw that an identical tunnel ran perpendicular to the one facing them. When Delgado looked to his left he saw an automatic appear momentarily in the distance as it crossed the intersection between another tunnel and that in which they were standing, suggesting a grid pattern.

'Quiet, isn't it?' Ash observed.

'Yeah,' said Delgado slowly. 'But for how long?' He took a few steps forward and saw that there were recesses around one metre deep that contained doors at regular intervals along the corridors. 'There's not many people down here considering this is where the action's supposed to be, that's for sure.' He paused.

'But then,' said Ash, 'perhaps these are not the *main* elevators. Perhaps these are simply the ones we came across first. The parts used to build the aircraft we've seen would need much larger elevators, nearer to the launch tubes.'

'Yeah, you're right. These are probably just personnel elevators.'

'So which way should we go?'

Delgado looked along the corridor opposite the elevator, then looked in both directions along the other tunnel. 'I haven't the faintest idea,' he said. 'If we work from the way the elevators are facing, then the launch tubes should begin in that direction.' As he pointed to his left he noticed signs on the tunnel walls, near the junction between the two. He walked over to the one nearest to him, but the words upon it were written in elaborate Seriattic script and he was unable to decipher their meaning. He drew some measure of consolation from the fact that even if he had been able to read the text there was no indication which way the signs were pointing. Perhaps this information was hidden in the indecipherable text . . .

He sighed heavily, walked a few paces along each corridor, then returned to the intersection. He closed his eyes, breathing slowly and remaining perfectly still, as if meditating. After a few seconds he opened his eyes, sucked briefly on his index finger and held it up in the air. 'As I thought,' he said, smiling at the coolness he felt. 'It's this way,' he said. 'The tubes are dragging the air through. Let's go.'

They paused at each intersection, but only met a variety of automatics going about their business. The units ignored them completely, blindly following their predetermined routes. A couple of times they heard voices in other nearby tunnels or within rooms they passed – mainly the distinctive growling tones of *mourst* – but they successfully managed to avoid direct contact with any Seriatts by ducking into the shadows of the door recesses they passed, or into adjoining tunnels.

At one intersection they heard a slow, deep bass throb that increased rapidly in both pitch and frequency until it faded abtuptly. A moment later a strong blast of warm air hit them, lasting several seconds before subsiding. It carried a pungent, charred odour.

Delgado leaned close to Ash. 'That must've been a launch,' he said. 'We must be getting close now.'

A large automatic came trundling along the corridor. Shaped like a squat, flat-topped pyramid, it was around a metre and a half high by a metre wide at the top, a metre and a half at the bottom and two metres in length. The machine was propelled at a quick walking pace by two narrow caterpillar tracks, one on either side, each of which was driven by three small wheels. At least one of these was badly in need of lubrication, and was emitting a regular, high-pitched squeak.

It appeared to be a basic courier. The position of hinges and latches indicated that one side of the machine opened completely, with the gatefold panels held in place by simple clips. Delgado judged from a certain, barely perceptible unsteadiness in the machine's movement that it was either completely empty or carrying a particularly lightweight load.

On hearing loud *mourst* voices they ducked quickly into one of the recesses and crouched in the shadows. They heard heavy footfalls as a group of *mourst* ran past the intersection with the tunnel ahead, shouting urgently. Delgado saw one of them: it was an enforcer, and his gun was drawn.

'I think they're looking for someone,' he said.

'Who could that be, though?' said Ash mischievously.

The courier reached the intersection between the two tunnels and halted briefly. Gears in the drive chamber beneath the cargo space wheezed and clunked, then the left track powered forward while the track on the other side moved in the opposite direction, turning the unit through ninety degrees. It rocked somewhat unsteadily as it performed the manoeuvre, the squeaking of the unlubricated wheel suddenly becoming short and insistent.

As the machine performed its laborious change of direction, Delgado stepped forward, reached out and deftly unclipped the hinged panel. The whole side of the courier was made from flimsy, lightweight metal sheets that flexed and boomed noisily as he folded the panels that formed the side of the unit up on to its flat top.

As Delgado peered inside, a strong smell of hot food hit him. On a large plate in the middle of the unit – the only thing the courier contained – were a variety of pulses in a rich, steaming sauce, and some chopped leafy vegetables. The bulk of the meal, however, consisted of different meats – steaks, ribs, chops, knuckles – all with generous proportions of fat. There were also portions that looked like poultry breasts and wings. All the meat appeared to have been very quickly cooked, and was almost raw, oozing blood.

'Wow,' said Ash softly. 'Would you look at that. My stomach could do with something substantial to digest.'

'You're not the only one,' said Delgado as he closed the side of the courier before it moved off again. 'But I'm afraid this isn't the meal we ordered.' He hastily clipped the latches shut and the automatic moved off once more. 'Come on,' he said, 'It's heading in the direction of the launch tubes. Let's follow it and see who's hungry.'

★

They followed the machine at a distance for several minutes, pausing as it turned at intersections, slipping quickly into recesses when it appeared to be stopping. As they penetrated deeper into the labyrinth of tunnels there were more people around. This, coupled with the increasingly strong odour resulting from the burning of fossil fuels, the occasional and extremely loud sound of aircraft being launched, and the strength of the breeze that accompanied each firing, indicated the tubes' proximity.

Abruptly, the automatic stopped by one of the doors and began to perform another of its clumsy changes of direction. Delgado pushed Ash back along the tunnel and into one of the recesses, making sure that they were far enough away that they would not be seen from the room, but close enough to see inside it when the door opened.

When the courier had completed its turn it rolled slowly towards the door, then paused. There was a faint buzzing sound within the room, and a few moments later the door opened. As the automatic moved into the doorway, Delgado peered inside.

A cream-coloured desk with smooth, rounded edges ran along half of the wall opposite the door. It appeared to be constructed from shiny plastic, metal or possibly enamel. Short diagonal slits in groups of six were cut into the front of the desk at regular intervals, presumably to provide ventilation for whatever technology was held within. The desk itself was fairly shallow, but banks of equipment and numerous instruments were set into the vertical surface rising from the back of it, which came almost shoulder-height to a human, chest-height to a full-blooded *mourst.*

Numerous *vilume* and several *mourst* peered at small screens and read data from the endless sheets of paper spewing from printers into untidy piles on the floor. The Seriatts looked at the screens, the slender black needles wavering over the white backgrounds of small, silver-rimmed dials, then compared this information to that on the printouts. Occasionally they moved sliders, pushed buttons or flicked switches as a result of their analysis, or simply screwed up the paper and tossed it into one of several large and overflowing waste baskets.

'Looks like he's the hungry one,' said Ash. A *mourst* had approached the courier and was beginning to unfasten the latches around the side of the unit.

'Get out of the way, get out of the way,' Delgado muttered as the Seriatt blocked their view.

Above the flat top of the vertical instrument panel within the room was a shallow window. The entire wall from the end of the desk was also transparent. Both window and wall were convex from their viewpoint, clearly forming part of the wall of the launch tube itself. From what Delgado could see, given his limited view, the rest of the interior of the tube seemed to be formed from fat, organic ligaments, between which were muscular walls, linked by a multitude of ridges, sinews and veins. It was like the oesophagus of some great creature. On the other side of the launch tube he could see large, oval holes through which the other two launch tubes were visible.

Delgado craned his neck for a better view and suddenly caught his breath.

'What's up?' Ash asked. 'You OK?'

'It's Michael,' he replied. 'Through there.' He pointed.

Ash stretched forward to see. In the launch tube furthest away from them, Michael was examining one of the racing machines, walking around it, tugging at ailerons and peering up its ass, before going to the other end and running his hands over its smooth snout.

'Looks like it wasn't what he ordered, either,' said Ash. The young *mourst* that had opened the courier was looking with disgust at the food the machine had brought him, and appeared to be complaining bitterly to his colleagues about the error. He walked off with the meal, and began showing it to them.

Beyond, one of the racing aircraft came into view in the nearest tube. Whether it was sliding on rails or seated on a moving carriage of some kind Delgado could not tell, but the aircraft emerged slowly from the right side of the large window, moving until central to it, obscuring the activities in the other tubes.

A number of *mourst* emerged from elsewhere in the launch tube and began working on the craft. Two of them, wearing one-piece protective suits complete with helmets and visors, manhandled a thick pipe from beneath the window to the aircraft. It seemed brown, moist and slippery, like a length of oversized intestine. One *mourst* propped a short ladder against the wing nearest to them and climbed up it. His colleague passed him the hose while continuing to support its obvious weight as it was attached to a sphincter-like orifice on the craft's fuselage, just behind the cockpit.

The pipeline secured and sealed, its ugly mouth gently persuaded into the opening on the aircraft, the *mourst* on the ladder nodded to a colleague within the control room. Delgado saw a *mourst* flick a series of switches, and a moment later the pipe began to writhe visibly, as if a high volume of fluid was passing through it into the machine.

As this happened, the young *mourst* returned to the automatic and placed the plate back inside it. Muttering to himself, he slammed the casing shut and slid open a panel on the unit's side. The *mourst* jabbed at controls Delgado and Ash could not see, then slid the panel shut again. When it stuck slightly, the Seriatt thumped it with a clenched fist.

'Nasty temper he's got there,' Ash observed. 'He must be *really* hungry.'

The *mourst* turned and walked back into the room, slamming the door shut once the courier had moved back into the corridor.

The automatic performed another of its slow turns, and began trundling along the corridor once more, squeaking noisily. Delgado glanced both ways along the tunnel. Seeing it was deserted, he moved swiftly out of the recess and edged sideways next to the courier, matching the machine's speed. Carefully he opened the access panel as the *mourst* had done, and saw a small backlit touchscreen and a few buttons. He studied the controls. All seemed to have multiple functions accessible via menu layers. The text on the screen made little sense to him, but as he moved sideways along the tunnel, followed by an amused Ash, he prodded at the tabs displayed.

Three options appeared: one word he recognised as the Counian word for 'human'. He pressed it as the machine stopped and prepared to turn a corner. The information on the display updated, with all text now in a script he could read. From then, manipulation of the device was simple, and he thanked the Andamour Council for its insistence that all programmable devices carry multi-language options.

Almost falling on a couple of occasions, Delgado tried to reprogramme the automatic as it made its way back to wherever the unwanted food had been cooked. Eventually, after taking several wrong turns with the menu system, the machine halted abruptly. There was a quiet wheezing sound from somewhere beneath it and a quiet ticking noise, like that made by a hot object cooling rapidly. Delgado cycled through a few more menus until he reached the option of JOB PARAMETERS. He delved into the submenus and made alterations to the machine's task priorities and scheduling protocols.

'You know what you're doing there, Delgado?' asked Ash as she kept watch in either direction along the tunnel.

'I think so. We'll have to just wait and see, though, I guess.' He slid the panel shut and unlatched the automatic's side. He then lifted the thin metal casing on top of the unit, bent down and reached inside. He removed the plate, wiped spilled sauce from inside the automatic on to the tunnel floor with the edge of his hand, then wiped his hand on the carpet. He looked at Ash. 'OK, get in,' he said.

'Get in?' She looked at the stained, sticky space within the automatic.

'Yes, get in. And be quick about it.' He reached out and placed his right hand gently but firmly on the back of Ashala's head, and pushed her down and forward into the courier's compartment.

She turned in the confined space and sat on her haunches, her knees tucked under her chin. 'I'm not keen on confined spaces,' she said, looking around with distaste. 'I'll do most things, but I'm not happy about this.'

'What about the *Talionis*?' asked Delgado as he, too, climbed into the machine. 'That's a pretty confined space. And with all that water pressing down . . .'

'That's different and you know it.'

'Well, we won't have to be in here for long, so quit moaning, OK?'

'Sure. Whatever you say. What have you got planned, anyway?'

Delgado reached out and pulled down the metal panel. It shut out all light except thin lines of brilliance around the edge that seemed too bright given the relative gloom in the tunnel. 'You've heard of the Trojan horse, right?'

'Of course.'

'Well, this is going to be the Trojan courier. We're going to give them a little something more than they expected for their lunch.'

After a few seconds the machine lurched and Delgado and Ash had to brace themselves against the sudden movement. The temperature inside the courier was high, the batteries powering the unit making the floor hot. The atmosphere was stifling, particularly given the lingering odour of the *mourst*'s unwanted meal. Within a few minutes they were both sweating heavily, rocking from side to side as the automatic made continuous adjustments to its course.

'Better get that gun of yours ready,' advised Delgado. 'You'll be needing it in a minute.'

Ash readied the weapon. Its small screen became illuminated, casting soft light across her glistening face. 'So when this *mourst* opens this thing up to see what its brought him this time, we let rip, right?'

'Right. If he ordered something else he'll come looking for it. If he didn't he'll most likely have a look see, anyway.'

'Out of curiosity.'

'Spot on.'

'This is all assuming you've programmed the courier correctly, of course.'

'Well, yes. Do you doubt my ability to re-programme an automatic?'

'Hey, Delgado, I'm just concerned I'm going to have to save your skinny ass again, that's all.'

They felt the automatic stop and perform another jerky turn. Delgado leaned forward, pushed the metal panel open slightly and peered out. 'We're there,' he said. 'Get ready.'

They heard the door to the room open. The automatic waited a few seconds before proceeding, then they felt another lurch and a slight bump as the unit passed through the doorway into the room. There was an increase in the noise level. Machines outside hummed and ticked, and printers squawked as they vomited paper on to the floor in tumbling heaps. *Mourst* and *vilume* conversation could be heard, interspersed by the odd sound of Seriattic laughter. As Delgado checked his small sidearm again, he licked his top lip; it was salty with sweat. Beside him, Ashala seemed more calm and relaxed than he could ever remember.

A *mourst*'s voice came close to the automatic, the figure's movement just visible through the slight gap between the metal panel and the main part of the courier's shell. There was apparently a response from someone else in the room, and the *mourst* paused in front of the automatic. Within the machine, Delgado and Ash peered out, waiting for their moment to come. The *mourst* laughed – the dark, husky sound of his kind – and muttered something to himself as he stooped to open the courier, probably complaining about the fact that the automatic's cover was not even latched properly. As he raised the metal casing, the full noise of the room burst on to them.

Delgado saw the *mourst*'s feet and shins in front of them, then the legs of others crossing the room, chair pedestals, more feet, an overflowing litter bin piled high with paper. Delgado held up a hand, indicating to Ash that she should hold fire. As the Seriatt folded the upper part of the panel in half and on top of the courier, the *mourst* was looking away from them, speaking to a colleague to his left. Behind him numerous *mourst* and a couple of *vilume* went about their business, ignorant of the presence of the two visitors. Even those looking past the courier did not see Delgado and Ash, who were hidden in shadow.

The *mourst* was younger than Delgado had realised, probably not even fully grown, merely an adolescent. His features were softer than those of other *mourst* they had encountered, the ridges of ligament at his neck less pronounced, his voice less abrasive, yet he possessed the same chiselled beauty as his more mature counterparts.

The young *mourst* looked down into the courier. He said nothing, clearly not comprehending what was before him. Then he cocked his head slightly, simply staring at the two humans squatting in the space where his meal should be. Delgado smiled thinly and felt a surge of emotion that transported him back to a time long past.

'Sorry about this, old chum,' he said. 'It's shame to ruin such a handsome face.' And with that he fired his weapon.

Due to the confines of the environment in which his gun would be used Delgado had set the weapon at relatively low strength, but had specified a very narrow spread, thereby increasing the efficiency of the lower amount of energy that would be discharged. He had also instructed the weapon to use IFPO – Intelligent Flux Projectile Ordnance – which possessed a range of attributes that enabled a skilled user to gain an advantage in otherwise difficult situations. In this case Delgado ordered the ammunition to postpone full formation for a fraction of a second. As a result, the only indication that anything had happened at all was that a hole appeared above and slightly to the left of the *mourst*'s right eye. No blood emerged from the wound, just a thin wisp of dark smoke.

For a second the *mourst* simply seemed to look down at them, but there was a certain vacancy to his stare, as if he were focusing just behind them. Saliva began to trail from his slightly open mouth, and he wore an expression a human might adopt if caught engaged in a particularly lurid sexual act.

Then, as the ammunition formed and unleashed its pent-up energy inside his skull, a certain acrid odour was evident, an odd combination of burning rubber and ammonia. The *mourst* teetered. Delgado glanced around the small area of the room he could see from within the courier. The Seriatt's colleagues continued with their work unaware that anything was amiss. Delgado reached out and gently pushed the swaying Seriatt with his right hand. The creature fell back, and landed heavily on the floor, a dead weight.

'Are we waiting until we can see the whites of their eyes, Delgado?' Ash whispered.

'Let's get as many of them as possible in one place,' he said. 'Easier to deal with that way. You should set that thing to a rapid-fire setting if you can work out how.'

Assuming the *mourst* had fainted or had a seizure of some kind, several other Seriatts rushed over and crouched next to him, a sudden cacophony of urgent, concerned voices almost drowning out the thin racket of the printers. Delgado saw one of the Seriatts point to the hole in the *mourst*'s head. Another *mourst* looked directly at the open side of the courier, but did not appear to see them immediately. Delgado smiled as the creature's posture changed, leaning forward to peer into the unit. The *mourst* pointed and said something, but no one seemed to hear him.

Delgado calmly adjusted his weapon's settings, and a very slight vibration ran through the gun. The *mourst* took a step forward, then said something else, this time more loudly. Others crouching next to the fallen Seriatt turned to look. One stood, another shouted an exclamation or warning.

'I guess now would be a good time,' said Delgado calmly.

'A very good time,' Ash replied.

They opened fire and stepped from their hiding place simultaneously.

The room became a scene of chaos and terror. Seriatts shouted, screamed or cowered; *vilume* tried to escape or hide, while *mourst* blundered stupidly towards the courier despite being unarmed. They were quickly gunned down, their cries of anger and defiance distorted into wails of agony. The temperature in the room rose rapidly, accentuating the thick stench of burning flesh, urine and faeces.

Within thirty seconds all the Seriatts Delgado could see were dead. He was uncertain how many, but he was also sure some had escaped. Ash was particularly enthusiastic, firing her weapon long and hard. Delgado made a mental note to keep out of her way: a friendly fire incident he could do without.

They stopped firing and Delgado looked around. The door into the tunnel was still open. Apart from the ceaseless grating of the printers and the endless tongues of paper lolling from them, the room was quiet and still.

'We better get this door secured,' said Ash. She shut the door, walked around the courier, closed the hinged lid and latched it, then pushed at the top of the unit. The flimsy upper two-thirds of the courier's shell leaned, but the machine did not budge. She crouched and pushed against the bottom of the device, but the battery housings were heavy, the caterpillar treads wider than she had estimated, and the unit extremely robust around the drives. It was solid, and would not move. She looked across at Delgado, who had walked across the room and was looking into the launch tube. 'For Christ's sake, would you give me a hand here, Delgado? We need to get this thing up against that door. It'll give us a little more time if someone tries to get in.'

'OK, calm down. Why not try and programme it so it moves itself into position? Save a hell of a lot of sweat.'

'No good. It's taken a stray round.' She pointed at a hole in the side of the unit; the control panel cover and the touch-screen beneath were shattered. 'It's going nowhere on its own. Now come on.'

Delgado walked over, and was as surprised as she at the courier's weight. It took them several minutes to push the machine into position to block the closed door.

They walked back across the room and looked through the window overlooking the launch tube. The aircraft in front of them was small, its wings and tail short. The fuselage was like two fat, partially merged cylinders, with an intake at the front and a propulsion outlet at the rear. The technology was ancient and brute, but would generate huge amounts of thrust. The intake at the front was an erotic oval mouth that would suck in air to be compressed, heated and forced out of the rear in a flatulent shaft of flaming gas and heat. The fact that the fuels that powered the machine were almost certainly highly volatile and difficult to use safely would add to the spectacle of the race: a cone of blue flame would always be more entertaining and dramatic than the vague red or purple shimmers produced by containment field generators. A thick hatch on top of the cockpit – a silvery bulge about one quarter of the way along the upper surface of the fuselage – was open.

The technicians were no longer working on the craft, having disappeared through a thick door a little further along the tube to Delgado's right. He walked to the door in the glass wall and tried it, but it was sealed. He looked at the aircraft again. As well as being attached to the tube's wall by the thick umbilical pipe connected earlier, several thick cables linked the tube floor and the aircraft's nose. Thin white vapour drifted downwards from a small exhaust flue in the side of its fuselage. Looking past the aircraft, Delgado could see only a short distance into the tube itself as it rose steeply a short distance away, the thin brown rails upon which the aircraft's cradle was mounted fading into the darkness. Small red lights set into the top of the tube cast an eerie glow, and reminded Delgado of the shaft into the Olympus Mons hangar.

He looked through the oval holes in the side of the launch tube at the others beyond. They contained similar machines, but these were partially obscured from view. There was still a certain amount of activity – figures in sealed suits manhandled pipes or peered at hand-held devices linked to the aircraft – but there were noticeably fewer personnel than before.

At first he could not see Michael, but then he appeared from the other side of the small racing craft as he climbed a ladder, becoming visible above the fuselage of his machine. He was a handsome young man, of that there was no doubt. His blue eyes appeared to shine, and stood out even across the hundred or more metres separating them. He was wearing what appeared to be a black racing suit. Its neck was close fitting, and appeared to have several open couplings at the top, just under the back of Michael's head.

Delgado narrowed his eyes and tried to focus his nobics on the youth. There was something puzzling about the admittedly distorted mental patterns Delgado perceived in him. He was not Myson's son, that was not in doubt. But there was a resonance. Although it was something Delgado could not pinpoint, it was oddly familiar. Perhaps Michael had not been the randomly chosen infant that suited Myson's means Delgado had always assumed. Could it be possible that Delgado knew Michael's father? It would make sense to some extent. Many would have been willing to give up their off-spring to serve Myson's purposes, in order to fast-track their way up the Structure hierarchy, but he could think of no one who would have had a child around that time. The feelings Michael's traces stirred were disturbing, and made Delgado feel somewhat unsettled.

There appeared to be something of an argument in progress, several *mourst* and *vilume* in elaborate robes voicing opinions through a clearly stressed *vilume* interpreter. Then he saw another figure.

'Well, I'll be.'

'What is it?'

'Osephius. See the guy standing on the far side of the tube with his arms folded and a bored expression on his face? That's him.'

'He doesn't seem to want to get involved in whatever's going on, does he? He's quite good-looking.'

Delgado snorted briefly. 'No, confrontation isn't exactly his style. He always was a sly one. He'd be the kind to incite a riot then watch from the sidelines as the police waded in.'

'You don't like him do you?'

'Is it that obvious?'

Michael opened the aircraft's hatch and looked down into the cockpit, then at someone on the tube floor whose legs were visible beneath the aircraft's nose. Michael was making movements with hands.

'What do you think they're talking about?' Ash asked.

'Looks like they're discussing the machine's movement through the air. The *vilume* translator's earning his pay, that's for sure.'

'Looks like a her to me.'

Delgado shrugged. 'Maybe, maybe.'

Michael climbed to the top of the ladder and clambered into the cockpit. For a moment he stood inside the machine, the top of the fuselage coming no higher than his thighs. He then crouched, and slid further down until his body was visible only from the chest up.

A young *mourst* wearing a small black headset appeared at the top of the ladder, carrying a helmet. Michael took it from him and put it on, tilting his head to one side and then the other as the *mourst* connected it to the couplings on the suit. Michael patted the *mourst*'s forearm as a gesture of thanks, then wriggled and writhed, sliding into the cockpit until he seemed to be almost lying down.

The *mourst* opened a small panel next to the cockpit hatch and plugged a narrow cable trailing from his headset into it. The Seriatt appeared to converse directly with Michael for a few moments, before closing and sealing the hatch. He then unplugged the comms lead, climbed down the ladder and removed it from the side of the aircraft. As he carried the ladder away, Delgado noticed that everyone else in the tube was leaving, passing through a door into a room similar to the one he and Ash were in. He then saw that the third tube also appeared to be deserted.

'Shit.'

'What is it?'

Delgado hurried to the control desk and studied the small screens, glancing briefly at the needles flicking back and forth across the small dials and the heaps of crumpled paper on the floor below the still clattering printers. The Seriattic characters revealed nothing.

'What is it, Delgado?' Ash repeated.

He strode to the window again. 'They're preparing to launch.' He closed his eyes and concentrated his nobics as much as he was able. He knew Cascari was close. He opened his eyes again. 'I've got to get into that aircraft.'

'But we don't know how long is left.'

'Long enough, I reckon.' He was leaning over the desk, concentrating on one particular screen, cycling through displays.

'What are you doing?'

'Trying to find human or Counian language options. There don't seem to be any.'

'Equipment's probably too old,' she said. 'Too expensive to update the languages on this stuff.'

'Delgado deftly touched onscreen tabs, trying to work his way through a maze of information sheets. 'Come on, come on,' he said. 'I really need to get that door open, right now. Hang on, I think I've got it.' He touched the screen again and waited. The display updated and he touched a few more tabs. The door to the tube in the corner of the room clicked. Ash reached out and pulled at the handle; the door opened easily.

Delgado rushed across the room. 'You coming?' he asked.

'What? You think I'm going to stay here? You're stuck with me for a while yet, Delgado.'

The air in the tube was noticeably warmer than in the control room, and felt slightly damp. There was also a faintly unpleasant odour.

A short flight of steps led from the control room to the tube floor. The aircraft sat on top of a fragile-looking cradle. Like the thin tracks upon which it rested, the cradle possessed the same organic appearance as the rest of the tube: deep brown-purple in colour, it looked like a mesh of rigid ligaments, riddled with veins of varying sizes.

The end of the tube was two hundred metres to the right, behind the aircraft, narrowing in a sphincter-like coil. Halfway between this and the rear of the aircraft was a door in the tube wall. It was presumably through this that the Seriattic technicians had departed earlier, although there was no indication of there being anyone in the room now, where it might lead or what it might contain.

The structures that formed the tube itself were much larger than they had appeared from within the control room. They were like fossilised arteries, stippled and blistered, although whether this was simply due to the heat of the aircraft's engines Delgado was unable to decide. Narrower veins and ridges trailed off the larger structures, merging with the floor and rising to form the slender tracks on which the cradle stood. The uneven floor also seemed to give way slightly underfoot as he walked towards the aircraft.

As he climbed the ladder that was leaning up against the aircraft's fuselage he opened a few extra sensory streams, despite their increasing instability. There was imminent danger, the intense traces he felt similar to those he had experienced prior to a major battle. It reminded him of long ago, on Buhatt and other worlds; back when he had been someone else.

He stepped on to the top rung of the ladder and then into the aircraft, so that he was standing on the small padded seat in the cockpit. He eased himself down into a sitting position. As Ash climbed the ladder, he felt around beneath the seat and found a release mechanism that allowed it to slide forward and down slightly, with a smooth motion and an oiled clicking sound. He manoeuvred himself into the cockpit as the seat moved, gradually leaning back until the seat locked in place.

There were two small triangular windows directly in front of him, although they looked more grey than clear, bearing a myriad of scars, scratches, pits and scores. Their small size and the fact that they would not provide an extensive or helpful view of the pilot's surroundings only emphasised the skill involved in surviving the sport. Without the benefit of artificial aids, flying in a straight line would be difficult enough, let alone landing or performing complex manoeuvres.

A series of smaller, circular portals ran along behind the two main windows, allowing the pilot to look to the side. There were two more towards the rear of the cockpit that would offer a limited rearward view. Cascari had been right: there was no ejection facility. Indeed, there did not even seem to be any method of exiting the machine in particular haste. It would be impossible to open the hatch at any kind of speed due to air pressure.

Ash leaned over the top of the machine and into the hatch. 'Comfortable?' she asked.

'Not really. I can't believe this is how they race. My feet are almost level with my chest. I've got to stretch my neck as much as I can to see through the windows, which are, in any case, virtually opaque. My elbows are digging into my ribs I'm so squashed into this seat, and I can only just reach the rudder stirrups. They must be mad.'

'Oh, I don't know. It doesn't look that bad to me.'

'You wait until you get in here. If you *can* get in here. It's going to be cosy, believe me.'

She stepped over, putting her right foot next to his right shoulder, then her left foot next to his left shoulder. 'You've had it too easy in the past, Delgado, that's your trouble. Slide forward a bit more will you?'

'I can't. This is as far forward as the seat will go. I'm not as tall as a *mourst*, remember?'

'OK, I'll squeeze in anyway. Hang on.' Ash edged herself down, grunting with the effort as she slid her legs past Delgado's arms. Eventually they were both crammed into the tiny cockpit, her thighs pressed against his neck, her legs just below the windows on either side of the instrument panels.

'I've always admired your calves, Ash' he said. 'You didn't know, did you?'

'Just keep your goddamn mind on the job in hand, Delgado. You think you can fly this thing?'

'Well, it's extremely basic. A bulky, heavy craft. Its surfaces are smooth but its aerodynamics are poor. The wings are too short to provide any real lift, and there's been little attempt made to increase the efficiency of the airflow over the fuselage. Sheer speed's essential if it's to perform effectively. It'll have a high stall speed, too. I guarantee you, it'll happily fall out of the sky at the drop of a hat.'

'Then just make sure you don't drop your goddamn hat, Delgado.' She reached up and slammed the hatch shut, and was immediately forced to angle her head slightly to one side due to the lack of space.

Delgado squinted at the row of instruments set into a curved black panel just centimetres in front of his face. 'How am I supposed to read these?' he said. 'They're so close to my face it's uncomfortable to focus on them.'

'Focus on my wonderful calves instead. If you want to swap places, I'm happy to do so because this isn't going to be a particularly comfortable ride for me, either.'

The instruments immediately in front of him displayed dark green Seriattic text, which changed occasionally as it updated; its brightness fluctuating along with an audible hum and a slight vibration. Above these, set deeper into the cockpit, next to Ash's knees, were two rows of three, small, chrome-rimmed dials, similar in appearance to some of those in the control room. The two on the right were slightly larger than the others. Fine black characters on plain white backgrounds were indicated by illuminated needles. At that moment, all registered zero.

He checked the main controls. 'OK. We have a joystick.' He gripped the contoured control loosely in his fingers. It was clearly designed for a *mourst*'s large hands and long fingers, but he could handle it easily. He moved the joystick gently; it was easy but firm. He heard dull clunking sounds as the aircraft's control surfaces moved in spasmodic throes, like the fins of dying fish. 'No hydraulics, huh. Great.'

'I wish you'd quit complaining, Delgado.'

'Sorry. This is the throttle.' He gripped a sliding handle set into the left side of the cockpit and pushed it forward very slightly, but with no results. 'Foot stirrups for the rudder controls. That's pretty much it.'

'But that's basically all we need, right?'

'And perhaps a bit of luck.'

Movement caught Delgado's eye and he turned his head, looking to the left, towards the control room. He could see figures moving around within it, tall silhouettes. A *mourst* enforcer stood in the doorway to the launch tube. He had a sidearm in his right hand but was looking back into the control room, apparently arguing with one of his colleagues. Through the shallow window above the control desks Delgado saw another figure stand upright.

A loud and regular bleeping, low in frequency but rising slightly in pitch with each note, was suddenly emitted by a speaker somewhere in the cockpit.

'What the hell's that, Delgado?'

'Damned if I know.' He looked at the instruments in front of him. Most were now blank, but one displayed a row of characters that changed with each beep. 'Looks like a countdown to me,' he said. 'You better hang on to your breeches. He looked back towards the enforcer who had walked down a few of the steps into the launch tube, but had stopped and was now talking to a *vilume* Delgado could see within the control room. The *vilume* beckoned the enforcer back urgently. The *mourst* looked at the aircraft once more before turning and walking back up the steps again with obvious reluctance. The moment he disappeared from view the door was slammed shut. A row of Seriatts watched impassively through the shallow window. Delgado waved cheerfully at them.

'Get ready,' he said. 'I don't think there's long left to go.' He craned his neck, looking to the right. Through the portals he could see the outlines of the other aircraft in their launch tubes, and could clearly sense the rising tension in their pilots. Michael's stream remained difficult to analyse completely. It was as if Delgado was somehow perceiving it in the wrong way. He could also sense Cascari somewhere nearby, almost certainly in another tube. He was also nervous.

As Delgado looked back towards the control room again he noticed harness clips protruding from the rear of the cockpit; it occurred to him then that they were not strapped in to the small projectile. He reached over his left shoulder with his right hand and pulled gently at one of the clips. A thick, padded strap extended smoothly from the rear of the cockpit past Ash's legs and diagonally across his chest, fitting into a catch by his right hip; a second strap crossed in the opposite direction.

'Hey, what about me?' Ash asked.

'Sorry, Ash, this vehicle was not intended to carry passengers. Can you move?'

She grunted slightly. 'Not a bit.'

'Then you've nothing to worry about,' he said.

He tugged at the buckles to tighten the straps, but due to lack of room in the cockpit and the restrictions imposed on him by the harness itself and Ashala's legs, he was unable to tighten it as much as he would have liked. Other pilots would have their harnesses tightened for them.

'You nice and secure now, Delgado?'

'Very comfortable, thank you.'

'Wish I could say the same. I'm getting a stiff neck already.'

The beeping suddenly increased rapidly in frequency, a series of extremely short notes followed by one long one.

'I think this is it,' said Delgado. 'Get ready.'

The Laboratory of Continuity Studies, Seriatt

The Continuity Scientists ran to the laboratory when informed of events by the *mourst* enforcer they had left watching over the portal. Upon their arrival, they were shocked by the sight that greeted them.

Hescar lay on the floor in front of the gate. His leather

clothing was ripped in many places. He looked much thinner than when he had left just two days before. Sherlaq knelt next to him. 'Fetch a physician,' she said. 'He needs urgent treatment.'

The *conosq* gently rolled Hescar over. His face was bruised, scratched and dirty; his left eye was swollen and he appeared to have lost some teeth on one side of his mouth. 'Hescar. Hescar, can you hear me? You are home again.' Hescar moaned and placed his left hand to his head.

The Oracles walked into the room. Silently, dispassionately, they approached the Continuity Scientists and looked down at the injured *mourst*.

'Can you hear me, Hescar?' Sherlaq repeated. 'Can you tell us what you saw?'

Hescar was uncommunicative for some moments. Then, when he eventually did open his eyes and look directly at her, she saw so much more than physical pain in his expression.

'It is no use,' he said, his voice little more than a hoarse whisper. 'There is no point.' He swallowed, closed his eyes and sighed wearily.

Sherlaq glanced up at her colleagues, then looked back to Hescar. 'What do you mean, Hescar?' she asked nervously. 'Why do you say this?'

Hescar chuckled weakly, a thin *mourst* cough. 'I have seen our fate,' he said. 'I have seen what the future holds. The Oracles are worthless. They know nothing. There is no future. Seriatt is doomed to ruin. It is unavoidable.' And then Hescar began to sob, the sound similar to *mourst* laughter, yet filled with immeasurable despair.

As the *vilume* physician entered the laboratory and began tending Hescar, Sherlaq stood and looked at Oracle Entuzo. 'Do you have any idea what he might have seen?' she asked.

'I do not,' replied the Oracle, still looking down at the *mourst*. 'He will have seen a specific future. Through the

Destiny Mask we Oracles see many futures. It is possible that we have simply not encountered the particular future he has visited.'

Sherlaq looked anxious. 'Is it possible that he has visited *the* future? The event that *will* occur?'

Oracle Entuzo looked at the Sherlaq. 'There is no single future, *Conosq* Sherlaq. This is what so many fail to appreciate. The future occurs only as a result of the actions we take now, and is not fixed. For example, there was a moment at which we had not reached the decision to send Hescar on his journey. Many futures were open to us then. Only when we made the decision that he should go did the moment of his return, and of telling us what he had seen, become more likely. It is thus with each moment that we exist, every decision we make. All contribute to the possibilities. Nothing is certain.'

'Then what should we do now, given what he has said?'

'We should tell the Administrators immediately,' said a *vilume* scientist. 'Action should be taken.'

'No,' Entuzo asserted firmly. 'The Administrators must not learn of this.' She looked at the scientists gathered around her. 'No one outside this room must learn of this.'

The scientists looked uncomfortable.

'Why do you say this, Oracle?' asked Sherlaq. 'Surely it is better that the Administrators be informed . . .'

'No. We tell them nothing. They will misunderstand and react inappropriately. We must speak to Hescar ourselves when he has recovered sufficiently to convey details of his experiences, then we will have a better idea of how to proceed.' She looked at the portal. 'Can this device be moved to a different location?'

Sherlaq looked at the machine. 'It would be difficult but . . .'

'But it could be moved?'

'Yes.'

'Very well. It should be taken to the Chamber of Visions immediately.'

Sherlaq looked perturbed. 'But why, Oracle? It is better that . . .'

'You will arrange for the portal to be moved to the Chamber of Visions,' Entuzo asserted. 'Now we know that it works effectively, the Chamber of Visions is where it truly belongs.'

'Very well, Oracle.' Sherlaq bowed slightly.

'And remember this,' said Entuzo. 'You are to tell no one. When Hescar is well enough to talk, I will speak with him myself. But no one else must know of his return, or what he claims to have seen. Do you understand?'

'We do, Oracle.'

But as Oracle Entuzo left the room, Sherlaq was uncertain whether she could keep her promise.

The Koss-Miet racing facility, Astragarda, Seriatt

The aircraft lurched and there was a faint click somewhere behind them, followed by a sudden and very loud humming. An amber light to the right of the throttle stalk became illuminated, then all other noise was drowned out by an incredibly loud roar. The entire aircraft began to shake, rocking on its delicate cradle so much that Delgado could no longer read the information on the small screen in front of him. His teeth clashed and he bit his tongue. He called to Ash to ask if she was OK, but he was unable to hear even his own voice in the cataclysmic environment.

He leaned forward as far as he could, looking towards the other two machines to his right. They were rocking visibly, a huge blue flame erupting from the rear of each. Their own aircraft lurched again and Seriattic text appeared on one of the displays in front of him.

Then, over even the immense noise of the engine, there was a slick, moist sound and a thick, pungent aroma. Darkness suddenly gripped the small aircraft as the tunnel walls contracted around the machine. The aircraft's hull groaned as the tract tightened its grip, the muscular tube wall squirming against the aircraft's windows.

The sound of the aircraft's power plant deepened, and in unison, the small ripples in the muscle gripping the aircraft moved towards the rear, then suddenly moved forward again. Delgado's guts seemed to rise in his body, and he felt intensely sick and dizzy as the launch tube expelled the capsule like a waste product.

Delgado moaned softly as the aircraft accelerated, pushed rapidly through the gut-like tube, the power of the engine pressing against his back and increasing the weight of his body. Within moments the aircraft reached an attitude of around fifty degrees, nose-high. Through the portals in front of him, he could see a small grey disc in the distance, quickly growing in size as the aircraft sped towards it. The circle of light continued to widen until the small machine was spat from the launch tube on a wave of hot gas and foul noise.

The sound of the engines faded substantially as, suddenly bathed in light, the capsule was released into the wide, open sky. Delgado felt lift in the aircraft as the air flowed rapidly over its smooth surfaces.

He tried to turn his head, but was restricted due to the limited space. 'You OK back there?' He called.

'Fine. Some ride, huh?'

'Damn right. Now we have to work out which of these machines Michael and Cascari are in.' He looked to his right. The two aircraft from the other tubes were powering through the air on columns of flame, undulating gently in the Seriattic atmosphere as they climbed steeply. Beyond them he could see two other groups of three machines, grey dashes in the pale sky. He watched them for a moment. They seemed to be turning away, their pilots coaxing them towards the coast.

Then, out over the bay, Delgado saw a pulse of bright light, and a shadowy circle hanging in the sky between plumes of frost-white cumulus.

It was the buoy.

'There's our primary target,' he said. 'If we don't get through that we've got no chance of getting to either of them.'

'Sorry, Delgado, all I can see from here is the back of your head. Did you know you're getting a bald patch?'

'They say baldness is a sign of virility.'

'Is that right? What's your excuse?'

The buoy flashed again, a stark signal. He eased the joystick gently to the right, rolling the aircraft on to one wing tip, then pulled back on the stick. He groaned as the speeding aircraft turned, and heard Ash exclaim behind him. Darkness encroached on his peripheral vision and specks danced before his eyes as blood drained from his head, his body pressed into the seat. He eased out of the turn and waited a moment to recover, then attempted the turn again. He strained his lower body. His eyes bulged and he felt perspiration on his forehead as he became several times his normal weight. It required immense effort to maintain the turn for as long as he needed to.

With the forces acting upon him weakening as he eased out of the turn, Delgado looked down to his right. Past the tiny wreaths of vapour dancing away from the wing tips in tight coils, he could see the launch tubes far below, their scale lost in the wider landscape; the grandstands were visible as small grey rectangles in patchwork fields.

'You still OK back there?' Delgado asked. This time Ashala did not respond. 'Ash? Are you OK?' No reply. Delgado assumed she had passed out during the turn.

But he had no time to worry about her now. She would regain consciousness soon enough. He looked towards the buoy ahead. He was far behind the other racers. If he didn't get through the buoy among the first half dozen machines he would not be catapulted on to the next, wherever that might be. He watched the movements of the small cluster of aircraft at the rear of the main group ahead of him. In a ragged group of eight, they looked like slivers of metal occasionally reflecting shards of sunlight, brilliant halos marking their engine outlets.

As the swelling circular buoy was partially obscured by cloud, Delgado extended his hyperconsciousness in an attempt to establish which of the machines Cascari and Michael were piloting.

Suddenly there was a loud thud and Delgado was flung against the harness, his head forced forward by the pressure of Ashala's body pushing against him. The switchback from powered to unpowered flight as the huge engine disengaged was like being slammed into a wall. The roar of the power plant was also replaced by the smooth sound of air rushing past the cockpit, with the occasional dull thump as wind buffeted the hull. The amber light next to the throttle was no longer illuminated, and when he looked ahead he saw that the engines of the aircraft ahead of him had also been extinguished: the initial launch burn had come to an end.

Delgado could feel his aircraft shedding speed rapidly, yet none of the other pilots seemed to be in a rush to re-ignite their engines, content for the moment to let momentum carry their machines towards the buoy.

Two aircraft to the left of the group drifted close together, one wing of each dipping slightly as they slid through the air. Delgado sensed intense Seriattic traces. The two aircraft jinked and dodged, then hurtled away from each other for a moment before rapidly closing again, their wing tips overlapping. Suddenly their wings touched, the briefest of caresses, and both machines coiled sharply away, seeking safety in clear airspace.

One of the two aircraft was clearly damaged, glittering flakes peeling away from its short wings like fish scales. As the aircraft began to lose speed Delgado closed on it rapidly. He could see it shuddering visibly as a result of the disrupted airflow, the pilot fighting to control the machine.

Without warning the damaged wing sheered away from the fuselage, reflecting regular flashes of light as it fluttered towards the ground, while the rest of the aircraft spun in tight circles. Delgado watched the machine fall until it was too far below him to see.

The other aircraft involved in the collision was now trailing a thin stream of pale fluid or vapour and had fallen behind the other machines. It was descending at increasing speed. The pilot dipped one wing and tried to turn the aircraft, but it lost height rapidly. He was skilful and got the machine back on a level plane within a matter of moments, but it was now facing the wrong direction and was far too low to have any chance of reaching the buoy. Ahead and to the left of the stricken machine the grey jags and ridges of the mountains waited to consume it. Apparently accepting his fate, the pilot ignited the burner and pushed down his aircraft's nose.

The other racers continued towards the buoy. Delgado knew instinctively that Michael and Cascari were among them, and with two of the aircraft now out of the picture there was a greater chance that they would all successfully get the slingshot they needed to reach the next buoy.

One by one each of the craft ahead of Delgado began to re-ignite their engines, their pilots beginning to use the raw power at their disposal as they jostled to try and improve their positions. Instead of prolonged applications of thrust, however, they used only sporadic bursts of power, firing their engines for only a few seconds at a time in an effort to conserve fuel.

But Delgado had no time for such strategies, and he gripped the throttle firmly in his left hand. He paused momentarily.

'Ash? You awake?' No reply came. Delgado gazed at the

waiting buoy, which was throbbing like a wound in the sky, raw and bloody.

Then he thumbed the burner ignition.

The acceleration was incredible. Delgado's stomach pitched. The craft around him rattled and shook as if the machine was falling apart. He heard a loud snapping sound just behind his right shoulder, but was unable to turn his head to look for signs of damage due to both the tremendous vibration and the proximity of Ashala's thigh. Everything outside the portals was blurred. The buoy was the only thing he could distinguish with any clarity, and even that was only a shuddering circle just above the nose of his aircraft.

After around twenty seconds Delgado took his thumb off the burner ignition button and was again thrown forward by the sudden loss of thrust. He heard a dull thud behind him as Ash's head lolled against the side of the cockpit.

He glanced around quickly. There were only three race capsules ahead of him. He turned his head and looked back as much as he was able. He saw a couple of aircraft behind him now, fighting for position, rapidly changing places as they tried to avoid being the last to reach the buoy. As he looked at the two machines, first one then the other fired their burners; Delgado heard the roar as huge wedges of energy burst from them, and the machines surged forward. Delgado extended his hyperconsciousness, and felt clear human tones in the traces he perceived. He smiled to himself. It was them.

With Michael and Cascari powering away from him he ignited his own burner again. Focusing on the glow of the other two aircrafts' engines, Delgado prepared to turn off his own engine the moment they did so. By the time they shut their power plants down, however, their speed was immense, and the buoy a huge circle in the sky, so close and so large that Delgado had to move his head to see its upper extremities, with its lower quarter hidden by his aircraft's nose.

The buoy seemed to be constructed from thick, gigantic

sheets of rusting metal, its surface stippled with the rivets linking the many plates from which it was made. The circle pulsed brightly as a regular throb of immense energy passed around its inner edge. Although the space within the buoy appeared empty, at close range he could see that the clouds beyond were somehow indistinct, rippling slightly as if reflected in a disturbed pool of water. Delgado could feel the buoy's pull acting upon his aircraft, and wondered at the tamed energies that were used to catapult the machines to the next waypoint.

He became aware of the other racers entering his peripheral vision, and glanced to either side. The three nearest machines were closing on him. Delgado looked towards Michael's and Cascari's aircraft and extended his hyperconsciousness, seeking traces of emotion, clues to their perceptions and decision-making processes in an attempt to predict their actions.

Due to Delgado's familiarity with him, Cascari's patterns came most easily. The young man was angry, bitter, determined. Although Delgado was also able to identify Michael relatively easily, his emotional state was harder to resolve.

As Delgado looked across at Cascari's craft, bright spikes of sunlight reflected off the metal frames around its windows. Michael's craft drifted towards Cascari's. It was not a move influenced by airflow or changes in atmospheric density, but a deliberate change of direction. As the two machines came closer together Delgado sensed the purity of Cascari's desire to take the place he believed was rightfully his. The intensity of his son's emotion surprised him.

He glanced ahead, at the shimmering centre of the buoy. They were approaching it rapidly even without thrust, their speed being shed less rapidly than before due to the buoy's pull. As a burner ignited on another race craft, Delgado gripped his own throttle control and thumbed the ignition several times in rapid succession, exclaiming each time his capsule surged forward.

He became aware of slight movement behind him. 'You awake now, Ash?' he called between bursts of power.

'Yeah. What happened?'

'You blacked out when I pulled a high-G turn.'

'Wow. Is that the buoy?'

'Well, if it's not, it's one hell of a doughnut.'

'Christ, I'm aching back here. Do you know which aircraft is Cascari's?'

'I think it's that one.' Delgado pointed through one of the scarred windows. 'If he's not careful he's going to kill himself. He seems intent on killing Michel before the race is over anyway. So much so I think he's lost sight of what we're trying to do here.'

Carefully, Delgado altered course, raising his aircraft's nose and guiding it to the left. The three aircraft were in a close group now, separated by less than fifty metres. Cascari and Michael were both slightly closer to the buoy. Delgado heard Ashala moan as he pushed their aircraft's nose down, aiming directly at the centre of the gigantic hoop.

Then, ahead of them, the leading race craft entered the field.

The noise generated by the buoy rose in volume and there was a momentary but noticeable increase in the speed at which the energy pulse circled its rim. The capsule within the field became a blurred shape, a ghostly, almost transparent form, before it greyed, faded and shimmered rapidly before disappearing completely.

Delgado blinked. Although the area of sky he could see through the buoy was the same as that he could see around it, apart from the slight distortion, the capsule that had just passed through it was no longer there.

He looked quickly to the left and then the right. He was mid-way between Michael and Cascari, but slightly higher, the three of them speeding towards the waiting energy field. With only a short distance to go there was no time for complex manoeuvres. Delgado could feel the field pulling his capsule forward, increasing the speed of his machine.

He began to feel dizzy and nauseous and knew instinctively that Michael and Cascari did too.

'I don't feel so good, Delgado.'

'It's OK. I think it's just the buoy. It'll pass once we go through. I hope.'

Delgado glanced behind him and saw the rest of the racers rapidly gaining on the leaders, their burners aflame. Delgado looked at Michael's and Cascari's machines with uncertainty. It was imperative that they all went through the buoy or that none of them did. He looked ahead again. The upper and lower extremities of the buoy could no longer be seen they were so close to it.

The three pilots lit their burners simultaneously and all three machines rushed towards the waiting field of energy. Ash and Delgado both gasped at the acceleration. Their's was the first aircraft to enter the shimmering field.

Delgado felt intensely sick and his skin tingled almost to the point of soreness. He felt as if his eyes were about to explode, and suffered a sudden and intense pain in his head. Hearing Ash gasp and swear, he assumed she felt the same, but did not feel able to ask her, so great and overwhelming was his own discomfort.

The capsule shook even more violently, and their universe shrank to the confines of the cockpit as the world beyond became little more than a murky smear. He exclaimed as the machine bucked briefly. His sense of orientation was completely lost, and for several seconds he felt as though he was in a wild, tumbling freefall, while behind them the aircraft's power plant continued to scream.

'What the hell's happening, Delgado?' Ash called from the back of the cockpit. She sounded as ill as he felt.

'I don't know.' He spoke falteringly, gasping for breath. 'Just got to sit it out. At least we're through.'

'Yeah, but . . . are they?'

It was a good question. Time stretched. Delgado leaned over and looked through one of the windows. He was just able to discern some blurred shapes, but no detail. Although the buoy's physical depth was at most a few metres, the aircraft appeared to be hanging at its centre, motionless in mid-air rather than moving through it. The inner rim of the buoy itself was a gigantic grey shape extending up and down to both sides. He could just about see the energy pulse at the hoop's uppermost edge. It did not seem to be moving. He could also see Cascari's and Michael's aircraft. They appeared to be suspended in time, no motion evident in their machines whatsoever. Even the ripples in the raging plume of blue flame at the rear of each were eerily still.

Both aircraft were relatively close, both slightly nose-high. Michael's aircraft was angled slightly towards Cascari's, one wing dipped, as if he had been about to make a manoeuvre of some kind the moment they had entered this state of apparent stasis. The vessels shimmered gently every few seconds, a vague shudder washing across them like heat haze, or like a stone breaking a reflection in water. Delgado craned his neck, searching the sky, but none of the other aircraft were visible.

He heard a popping sound, at first very faint, but increasing in volume as the seconds passed, until it was a deafening series of explosions the source of which he could not establish. His vessel began to jar violently with each immense report, his body thrown upward in the loose straps, his head banging on the cockpit hatch above. He heard Ash cry out with each lurch.

He looked to his left expecting to see the other aircraft experiencing the same punishment, but they remained immobile, motionless in the transitional interzone that existed at the centre of the buoy. The craft lurched again and the noise ceased abruptly.

Delgado glanced around, trying to work out what was

happening. As he looked at the buoy it seemed to stretch and separate, as if becoming two buoys from the body of one. Then there was a wet slapping sound and suddenly the immense airborne structure was gone.

The aircraft pitched forward, and suddenly he found himself in free flight again, the aircraft's speed immense. He peered through the main portals in front of him. A city – whether or not it was the one that they had previously visited he did not know – was spread like a thickly textured carpet before him. He caught a glimpse of the tail of Cascari's aircraft's as it descended, chasing Michael's steeply towards the ground.

'Hang on,' he called. 'This could get a little bumpy.'

'Bump*ier*, you mean? Great.'

Delgado rolled their own machine on to its back, and he looked up through the slit window in the hatch above his head. He caught a brief glimpse of the other two aircraft as they slashed diagonally across his line of vision, diving towards the ground. Flame erupted from their engines like elaborate plumage. Then they were gone, out of sight.

Both he and Ash moaned as Delgado pulled the joystick towards his waist. Then his vision darkened as blood flooded his brain.

Delgado snorted like a pig as his aircraft turned sharply and plummeted towards the ground. He yelled as the capsule shuddered violently and his left knee smashed against the bank of small dials next to it. Rods of pain shot through his leg, and the casing surrounding the dials fell apart, the three slender needles darkening abruptly.

The city filled the two main portals in front of him, the white and pastel shades of the elaborate Seriattic buildings intersected by the canals and roads. He glimpsed a vessel on one of the canals, a shining black, multi-masted ship. The thick canvas of its great sails billowed, and its prow cut a deep, clean wake through the water.

He searched for the other two aircraft, clumsily altering the pitch of his own machine as it dropped through the sky. At the same time he extended his hyperconsciousness, seeking the other two men. He sensed anger, confusion, arousal and fear, but these were entwined with other traces, for which he was unable to establish individual sources, or estimate the potential meanings of their different combinations.

He moaned gently as he raised the nose of his aircraft to an angle of around forty-five degrees. The vessel protested as he performed the manoeuvre, its stressed superstructure making discontented noises. Behind him, Ash, crammed into the limited space at the rear of the cockpit, gasped and swore as G-forces played upon her.

A shard of sunlight reflected off something to Delgado's left, low in the sky. He turned his head, searching frantically; and then he saw them – two dashes speeding low over the rooftops, one chasing the other hard. Delgado glanced from altimeter to air-speed indicator and deftly pushed the joystick forward again. The ground rushed up at him and he saw small motor vehicles on the roadways, Seriatts on sidewalks.

He groaned deeply as he checked his descent, his weight increasing as he eased out of the dive. Dancing sparks mottled his vision and a dark cloak began to envelop him. He fought to maintain his grip on the joystick with both sweat-slicked palms. The aircraft levelled out below the rooftops of the highest buildings, and he was immediately forced to roll the machine on to its side, turning hard to avoid a spiral tower of multicoloured glass that flashed beneath him in a blur of diffused colour and light.

He saw the other two craft speeding over the rooftops, jinking to avoid towers and creating curlicues of smoke as they sped through the dense black emissions rising from tall brick chimneys. Confusion and fear were distinct in the traces of the two young men now, their separate states for some reason clearer, more easy to distinguish: Michael's emotional strands were potent and fluctuating rapidly; Cascari was dominated by steady, unwavering determination, and a grim resolution to see his actions through to their ultimate conclusion at whatever cost.

'What the hell's going on, Delgado?' Ash called.

He shook his head. 'I don't know. Cascari seems intent on killing Michael no matter what. We've just got to hope we can stop him killing himself in the process.'

'You think we can still get to the end of the race?'

Delgado shook his head. 'No. We've used too much fuel, lost too much altitude. When all our fuel is gone we're just going to have to land wherever we can. If there's anywhere suitable, that is.'

They were moving at incredibly high speed for such low altitude. Occasionally a spurt of flame would erupt from the rear of Michael's aircraft, immediately followed by a corresponding burst from Cascari's machine. As a result, the distance between the two vessels was relatively consistent.

Delgado ignited his aircraft's burner once more and felt a firm shove in the back as the immense engine pushed it through the air. He descended slightly until his aircraft was directly behind the other two machines and equidistant from them. Their engine outlets gaped like mouths before him, occasionally spewing fire. Delgado thumbed his burner ignition for longer than the other two men to reduce the distance separating them, until his aircraft was only around three lengths behind theirs.

Realising he was catching them too quickly, Delgado briefly applied the airbrakes to shed some speed. The metal assemblies rose from the wings with a faint whine, the aircraft juddering as a result of the increased drag. Michael's aircraft suddenly banked hard right, its burner lit. Cascari responded quickly, his aircraft curving in front of Delgado's.

Delgado's machine skidded on the air as he tried to maintain his relative position, chasing hard as they descended towards the city, which rushed up in a blur of russet and grey slate and glass-domed roof gardens.

The three aircraft turned left and levelled out, their shadows crossing courtyard, street and waterway like spectres, shock-waves dragging roof tiles clattering from buildings; window shutters slammed, shattering panes of glass; frightened animals scurried and cried.

One after the other the burners ignited again as the machines flashed over a road intersection, then turned above one of the wide canals. In triangle formation, with Delgado at the rear, they sped over pleasure cruisers, barges and tramp steamers on the waterway. A light flashed on one of the instrument panels in front of Delgado's face. He looked at it momentarily but was unable to establish whether or not it was important. When he looked up again the other two aircraft had climbed steeply, and directly in front of him was a three-span suspension bridge, its wires taut like harp strings.

There was no time for Delgado to react; the bridge swelled rapidly. He licked dry lips as he gauged the distance between the bridge and the slab of glistering water beneath it. The quality of light made the amount of space available to him virtually impossible to judge. On the other side of the bridge he could see a huge, lumbering paddle steamer, twin funnels belching gouts of dense black smoke, gems of water cascading from its paddle wheels. It was difficult to estimate the vessel's size and distance from the bridge, impossible to gauge its speed.

'Pull up, Delgado,' yelled Ash, behind him. 'Pull up. Delgado!'

The aircraft approached the bridge with alarming speed. As the sun was obscured by high cloud the light changed, the canal and bridge merging to become a single band of grey. The space stretched like a wide mouth. Delgado eased the aircraft down until it was skimming the canal. Ash was shouting increasingly urgently behind him. As the fragments of light reflected by the water's rippling surface became a single sheet of silver, Delgado held his breath.

He passed beneath the bridge in an instant, a band of shadow crossing his machine. As the paddle steamer grew large in front of him, he saw a group of people standing on one of the upper decks; one of them was pointing, mouth open. Delgado fired the aircraft's burner and pulled back on the joystick.

He heard Ash moan as his own stomach sank and the aircraft climbed sharply, passing through the smoke rising from the vessel's funnels. A few seconds later he levelled off and banked his aircraft on to one side to look down. The paddle steamer was just a small dash slanted diagonally across the waterway, seemingly about to collide with one of the bridge's uprights. He levelled the craft and searched the sky, seeking Cascari and Michael. He spotted their machines and charged after them.

He could feel that his fragmented nobics were failing to control his adrenalin properly, feeding it to him in sudden, intense bursts instead of a steady and moderate flow that would enhance his abilities while avoiding the dangers of saturation. As a result, he was more tense than he wanted to be, and aware that he was prone to taking high-risk gambles.

He coaxed his aircraft back into composure and turned left. The sun was behind him now, which made spotting the other two machines easy. Cascari was closest, about two thousand metres away. Delgado could see his aircraft speeding low over the city, its tiny shadow a dark and trembling blur, shrinking and swelling as it passed from rooftop to street to courtyard. Michael's aircraft was at greater altitude but further away, casting a larger, less defined shadow in a pale grey smear across dark, scree-covered slopes.

Delgado ignited his aircraft's engine. Almost instantly the machine lurched, surging forward, then stopped abruptly. The power plant beneath him faltered, emitted a particularly unhealthy noise that was a combination of grinding metal and a series of loud bangs, then fell silent. Delgado thumbed the ignition button several times but heard only distant clunks somewhere behind him.

'What's the matter, Delgado? You all out of gas?'

'It would seem so.'

'So what now?'

He raised the aircraft's nose. 'We'll have to try and gain some height while we've still got some momentum.'

'But that'll slow us down.'

'Yeah, but it'll give us a better chance of finding a suitable landing site, or a little extra speed if we need it when we're coming down.'

'Well, I can tell you, Delgado, I'm all for getting out of here asap. My neck's killing me.' She exclaimed and cursed as the aircraft bounced through pockets of air.

Delgado craned his neck as his aircraft gained altitude, peering down at the other two machines. As he watched, they ignited their burners almost simultaneously and accelerated visibly. Cascari's burner extinguished, re-lit with an odd blue-grey flame for a moment, followed by billowing grey clouds. After that the outlet at the rear of his vessel remained dark.

'Look's like Cascari's out of fuel too,' he said.

'Great. Let's meet up on the ground and have a picnic.'

'I'll do my best to ensure we meet up on the ground, but I'm not sure we're in store for a picnic any time soon.'

As their own machine shed the remainder of its useful speed and began to stall, its nose dropping, Delgado looked at Cascari's craft. He was not far ahead, and also appeared to be trying to climb without power.

Cascari began to turn his aircraft back towards Michael's, making the best use he could of the speed available to him; but without power his options were limited. He had only one chance to knock the other man from the sky – and Delgado sensed that in his current state, with his intensity of feeling, that was exactly what he would attempt to do. His own fate was unimportant.

Delgado watched as Cascari brought up the nose of his aircraft and climbed, trading speed for altitude in his search for a place to set his machine down. Delgado allowed his own aircraft's nose to drop until it was descending at an angle of around forty-five degrees, its speed rapidly increasing, then pulled back on the stick a little. He watched the two aircraft being piloted by the younger men. Cascari was on an intercept course, rapidly closing on Michael, who was also searching for somewhere to land.

Delgado glanced around. There were few open spaces that looked large enough to take an aircraft. To his left there was a large grassy area – possibly a playing field or park – which was virtually clear apart from a few trees in widely spaced groups, but given his altitude it was too far away to reach. There were one or two other possible places such as wide roads, but they seemed unlikely to provide even remotely soft landing sites and landing without undercarriage of any kind was likely to be rough wherever it was attempted.

Michael turned hard left as Cascari's aircraft flashed past the nose of his own. Both pilots were struggling to maintain speed and height without power, the residual momentum declining after each loop or turn.

Having descended from a greater altitude, however, Delgado had more speed. As he covered the remaining distance separating his aircraft from those of the two younger men, Cascari again sliced through the air towards Michael, who manoeuvred his own, now cumbersome, aircraft out of the way at the last moment. The two vessels were like dinosaurs dying from wounds suffering during combat, continuing to follow their instincts, yet doing so in an increasingly lethargic manner as their life force ebbed away.

As Cascari turned and again tried to collide with Michael's craft, Delgado passed between them, the other two machines bucking in the turbulence the passing of his aircraft created. Delgado pulled back on the stick, dragging his aircraft through a tight loop. As the nose of his aircraft dropped and the sound of rushing air grew louder, he turned towards Cascari's aircraft. Cascari did not see him approaching from his rear right quarter, and as the young man turned to cut across the nose of Michael's machine, Delgado's aircraft entered the airspace between them.

Michael was forced to turn hard right. Delgado turned his head to look back towards Cascari's craft and yelled aloud as the underside of the other machine filled the sky in front of him. There was an absurdly dull thud and a jolt as the two machines collided. Sky appeared in front of him again as Cascari's aircraft coiled away.

Cascari's aircraft adopted a course similar to Michael's, albeit at a slightly greater altitude. Delgado cautiously turned his own aircraft in a laborious arc intended to try and maintain as much speed as possible. When he levelled the wings, the three aircraft were descending, lacking the height and speed necessary to perform all but the most basic of manoeuvres, which were themselves not without risk.

Delgado looked ahead. There were now no large clear areas visible where one aircraft might be able to land, let alone three. The buildings of the city were densely packed; monorail tracks intersected at a complicated junction that looked like the half-built web of a giant spider, its threads curving to distant points across the city. A canal ahead seemed to offer the best opportunity.

'You fancy a swim?' Delgado asked.

'Why? What are you planning, Delgado?'

'We're going to have to ditch. In the canal, up ahead.' He pointed.

'Are you serious? There's no other option?'

'Take a look around,' he said. 'It's all too built up. We could try a road but we don't have the power necessary for a controlled landing. At least water will give a little.'

'Well, I can't see too much from back here, Delgado. All I know is that if we're ditching we're going to need to get out of here fast.'

'See if you can open the hatch now,' he said. 'It'll save time when we hit.'

'I don't much like the sound of "hit", Delgado.'

'You know what I mean.'

'Yeah, and I still don't like it.' She looked up at the hatch above her head, reached up and tugged sharply at the release handle. There was a sudden, sharp cracking sound and a line of light appeared around the edge of the hatch. The sound of rushing air suddenly increased in volume, and she felt a cool draught on her face. 'I can't open it,' she said. 'There's too much pressure.'

'That's OK. But when we ditch, open it and get out. We don't know how long this thing'll take to sink, and once the water starts coming in through that hatch we've had it.'

Delgado smiled as, in front of him, the other two aircraft arrived at the canal and performed tentative ninety-degree turns to position themselves above it: they had made the same choice as he. A few moments later Delgado copied their manoeuvre, following them towards the shimmering water. He looked out of the windows to his right as he covered the final few metres. People were standing on the canal-side path, pointing at the three race craft gliding silently towards the water.

Suddenly, Delgado realised that he had misjudged their height and that the aircraft was lower than he thought, and the water seemed to rush up. Ahead, the other two machines had already entered the water, huge plumes of spray rising from their rear ends as they ploughed deep liquid furrows.

Abruptly, Delgado's aircraft drifted to the right in a gust of wind, heading towards the canal bank. He yanked the joystick to the left, but the action appeared to have little effect. There was a loud bang, an agonised, metal-tearing scrape, and both he and Ash cried out as the aircraft's underside slammed against the canal bank, bouncing unenthusiastically.

The impact knocked the wind from Delgado, and he struggled to regain his composure sufficiently to control the vehicle. It was too nose-high, going too slowly for him to do anything but try to make the best of a bad situation that had suddenly got much worse. The aircraft reached an altitude of about twenty metres and was more or less above the centre of the canal when, with the joystick slopping about uselessly, it lost most of its remaining forward motion.

The aircraft began to slide backwards through the air, rapidly gaining speed as it was dragged by the weight of its engine. In a desperate attempt to soften what would undoubtedly be a very hard landing, he thrust the joystick forwards.

The aircraft was slightly nose-down when it slammed against the water, halfway through performing the manoeuvre Delgado had attempted, having regained only a little forward speed.

The impact sent a sheet of pain up his spine and he lunged forward in his seat, the straps yanking at his shoulders. His teeth snapped shut and he groaned, tasting blood. Behind him Ashala cried out, her knees banging against both sides of Delgado's head as the aircraft skidded across the surface of the canal, which was much less smooth than it had seemed from the air.

The dying vehicle bounced across the choppy water with great thuds and bangs that boomed and reverberated through the machine's thin hull as it rapidly shed its little remaining speed. Delgado banged his face on the edge of the screens in front of him and hit the side of his head against Ash's right knee. Although he could not see, he suspected that the aircraft's hull had been breached somewhere near his feet, as there was a definite increase in the volume of sound from outside the craft, and something sharp was pressed hard against his right ankle. It did not hurt but felt warm, with a slightly dull, throbbing sensation.

Spray splashed up on to the portals until he could see practically nothing outside the cockpit. Eventually the vessel came to a stop, pitching and rolling on the swell of the canal, which had been aggravated by the arrival of the three racing machines. Lines of sunlight reflected off the water and undulated across the cockpit ceiling. They were somehow calming and serene given the recent violence of the environment.

Water lapped glumly against the aircraft in regular flops somewhere beneath him, and he heard bubbles escaping from somewhere within its hull. The craft creaked and groaned gently. Through the portals in front of him he could see the water lapping gently against the aircraft's nose, and a crowd watching from the bank. There was an enormous gulping sound, and a huge bubble surfaced directly in front of the vessel. Ahead of him, the other two aircraft were sinking rapidly in a seething white mass of water. Of Michael's vessel, only the scarred tail remained visible as the craft sank. He could hear water spraying somewhere behind him. His wrist throbbed, and when he looked down at it he was surprised to find that it was cut. He pressed three fingers against it in an attempt to halt the bleeding, and generated a batch of temporary nobics to help the healing process. Outside, the water was almost level with the bottom of the portal, the aircraft's nose now fully submerged.

He looked up and saw Ash standing on top of the aircraft, shrouded in a blaze of bright sunlight. She was calling and beckoning to him. '. . . the hell out of there, Delgado.' The words burst into his consciousness as if a door had suddenly been opened.

He released his harness, reached up and wriggled his hips to free himself from the narrow cockpit, then hauled himself up into the open air. He felt a cool wind across his face, and heard a lone voice shout on the canal bank. He struggled to push himself up and hoisted his feet from the cockpit so that he was sitting on the aircraft's roof. He looked down at the vessel's nose, which was now just visible beneath the grey-green surface of the canal. The tail was much deeper, dragged down by the weight of the engine. Along the side of the aircraft were huge dents in the fuselage and serrated ribbons of metal peeling away.

He saw Cascari and Michael swimming clumsily towards the shore, weighed down by their sodden clothing and boots. A couple of *mourst* were clambering down the steep canal bank to help them from the water. Delgado's aircraft shuddered, and a broad mass of bubbles appeared at the rear of the vessel like gratefully released flatulence.

'Come on, Delgado,' Ash called. 'We better get off this thing before it takes us down with it.'

He reached out and took the hand she offered to help him to his feet; it seemed small and fragile. They both jumped into the water, and were almost overcome by its coldness.

Delgado and Ash lay on the canalside, the sun hot on their faces. Their sodden clothes steamed gently. They were surrounded by Seriatts on three sides and a steep bank dropped away to the canal directly in front of them.

Delgado squinted and raised one hand to shield his eyes from the glare. The Seriatts looked down at them in silence, their alien expressions unfamiliar and unreadable. He could hear a couple of raised voices from behind those he could see. He felt that they were calling to someone or something, but he was unable to tell who or what this might be.

He felt an odd dislocation of self, as if having an out-of-body experience. For some reason he felt physically fine, if slightly dizzy, but he also felt unable to react to the situation in any way. Like a child in an unfamiliar environment or in the company of total strangers, he simply felt compelled to wait for something to happen. The ability to refer to the parametres of his existence seemed to have been taken from him, the capacity to verify himself eroded by some mysterious force. He could remember nothing of getting to the canal bank. He did not know if he had swum the whole way himself, or whether he had passed out in the cold water and been dragged to the shore by Seriattic hands. The previous few hours seemed like a dream. Perhaps they were. Perhaps this was. He could not tell.

He looked to his left. Ash lay on the bank next to him. Her eyes were closed and she appeared to be breathing heavily. She was frowning slightly. Delgado was struck by the smoothness of her skin.

'You OK?' he asked softly.

She nodded slightly, but kept her eyes closed. 'Yeah,' she said, her voice slightly hoarse. 'Worn out and hungry, but otherwise OK. What are we going to do now, Delgado? This isn't exactly how things were supposed to go, right?'

'Right.' He closed his eyes again. 'How many Seriatts do you think are around here right now?'

'About fifty.'

'Fifty, huh? You see many *mourst*?'

'No. What are you thinking about, Delgado?'

'Well, *mourst* are the ones we've got to worry about. *Conosq* and *vilume* we can overpower more easily. *Vilume*, anyway.'

They heard more raised voices, coarse *mourst* tones.

'If you're thinking of making a run for it, I'd make it quick,' she said calmly.

Delgado heard closer voices and looked up. The Seriattic crowd fell silent, parted, and two *mourst* enforcers appeared.

'Too late,' said Ash quietly.

The enforcers looked like hardened veterans. Something about them reminded Delgado of long-serving purifiers or

PPD invigilators: there was a coldness, a certain insulating detachment from their duties. Their scuffed but supple leather uniforms creaked as they moved, and perfectly matched the contours of their *mourst* physique. They seemed to be of equal rank. One of them was chewing something lazily. They simply looked down at Ash and Delgado as if they were a couple of corpses. The one that was chewing poked at Delgado's right shoulder with a calf-high boot with three silver buckles on the outside, then looked at the other *mourst* and said something under his breath. The other did not reply, but simply continued to look down at the two people before them.

These two enforcers were joined by a third, who pushed his way through the crowd. He spoke rapidly and somewhat breathlessly, as if he had been running for some time. Delgado tried to read their traces, but the ageing, fragmented nobic evolution within him began to snag, spurring worrying, paranoid conjectures, possibilities based on insubstantial information. Despite his best efforts, these were difficult to suppress.

'Listen,' said Ash. 'Sounds like an aircraft.' One of the *mourst* leaned down and roared something in her face in Seriatt, his nose wrinkling to reveal his sharp, yellowy incisors.

Delgado listened. She was right. It was faint, but quickly getting louder, and a few moments later a large copter was a dark silhouette above the *mourst*, blotting out the sun. Its long rotor spun rapidly above its smooth, bulbous body, a shimmering blur distorting the sky, releasing fat chunks of sound as it kept the vehicle aloft. The fans that gave the machine forward motion were housed in large circular assemblies behind the machine's broad body, and emitted a thin, nasal whine that contrasted with the brute force of the lift engine.

The three enforcers looked up at the aircraft, as did the rest of the crowd. Delgado raised his head and looked towards the canal. The slope down to the water was steep and dusty and several large boulders protruded from the hard, sun-baked earth, as did occasional clumps of tough-looking dark green foliage. At the water's edge the slope was more shallow, covered in an area of glossy slime and muck that suggested the canals were tidal. The racing aircraft was by this time completely submerged.

He looked up. On the opposite canal bank more Seriatts were standing in clusters of five or six. While some were looking and pointing at them, others were paying attention to other sections of the same path. This was presumably where Cascari and Michael were. He extended his faltering hyper-consciousness. The traces emitted by Cascari and Michael were strangely combined. He assumed this was due to the increasingly strange performance of his nobics. At least he was certain they were both still alive.

Some of the Seriatts surrounding him were looking down at him, others were still looking up at the hovering aircraft. One of the three enforcers had one finger pressed into his left ear and was gesticulating broadly while looking up at the machine, clearly communicating with its crew.

Delgado rolled on to one side. 'Come on,' he hissed. 'Into the water. Quick!' He scrambled for the slope leading down to the canal. His wet clothes were cold. He grunted and grimaced and a thin trail of snot emerged from his left nostril. He heard a couple of shouts, the unmistakable barks of the *mourst* enforcers, but ignored them and continued to drag himself down the slope using his forearms, pushing hard with his legs.

He reached the edge of the slope and pulled himself down the final few metres, grateful for the ease with which he slid towards the water. He heard more *mourst* shouts over the sound of the hovering aircraft, and desperately clawed his way down the bank. As his speed increased it became more difficult to control the direction in which he was going. A large boulder loomed. He pushed against smaller rocks in an effort to avoid it, but he hit it heavily on the left side of his face and his shoulder. He groaned and felt nauseous as an oddly dull pain washed through him. He turned and looked for Ash, but she was at the top of the slope, a *mourst* enforcer kneeling next to her.

A buckled boot raised a cloud of dust as it stamped down in front of Delgado's face. Slowly he looked up, wincing against the sun and the pain in his head. The *mourst* enforcer was just a black shape against the brilliant blue sky. The copter appeared above the Seriatt like a mutant insect. The *mourst* leaned down and placed something against Delgado's temple. He cried out as an agonising jolt shot through his head, and his consciousness was lost.

Structure Tactical Training Installation, Thursemiol, Fahoun system

The ground appeared to shimmer slightly as the imps ran towards the approaching Lyugg tanks, the small chameleon pacs on their leather belts – their only item of clothing – rendering them virtually invisible against the hard, dry earth. The creatures were revealed momentarily each time they fired their short-stem Hi-Mag weapons, but despite the numbers being mown down by the flaming tongues of energy lashing from the muzzles of the machines they were attacking, they remained focused on their objective.

The tank crews battled hard, but the imps were too numerous and too determined. Within minutes of jumping from the snubship that had carried them from behind Structure lines to the drop zone between the trees in the valley and the incoming Lyugg hardware, the imps had blown the tanks' hatches, overwhelmed and killed the crews, robbed them of their distinctive jewellery, and set fire to their mutilated corpses.

With newly acquired chains in precious metals now draped around their necks like trophies, and chunky stone-encrusted rings jammed halfway up their fat, hairy fingers, the imps growled and spat and masturbated in celebration of their victory, their dark eyes reflecting the golden flames rising from the open hatches of the tanks they had disabled.

The imp chief strode to the brow of the hill and looked down towards the bay. The Lyugg base sprawled, squid-like, before him, grey prefabricated storage, arms and control facilities at one end, the slender jetties of the port extending into the sea at the other. According to the briefing, this was a particularly important installation for the Lyugg, the hub from which they supplied their forces in the Dinsic region, and home to their short- to mid-range strike craft. It was therefore particularly important for Structure to capture it.

Some of the buildings were already burning as a result of strafing by Structure xip fighters. Vehicles were speeding along roadways, while panicked Lyugg operatives ran between buildings or bunkers. All were targets, and the potential for violence in the next few hours aroused the imp chief greatly. Ignoring the strange tingling sensation in his brain, and a sudden urge to return to the dust-off point, he turned and growled orders at those who had gathered behind him. Then, with a throaty cry, he turned to lead his troop in a charge down the hill to attack whatever unfortunate creatures they might encounter.

With the tanks disabled and the imps heading towards the base, the way was clear for the deployment of the grunts, with wave after wave of them spewing from lines of slowly descending snubships. As more xip fighters flashed overhead on their way to strafe further targets, three dragons flanked by wyverns emerged from the forest at the foot of the hill. The dragons' caterpillar tracks clattered and squealed as the angular machines began to climb the slope like mechanised dinosaurs, their exhaust vents spewing dense black smoke as they powered up the incline. The wyverns strode gingerly on their mechanical legs, their long, segmented tails raising clouds of brown dust and dragging generous lengths of foliage behind them.

The wyverns' numerous weapons clusters rotated rapidly as they searched for targets. An array on one machine turned skywards and locked on to an unidentified object: a sphere dropping towards the ground, its glossy black surface reflecting cloud as it descended. The wyvern's primary combat core calculated its rate of descent as twenty metres per second. It was about to attack it as another wave of xips passed between the wyvern and the target, forcing the weapons core to hold fire, and causing the wyvern's tracking systems to lose contact with the inbound object for a moment.

When it was just metres from hitting the ground, the sphere turned through ninety degrees and passed between a wyvern and one of the dragons, reflecting the ground below it in a rippling blur. It then climbed to pass over the trees covering the steep slope at immense speed, aiming for Structure's Forward Command Point, which lay beyond the escarpment. Having gained track on the object again as the sphere climbed, the wyvern released a rapid volley of shots. But the orb was moving too quickly, and disappeared over the brow of the hill unscathed. It sped towards the fortification at the bottom of the hill, came to an abrupt halt above the main compound, then dropped vertically until it was only around half a metre above the ground. There it stopped, silent, motionless.

A slender fissure appeared pole to pole in the sphere, fracturing the image of the armoured temporary buildings reflected in its glossy surface. The split widened, and thousands of Lyugg scarabs spilled from the orb, tiny mechanical creatures spreading throughout the Structure base, disabling electronic systems and attacking personnel with microblasters.

As the scarabs continued to overrun the Structure position, Lieutenant Carter removed his visuals visor and looked towards Commander Harrison, who was seated to his right.

'You see where you went wrong, Carter?' Harrison said as he removed his own visor.

'Yes, sir.'

'Yes. You failed to devote adequate resources to incoming airborne attacks and you were defeated as a result. This facility will be overrun with Lyugg forces within minutes. Some of the cores under your command were aware of the danger, but you failed to respond to their warnings. This is partly due to your character, Carter. You don't like taking advice from AIs. I can understand this to a certain extent, but you need to overcome it if you are to become a successful operational commander. The other problem was that your imps were poorly controlled. The chief decided to attack the rest of the installation on his own because your own concentration lapsed after successfully tackling the tanks. Your failure to manipulate him successfully meant that you did not have time to apply effective close-air support.'

'I tried to influence them after they'd dealt with the tanks but the chiefs didn't respond.'

'Well, they have a tendency to do that, Carter. They often seem to be able to sense an inexperienced hand. But this is why we use real imps in a physical environment against constructs, with AI-controlled hardware, rather than use a full simulation. No matter how well programmed, simulations never seem to realistically reproduce imps' genuine unpredictability and resistance. They have been designed in such a way that they are extremely determined creatures, and while this can be very useful, one has to know how to handle them.'

'I understand, sir.'

'Good. It's important that you learn the value of AIs and the various techniques that best facilitate successful imp manipulation. If this were a real combat situation rather than a staged incident, you and all under your command would be dead by now.' They watched the scenario continue through the thick window. The Lyugg scarabs tore the Structure installation apart quickly, allowing the simulacrums of Lyugg infantry through to attack. It was clear that in this instance, Structure was beaten.

The door into the observation room overlooking the terrain where the combat was taking place opened behind them. A young communications officer rushed in, red-faced and breathless.

'Sorry to disturb you, Commander Harrison,' the young man gasped, 'but Commander Monroe says there's something out to sea. He's not sure what it is and he wants you to come to the observation deck right away.'

Harrison sighed as he stood. 'Very well, very well. Let's see what all the fuss is about. Thank you, Mullins.' He looked at Lieutenant Carter. 'I shall leave you in control here, Carter. See if you can get them to stop what they're doing and return to their respective camps. We'll repeat the scenario tomorrow and see if you've learned anything.'

'Very good, sir.'

Harrison left the Combat Simulation Control Suite and followed Mullins along the corridor towards the elevator that would take them up to the Observation Deck, wondering if the situation was as serious as the young officer's urgency seemed to indicate.

Mullins opened the elevator door and stepped back to allow Harrison to enter. 'There you are, sir,' he said. 'She'll take you right up.' He took a few more steps back and knocked against a fire extinguisher, which fell to the floor sending a jet of white foam across the maroon carpet. Harrison raised an eyebrow as he stepped into the elevator and Mullins scrabbled to bring the extinguisher back under control, spraying even more of the foam across the floor. Mullins was a good lad, but he did have something of a habit of breaking things and causing mishaps.

The elevator ascended quickly and the door opened. The

entire wall of the circular observation room was transparent blastplate, and when Harrison stepped out, directly in front of him he could see that, three hundred metres below, the clean-up operation was beginning following Carter's attempt to resist the Lyugg forces. Beyond, the forest was a swathe of green that coated the undulating hills, while to the right the rest of the Structure training facility stretched away like a scab on the otherwise undamaged landscape.

Harrison walked to the left in search of Monroe, and found the grey-haired officer looking out to sea through a pair of large teleculars.

'What's the problem, Monroe?' Harrison asked. 'Mullins said it was urgent in the extreme.' He tried to keep his irritation at being dragged out of an instructional session out of his voice. Monroe was cantankerous and stubborn, but wasn't known to waste time.

'Here,' said Monroe, handing the teleculars to Harrison. 'Have a look and see what you think. I can't make head nor tail of it.'

Harrison put the teleculars to his eyes, their motors wheezing softly as they adjusted automatically to his vision. For a few moments all he could see was the gunmetal chop of the sea, undulating beneath the equally bleak, overcast sky, but as he scanned the area strange objects came into view. They were like sea anemones that had somehow drifted from the sea bed, rising through the depths to float a few metres above the waves, changing colour frequently. At first Harrison could see only half a dozen or so, but more emerged from the water as he watched, rising into the air and holding their position in relation to the others.

'You see 'em?' Monroe asked.

'Uh huh.'

'What d'you think they are?'

'Search me. Organisms? Remotely controlled machines of some kind?'

'That's what I thought. Strange thing is, they're not showing up on the scanners. You seen anything like it before?'

'No. How far out are they?'

'About a hundred kilometres, maybe a little more.'

'You sent anything out there to investigate?'

'A GPC's just been diverted. ETA's less than a minute.'

'Do you think they could have anything to do with that meteor hit we picked up near the pole a few weeks back?'

Monroe shook his head. 'Nah. It could've disturbed something on the sea bed, I guess, or triggered some undersea volcanic activity that triggered something else in turn, but the sea's pretty deep up there. I doubt it would have had the speed necessary to hit with sufficient force to cause a serious seismic shock by the time it reached the bottom.'

'Hmm. It's weird all right. Hey, the GPC's arrived.' Harrison watched as the General Patrol Craft circled the hovering objects, gradually descending until it was holding station just twenty metres or so above them. 'Contact them. Let's find out what they can see.'

Monroe reached out to the comms unit and opened an external channel. 'Monroe to GPC four eight seven. Report, please.'

'It's kinda difficult to say what they are, sir,' came the reply. 'They're just . . . hanging there.'

'Do you think they're organic?'

'Can't tell, sir. They look organic. But my gut instinct tells me otherwise.'

'Could be some kind of life form we've not yet documented here,' said Harrison quietly. 'Hang on.'

'What's happening?'

'One of them is rising towards the GPC.'

'Raise your shield, four eight seven,' ordered Monroe.

'Shield active, sir.'

Harrison watched as the object approached the aircraft. 'It's no good,' he said. 'That thing's passed straight through the shield and attached itself to the hull. The shield didn't do a thing.'

'One of them has attached itself to the ship, sir,' reported the GPC pilot. 'Instruments are going haywire.'

'More of them are rising towards it,' said Harrison. 'My God, they're swarming all over it.' Monroe ran and grabbed a second pair of teleculars from a nearby storage cabinet. They could only watch as the mysterious objects smothered the machine, their tentacle-like structures lengthening, becoming attached to every part of its surface.

'I'm losing control, sir! Systems won't respond. Jesus, they've . . .' White noise suddenly replaced the pilot's voice.

'Four eight seven, report,' Monroe yelled. 'What's happening?'

No response.

The GPC began to turn slowly on its axis. The nose dropped slightly and it pitched to one side. Several of the objects moved towards the large round turbine housings on either side of the GPC's short tail, extending their tentacles into the fans. The turbines began to emit dense, black smoke. One of the fans shattered, and then the engines exploded, fireballs rising into the sky behind them. The GPC dropped suddenly towards the sea. It hit the waves hard, but sat on the surface, bobbing on the swell. Then there was another large explosion from just below the waterline, and the GPC began to sink quickly.

'They brought it down!' Monroe exclaimed. He reached for the comms unit. 'Air Control, scramble a dozen xip fighters immediately.'

'Oh my God,' muttered Harrison quietly.

'What's happening?' asked Monroe, putting his teleculars back to his eyes again.

'They're becoming detached from the GPC and are rising into the air again. They're heading this way.'

As the objects accelerated rapidly towards the Structure

training facility, Monroe sounded the alarm. But as Harrison watched them approach, somehow he knew they would not be able to stop them.

Seven

a gift from amazonia

Unknown location, Seriatt

Shuddering. Noise. Delgado opened his eyes and found that he was aboard the copter.

Sunlight stars reflected off transparent blue-tinted panels in the copter's roof. Through them he could see the rotor's wide blades shimmering. He raised his head. He was strapped into a stretcher fixed to the bulkhead at the rear of the aircraft's passenger compartment. Restraints across his chest and upper arms, thighs and shins severely limited his ability to move. He tried to raise his wrist to look at it, but it was stiff and unresponsive. His clothes, which were almost dry now, were covered in a layer of grey-brown dust as a result of his bid to escape. The cloth at one knee was slightly torn. A *mourst* enforcer sitting at the foot of the stretcher looked at him dispassionately for a moment, then looked away again. The copter's motion made the *mourst* tremble as if he were cold.

Delgado looked to his left. Ash lay on a similar bunk on the opposite side of the cabin. Although he could tell she was not dead, she was either asleep or unconscious, but he did not know which. Two other Seriatts – one *mourst*, one *vilume* – were sitting in the cockpit flying the machine. Each wore a thin, seemingly insubstantial helmet linked to a central console via numerous coiled cables that emerged from a slight bulge at the back. The *vilume* seemed to be the pilot. Occasionally one of them would speak a few words, but it was unclear to Delgado whether they were communicating with each other or someone on the ground. Other than this, there was no conversation aboard the aircraft.

Delgado craned his neck as far as he could in an effort to see through the cockpit window, a slightly tinted transparent quarter-sphere that formed much of the front of the machine. They were flying low and fast, speeding over the treetops of a lush forest. They seemed to be heading for the coast, which he could see in the distance. Two other copters were flying not far ahead.

Delgado lay back down again, blinking rapidly as he tried to extend his hyperconsciousness in an attempt to reach Cascari, or even gain some idea of Michael's condition in case this might give him some kind of clue to Cascari's location or health. His efforts were to no avail. He was too weak or tired to reach either of them. It was possible that they were simply not physically close enough for him to make contact. If this was the case, then they could not be aboard the other two aircraft, unless his nobics were failing him to a greater extent than he had previously realised. Frustrated and feeling the onset of despair at their situation, he closed his eyes. Within seconds the need for sleep was too great to resist, and he had been dragged into the peaceful respite offered by temporary oblivion.

When Delgado woke again he raised his head and looked to his left, licking his dry lips. Ash had not moved. Through the front of the copter he could see that it was now dusk. The machine was crossing a coastline, only the glistering lustre of the sea now visible ahead. It shimmered softly as night approached, defining edges blurred in the fading light.

Delgado looked at the *mourst* sitting by his feet. 'Could I have something to drink?' he asked. 'Water? I thought Seriatts were supposed to be hospitable.'

The *mourst*'s sharp, wide lips curled. 'You speak out of turn, human,' snarled the Seriatt in poor Counian. 'You will come to regret this. When we reach the Shadatz camp you will truly learn of our hospitality.'

Delgado rested his head and closed his eyes once more. There was nothing to do but wait.

En route to Shadatz Corrective Centre, Seriatt

Other than the thin orange glow cast by the instrument illumination in the cockpit, the interior of the copter was completely dark when Delgado next opened his eyes. If he stared hard he could just make out the rotor column through the ceiling panels, fat and black against the midnight blue of the sky. Beyond the rotor, thin strands of cirrus cloud were just visible.

The *mourst* enforcer sitting at the foot of the stretcher was asleep, his arms folded across his broad chest, head lolling back against the bulkhead behind him. His mouth was open. He was snoring loudly.

Delgado raised his head and looked towards Ash. She was awake now, and looked back at him. One of her eyebrows was cut and slightly swollen.

'Hey, Delgado,' she said softly. 'How's your head?'

'Fine. How about you. What happened to your eye?'

She jerked her head to one side. 'Our friend here thought I needed a lesson in Seriatt,' she said. 'I don't think it's all he's got in store for me, either. He's already showed me his status among Seriattic *mourst*, if you know what I mean.'

'Jesus.' Delgado let his head rest on the bunk. 'I'm sorry about all this,' he said.

'What? You're kidding me, right?'

'You shouldn't be here. There's no need for you to be here. This is something Cascari and I had to do.'

'Don't get all gooey on me now, Delgado. I came by choice, remember. Besides, you're getting kind of downhearted aren't you? You know what they say: it ain't over till the fat lady sings. Well, I sure don't hear no singing just yet.'

'Oh boy,' said Delgado, 'but what I wouldn't give right now for a fat lady.'

The straps restraining them felt tight as they both laughed.

'Any idea where we are?' she asked.

'No. I can't see much. All I know is we were over the sea, now we appear to be over land again.'

'How long do you think we've been airborne?'

He shook his head. 'No idea. But it was broad daylight when we were by the canal. Not long after midday by my estimation.'

'How long are the days here?'

He shook his head again. 'No idea.'

He craned his neck to look through the copter's front window. Strobes on the other two aircraft emitted regular red flashes that briefly illuminated the underside of each aircraft, momentarily revealing their positions. Delgado refocused: in the distance, beyond the other two copters, the moonlight-frosted crests of the waves ended abruptly at another coastline. Cliffs rose vertically from the water and, on the land beyond, creamy clots of light indicated an installation or settlement.

He felt the copter rise, then it turned steeply to the left, and Delgado was forced to let his head fall back, his feet tipped higher than his head. Only when the aircraft levelled was he able to look out again.

The three copters were heading towards two converging lines of red lights, at the end of which was a large circle of green lights. Around this were various buildings, pathways and roads, all of which were illuminated by the bleak grey light cast by floodlights at the tops of tall poles. The copters descended slowly and smoothly, and the skilful *vilume* pilot landed the machine gently within the green circle a few minutes later. The engines were turned off and the rotor quickly slowed.

The *mourst* guard at the foot of the stretcher into which

Delgado was tied woke abruptly, and rubbed his coarse face with his equally coarse palms in an effort to wake himself.

'Hey, sleepy head,' Ash said.

The *mourst* stood, shouted something, then kicked her in the temple. Her head lolled and she remained motionless.

In the cockpit, the *mourst* and *vilume* pilots unplugged cables and removed their helmets. They were apparently grateful to do so, rubbing eyes and ears and massaging their scalps.

There was a slick, liquid sound, and the window near Delgado's head and on either side of the copter's forward compartment re-formed into steps down to the ground.

'*Cournie fog-moi nesh'nia,*' said the guard at the foot of the stretcher. He was looking past Delgado, apparently speaking to someone outside the copter.

'*Fegent proq'niess dil-occ,*' said the unseen Seriatt. It appeared to Delgado to be a question, but he could not be certain. The *mourst* in front of him replied briefly, and the next moment Delgado's stretcher was being manhandled from the aircraft, tipped precariously to one side in the process in order to get through the opening.

As he and Ash were manoeuvred clumsily from the vehicle, Delgado looked around. The other two copters were quite a distance away, but he could see similar stretchers being extricated from them, a seemingly equal level of clumsiness being exercised in both cases. The stretchers were placed on the floor a few metres away from each copter, and the three groups of Seriatts came together between the three landed aircraft. They stood in a group, talking, exchanging small items of food – possibly confectionary of some kind – occasionally making the strange throaty sounds Delgado knew were *mourst* laughter. They did not seem to be talking about their four passengers.

There was little other activity. The majority of the surrounding buildings – the exceptions being the smaller huts – were dark, as if unoccupied. To Delgado the place looked like a military base, but something about the atmosphere and the way in which things were taking place suggested to him that this could be an unofficial, clandestine operation of some kind. There was one thing of which he felt certain, however: they had not been bought here to receive medical attention.

Delgado heard a noise to his left. He looked and saw a *mourst* emerge from one of the buildings, the light in the doorway briefly forming a radiant aura around him. As the *mourst* walked across the courtyard, the footfalls of his boots making loud reports echoing off the surrounding buildings, he began to address the group of Seriatts. When he had finished speaking one of the Seriatts stepped forward and seemed to challenge him. The other *mourst* made an apparently dismissive gesture in the air with one hand and said something else, then the group of Seriatts split into three, returning to the stretchers.

The *vilume* pilot bent down and touched something on the side of the stretcher near Delgado's head. Another did the same to Ashala's stretcher. He heard a faint humming and felt a tingling, and a moment later the stretcher began to rise smoothly from the ground. The *vilume* and the *mourst* pilot stood by the stretcher at Delgado's head, while the *mourst* guard stood at his feet. They pulled lengths of cable from within the stretcher and, seemingly effortlessly, the four captives were taken away from the copters and along the deserted paths leading away from the landing site. Stirred by their passing, slender strands of mist curled lovingly around the floodlight poles like cats' tails in the cold night air.

As the four stretchers converged, Delgado tried to make eye contact with Cascari, but the young man looked at him only briefly before looking away again. Although there was anger in his expression, there was also great fatigue, the kind of soul-sapping weariness that makes any decision or rationality seem impossibly difficult. It was as if he had finally realised, or been forced to realise, that his goal of killing the person who he believed had the potential to deny him his rightful *mourst* position was unachievable, and that, instead of cementing his own position, he had perhaps put all their lives in danger.

They reached a large building, and were taken up some grey stone steps into a warm corridor. It was narrow, but just long enough for the four stretchers and the Seriatts guiding them to fit. Delgado's stretcher was at the front. Craning his neck he saw a single wide door in which there was a long, rectangular window. Through it he could see a *mourst* leaning back on a chair, his feet resting on the broad wooden desk in front of him, hands linked behind his head; he appeared to be asleep.

The *mourst* guard at the front of Delgado's stretcher reached out and rapped on the window with his knuckles. The sleeping *mourst* started, slid his feet off the desk quickly, sat upright in his chair and looked around the room with blood-shot eyes. He reached out to what looked like a comms screen, but it was blank. It was some seconds before he realised that it was not this that had not woken him.

The *mourst* at Delgado's feet rapped on the window again. His counterpart within the room turned and looked at him for a moment, then pushed his chair back from the desk, stood and walked across to the door.

He was overweight for a *mourst*. His plain white button-down shirt with its stained front was too tight around his belly; his trousers were too low at the waist. Excess flab jarred with each step. His face was coated with an abrasive layer of dark stubble. As he walked, he stuck a finger into his left ear and scratched around, extracting grime and flicking it to the ground.

He touched something next to the door and leaned forward slightly. His voice emerged from a single speaker in the corridor, thin and metallic in tone. 'Yes? What is it?' The *mourst* was speaking Counian. He looked agitated, but whether this was because he had just been woken or because he was puzzled by the situation that confronted him, Delgado was unable to decide.

'*Eggec hid mour pas,*' said the *mourst* enforcer at the foot of Delgado's stretcher.

'Are you able to speak Counian?' asked the other Seriatt.

The enforcer sighed heavily. 'Only if I *really* must,' he said.

'Counian is the official language now. You know that.'

'That doesn't mean I have to like speaking it, though, does it? I am a Seriatt. I have my own language. As do you. What is your name?'

The *mourst* within the room looked nervous, as if realising that this was someone important, without knowing who. 'Acting Superintendent Otonz,' he said, glancing at the others in the corridor. 'I'm currently in charge of this facility.'

'I am Major Throubesh of the ZeeS4,' said the *mourst* at the head of Delgado's stretcher. Otonz was clearly unsettled by this statement. Delgado knew the ZeeS4 was a notorious group within Seriatt's military unit whose jurisdiction covered interplanetary as well as domestic affairs. Its members were the equivalent of Structure's PPD, Reactionary Forces, Enlightenment or the Assimilation Group depending on the task and location in question. 'Are you a pacifist *mourst*, Acting Superintendent Otonz?'

The Acting Superintendent ignored the question. 'The arrival of these prisoners is unscheduled, Major Throubesh,' he stated. 'Who are they? What are they doing here?' He gesticulated towards the stretchers, his natural *mourst* instincts preventing him from backing down having suddenly found himself in a confrontational situation.

'These prisoners are suspected subversives, saboteurs,' said Throubesh, slowly and calmly. 'They murdered one of our colleagues.' Someone at the rear of the corridor said a few quiet words. Throubesh half turned, then looked back at Otonz. 'And a *vilume*,' he added, apparently reluctantly. 'Then these three got into today's race,' he motioned towards

Delgado, Cascari and Ashala, 'and attempted to kill this one.' Throubesh pointed to Michael. 'He claims he was officially registered to race, and that he has come from Earth to take his place within Seriatt's Royal Household. Our intelligence on this is incomplete. As for the others . . .' He shrugged. 'We'll find something,' he said. 'ZeeS4 can always find something.'

'That one looks human,' said Otonz, pointing at Delgado. 'And that one.' He pointed at Ash.

'That's because they *are* human, Acting Superintendent Otonz.'

'What about the other two?'

'This one claims to be half human, half Seriatt, despite the fact that he appears human. While this one clearly has some *mourst* blood in him, although its purity is in doubt.'

Acting Superintendent Otonz looked less certain to Delgado, but did not challenge Throubesh. 'Why have they been brought here?' he asked. 'If they have arrived on Seriatt only recently they should still be in quarantine.'

Throubesh shook his head slowly. 'We need to interrogate them, find out what they know, who they are working for and what they are doing here.'

'We don't have the facilities to do that.'

'Facilities we do not need,' said Throubesh grimly. He glanced briefly back at Delgado, then at the other stretchers. 'We will find other methods of acquiring the information we require. Now open the door, please, Acting Superintendent Otonz. We have travelled far and are tired. My patience is wearing thin with this conversation.'

Otonz stood firm. 'I can't do that,' he said. 'There are no interrogation facilities here. No room whatsoever, in fact. You'll have to take them to Goshimez if you want to interrogate them. There are proper facilities and sufficient accommodation there. You can't do it here.'

Delgado could see Throubesh's reflection in the glass of the door. While he carried a lot of weight for a *mourst*, his stockiness implied physical strength rather than mere excess weight. A thin scar ran from just below his right ear down almost to the end of his chin. His expression was hard and cold. Delgado suspected that it changed little whatever his mood.

Throubesh took a step closer to the door so that his face was almost pressed against the thick glass separating him from Otonz. He spoke quietly and evenly, but with ominous restraint. 'You will open this door, Acting Superintendent Otonz, or I will personally pull your guts out through your backside and stuff them down your throat until you choke. Then I will let my officers here eat you. Do you understand me?'

Otonz swallowed, glanced at the rest of the surly *mourst* in the corridor, and then looked back at the major. Delgado watched the two of them. Throubesh appeared to be the type who would carry out such a threat with zeal. He also suspected that Acting Superintendent Otonz believed this too. Other than the slight creaking of the enforcers' leather uniforms, there were a few moments of tense silence. Throubesh remained motionless, simply staring through the glass. Otonz fidgeted and looked uncertain. Delgado sensed that the Acting Superintendent was simply being awkward. There was room for them, but he just didn't want to let them in for some reason. And while Otonz knew he was not being particularly convincing, he was not sure how to get out of the situation with face now that he had made a stand. His *mourst* pride would not allow him to back down with ease.

'You understand that if I let you in here I can't put them in separate cells,' said Otonz eventually. 'I can't guarantee that if they're left unattended they won't harm each other, and I won't be culpable in any way for their well being or security, Major Throubesh. I have neither the facilities nor the personnel. They are your prisoners, and you will remain responsible for them at all times. Agreed?'

'Just open the door,' muttered Throubesh.

'Very well,' said Otonz. 'I shall let you in. But remember: they're *your* responsibility.' He pulled a black leather wallet from an inside pocket and struggled with the huge number of key-cards it held. After several incorrect attempts and a great deal of frustrated fumbling, the guard unlocked and opened the door, allowing the ZeeS4 major and those in his charge to enter. When all the stretchers were in he closed the door again and locked it.

Throubesh walked calmly over to the Acting Superintendent, his broad, leather-clad shoulders partially obscuring Otonz from Delgado's view. Throubesh reached out and gripped Otonz around the neck with one muscular hand and pushed the guard back against the wall. Otonz's half-hearted attempts to fight back were pathetic and futile, particularly for a *mourst*.

The two Seriatts stared at each other. Both were salivating and growling, baring sharp incisors. The ridges of ligament at their necks were red and angry, thickening them, although Otonz was obviously reacting to the intimidation rather than attempting to intimidate Throubesh in return. Delgado glanced at the other *mourst* officers he could see. They appeared to be slightly agitated.

Throubesh looked down at Acting Superintendent Otonz and inclined his head slightly. Otonz was clearly struggling for breath, his face quickly reddening. All the others in the room watched in silence as, slowly, Throubesh raised his other hand. Gently he curled one slender finger around the elaborate necklace Otonz was wearing, and lifted it away from his skin.

'So,' he murmured, '*timauna thenetec gadar.* Somewhere a *vilume* and a *conosq* wear identical braids and the three of you form a happy *timauna*, no doubt. You have *driss thenetec gadar nim cor*? Offspring of which you are no doubt proud. Are they *mourst*? *Vilume*? *Conosq*?' He made the odd growling exclamation of a *mourst* expressing humour. 'You are a pathetic slob of a *mourst*, Acting Superintendent Otonz. A disgrace to the rest of us, like so many who have embraced the offerings of the Andamour Treaty and adopted the Counian language the Council has imposed upon us. Yet there remains purity in you. I see that. You have not completely abandoned your Seriattic culture.' Otonz was able only to stare at Throubesh as he slowly strangled him. Throubesh leaned even closer to Otonz. 'If you trouble me again, Acting Superintendent Otonz,' Throubesh snarled, 'I will find you and your family and I will impale each of you on a spit. I will turn you well away from the flame so that you cook slowly and retain your juices. I will baste you with exotic oils and dust you with fine herbs.' He leaned even closer. 'And then I will consume you,' he whispered. 'Do you understand me?' Otonz nodded weakly, his movement restricted by Throubesh's fist. The ZeeS4 officer released him, and Otonz dropped to the floor, doubled over, gasping and coughing.

Throubesh patted the Acting Superintendent's back and walked away from him, returning to the stretchers. He swaggered around them, looking at each of his prisoners with an air of extreme superiority. 'We need a cell,' he called back to the slowly recovering Otonz. 'If you say you are short of space then one will do. If they kill each other while awaiting interrogation it will be a pity, but only because I should like to kill them myself.' He stopped next to Delgado and bent at the waist examining Delgado's face closely. 'Humans have a particularly low pain threshold as I recall,' he said. 'And members of ZeeS4 enjoy so little recreation.'

They were carried through a series of white corridors to the cell. Any attempt to look at their surroundings was met with a slap around the side of the head and an incoherent string of throaty growls from the *mourst* steering the stretchers. Forced to stare at the light strip in the ceiling, Delgado's only real impression of the place was that it was very clean: the walls and ceiling were white, the smell of disinfectant was strong; the silence was intimidating.

The *vilume* appeared to maintain a distance at the rear of the group, as if she sought to disassociate herself from the acts of her colleagues. Her slender figure came into view occasionally as they proceeded through the chain of corridors. On the two occasions Delgado managed to glance in her direction, she returned his gaze. He was unable to decide whether she might be sympathetic towards them, however, as the expression on her narrow, fragile face was aloof and dispassionate.

Eventually the group paused. Delgado heard the hiss of a door opening and the stretchers were manoeuvred into a small room, which was also painted white.

The door was closed and a series of commands were entered into the stretchers via small touchtabs at the end of each one. The Seriatts stood back, and a few seconds later the stretchers began to tip silently, the feet of each prisoner lowering towards the ground. Eventually the stretchers were vertical, the prisoners effectively standing on the small blocks that protruded from the stretcher beneath their feet. They looked at each other and glanced at their Seriatt captors with uncertainty, but none of them spoke. Michael glared with rage at anyone who looked at him, his face red with anger.

Delgado glanced around the cell and took in as much as he could. It contained only a single bunk, a wash basin and a latrine. There was no window, only a featureless, glossy black panel – possibly a one-way observation window – on one wall.

The Seriatts stood around, arms folded or leaning against walls, apparently waiting for instructions from Throubesh. The major's eyes were filled with the superiority and confidence that results from having the upper hand. He strolled back and forth in front of the four restrained people, hands clasped together in front of his rugged chin as if in prayer. He stopped in front of Delgado and rubbed his eyes with his fingertips, then let his hands drop to his sides.

'I am Major Throubesh of the ZeeS4,' he said in human, speaking with bizarre warmth. The *mourst* smiled as if they should both recognise his name and be grateful for being in his charge. 'You are my prisoners. I will tell you what we know. We know that you all have a connection with Earth, a planet with which Seriatt currently has a rather tense relationship. We know that there were several murders within a short space of time at the Koss-Miet racing facility in Astragarda, where you gained illegal access to racing aircraft. You then engaged in, well, aerial combat.' He glanced behind him at his colleagues as if this was some kind of joke. While there was polite laughter from the *mourst*, the *vilume* seemed unimpressed. Delgado surmised that perhaps she was the only one among them who could afford to express such indifference. 'However,' Throubesh continued, 'whether you have a link to each other or are simply individual renegades is something about which we are less certain. It is this, along with a few other issues, which we intend to settle one way or the other while you are here.'

'I demand to see your Commanding Officer,' shouted Michael. 'This is a disgrace. I demand to be released at once. If you contact Arbiter Messinat at the palace she will confirm that I am who I say I am, that I was taking part in the race as a result of an agreement with the Andamour Council and that I am the rightful heir to the position of Monosiell.'

Major Throubesh smiled a bitter *mourst* smile and walked across to Michael. He stood in front of the young man, rocking on his heels. 'You have spirit. I like spirit,' he said. 'It makes certain aspects of my work so much more satisfying. Don't you agree?' He half turned and looked at his colleagues again. They made quiet noises of affirmation. 'However, at this moment in time I do not feel particularly disposed to contact the Royal Household. They are impotent. Matters of such importance should be handed over to the military, not be controlled by Andamour Council puppets.'

Throubesh paused, seemingly calming himself. He yawned widely, revealing his formidable *mourst* teeth. 'At the moment I am too tired to deal with you,' he said. 'And my staff need food and rest. We will return later, whereupon your interrogation will commence. If you wish to harm yourselves please be thorough, but have consideration for those who will have to clean this cell after you. But before I leave,' he said, 'I will show you something.' Throubesh looked at one of his officers. The other *mourst* stepped forward, half unzipped his leather tunic and produced a small, slim rectangular box from an inside pocket. He handed it to Throubesh then took a step back. Throubesh turned and placed the box on top of the bunk and touched it with the tip of one finger. A large display was projected above the device.

It was a room. Strips in the walls provided inadequate illumination. In the centre was a wide marble slab on top of a circular pedestal. In one corner was a brazier, from which three short rods protruded. Deep within the mound of coals upon the brazier there burned a fierce orange core. A slender rope of dark smoke rose towards a hole in the ceiling, the area around which was blackened with carbon. Next to the brazier a *mourst* stood solidly, arms folded across his chest. Aromasense units in the small projection device released a thick stench of shit, sweat and fear.

A young *mourst* was tied to the slab by shackles that encircled his wrists and ankles. His flesh was red where the metal had rubbed him. The shackles were linked to lengths of chain too short for him to be able to move his limbs more than a few centimetres in any direction. He was sweat-soaked, grimy, covered in bruises and weals.

Next to his right thigh a large knife lay on the slab, just out of reach of his fingers. Next to it was a jar of what looked like salt. Slithers of flesh seemed to have been sliced from his abdomen and face, revealing the pink, raw tissues beneath. Other than the slight rise and fall of his chest, he remained motionless.

Off camera a muffled voice could be heard. Although the precise words were difficult to distinguish, the tone of the voice was soft, calming, like a parent talking to a young child. There was a question, a pause, then the sound of an impact. This was followed immediately by a thin squeal, a whimper, a series of incomprehensible, breathy words. Another blow. More cries.

The *mourst* on the slab raised his head to look across the room, at whatever was taking place out of shot. His face was hugely swollen and bruised, grotesquely distorted. Above his left eye – itself two thirds shut – was a deep cut. His mouth was just a black circle in his face, all fleshy tissues burned away. His lips were gone, the inside of his mouth a charred void; the edges were ragged with hard, blackened points of burned skin. He moved his head and neck as if trying to say something, but no noise emerged. He seemed to try to swallow, then allowed his head to fall back, defeated.

The calm off-screen voice called to the other *mourst*, who turned and drew one of the rods from the brazier. One half remained black, obviously cool enough to touch with bare hands, while the other half was so hot it glowed. Carrying the rod carefully, the *mourst* crossed the room until out of sight.

The weaker voice cried out, terrified. More unintelligible words streamed forth, becoming increasingly desperate. Then there was a scream of agony the like of which Delgado had not heard for a very long time. It faded quickly – too quickly – and became a continuous string of choking, gagging moans.

Then silence.

A cloud of thin grey smoke drifted across the display and a new rotten and corrupt smell permeated the cell. There was a dull, muffled sound. Suddenly Throubesh appeared close to the camera, the glowing iron clutched in one hand. He was looking towards the floor, his face dispassionate. He turned his head and looked directly into the camera. 'A pity,' said the on-screen Throubesh. 'I had so looked forward to chatting with him.' As his mouth stretched into the wide, sour *mourst* smile, he placed a thin sliver of dark, moist flesh into his mouth and began to chew.

Throubesh turned off the display, picked up the box and handed it back to his officer. He turned and smiled at his prisoners. 'A personal favourite,' he said. 'All the action takes place out of sight. It's so much more effective, I find. Adds so much more tension. The imagination is an enemy, after all. He tasted good. He was young and tender. His friend I cooked, but I found I prefer the taste of raw meat. I am sure,' said the Seriattic major, 'that you will cooperate fully with my questioning when I return in the morning. However, if you do not, then you may face the same fate.' He looked at each one of them in turn, but his eyes rested on Ash the longest. As she stubbornly returned his gaze, Throubesh walked over to her and traced a line down her chest with one finger, his long, black nails teasing her tunic buttons. Delgado and Cascari were tense, and Ash was red-faced but desperate to hide her fear. 'I understand human females are particularly succulent,' he said, 'if a little fatty.' Abruptly Throubesh turned. 'Come'. He beckoned to his officers. 'We will return when we have slept.' With that he left the room, followed by his entourage of *mourst*. Delgado noticed that the *vilume* was nowhere to be seen.

Behind the departing Seriatts the thick cell door slid shut, the sound of the locking bolts that would secure it sliding into place with firm thuds.

The edge of the Fahoun system

When they had destroyed the source of the vessel that had attacked them as they emerged from their haven, they left the planet beneath whose seas they had multiplied, and gathered together at the predetermined point in space. There were thousands of them, identical, still growing as they prepared for the coming battle, pulsating through the spectrum. Within them, tens of thousands of cells started to divide, and the final stage of the process began.

Shadatz Corrective Centre, Seriatt

There was great tension in the small room. Cascari and Delgado stood together, facing Michael on the other side of the bunk. Ash was leaning against the wall near the door.

'Well, this is a twist of fate,' said Michael, chin high, arms folded. 'The last thing I expected was to be held in a Seriattic military cell with you three.'

'This isn't exactly what we had planned either,' said Ash.

'Just what *did* you expect?' Cascari asked Michael bitterly. 'Did you really think you could just come here and that the Seriatts would accept you as Monosiell? You're obviously human. A pawn for Myson.'

Michael snorted. 'But I'm not,' he said coolly, smiling. 'My Seriattic heritage has been proven, and the Seriatts have accepted that proof. They had no choice.'

'What do you mean?' asked Delgado. 'What proof?'

'Tissue samples were analysed by independent scientists appointed by the Andamour Council. They proved that I'm half Seriatt, that my mother was Vourniass Lycern, the *conosq dis fer'n'at*. They compared my cells to those of hers they had in storage at the biotechnology centre where she conducted her research.' He was calm, cocky.

Delgado shook his head, frowning. But when he spoke it was more quietly than before. 'No. If tests were conducted and they did yield those results then Myson must have had his biotechs mess with you, fixed it so you *appear* to be Lycern's son. But you're not. They took some cells from Lycern's body, cloned them, implanted them into you, merged them with your own, somehow. I don't know the ins and outs of all that stuff, but it must be something like that. You're human. Cascari is my son. Mine and Lycern's. I know he's our son because I was there when he was born, and he wears the pendant taken by Ash from Lycern's body after Myson had her killed.' He looked at Cascari and jerked his head in Michael's direction. 'Show him.'

Cascari unbuttoned his tunic and raised the white T-shirt he wore beneath; he lifted the pendant from his chest, showing it to Michael. It was a beautiful beaten-silver square, approximately seven centimetres along each side. Slender lines of amber glass curled across its surface to form loops. In the spaces within the loops were tiny but incredibly detailed engravings. Michael leaned forward slightly, frowning as he tried to discern the minute images. They were depictions of different Seriattic events: *mourst* in combat; a *conosq*, *mourst* and *vilume* engaged in the full mating act of *driss lousoue*; a ceremonial event of some kind.

Michael shook his head and stood upright again. 'Exquisite,' he said flatly. 'I don't know where you got that trinket, Delgado, but it means nothing. Do you really think the Seriatts would have accepted my coming here if the evidence was controvertible? The proof was such that the Andamour Council put them in a tight spot. If they refused to accept my case then sanctions would be imposed and they'd be economically ruined in a very short space of time. Do you know how much trade between Seriatt and Lyugg is worth? They couldn't afford to risk losing that.'

'So you're here through bribery, huh? What a surprise. Myson's probably got half the Andamour Council in his pocket,' said Cascari. 'So whatever he says goes.'

'You don't look that welcome to me,' said Ash. 'They've hardly put a garland of flowers around your neck, have they?'

'That's because of your interference,' spat Michael, seemingly losing control for a moment. 'If I'd completed that race, proceedings would have gone to the next stage. They would've been forced to begin negotiating terms for my accession. That race of theirs is a *mourst* ritual. Any way they can find of keeping us out that the Andamour Council can't dispute, the Proctors and Arbiters will use to try and get a Monosiell of their own in place so *they* can have the real power. And you gave them exactly that.' He looked at Delgado and waved a hand in Cascari's direction. 'Did you really think you could pass him off as royalty?'

Delgado took a step forward. Despite his efforts to remain calm he could feel himself becoming angry, frustrated by the strength of Michael's arguments. 'Cascari is the rightful heir to the position of Monosiell,' he said. 'I was there when he was born to Lycern. Ash took the pendant from her and placed it round his neck herself.'

Michael laughed briefly. 'You sad, deluded . . . you really believe all this horse shit, don't you? You're mad. I've heard about you, Delgado. You're a bitter old veteran who went too far, and lost everything. You've got a whole lot of ruined nobics in your head and they're screwing you up.' He tapped his temple. 'You don't know which are your own memories and thoughts and which are just the nobics playing tricks on you.' Delgado gazed at him. He knew he could be right. 'I'm here because I'm meant to be here,' Michael continued with conviction. 'This is the opportunity I've been waiting for my whole life. To be what I really am. To give my father the key to peace and stability that he's sought for so long.'

Delgado laughed. 'Peace and stability? Christ. You only *think* it's what you've been waiting for. Myson's a maniac. He's been grooming you, feeding you stories of Seriatt, making you *believe* it's all true. It's not. It's a lie. The only reason you're here is because he wants something, and when he wants something it doesn't matter what he has to do to get it. When Myson realised he wasn't going to get a real link to Seriatt through Lycern, and that the child she'd given birth to was gone, he chose you, for whatever reason, to take on the role instead. Besides, Myson's infertile. You didn't know that, did you? I bet the tests you claim proved that Lycern was your mother didn't prove Myson's your father, did they?'

Michael tried to maintain his composure, but was obviously rattled. 'Why would they perform a paternity test?' He shook his head, and glanced at the floor. 'Anyway, it doesn't matter what you think, or what you think you know. Do you really *believe* you can stop us?'

'Yes. Cascari's entitled to the seat of Monosiell by birth, and he has to take it. We have to stop Myson gaining influence on Seriatt, stop his arms deals with the Sinz, stop him gaining access to the Seriatts' time-travel technology.'

'How did you know about that?' said Michael, looking surprised. '*No one* knows about that.'

'Apparently that's not the case, now is it?' said Ash.

Delgado sensed growing unease in Michael as doubt began to creep in. There were several moments of tense silence.

'All right,' said Delgado. 'Let's make a deal.'

Michael snorted derisively. 'A deal, Delgado? What kind of a deal? What do you think you have that I could possibly want?'

'A chance to get out of here before Throubesh comes back and begins having fun with you. You might claim to be half *mourst*, but you don't look to me as if you'd stand much of his attention. We're going to try to get out of here. If you want to you can come with us.'

'And you want what from me in return?'

'Access to the Seriatts. You're here with the backing of the Andamour Council. If we get you out of here in one piece, then you must allow an Oracle to ascertain which of us is telling the truth. Whether the position of Monosiell rightfully belongs to you, or to Cascari.'

'And if I decline your kind offer? What then, Delgado?'

'We kill you before we leave and take our own chances. We might not get to the Seriatts but at least that way Myson's out of the picture. Although I've no doubt that would only be temporary. I guess it all depends on how confident you are about what you claim.'

Michael blinked, looked at each one of the three individuals before him. 'Well, you have considerable combat experience,' he said. 'So I guess my chances of getting out of here in one piece are that much greater if I work with you. I doubt very much that the ZeeS4 officers who brought us here have informed the palace of my whereabouts. They're probably not even aware who I am.'

'So it's a deal?'

Michael nodded. 'It's a deal.'

Upon hearing the footsteps in the corridor outside Delgado shouted for help in Counian. In front of him Cascari was lying face down on the blood-spattered cell floor, motionless. Ash and Michael stood on opposite sides of the room, watching.

A few moments later a square area in the top half of the cell door began to shimmer, as if its very fabric was softening. Eventually, the metal looked like a sheet of thick ice, frosted and rough, and the silhouette of a head became visible through the opaque panel. Although it lacked detail, Delgado could tell by its shape that it was a *vilume*. He assumed that from the other side the panel was transparent, and that the Seriatt could see clearly into the cell.

'Please. He needs help,' said Delgado, kneeling and leaning over Cascari's body. He looked up. 'There was a fight. These two . . .' He motioned towards Cascari and Michael. 'He fell and hit his head on the edge of the bunk. I think his life is in danger.' The *vilume* looked at the place Delgado indicated. There was a smear of blood on the corner of one of the bars forming the bunk's metal frame.

The Seriatt's voice – crisp yet warm – was amplified slightly by a comms device Delgado could not see. 'Step away from the door. Move over to the other side of the room.'

Delgado stood, and he, Michael and Ashala did as instructed. They heard bolts in the door release as the Seriatt unlocked it. It opened slowly, and the *vilume* stepped cautiously into the cell.

The *vilume*'s face had some male qualities, but a very delicate bone structure and fineness of features. The masculine aspects of the *vilume*'s appearance unnerved Delgado, as he realised that he found this intersex Seriatt extremely attractive. One moment the *vilume* appeared male to him, the next female. He was unsure how he perceived the creature, but given the emotions the Seriatt seemed to be stirring in him he found himself reluctant to consider the *vilume* as being anything but female.

Watching them intently, the *vilume* closed and locked the door behind her, then slipped the key into one of the folds of her floor-length robe. She crouched next to Cascari, cocking her head to one side as she looked at him, glancing warily at the others. As the Seriatt moved to roll Cascari over, Delgado leaped towards her.

He crossed the room before she was able to react, moving behind her and curling his right arm around her neck. He clamped his left hand firmly over her mouth, then dragged her backwards towards the corner of the room so that anyone passing the cell would not see the commotion within. As the *vilume* became increasingly red-faced, muffled protestations bled from between Delgado's fingers. The Seriatt clutched desperately at his arm and tried to pull it from her neck. She also tried to resist the movement across the room, but her feet could not gain purchase on the smooth floor.

As the Seriatt thrashed, Ash helped Cascari to his feet. The young man dabbed at his bloodied nose and muttered something.

'Sorry about that,' grunted Delgado, as he continued to wrestle with the Seriatt. 'Hit you a bit harder than I'd intended. I had to make sure it bled properly, though.'

'Yeah, I guess so.'

As Delgado continued to struggle with the increasingly agitated *vilume* he glanced at Ash, Cascari and Michael who were watching. 'Well, give me a hand here will you, for Christ's sake?'

Simultaneously the three others stepped forward as if this had not occurred to them before. Cascari and Michael each reached for one of the *vilume*'s slender ankles, while Ash grabbed one of the Seriatt's wrists, but they were difficult to grip so frantic was the *vilume*'s struggle.

'Live one, isn't she?' shouted Michael as they grappled with her.

'Maybe she's heard about the kind of thing that happens to Structure prisoners,' said Ash.

'We need to get this gown off her,' said Delgado. 'Then we can get her on to the bunk, wrap her tightly in the sheets to keep her still, stick something over her mouth to stop her squawking.'

The *vilume* managed to free her right ankle from Cascari's grip and kicked out at him; her toe connected solidly with his bottom jaw and he recoiled as he bit his tongue.

With a great struggle they managed to get the Seriatt's gown off and cast it to the floor. The *vilume* was surprisingly thin and bony when dressed in only the underwear worn beneath the heavy garment.

'Get her on to the bunk,' instructed Delgado.

With an effort that seemed utterly disproportionate to the *vilume*'s slight frame, they finally managed to heft her on to the narrow bed. While Cascari pinned down both her ankles Delgado tore a long strip from one of the sheets and tied it around her head, pulling it tightly over her mouth as a gag. Michael removed his hand from her mouth at the last moment, and Delgado tied the gag tight enough that she would not be able to bite through it. She writhed furiously, hoarse rasps sizzling in her throat as she continued to struggle, her eyes burning with rage.

The gag in place, Delgado and Cascari quickly turned the *vilume* over, pulling the sheets tightly around her body, and then tied knots in them. When satisfied that she was held securely, they turned her so that she was facing the ceiling. The slender *vilume* began to thrash more wildly than ever.

Delgado walked over to the gown, picked it up and began searching through it. 'Where did she put that key?' he said. 'This thing's got more pockets in it than a Maatine vendor's trading gown.' After considerable searching he produced the key from one of the pockets and held it up. 'Here we are,' he said triumphantly. 'Our passport to freedom. Well, the corridor outside, at least.' He threw the garment to Ash. 'Here. Put that on.'

She looked at him. 'Let me guess. You want to me distract the *mourst* in that control room or whatever it is, right?'

'Aw, come on, Ash,' said Delgado. 'You know how good you are at that kind of thing.'

'Look, Delgado,' she said. 'I'm happy to have a go, but I mean . . .' She held up the *vilume*'s hooded robe. Even with her arms at full stretch the garment still trailed on the floor. 'This thing's just too darn big for me. You think he's not going to be suspicious of the fact that it's dragging along the floor and he can't see my hands because the sleeves are so long?'

'Look, put up the hood so he can't see your face, tuck one cuff inside the other so he can't see your hands and dazzle him with your charms. That's all there is to it. You can do that, can't you?'

'To be truthful it's more your size. Maybe you should be the one to do all the dazzling, Delgado,' she suggested.

He shook his head. 'No can do. I've got to take him out. I can hardly do that in a fancy dressing gown now, can I? And then I have my reputation to think of.'

'Whereas my reputation's worth jack, is that it?'

'I didn't say that.'

On the bunk the restrained Seriatt squirmed and made

frustrated noises. Delgado leaned over the Seriatt and looked into the *vilume*'s eyes. 'Look, I realise this is probably annoying, but you've just got to be grateful we didn't kill you. Thing is, I think we've done a little too much of that already. You understand?'

The *vilume* wriggled and tried to kick her legs, despite being bound tightly in the sheet.

They left the cell and made their way back towards Otonz's office. It was late, the lights were dimmed and the white-walled corridors empty. Ash walked ahead, wearing the *vilume*'s gown. They had managed to shorten the length of the garment she wore a little by tucking part of the back into Ash's waistband. It now dragged along the floor no more than the robes worn by other *vilume*. The hood was raised to hide her face, and her hands were hidden within the cuffs. Although slightly short, she could pass for a *vilume* – briefly. While this appeared to be a relatively low-security facility, Delgado believed that having an apparent *vilume* leading them should buy some time if they bumped into any other Seriatts.

They passed a room filled with Seriattic noise. It seemed to be a combination of *mourst* and *conosq* laughter. They sounded slightly drunk. The four turned another corner, and were in the corridor leading to the office of Acting Superintendent Otonz.

'You go and see how the land lies,' whispered Delgado. 'We'll wait here. If he sees us we'll have no chance.'

Ash walked ahead while the others waited at the corner. She paused at the door, peered briefly through the window into the room, then rejoined them.

'He's asleep,' she whispered. 'Snoring like an oaf.'

'Do you think you can get him to open the door?' asked Delgado.

'Ask me again later,' she said in hushed tones, glancing back towards the door, 'when we're outside. You wait here. I'll distract him. When the time is right, you make your move.'

She walked the short distance back to the door. When she reached it she touched a button to one side and a faint buzzing sound could be heard. Although she did not move her head, Delgado knew from a shift in her mental patterns that Acting Superintendent Otonz had successfully been roused.

At the end of the corridor Otonz's bulky shape appeared in the window in the door. Delgado tensed – this was the key moment: if Otonz realised she wasn't a Seriatt before the door was open they were done for. The *mourst* looked down at Ashala's hooded form with an expression Delgado was unable to assess, but he noticed that despite being less pronounced than in other *mourst*, the ridges at Otonz's neck were slightly swollen, indicating some arousal.

Otonz reached out with his right hand. There was a faint click, and the sound of the Acting Superintendent's breath was suddenly audible, even twenty metres or so along the corridor. 'What do you want?' His tone indicated that he was only half interested. He was probably already entertaining fantasies about what might occur between himself and this *vilume*.

'We believe there is a problem with the communications relay in your office,' said Ash, keeping her head bowed slightly so the *mourst* could see only the lower part of her face. 'I have to investigate and report to my superior as soon as possible.'

Otonz looked uncertain. He licked his lips, rubbed the palm of his right hand across his face as he carefully appraised the situation. He glanced behind him, then looked back towards Ashala. 'What kind of problem?' he asked. 'I have not been notified of a problem and have experienced no comms errors.' Delgado saw a tiny globule of spittle launch from Otonz's mouth as he spoke.

'The problem is unspecified at this time, and although it may not affect your personal communications it may help us to trace the source if we can check your output log. We need to discount your office as a possible source.' Delgado watched Ash intently, and with more than a little admiration.

'I am not sure,' said Otonz. 'I think I would have been told of this earlier if it were so important.'

'The problem has only just become apparent and is spreading rapidly,' she said. 'There has been time to inform no one of the situation.' She softened her voice slightly, almost imperceptibly. 'Someone of your position would otherwise have been notified long ago.' Otonz moved slightly, as if shifting his weight from one foot to the other. He stood a little more upright and stuck out his chin. 'If we do not act quickly,' Ash continued, 'the entire base could lose communications capabilities. Do you wish to be held responsible for that?'

Otonz sniffed sharply as he apparently came to a decision, then reached out to the door release. Delgado edged back to make sure he would not be seen, and indicated to Cascari and Michael that they should be ready. Then there was a loud click as the door to Otonz's office was unlocked.

Delgado leaned forward just enough to be able to see along the corridor. Otonz was standing in the doorway. Ash's slight frame was dwarfed by his bulky, somewhat angular form. Delgado noticed that there had been a change in his expression: a grotesque, Seriattic smile on the *mourst*'s face.

Her head still bowed, Ash conversed quietly with Otonz for a few moments, but their voices were too hushed for Delgado to hear. Ash drew her right hand from within the left cuff of the robe she wore and touched Otonz's arm. The *mourst* looked at her hand and seemed to realise that it was somehow unusual, but failed to recognise it as human.

As Otonz opened the door wider, Ash said something else and looked up at the *mourst*, simultaneously making a signal to Delgado with her right hand.

But by that time Delgado was already running along the corridor, with Cascari and Michael close behind him.

As Otonz turned to close the door, Delgado used all his

momentum and threw himself at the *mourst*. He hit Otonz in the chest and the Seriatt grunted and staggered back, arms flailing as Delgado pushed him up against the wall. Delgado's right forearm was pressed against the *mourst*'s throat. While Delgado knew Otonz was physically stronger, he also knew that the Acting Superintendent did not appreciate this fact.

'How do we get out of here?' Delgado demanded aggressively, increasing the pressure on Otonz's neck. The *mourst* made a series of short, incomprehensible sounds. Otonz, his head pressed to one side against the wall, glared sideways at Delgado with fearful, bloodshot eyes. 'What is the procedure for opening the doors?' Delgado demanded, nodding towards the door next to them. Otonz hissed and burbled. He shuffled his feet and tried to move his head, but Delgado held him firmly in place.

'I think he'd tell you if he could, Delgado,' said Ash without looking up: she was sitting behind Otonz's desk, opening drawers and peering into them.

Delgado eased the pressure on the *mourst*'s neck slightly. Otonz gulped air gratefully, his eyes watering, pale secondary membranes sliding repeatedly across them. Delgado was aware that Cascari and Michael were standing close behind him, and could hear Ash continuing to rifle through the Acting Superintendent's desk. 'I'll ask you again,' said Delgado, making an effort to speak calmly and clearly. 'What is the procedure for opening the doors and getting outside?'

The podgy *mourst* looked at him with puffy and red-rimmed eyes. His lips were slightly pursed and he was trembling slightly. Delgado reached around and pulled the small blade from his waistband. Its sharp edge glinted. Delgado did not take his eyes off Otonz who stared fixedly at the blade as it was held up in front of his face.

'The sharpened edge is such a basic weapon,' said Delgado. 'I've always had a fondness for it. Basic but effective. They don't block or fail to charge or misfire and blow half of your head off. And they're quiet, too. If you can stifle the victim's screams you can kill and be gone in moments.' Otonz flinched as Delgado pressed the blade against his neck. He smiled, and applied pressure until a thin line of blood appeared. 'I'll ask you a final time,' Delgado said calmly. 'How do we open these doors?'

Otonz swallowed dryly, licked his lips and looked from Delgado to the others in the room. Tiny pearls of sweat shone on his broad, dark-skinned forehead. His breathing was shallow and rapid. He looked at Delgado. 'A menu,' he said hoarsely. 'Go through Sec4 on the screen over there and input the passwords.'

'Show me,' Delgado snarled, yanking Otonz towards the desk.

The fog was thicker than when the copters had landed, coiling around the buildings and the floodlight towers. The light cast by the floodlights painted grey smears in the fog, but the strength of the light they emitted was almost completely absorbed by the brume, making them ineffective. This suggested to Delgado that such thick fog was the exception rather than the rule around the base. He considered that this was just his kind of luck.

The three copters sat like gigantic, bloated toads in the murk; their smooth shapes occasionally broken by fragile antennae clusters, variously sized domes, and angular protuberances of unknown purpose. The huge, dormant rotors arched down towards the damp surface of the landing site like long, tired limbs.

Crouching between two refuse containers at the edge of the courtyard, Delgado, Cascari and Ashala stared across at the machines. The night air was cold, and clouds of breath-mist formed briefly in front of their faces before being lost amid the fog.

'See anything?' whispered Delgado. There were no replies. 'Good. We've been lucky.'

'So far,' said Michael from behind them.

'Quite, quite.'

There was sudden noise as the large shape next to Michael moved. Otonz groaned as Delgado leaned back and dug his right elbow into the *mourst*'s ribs. Otonz was lying on his left side on the slightly damp ground. His feet were free, but his fat hands were bound behind his back with copious lengths of broad tape, reels of which Cascari had found in Otonz's office. The *mourst*'s eyes bulged over the top of another length of tape pressed firmly over his mouth, which moved in and out in time with his heavy breathing. Small drops of condensation formed on it as he exhaled through his long, *mourst* nostrils. The left side of his face was speckled with small indentations and particles of grit where it had rested on the ground.

'Remind me again,' said Cascari, frowning hard as he looked over his shoulder at the Acting Superintendent. 'Just what the hell did we bring him along for? He'll slow us down at best, and at worst raise the alarm before we can get out of here. We should've left him behind.'

The soles of Delgado's boots crunched on grit as he twisted to look at the *mourst*.

'He might know the local terrain,' whispered Delgado. 'It's all very well saying we're going to fly out of here, but we won't know where we're going. He might just be able to help us.'

They fell silent again, staring into the mist, almost holding their breath as they listened for any sound. Delgado stared into every shadowy nook in search of cameras, drones or guards, but the area seemed deserted. The Seriattic night was silent and still, apart from the swirling fog.

At Delgado's command they shrank back into the shadows cast by the refuse bins, hunkering down to make themselves as small as possible to discuss their plan of action. Suddenly voices exploded into the night and there was laughter and heavy footsteps crunching on the courtyard. Cascari and Delgado pressed themselves against Otonz to ensure he would not be seen even if he was stupid enough to try and raise the alarm.

Delgado looked into the fog, watching intently, but could see nothing. Then two *mourst* emerged from the murky layers. They seemed to be low-ranking guards. Basic weapons of the short-stem type were slung over their shoulders. They wore ill-fitting armour comprised of chest and back plates, shin, arm and shoulder guards. There also appeared to be attachments for helms of some kind at their shoulders and behind their heads, but these were apparently elsewhere.

They were casual, joking and laughing in short, gruff coughs. One – the taller, slimmer of the two – seemed to be recounting something in Seriattic to the other, who was looking up at his colleague with what Delgado assumed was admiration, although he found the *mourst*'s expression impossible to read. Younger, a lack of confidence indicated by his somewhat slouching gait and apparent awe, he growled at occasional points in his colleague's story, as if agreeing or otherwise.

Delgado spoke to Cascari. 'Can you translate any of that?'

Cascari listened for a moment then wrinkled his nose in an expression of uncertainty, in which Delgado always saw an odd mix of human and Seriatt. 'Something about an urgent alliance the older one's had,' he said. 'An act of *driss lousoue*.' He paused again, listening for a moment longer. 'He's proud of what he is referring to as his "achievement".' He jerked his head towards the guard. 'And he's boasting to his colleague about his union with the *conosq*.'

Delgado eyed the two *mourst* carefully, then slowly got into a crouching position. He was preparing to run.

'What are you planning?' asked Cascari.

'I'm going to get those weapons. The ZeeS4 took ours, remember?'

'Why?' asked Cascari. 'They're heading for that prefab. In a few moments they'll be in there, then we can get aboard the copters and fly out of here.'

'We *need* those weapons,' asserted Delgado. 'We have no firearms whatsoever. They'll be easy meat. It won't take long. You want to give me a hand?'

'If you insist.' He stood next to Delgado. 'A father and son team,' he said, patting Delgado on the back. 'Just like in the Hornets.'

'Oh please,' groaned Michael from behind them. 'You're making me feel ill.'

Ash leaned over to him. 'Shut your mouth,' she hissed. 'Or we might decide our deal's off.'

As the *mourst* approached the prefab, Delgado whispered to Cascari. 'We'll take a bit of a detour, run along that verge there,' he indicated a strip of grass behind the two parked copters. 'It'll take a bit longer, but we heard them before we could see them,' he pointed at the *mourst*. 'If we go running across the courtyard they'll have time for a drink and a snooze and still be able to shoot us before we get there. You ready?' Cascari nodded eagerly. Delgado turned to the others. 'While we're dealing with them you get into one of the copters and make ready to get out of here. We'll probably attract considerable attention, so we don't want to hang around.' Delgado glanced around the courtyard. There were no other Seriatts in sight. 'OK,' he said, 'let's go.'

He and Cascari started running.

As Delgado and Cascari sprinted towards the two *mourst* they could hear only the soft sound of their footfalls on the damp grass and their own breathing. They passed close behind the copters, taking advantage of the short, faint shadows the bulky machines cast.

As they closed on the two *mourst* they were on the shallow steps leading up to the prefab door. The taller, older one was still recounting his tale as the younger guard half turned, reaching for the door handle. Seeing movement, he looked past his colleague. When he saw Delgado and Cascari approaching, his expression changed and the other *mourst* turned to see what had caught his attention. Before the Seriattic guards had time to reach for their weapons, Delgado and Cascari had launched themselves at them.

The two *mourst* groaned heavily as they hit the ground. Their weapons were flung from their shoulders and went skidding and spinning across the courtyard. Cascari had attacked the younger of the two and suddenly found himself lying awkwardly on top of the *mourst* like an inexperienced lover. He looked for the guard's lost weapon, but it was just out of reach and he had to scrabble off the Seriatt and along the ground in order to get it. He could hear the cursing *mourst* struggling to his feet behind him.

Cascari grasped the weapon's muzzle, jumped to his feet and swung the gun around at arm's length. The weapon's butt caught the young *mourst* a strong and sickening blow on the jaw. The Seriatt cried out and fell to the floor, his long hands clasped to his face. Cascari stepped up to him as the *mourst* lay on the ground, and clubbed the young Seriatt with the gun. He glanced across the courtyard and saw the others making their way towards one of the three copters, Ash encouraging the staggering Otonz by giving the *mourst* frequent shoves in the back.

A short distance away Delgado and the taller of the two *mourst* seemed to be engaged in some kind of carefully orchestrated ritual dance. Half crouching, they circled slowly, hands either flattened and rigid or fists clenched. Although the *mourst*'s weapon lay just a couple of metres from them, neither would be able to get it before being overpowered by the other.

Cascari looked at Delgado. Although the older man seemed tired, he was clearly skilled in such martial arts. Despite Delgado's skill and experience, however, the *mourst* confronting him was young and fit, quick of mind and lean of limb. The guard was continuously mumbling quietly to himself an ancient ritual chant his species learned from the *conchey trinzig diasii*, and often used as a source of support in combat.

Cascari looked towards the copter the others were now boarding, back to Delgado and his adversary, then down at the short stem weapon he was holding. He turned it over in his hands. It was relatively insubstantial, very light in weight and seemed to be basic in design. There were no data screens or AI core and the ordnance appeared to be the equivalent of hi-kompression rounds. Dumb ones, probably. But at this range the intelligence of the ammunition wouldn't be an issue anyway.

He looked around the weapon's hand-grip, released a transparent plastic catch and flicked up the switch beneath it. The palms of his hands began to tingle satisfyingly. There were one or two rotary controls with small characters on them. Although he was unable to identify what they might do, he nonetheless rotated each of the controls in either direction a couple of times, unsure whether or not they would improve its performance.

He looked up at Delgado and the *mourst* guard once again. Still they circled each other, as if demonstrating an ancient courtship dance. They evidently recognised each other's skill in whatever slightly differing forms of combat they were utilising and, although occasionally one or the other of them would kick out, the potential blow was always blocked by the other. It was a fight going nowhere, fast.

Cascari looked across at the copter again. All were aboard now. A faint light was visible within the cockpit and he could see a moving silhouette. It appeared to be Ash. In front of him the two men continued their laborious non-fight. Cascari saw the opportunity to escape beginning to slip by and realised that he had to make a decision. It risked raising the alarm, but surely one shot could go unheard, or be mistaken for something else. Couldn't it?

He raised the gun to his shoulder. The two combatants either failed to notice or were not prepared to risk looking away from their opponent for even a moment.

Gently, when the *mourst* was directly in front of him, Cascari squeezed the trigger.

The gun released a potent stream of composite energy packets in a raging torrent. Recoil thumped the weapon's butt hard against Cascari's shoulder, shoving him bodily backwards. He closed his eyes instinctively as brilliant flashes exploded just in front of the gun's muzzle. He heard nothing above the sound of its release. He stopped firing and opened his eyes, blinking rapidly at the cloud of thin, acrid smoke hanging in the air just in front of him, its dark, dense composition a contrast to the pale grey fog.

The guard was dead, having apparently been dismembered by the gunfire. There were some scorched clothes on the ground which looked like the remains of his uniform, some charred shapes that may or may not have been body parts, and a large hunk of partially clothed meat that appeared to be the torso and legs, although Cascari could not be sure whether this was the case.

He looked up and saw that one of the copters was burning, apparently having been the recipient of a few rounds. A broad section of the tail was glowing orange, and in the space of just a few seconds the delicate framework became visible as the outer skin disintegrated, consumed from within by fire. The fragile supporting structure weakened quickly, and the rear half of the tail and the secondary rotor assembly collapsed, crashing to the courtyard and scattering across the ground in a wash of bright sparks. There was a fiery glow in the cockpit and small explosions began to punctuate the quiet night as various gas- and liquid-filled containers reached critical temperatures. A klaxon suddenly began to sound from elsewhere in the complex – a loud, shrill tone demanding attention. Lines of previously dormant floodlights became active, painting bright strips in the fog.

Delgado walked towards him. 'Should I consider myself lucky or did you mean to miss me by millimetres like that?'

Cascari briefly examined the weapon again. 'Let's just say I wouldn't advise anyone to choose one of these things if they were looking for a weapon of accuracy. They have sidearms, too, look.' He pointed at holsters worn at the waist by both *mourst*. Delgado took the weapons from each Seriatt, looked at them briefly, then placed them in his tunic pockets.

He turned and looked towards the copters. 'We better get out of here,' he said. 'We'll give that thing a wide berth in case it decides to blow.'

The two men began to run quickly towards the machine the others had boarded. They were already able to feel the heat from the burning copter. Vents immediately beneath the main rotor of the aircraft the others had boarded exhaled clouds of dense smoke and brief gouts of flame as Ash brought the machine to life. Even over the noise of the other, gradually disintegrating copter, there was an audible wheezing sound as the rotor struggled into life. By the time Delgado and Cascari had reached the open hatch the rotor was spinning rapidly, causing a great downdraft that sent huge swathes of mist across the courtyard and fanned the flames of the aircraft burning nearby.

As the two men clambered up the steps to board the shuddering craft, half a dozen *mourst* appeared from one of the prefabs to their left. Delgado glanced at them. They were looking at the burning aircraft. One of them pointed towards it while the others remained motionless. They did not seem to have noticed the fact that the second copter was about to take off.

Delgado clambered into the aircraft. Michael was sitting on one of the bench seats and Otonz was lying on the floor, frantically kicking his legs. Delgado crossed the passenger compartment to look quickly out of the window on the other side, and saw the burning aircraft slump forward and down as its short landing struts collapsed. The fuselage buckled as it impacted the ground and a couple of small cylinders strapped to its side fell from their cradle and exploded impressively. As balloons of fire rose rapidly into the sky, the flames eating the machine seemed to attain new hunger.

Delgado turned and climbed through the central bulkhead into the cockpit.

Ash was sitting in the pilot's seat, wearing one of the helmets. A dark reflective strip covered the top half of her face. She looked at him and smiled.

'What took you so long?' she said.

'You know what these Seriatts are like,' he replied as he settled into his seat. He handed her one of the guns taken from the *mourst* guards. 'Always got to make a song and dance about everything. We ready to lift?'

She tucked the gun beneath her belt. 'Almost. Another fifteen seconds or so.'

'I'm not sure we've got that long.'

'I guess we'll soon find out.'

Delgado looked ahead. More guards had joined the first group outside the prefab. These seemed to be more aware of what was happening than their colleagues and were possibly of higher rank. One of them certainly seemed to be giving orders to the others. Two or three of them had weapons.

'We're are almost ready to go,' said Ash. 'Rotor's almost up to speed.' She rapidly touched control tabs, cycling through displays. 'OK. You guys ready? I have a feeling this could get a little rough.'

Delgado turned and peered back into the passenger compartment. Michael and Cascari were sitting at opposite ends of the bench seat, looking out of the aircraft like a couple after a row. Otonz continued to wriggle around on the floor.

Ash gripped the main control stick firmly but gently in her

left hand, while gripping another, smaller joystick in her right. She increased power and the vibrations running through the copter increased in intensity. The aircraft began to feel distinctly buoyant as it reached the verge of flight. There was a large explosion from the gradually disintegrating copter in front of them that scattered shards of glass and metal across the nose of their own machine.

The copter lurched and rose abruptly. Ash simultaneously manipulated physical controls and a multitude of virtual interfaces, as if taken by surprise by the suddenness with which the aircraft had taken off. As the machine climbed, Delgado saw something emerging in the mist along one of the roads intersecting the prefabs. It was an articulated vehicle of some kind, a long, three-part ladder on the top of its broad body. Various *mourst* hung from its sides as it rumbled on caterpillar tracks towards the burning copter.

He looked back towards the *mourst* guards and saw three or four of them – their silhouettes bulky with armour – beginning to ascend slowly, apparently wearing lifters of some kind. There were flashes around the copter and a series of dull thuds: they were being shot at.

Delgado glanced at Ash. She seemed to be concentrating hard, her lips moving slightly as if muttering to herself. Perhaps she was cursing. Or praying. Delgado realised that he did not know whether she had any religious beliefs.

Her head occasionally moved in sharp jerking motions as she manipulated the data being fed to her. As they reached a height of around forty metres, roughly level with the ridge of one of the higher roofs, the copter lurched. Delgado instinctively reached out with his left arm to support himself as the machine tipped precariously to one side. It rolled rapidly to an alarmingly steep angle of around sixty degrees before Ash was able to correct it, bringing the machine level again by descending slightly.

She was frowning, cycling rapidly through information

sheets. Delgado leaned forward and saw the airborne *mourst* rising to the same height as the copter, but maintaining a reasonable distance away from it. Their stubby rifles released more flashes of brilliance. There were further dull thuds as the copter's armoured hull took hits. Ash raised energy shields.

'What's wrong?' Delgado called across to her.

'I don't know.' She tried to gain altitude but again the copter began to tip to one side. The *mourst* continued to fire at the hovering copter, beginning to move cautiously towards the machine as it became apparent that return fire was not forthcoming, and the craft was apparently in some difficulty. 'It's as if this thing's caught on something. Tethered to the ground somehow.' She wrestled with the controls for a few moments more, then abruptly tore the visuals strip from her head. 'You take control,' she yelled, unfastening her harness. 'There's something I need to check.'

'I can't fly this thing,' protested Delgado.

'I'm not asking you to fly it, Delgado. Just hold station, that's all.' She flung the visor into his lap. 'Wear that and take the controls while I go back here for a minute.' She indicated the passenger compartment. Before Delgado could respond she had plunged through the bulkhead.

Delgado looked down at the visor in his lap, and then from one hand to the other as he tightly gripped the controls. 'How the hell am I supposed to put that on now?' he asked himself quietly. He glanced from window to instrument panels to controls to visor. He paused, judged the machine's stability, then let go of the main control for a fraction of a second. To his surprise nothing happened. There was no noticeable pitch, yaw or roll, no sudden loss of altitude, no drama of any kind. He released the controls again, grabbed the visor and quickly put it on to his face. He felt instantly sick as a river of overlays surged into his brain: datasheets, stat analyses, weapons controls, array after array of deeply complex system interfaces he had no hope or intention of trying to analyse or manipulate.

He pulled the visor from his head and flung it on to the pilot's seat: it seemed there were things that he would never be able to do again, skills lost; never to be recaptured.

He glanced behind him. Ash had opened the copter's hatch, the fluid material melting back into its source gland. A draft of cool air hit him and wind buffeted around the inside of the copter as, watched by Michael, Cascari and the restrained Otonz, Ash's hair ruffled and flicked across her face in the downdraft as she hung on to part of the aircraft's interior with her right hand, and leaned out through the open hatch, and down to look some way underneath the copter's hull.

Delgado looked ahead again and adjusted his grip on the controls, trying to maintain the vehicle's attitude. Ahead, the airborne *mourst* were getting closer, now only sixty or so metres away. He could see faint spectres of transparent blue flame writhing behind them as their airpac thrusters pushed them through the sky. Their weapons' discharge continued to be safely absorbed by the copter's shields, but their unchallenged attack was beginning to compromise the strength of the aircraft's defences, and before long the shields would weaken and disengage completely. Soon they would be so close that the shields would be useless anyway, unable to absorb and dissipate the energy effectively at such close range.

Delgado glanced back and saw Ash haul herself back inside the copter. He frowned as she rolled Otonz on to his back and sat astride him. She grabbed one of the short-stem rifles captured from the guards and busily adjusted its controls. Delgado glanced forward, then looked back over his shoulder in time to see Ash shove the rifle down the front of Otonz's waistband. She stood, and beckoned to Cascari and Michael. The two men leaned towards her. Having apparently communicated her intentions, they struggled to manoeuvre Otonz around so he was lying sideways to the door. Wind howled around the interior of the aircraft as the huge rotor thundered above.

Delgado looked ahead, deftly corrected the copter's drift. A huge explosion suddenly filled the cockpit with a rich red-orange light as the other copter on the ground exploded, miscellaneous debris flung into the air by the blast. Delgado heard a series of loud metallic clunks and bangs as pieces of wreckage too small to be stopped by the copter's shields made contact with its underside. The airborne guards were so close now he could almost read the names on their armoured breastplates.

He heard another faint explosion somewhere immediately behind or below, and instinctively looked back. He knew there was something different, but for a moment did not appreciate exactly what it was.

Then he realised: Otonz was no longer there.

Ash resealed the hatch and clambered back into the cockpit. She grabbed the visuals visor from Delgado and sat in the pilot's seat.

'You managed without me?' she asked brightly.

'Where's Otonz?'

'Too much ballast,' she said as she retook the controls.

'You've thrown him out, haven't you?'

'We were tethered to the ground by a thick pipe or cable of some kind,' Ash explained. 'A fuel line or data link, something like that. Whatever it was, it was stopping us from lifting.'

'So you just threw him out?'

Ash glanced across at him, frowning. 'What the hell are you worried about, Delgado? You would have killed him if you felt it was necessary. Hell, you've killed plenty of people before now when it *wasn't* necessary.' As she spoke she powered the copter directly towards the airborne *mourst* in the air ahead of the aircraft.

Delgado pulled a face. 'I can't argue with that, I guess. What did you do? How did you sever the link?'

'I once read about those guns on a Structure intelligence site

I gained access to. They have a suicide setting, for use if the operative is captured or surrounded by the enemy. It's something to do with *mourst* honour, apparently. It can be set with a delay so it blows up in the captor's face.' She looked at Delgado as if that would be explanation enough, but the way he looked at her indicated that it wasn't. 'So I set it and pushed him out. He landed near the point at which the cable was joined to the ground and the explosion broke the link.'

Delgado wasn't sure whether he was amazed at what she had done because he admired it, or whether he was simply surprised that she had done it at all.

Ahead of them most of the airborne *mourst* descended quickly as they saw the copter rushing towards them, but one of them tried to gain altitude. He was too slow, either having insufficient power in his liftpac to climb, or failing to react quickly enough. The copter's broad rotors sliced him in half at the waist. His legs bounced off the top of the aircraft and plummeted towards the ground, while the upper half of his body – driven by the still firing liftpac – rose quickly before altering course and eventually plunging downwards after the legs, as if somehow seeking reunification.

Another *mourst* moved first one way then the other, almost as if his liftpac was malfunctioning or he lacked the experience necessary to control it properly. In the end he simply collided with the copter directly in front of Delgado. The bubble gave slightly as a result of the impact. With the shape of the *mourst*'s body impressed into the transparent substance, Delgado caught a glimpse of the Seriatt's face before he fell. He looked young, inexperienced, scared. The canopy regained its original shape within a couple of seconds of the Seriatt falling away from the copter, and the image of the young *mourst* was gone.

The copter was climbing rapidly now, the flames and carnage just a coloured glow somewhere beneath them, casting a fiery hue across the Seriattic night.

'So which way you wanna go, Delgado?'

'I don't know. We don't know where we are, do we? The idea of bringing Otonz along was so he could act as a navigator.'

Suddenly there was a huge explosion somewhere towards the rear of the copter. Physical instruments in the cockpit shattered. Electrical circuits sparked and fizzed and the lights went out. The copter's engine groaned desperately and loud irregular bangs indicated a terminal injury. The aircraft began to descend at increasing speed.

'What the hell was that?' yelled Delgado.

'I don't know,' Ash replied coolly. 'But it was goddamn effective whatever it was.' She was grappling with the controls, manipulating interfaces in an attempt to retain control. 'Got a lot of systems damaged here,' she said. 'I'll just have to go with what I've got.'

Cascari leaned through from the passenger compartment as the emergency lighting was activated. 'What's going on?' he called above the engine's death throes.

'Looks like we're going down,' said Delgado. He paused as the copter shuddered violently. An alarm sounded briefly before being silenced by Ash. 'Tell our Structure friend back there to get ready. But try not to tense your muscles. Just relax. Otherwise you increase the risk of serious injury.'

Cascari nodded and feigned a salute. 'Thanks,' he said. 'Don't tense muscles. Relax. Right.' He withdrew back into the passenger compartment.

Delgado could see little other than layers of mist now. He had no idea how far they had gone, whether they were still over the installation or beyond its perimetre. He could see no ground detail. They could be at an altitude of five hundred metres or just fifty – there was no way of knowing. He looked at Ash. 'How long have we got?' he asked.

She did not respond, but continued to fight the machine. Sweat on her forehead glistened in the glow cast by the few still-functioning screens around her. She rocked her head slightly as she manipulated datasheets, as if making a series of categorical refusals.

As Delgado opened his mouth to speak again there was a tremendously loud but dull crump, followed by an even louder scraping sound. The copter shuddered. Delgado and Ash lurched forward in their straps. Delgado saw something out of the corner of his eye and looked over his shoulder. A person's back – it was impossible to tell whether it was Michael's or Cascari's – was wedged in the opening between the passenger compartment and the cockpit. It fell away from the opening as the copter lurched once more.

Quiet suddenly returned as the machine became airborne again. Delgado looked at Ash and saw her muttering to herself. There was a loud rushing sound, like fast flowing water or a stiff breeze, and the copter shuddered. Treetops? There was a series of stronger vibrations and several loud bangs. The copter began to tip to the left. Ash tried to correct but the machine did not respond. She yanked fiercely at the joystick as if brute force alone could persuade the stricken vehicle to comply, but her efforts were futile.

Delgado looked out of the window next to him and saw slender branches whipping against the copter's side in the darkness and mist. Something from the opposite side of the cockpit fell past him as the aircraft reached ninety degrees. He could hear the rotors chopping at the flora. Clutches of wire and data ribbons fell from their hiding places and hung in the air. Particles of dust and grit fell through the space separating Ash and Delgado. There was an incredibly loud bang and a violent lurch and suddenly the copter's main engine began to scream. Delgado was pressed against the side of the cockpit. He experienced a dizzy, falling sensation. He heard a shout. A sudden and tremendous jolt. He looked towards Ash and she mouthed something at him.

Then blackness came.

★

Delgado's consciousness returned slowly, small packets of information occasionally filtering through. The ground beneath him felt soft and damp. It smelled of earth and corruption. His head ached dully. He licked dry lips and swallowed.

He opened his eyes and found he was lying on a carpet of fallen leaves that were various shades of brown, russet and gold. Delgado pushed himself slowly to his feet. His forehead was pounding. He deftly probed the area above his eyes with the fingertips of his right hand. He felt no pain, but when he looked at his fingers they were red with partially congealed blood.

He saw Ash and Cascari making their way towards him. Behind them the copter was a fiercely burning carcass of distorted metal and plastic lying on its side. The heat was intense. Branches and twigs cracked and popped in the flames in a loose off-beat rhythm. The thick plume of dark smoke rising from the pyre was visible despite the fog and darkness.

Ash's face was scratched in several places and she was limping slightly. She was also holding her left arm at the elbow. Cascari had a bruise on his left cheekbone and his left eye was slightly bloodshot. His left ear was also scratched, and the hair above it was matted with blood.

'Trick or treat?' said Delgado grimly as they got closer. Neither of them smiled.

'We're screwed,' said Cascari bitterly. 'Big time.'

'Where's Michael?' Delgado asked.

'He made a run for it,' said Cascari. 'I'm not sure whether he was thrown clear or what, but he sure made a quick getaway.'

'Which way did he go?'

Cascari pointed past the nose of the burning copter. 'I couldn't see him for long. He just disappeared into the darkness.'

'Did he look injured?'

'Well, his legs were working fine, that's for sure.'

They began to walk away from the heat of the burning copter. Delgado looked at Ash. 'Any idea what happened?'

She shook her head. 'It was probably a SAM of some kind rather than anything more advanced. It doesn't really matter, does it? They hit us in the ass and down we went.'

'I guess not. Whatever happened, we're here now.' They paused by a closely packed group of trees. 'Have you any idea how far we flew? What was our direction of travel? Our speed? We might be able to work out our location in relation to the coast.'

'Which coast, though, Delgado?' Ash said. 'We crossed a coastline on our way to the base, remember? For what it's worth, if my reckoning is correct we're only a few kilometres from the base. If I managed to maintain a relatively straight course it's somewhere in that direction.' She motioned behind and to her left, but it was a vague gesture. 'How far it is I couldn't say. I think we might have covered three kilometres, but it might be less. We were airborne for only a short time.'

They all flinched as the burning copter suddenly exploded. Fat golden sparks rose high into the air then fell back towards the ground in elegant arcs, igniting trees and hitting the damp forest floor like gobbets of molten glass. Simultaneously, it seemed, their approach covered by the sound of the explosion, three copters appeared above the trees, solid shafts of brilliant white from their searchlights penetrating the foliage. The forest floor seemed to undulate as trees cast dark shadows that stretched and contracted in the glare.

Delgado signalled urgently and they pressed themselves against tree trunks. He peered around a tree, pressing his left cheek against its rough bark. The searchlights continued to bleach the forest. The noise of the copters on which they were mounted was overwhelming and the tree branches directly beneath the aircraft bent towards the floor in the immense downdraft. Delgado shielded his eyes and squinted as he looked up towards the hovering machines. He was just able to discern their outline, but his view was distorted by the brilliant lights and shivering trees. From what he could see the machines were different to the copter in which they had attempted to escape, narrower, sleeker, as if designed for speed rather than capacity.

He saw a shape, a changing silhouette, as a line was dropped to the ground from the copter. More lines dropped from other machines, and then figures slid down them to the forest floor, where they were immediately absorbed by shadow. They were slender and agile, not the bulky armoured guards he had seen earlier, possibly some kind of special forces.

Delgado glanced from one line to another and saw figures dropping down all of them, three, six, nine from each copter.

Delgado attracted Cascari's attention. 'Here, you'll need this,' he shouted. But his words were absorbed by the thunder of the copters above. He threw the second sidearm taken from the *mourst* guard. Ash already had hers drawn.

Delgado crouched, slowly raised his own rifle and activated the weapon. He looked along its short barrel, trying to spot potential targets by eyesight alone, but the constant shifting between darkness and brilliance made it virtually impossible for him to aim visually due to the constantly changing shadows. He released one or two rounds towards shimmering, ghostly shapes and quivering branches, but he was unable to tell whether or not he had hit anything.

He looked across at Ash. She looked concerned, and was mouthing something to him, pointing towards the copters, but he could not hear her above the noise of their engines. He shook his head. She shrugged, turned and aimed at one of the hovering copters, then fired a few concentrated rounds. The searchlight went out and she stopped firing briefly before resuming her assault, this time aiming at the other two copters. A few seconds later the two remaining searchlights were gone and the forest was plunged into relative darkness once more, the only light now being cast by the still-blazing wreckage to their left. All three aircraft seemed to climb quickly away from the forest canopy, the noise of their rotors lessening slightly.

In the trees, Delgado could see nothing distinctly alien to the forest environment. Then there was a brief but definite movement and he sprayed the area with ammunition.

There was an indistinct shimmering, a vague distortion. Cascari and Ash both fired a long burst of high intensity rounds that ploughed through the forest.

Delgado glimpsed movement in the corner of one eye. He turned swiftly but saw nothing. Suddenly a mass of Seriattic *mourst* seemed to rush at them from every direction like animals rising from the ground, and they were completely overwhelmed.

Eight

the progeny of Zeus

ZeeS4 headquarters, near the Seriattic Palace

When Delgado woke he found himself tied to a stretcher, being carried by *mourst* ZeeS4 officers through a labyrinth of dark, narrow corridors. Small oil lamps set in black iron sconces cast ineffective smears of piss-yellow light for short distances down the dark walls. A bitter odour of corruption was pervasive. He felt a certain sense of oppression that gave him the impression he was underground. The number of footsteps echoing through the corridor indicated that there were many people around him. He felt that Ash and Cascari were nearby, probably on stretchers behind his own.

They reached a thick steel door coated in a thin layer of rust. One of the enforcers walking in front of the stretcher produced a long metal key and unlocked the door, the mechanism within the lock clicking noisily. The door opened to reveal a cell. They were taken inside, untied, and made to get off the stretchers. Delgado looked across at Ash and Cascari: Ash looked utterly exhausted, as if all the recent events had suddenly caught up with her, and she held his gaze only momentarily before looking down at the flagstone floor. Cascari looked defiant and angry, although there was also weariness in his eyes. He realised that they both looked as though they had lost weight. Their hands and feet were then tied with strips of cloth to metal hoops set into one of the damp, moss-covered walls.

A *mourst* took a couple of paces across the cell and stood directly in front of Delgado and Cascari. Delgado judged from his appearance, a certain nobility in his general demeanour and the elaborate robes he wore, fashioned in a deep red, velvet-like material with gold edging, that he was not a member of the ZeeS4, or any other part of the military, but possibly a diplomat, Proctor or Arbiter. For several moments the *mourst* silently appraised Delgado and Cascari in turn, his mysterious dark eyes moving from one to the other of them. The Seriatt then turned and barked something Delgado did not catch at another *mourst*, who immediately scurried from the cell, slamming the metal door behind him.

Another *mourst* arrived as their bonds were being secured. He was smaller than the others, and, like the diplomat, clearly not a member of the ZeeS4 or an enforcer. He was carrying a black, rectangular box with hinges along one corner and a catch on one side. He sat down at a small wooden desk in the corner of the cell, placed the box upon it, and let the side facing him fold down on to the desk. Long, round ivory-coloured keys protruded from the front of the unit, which had a single narrow slot in the back. Like everything else Delgado had seen on Seriatt, the quality of this device's construction was superb. The *mourst* took a stack of thick, beige rectangular cards from a drawer in one side of the box, pushed one into a slot on the front of the machine, then trailed the rest down the side of the desk, putting a stack of them on the floor next to his left foot. The cards appeared to be perforated to enable easy separation.

As the *mourst* began to type, the keys clunked noisily and the cards began to shuffle across the desk and from the stack on the floor in synchrony with each keystroke. Having passed though the device, they emerged from the slot on the back having been impressed with a pattern of small indentations on one side, then moved gradually towards another stack on the floor behind the desk, each card folding neatly into position on top of the previous one. Delgado surmised that the *mourst* was transcribing events.

The diplomat and the ZeeS4 officers were arguing. Although the diplomat spoke in Counian, the ZeeS4 officer spoke in Seriatt. Either he was incapable of speaking Counian or – as Delgado suspected – there was a reluctance within the military to accept the new official language imposed on Seriatt by the Andamour Council.

'I will not allow you to interrogate them,' said the diplomat. 'There are too many uncertainties and possibilities.' The *mourst* growled something in response. 'It is not my concern what Major Throubesh has instructed. You will not harm them.'

The argument stopped as the cell door opened. Two *mourst* entered, followed by two *vilume* whose robes, although in the traditional *vilume* style, somehow seemed to be superior to those of other *vilume* Delgado had seen, the fabric thicker, the detailing more elaborate.

They were in turn followed by Michael and Osephius.

Osephius walked up to Delgado and stood directly in front of him, his hands clasped behind him. The transcription device began to clatter once more as Osephius spoke. 'Well, well, well,' he said, 'Alexander Delgado. We met briefly on *Zavanchia*, but, before that, how long was it since our last meeting?'

'Not long enough,' said Delgado.

Osephius smiled broadly. 'It's comforting to know that some things don't change. You're still the epitome of arrogance, Delgado. I'm glad we've met properly again after so long. Our last, brief meeting was, well, a little sour.' He looked at Cascari, then took a step towards him. 'This must be the half-Seriatt they say you're claiming has the right to take the position of Monosiell. You and the Mars Militia have been a considerable irritation to Structure for a long time, but I must say this is one of the most audacious stunts your little group has ever attempted to pull off.' Osephius leaned back, peering at Cascari with a frown, like an artist appraising his own work with a critical eye. 'He certainly *looks* like a hybrid, I'll give you that. You must have a fine biotech in your group to achieve such a skilful blend of Seriattic and human features.'

'I look like this because I'm half human, half Seriatt,' spat Cascari. 'Not a fake like him.' He jerked his head in Michael's direction.

Osephius smiled again, and half turned to look at Michael, who was standing behind him near the door. 'And he has his father's temperament, too. How touching.'

'Let the Oracles examine him,' said Delgado. 'They'll confirm our claims.'

Osephius turned to face him again. 'All in good time, Delgado. Have patience.' He took a few paces towards Ash. She looked up at him, her expression bitter. 'And look,' he said, smiling, 'a beautiful maiden to complete the trio.' He reached out and stroked Ashala's right cheek with the back of his left hand. When it neared the corner of her mouth Ash turned her head and bit into his flesh. The bite was deep enough to draw blood. Osephius yelled and stepped back, yanking his hand from her mouth and immediately slapping her across the face with his right hand. Several *mourst* stepped forward as Delgado writhed, instinctively trying to kick out, but he was prevented from doing so by the bindings at his ankles and the futility of his struggle quickly became clear.

Michael laughed as Osephius examined his wounded hand, scowling fiercely. 'Is that what they call a love bite, Osephius? I think she rather likes you. I told you she was feisty.'

'Indeed. Perhaps I'll give her something more to think about later. A little more than a bite, perhaps.' He glared menacingly at her.

'Now, now,' said Michael. 'Let's not get overexcited. We have business to deal with. Some myths to dispel. The Seriatts have become aware of your claim,' he said, addressing

Delgado, 'and are insisting that the possibility that you are telling the truth be examined. It's immensely frustrating but they continue to resist my father's advances. Matters are complicated by the fact that somehow your existence has also been leaked to the Andamour Council – your antics during the race were caught by one of the news teams apparently – and they are trying to prevent you being given any form of audience with the Oracles. This has in turn led to some speculation among the Seriattic hierarchy that there may be some legitimacy to your claim, and that the council is merely acting in Myson's interests. We have to establish that you have no claim to the seat of Monosiell here, now.'

'But he does,' stated Delgado. 'There is no doubt.'

'No doubt in your crazed mind, Delgado, I'm sure. But the rest of us prefer reality to fantasy.'

Suddenly the cell door opened again and the *mourst* who had left earlier hurried into the room, hot and slightly flustered. As soon as he entered the cell he immediately turned to face the door and knelt, as did all the other Seriatts present. The transcription machine felt silent as the transcriber manoeuvred his way clumsily from behind his small desk to kneel on the stone floor.

Then a *vilume* walked through the door: it was one of the legendary Seriattic Oracles.

The *vilume* looked female at first glance, but was taller than any *vilume* Delgado had ever seen, even more aloof and serene than her counterparts. Her face was gaunt, her features appearing elongated, and her skin was a very pale grey. She wore a black, floor-length robe in the typical *vilume* style, fashioned in heavy fabric with a slightly coarse nap. On her head she wore a tall, round hat in similar material, with a narrow, round-edged brim at the top. Beneath it her black hair was combed back across her head. Several other *vilume* followed the Oracle into the cell, clearly prepared to attend to her every need. They stood quietly together in the corner, waiting until they were required. Delgado heard the higher-ranking *mourst* welcome the *vilume* in Counian as 'Oracle Entuzo'.

The Oracle looked in Delgado's direction. Her completely black eyes seemed to look through him. Then the *vilume* looked at Ashala. 'I sense something in this one, Lord Valecch,' Entuzo said, her warm voice possessing a distinctly male timbre that countered her female appearance. Ash glanced uncertainly at Delgado. 'She has . . . depths,' continued the Oracle. 'I am intrigued. I take it she is the one with which I am to commune?'

'No, Oracle,' said Valecch, 'she is merely a companion of the two males.' He indicated Delgado and Cascari.

'"Merely a companion,"' muttered Ash grimly. 'Well thank you very much.'

'This surprises me,' said Entuzo. 'But I will do as you wish.' The *vilume* looked at Ashala for several more seconds, then reached out and placed the palm of her left hand on Ashala's cheek, which was still red from Osephius' blow. The Oracle's fingers were pale and bony, their long, curling nails painted with intricate patterns in bright and sparkling colours. The wide cuff of her robe sleeve fell open as she reached out, revealing a skeletal arm. 'For you I see a great future,' she said softly. 'A future of immense importance.' There was a pause. The Oracle breathed deeply, her black eyes staring. 'But it is not here,' she continued. 'And not now.'

'Gee, thanks,' Ash whispered. 'A promise of hope from the Grim Reaper. I'm touched.'

Without responding, Oracle Entuzo turned and took a step towards Delgado. The *vilume* reached behind him and placed her cold fingertips on the back of his head, the ball of her thumb touching the nape of his neck. The Oracle stared intently into his eyes, and Delgado began to perceive a strange hollow sensation in his brain that seemed to spread from the points at which the *vilume*'s fingertips made contact with his head. The *vilume* adjusted her grip and began muttering an incantation in a strange, mellifluous language that was neither Seriatt nor Counian.

As the hollow sensation spread, the *vilume* took another step closer, until she was pressing her forehead against Delgado's. It was like a block of ice, and Delgado gasped as his head was filled with an edge of cold pain. Bizarrely, he found himself becoming sexually aroused, but whether this was due to the close proximity of the *vilume*, despite her ghostly, androgynous appearance, or merely some side-effect of whatever process she was performing upon him, he was in no condition to assess.

Delgado became numb, and felt himself enter a state similar to the suspended consciousness that occurs within a deepsleep chamber. Time seemed to freeze. He was aware of his surroundings, but somehow displaced from them. He heard a shrill sound like distant bells peeling. He could see the *vilume*'s lips moving as she continued to chant, but he could hear only the faint, tremulous clamour. Her wide, black eyes stared into his.

Abruptly, after a period the duration of which Delgado was unable to determine, the *vilume* released him and took a step back. She looked at him coldly. 'This one believes what he has told you to be the truth,' she said.

'But, with all due respect, it cannot be the truth, Oracle Entuzo,' said Osephius.

'The truth is not mine to give, human,' the *vilume* stated, continuing to stare at Delgado. 'Only facts can I offer. This human male believes what he has told you to be the truth. That is a fact.'

'But it can't be so.'

'All individuals' truths are unique. His truth may not necessarily be your truth. Personal belief can sometimes become truth. Perhaps this is where the discrepancy lies.'

Osephius looked flustered, and as if he were struggling to remain patient.

'Can't you separate the truth from the fact?' interjected Michael. 'You must be able to establish the *reality*.'

'If this were possible,' the *vilume* replied dispassionately, 'then my task would be so much simpler. And perhaps the understanding of others greater. I can offer only analysis, not categorical statements. As with truth, realities are numerous, subjective and variable.' She turned to face Michael. 'I will try to assess your facts next,' she said. 'Perhaps we will be able to determine whether they are linked to his.'

The transcription machine's constant chatter ceased in expectation as the *vilume* performed the same ritual on Michael.

After a few minutes the Oracle released him, took a step back and looked impassively at Michael. 'There are facts,' she said softly, almost drowsily, as if the act was tiring her. 'You are unsure of the other's claims. And there is mistrust, uncertainty of the motives of your counterparts here.' Michael glanced uneasily at Osephius, who simply raised an eyebrow. 'I also feel a link between you and this human.' She indicated Delgado. 'But the details are elusive and I am uncertain of the potential. However, it is clear that there is strong *mourst* in you,' the Oracle continued. 'Indeed, despite your physical attributes I am certain that your blood is of the same line as the Royal Household. I have no doubt. You are the offspring of *Conosq dis fer'n'at*, Vourniass Lycern.'

Michael and Osephius looked at each other and grinned with triumph. 'You see, Delgado,' said Michael. 'There's your proof.' He looked at Lord Valecch. 'Contact the Andamour Council, the Seriattic Arbiters and Proctors, and General William Myson on Earth,' he said. 'Oracle Entuzo has confirmed my status as *m*'

'However,' Entuzo interjected, 'I must also join with this one—' she indicated Cascari '—to gather all the facts before any final assertion is made.' As she stepped towards Cascari the young man maintained his expression, refusing to show signs of being moved or disturbed by the events. As she had done with Delgado and Michael, the *vilume* sorceress first grasped the back of Cascari's head and neck and the pressed her forehead against his. She resumed her incantation, which became increasingly loud and intense, a deep and resonant drone.

Then, abruptly, she relaxed. 'It cannot be done,' she said. 'His mind is constrained by hatred and bitterness. His Seriattic heritage is clear in his physical characteristics, but I cannot be certain of his birth line as I am unable to commune with him sufficiently.'

'No!' Delgado yelled, unable to contain himself longer, yanking at the bonds restraining him. 'He is the son of Vourniass Lycern. I am his father.'

'I can only relate fact,' reasserted Oracle Entuzo calmly. 'He may have Seriattic appearance, but this one—' she pointed at Michael '—has *dis fer'n'at* blood.'

'I was present at his birth,' Delgado shouted, his face red. 'Vourniass Lycern, the *conosq dis fer'n'at*, gave birth to him and I am his father. These are *all* facts.'

'I cannot be certain of his background. He is too closed. There are too many variables, too few certainties.' She stepped back away from Cascari. As she drew her hand from behind Cascari's neck one of her long fingernails caught the chain he wore and pulled it from his tunic. It fell in front of his chest. Even in the dull light of the cell the silver pendant glinted as if enchanted. Upon seeing it, the Oracle immediately bowed low before him, hands palm-upward in a gesture of obsequiousness. Upon seeing the pendant themselves, every other Seriatt in the cell did likewise.

'What does this mean, Oracle Entuzo?' whispered Lord Valecch as they knelt before Cascari. 'How can he have a *cursilac* medal if he is not of royal blood?'

'It can mean only one thing,' replied the Oracle. 'The link is clear now. My powers of sight must be diminishing.'

'What, Oracle?' asked Valecch. 'What does it mean? What is the link?'

'Given the purity in the other, the claims these have made and my perceptions of the older human male, the answer is clear. He fathered both, and they are born of the same *conosq*.'

Despite the protestations, denials and counterclaims made by Michael and Osephius following Oracle Entuzo's assertion that Michael and Cascari were brothers, the Seriatts proclaimed that Delgado, Cascari and Ashala must be released. They were then taken to Seriatt's Royal Palace in an air-conditioned limousine carriage with glittering metallic black coachwork, drawn by a team of four muscular bi-pedal creatures like hideous ogres with heavy brows and thick, muscular thighs. Linked by a leather bridle with shining metal studs and hoops, the team of creatures moved with athletic grace despite their size, hauling the vehicle with ease, steered by a skilful *vilume* driver sitting at the front of the carriage. Delgado could not tell whether the grotesque creatures were artificial constructs, genetically engineered, or merely tamed animals.

Within, the carriage was spacious and opulent, with studded cream leather seats and detailing in polished stone and coloured glass. All pedestrians stopped and watched as it proceeded through the streets, the other traffic parting swiftly to allow it to pass unhindered. At their insistence, Michael and Osephius were conveyed to the palace in a separate carriage.

Delgado stared intently out of the window, trying to rationalise what the Oracle had said.

Ash, who was sitting next to him, placed one of her hands on his. 'What are you thinking?' she asked softly.

'What am I thinking? I'm thinking that I tried to kill him. My own son. My *other* son. All these years he's been with Myson, raised in that perverse environment. I was trying to kill him when I should have been trying to save him.' He looked at her. 'But it all makes sense now, doesn't it?'

Ash looked into his intense eyes and saw the anguish he felt. 'It makes sense,' she agreed. 'It doesn't make it easy, but it does make sense. Myson wouldn't have hammered on at the Andamour Council all these years unless he felt he had a genuine case. Lycern had twins. Myson took away the first-born . . .'

'While I was unconscious, and you and Bucky found Cascari in the rubble after you crashed in. Both you and Myson assumed you had the only child.'

'Maybe if Michael looked like a *mourst*, as Cascari does, we would've realised what had happened sooner.'

Delgado looked out of the window again. 'Maybe,' he said. 'Maybe not. Maybe we didn't want to see the truth.'

'Maybe we just wanted to see our own truth, if what the Oracle said is anything to go by.'

'Of course, you realise it could all be a trick,' said Cascari. He was sitting on the opposite side of the carriage, looking bitter and angry. 'How are we to know this Oracle hasn't got a vested interest in saying Michael is Lycern's, too? Maybe he doesn't look like a *mourst* because he isn't a *mourst*, like we've always said. Perhaps Entuzo's got her own reasons for saying I'm not the only one. Now *that* would really make sense.'

Delgado looked at Cascari, and saw the emotions smouldering within him as he struggled to come to terms with the situation. Delgado shook his head. 'It's no good trying to deny it now, Cascari,' he said. 'It's the final piece of the puzzle, the reason for all the things I've felt over the years that I couldn't explain. I knew something was missing. But I always thought it was Lycern.'

Ash took her hand from Delgado's. 'So what do we do now?' she asked.

'What do you mean?' asked Cascari, frowning.

'Well, this changes everything. Right?' She looked from Cascari to Delgado.

Delgado shrugged, but continued to stare out of the window. 'Does it?'

'Of course it does.'

He looked at her. 'What does it change?'

'You're his *father.*' She looked at Cascari, almost pleading. 'He's your *brother.*'

Cascari looked at Delgado. Delgado looked back out of the window. 'For me to be his father, he would have to be my son. Biologically he's mine, but that's all and it's not enough. He's Myson's. You can see it in his actions, you can hear it in his voice. It's in the ethos he clearly lives by. Nothing has changed.'

Ash looked at Cascari, but he simply stared back at her, his gaze icy.

They arrived at a set of large, black iron gates set into a white wall of chalky texture. The gates opened automatically and the carriage proceeded along the driveway beyond, its wheels crunching noisily on the gravel. The driveway curved gently to the right through broad, well-kept lawns towards a wood about half a kilometre away. It emerged on the other side of the trees at a wide gravel area in front of the palace entrance. The heavy door next to Cascari slid open with a smooth, easy movement, and the three of them stepped from the limousine.

The palace was a low but very wide building, apparently circular in shape. Other than pointed towers rising from either side of the main entrance, it was only two or three storeys at the highest point.

On either side of the main entrance stood a *mourst* guard in what Delgado took to be some kind of ceremonial uniform, consisting of tunic and kilt fashioned from soft black leather. Lines of bone were attached to their chests like ribs, and across their shoulders and down their limbs black metal plates were attached to the leather like an exoskeleton. At their sides they wore large curved scimitar-like swords, and long spears were strapped to their backs. Delgado noticed that they were adorned with multiple piercings, and that their dark, coarse skin was embellished with subtle tattoos in dark red and gold.

The palace itself seemed to be made of the same chalk-like stone as the wall surrounding the grounds. Stone-framed, Gothic-style windows with innumerable stained-glass panes, divided by shining lines of pewter-like metal, stretched almost to the roof from just above the narrow strip of neatly trimmed lawn between the palace and the driveway. The windows seemed to glisten, as if somehow alive with the very quality of the light passing through them. Between the windows, mosaics of glass and polished stone were set within frames of seemingly random shapes on the palace wall, along with carvings of strange creatures.

To their left, the carriage carrying Michael and Osephius came to a halt. As they alighted, Lord Valecch, who had ridden in a third, far less luxurious carriage, hurried up to them in a manner that indicated it was not good etiquette to do so, hands palm-upward, stooping as low as he seemed able without getting on all fours. 'Highness,' he said. 'Highnesses.' He addressed both Cascari and Michael, but was clearly uncertain which should take priority. 'We should enter immediately. The Administrators have assembled and are waiting.' Cascari and Michael glanced coldly at each other, but followed Lord Valecch without speaking.

As they walked into the palace, followed by a group of *mourst* enforcers, Osephius moved close to Delgado. 'Watch your back, Delgado,' he said quietly. 'We're not going to let this go without a fight. There's too much at stake.'

'Myson's offered you a nice little reward for being Michael's guardian, has he? A Seriattic continent of your own to rule, perhaps? Hoards of *conosq* to quench your most basic desires? Funny. He gave me a mission I couldn't complete once. You may remember it.'

'Don't judge all men by your own standards, Delgado.

Besides, that was your own doing. How you could have had intercourse, if that was what you would call it, with one of those repulsive creatures has always astounded and disgusted me, and many others. You must have been out of your mind even then.'

Delgado leaned close, and whispered: 'There's no way you're getting what you want. I'll die before I see Myson gain power here.'

'I'll hold you to that, Delgado.'

There were no doors to the palace entrance, just a stone archway the same shape and proportion as the windows. Inside, the palace was a cool contrast to the heat of the Seriattic day. The floor of the circular room they entered was made of highly polished wood; the walls were painted white and the ceiling was quite low, with swathes of plush fabric stretched from its perimetre to the central point. There was a notable lack of the kind of valuable objects and demonstrations of luxury that seemed to be associated with all the other palaces Delgado had encountered, but the air of wealth and affluence was perceptible nonetheless.

The party followed Valecch across the spacious entrance hall, and into a long, wide corridor on the opposite side. The floor in the corridor was laid with a plush red carpet, the deep pile of which absorbed the sound of their footfalls. Sets of double doors were spaced at regular intervals on either side of the corridor. Between these doors were framed sheets of silver metal, upon each of which was engraved a single scene. Only when he saw an image of a group of *mourst* in combat did Delgado associate these images with those upon Cascari's pendant.

Valecch stopped at one of the sets of doors and looked back along the corridor. Delgado looked in the same direction. While initially the *mourst* appeared to be waiting for the rest of the enforcers to catch up, he seemed to be looking past rather than at them. Delgado looked towards the palace entrance and saw a flickering shape move past it. It was like some strange and elaborate machine on a cart of some kind, but the detail was washed away by the glare and he was unable to discern what it might be.

Delgado looked back to Valecch and saw the *mourst* give a firm pull on a red and gold rope hanging next to the door, stooping to pull it to its entire length. When he released it, the rope slid quickly back up as if on a pulley. There was a momentary pause, then muffled, wooden clunking sounds could be heard above the ceiling as wheels turned and linkages shifted. Then, somewhere beyond the wooden doors, a sombre bell tolled once.

Valecch faced the group standing behind him. 'I must warn you,' he said, 'unless you are addressed directly, you must remain silent. I cannot emphasise the importance of this enough. Do you understand?' They nodded. 'Good. We must enter now.'

Valecch turned and opened the door slightly. He took a step forward, and exchanged hushed words with a *mourst* standing just inside. After a few moments of discussion, first one door, then the other was opened fully, and they were able to see into the room beyond.

There was a long, rectangular table, the grain and knots in the pale wood visible through its thick, clear varnish. It stood out in the room against the ceiling, which was a rich, deep red, and the cream, pleated curtains which covered the walls. Around the table sat a dozen or so Seriatts, a mixture of all three species. Delgado tried to avoid making eye contact with the *conosq*. The strength of feeling they stirred in him was surprising. The Administrators appeared to be the equivalent of Earth's planetary council: a body of high-ranking officials who made important decisions.

Delgado tried to extend his hyperconsciousness to gain some clue to the Seriatts' thoughts and intentions; but their traces were too pure, too alien, and his nobics now much too weak for such intensive processes. His mind was overwhelmed by the confused patterns that rushed through him.

All those seated around the table stared intently at Cascari and Michael. Delgado looked towards Cascari who was standing to his left. The pendant around his neck seemed to stand out against his grubby tunic as if it was more than just a piece of jewellery. Next to him, Michael stood proudly, head high. Looking at him with fresh eyes, Delgado would have to admit that he was a fine young man. A young man of whom any father would be proud.

Valecch cleared his throat and stepped forward to address the gathering. 'Proctors, Arbiters, Oracles . . .' He held his hands palm-outward and stooped briefly, then seemed to focus on a beautiful *vilume* at the head of the table opposite them. 'Arbiter Messinat, I know you have all been informed of the dramatic developments that have occurred. Oracle Entuzo has long been predicting the arrival of a Saviour. It appears that, given the circumstances, we may have two Saviours.'

A *mourst* on the far side of the room suddenly stood. 'I will not accept this, Arbiter Messinat. I will not. These humans cannot be our *Saviours*. They have come to us for their own gain in the human way we know. They have been sent by their General Myson. Have we learned nothing of these creatures? We cannot allow ourselves to be forced to accept the bidding of the Anadamour Council.'

'The facts cannot be altered,' said a *vilume*, calmly but adamantly, her enunciation of the words crisp and precise, 'or the evidence that has been presented to us. Oracle Entuzo – one of our finest seers – has communed with both the human male and both of the half-*mourst*. Based on her testimony we must accept that they are telling the truth. One of them is human in appearance, it is true, but Oracle Entuzo is confident of his Seriattic lineage, and his relationship to *Conosq* Lycern. The other wears a *cursilac* medal.' She gestured towards Cascari. All in the room looked at the pendant. 'This could not be obtained other than by coming into contact with a member of the Royal Household. And, as we know too well, it is an unfortunate fact that Vourniass Lycern left this palace – the only *conosq dis fer'n'at* ever to do so. The human female is adamant that she placed the medal around the child's neck at birth, having taken it from *Conosq* Lycern's body. Oracle Entuzo has not communed with this human, but believes she is stating fact. She is certain that both of the half-*mourst* are *Conosq* Lycern's offspring.'

'What about forgery, Arbiter Messinat?' growled Proctor Coortien, his *mourst* face even more sour than usual. The Seriatt gazed intently at Cascari, then Delgado. 'It could be a counterfeit medal, designed to enable infiltration of our innermost chambers in this very manner. I have never trusted humans. It is a trick. Perhaps our Lord Valecch is a co-conspirator.' He slapped his hand on the tabletop as if to physically validate his statement. Lord Valecch looked at the *mourst* with what Delgado assumed was the Seriatt equivalent of a scowl.

The *vilume* looked at the pendant, at Cascari's face, then at Michael. 'Oracle Entuzo has studied the artefact closely, Proctor Coortien,' she said quietly. 'The medal is genuine.'

'This is preposterous,' spat another *mourst*. 'You cannot seriously be suggesting that either of these *creatures* is entitled to the seat of Monosiell! They are human, Arbiter Messinat! *Human*!'

As if maintenance of her composure was becoming difficult, Arbiter Messinat closed her eyes, breathing slowly and deeply. 'Part of them may be human, Proctor Coortien,' continued Messinat with patience, 'but Oracle Entuzo has established that the *mourst* aspects of their personalities are far stronger.'

A *vilume* sitting at the far left corner of the table raised a hand. Her heavy-lidded eyes made her look drowsy or drugged.

'You have a contribution, Proctor Rümini?' said Messinat.

Rümini spoke slowly and quietly. 'I wonder if there might

be strategic value in one of these—' the *vilume* waved a hand vaguely '—*mourst* assuming the position of Monosiell? Something we may negotiate to our advantage? Perhaps it is time to consider entering into some form of alliance with the humans.'

Several *mourst* and *conosq* at the table immediately voiced dissent.

'I believe such a possibility has long since been lost, Proctor Rümini,' said Messinat.

'But surely it would be beneficial to both worlds,' Rümini insisted. 'Better understanding would almost certainly ease tensions if a position of power . . .'

'Or perhaps the Monosiell could feed his human counterparts information, Proctor Rümini!' gasped Proctor Coortien, spittle flying from his dark, contorted mouth. He banged the table with his fist a second time. A couple of nearby *vilume* flinched visibly.

'Thank you, Proctor Coortien. Your contribution is, as ever, most useful.' Arbiter Messinat stared at Coortien until he was forced to look away.

'Of course,' said Proctor Rümini, continuing as if Coortien had not spoken, 'when I say a position of *power* . . .'

Another *conosq* interjected. 'Your point is a valid one, Proctor Rümini, but Seriatt's relationship with Earth is not the true problem here.'

'Then what is the problem, Arbiter Shorial?' said Messinat.

Arbiter Shorial clasped her long fingers before her, her silver nails reflecting gems of light. 'It is very simple, and surely obvious.' There was a pause; Shorial looked around the table. 'Perhaps not,' she said. 'The problem is this: while it is true that we need a new Monosiell of acceptable heritage, we need only one.'

All at the table looked at Cascari and Michael.

'Then how do we decide which of them should become Monosiell? What are the alternatives?' asked Rümini.

'Invoke *di-fio nu'compria*,' spat Coortien. 'It is the only way.'

Messinat glanced at Coortien with apparent impatience. 'Perhaps Oracle Entuzo could enlighten us,' said the Arbiter. She looked towards the *vilume*. 'Oracle, can you advise us which of them it is? Can you see their fate?'

Oracle Entuzo gazed at Michael and Cascari. 'There are fragments only,' she said quietly. 'Many possible destinies for both. Too many to state with certainty what the genuine future of either may be.' The Oracle looked at Ashala, seemed about to say something, then decided against it. 'I fear I am unable to help,' she admitted. 'Unless . . .'

'Unless what, Oracle Entuzo?'

'Perhaps the Destiny Mask can enlighten us. I have never attempted to focus on a human mind, but as they are half-*mourst* . . . it is a possibility.'

Delgado, Osephius and Ashala sat in a plush auditorium overlooking a circular chamber. In front of them was a polished wooden balustrade adorned with brass detailing; the wooden walls were panelled; numerous candles cast gentle warmth and light.

They were surrounded by the Seriattic Administrators. The *vilume* and *conosq* Proctors and Arbiters were largely impassive, but the dissatisfaction of their *mourst* counterparts with the situation was clear. Two *mourst* enforcers stood near the door, watching the humans carefully.

Delgado looked at Lord Valecch, who was sitting to his left. 'What is this place?' he asked. 'What's going to happen here?'

Valecch leaned close to him and whispered, as if wary of being seen talking by his counterparts. 'This is the Chamber of Visions. The Oracles' most sacred place. Here they see potential futures, and attempt to predict coming events. Soon you will see. Oracle Entuzo will attempt to focus on the two half-*mourst* to try and establish which of them should become Monosiell, and perhaps what other possibilities the future holds. We have seen many great and unexpected prophecies here.'

'And were they accurate?'

The *mourst* adopted a brief expression Delgado was unable to read. 'Some of the Oracles' predictions have proved disturbingly so.'

'And what's that?' Although he knew instinctively, Delgado pointed to the large object several metres from the head of the couch. Around three metres wide, nine high and four deep, its upper edge came almost level with the lowest part of the balustrade. The structure was mounted on a brown base, the texture of which was similar to the inside of the tubes from which the racing aircraft had been launched. The front of the object formed a rectangular frame which seemed to be fashioned from a crystalline substance, like slender pipes of solidified amber flecked with shards of silver. The material was smooth, but there were occasional lengthy extrusions, like trails pulled from hot glass that had cooled and hardened. The amber framework appeared to be luminescent, and a series of tiny bright sparks danced inside the tubular structures. Within the perimetres of the delicate frame was a faint, shimmering sheen, like a film of sparkling dust on water. It seemed to swirl and ripple as if disturbed by gentle eddies, and reminded Delgado of the buoys used to catapult the race aircraft between waypoints. Behind the frame the object was rounded, covered with swellings of various sizes.

Lord Valecch seemed to become excited. 'That is the gate to all our destinies,' the *mourst* said. 'Our finest Continuity Scientists have laboured long to manufacture it, having taken minute samples of the Destiny Mask and attempted to extrapolate its properties. With that gate, the answers to many of the most difficult questions will be ours, and with far more certainty and clarity than is currently possible through use of the mask.'

Delgado stared at the gate. It looked so simple, yet its power and potential were immeasurable. 'And it works? It enables time travel?'

Valecch looked at the machine. 'We do not yet know,' he said. 'We believe it is in a constant state of flux, joining any number of time-space locations at any given moment. A similar, temporary gate appears at the other end. In many ways it is therefore random, and must be used with care. One brave *mourst* has entered it, but he has yet to return.'

'Why send a *mourst* rather than an Oracle?'

Lord Valecch clasped his hands in front of his face. 'Our Oracles are too precious to risk,' he said. 'Without them our futures would be completely unknown. Only when we are certain the gate is safe will we be able to consider allowing Oracles to use it. And even then it may be decided that we have to send trainees.'

Delgado and Ash looked at each other. The importance of the time machine could not be underestimated. When he glanced at Osephius, who was sitting to Ashala's right, Delgado saw that the Structure man was also gazing at the device with clear longing.

A door opened on the right side of the Chamber of Visions. Eight *vilume* entered, followed by Oracle Entuzo, who was in turn followed by Michael and Cascari. Entuzo lay on the black couch at the centre of the room, while Michael and Cascari were instructed to sit on either side of her on high-backed leather chairs. They gazed uneasily at each other as Entuzo's attendants fussed around the Oracle and lit the candles beneath the numerous oil bowls situated around the chamber. As the oils began to warm, the room filled with a smooth and sweet aroma.

Delgado looked back to the rest of the chamber and saw that almost all activity had ceased. Most of Oracle Entuzo's attendants were standing quietly around the chamber's perimeter. Only one of them – who Delgado assumed was the most senior – was still active. The *vilume* walked to the wall and touched a small dark square. A panel immediately slid open to reveal one of Seriatt's most renowned objects: the Destiny Mask.

The *vilume* put on the black gloves that lay in front of the stand on which the mask rested, then carefully picked it up and carried it across to Entuzo. The *vilume* placed it gently on the Oracle's face.

As the attendant moved away, Delgado heard a very faint, high-pitched sound, and then saw the mask begin to glow slightly. He felt a slight tingling sensation, like a wash of static electricity. In the Chamber of Visions, Entuzo opened her mouth slightly, her fingers trembling. She arched her back, the couch automatically adjusting to her new posture. Entuzo licked her lips, swallowed, and gripped the leather. The mask glowed more brightly, then seemed to soften, melting down the sides of the Oracle's face until, like an advanced visuals visor, it merged with her skin to form a hard and glossy golden shell.

The Oracle moaned more deeply than seemed possible given her slight physique, and began to writhe on the couch, continuing to grip it with her long fingers, her elaborately decorated nails pressing into the leather.

Then, above Entuzo's body, a grey, barely perceptible mist began to appear. It was so faint that at first Delgado was uncertain whether he was imagining it. Then shapes began to form in the haze, unclear, fragmented images. There seemed to be buildings, moving figures, vehicles and faces, but all were too blurred and vague to identify what or where they might be.

Delgado stared. 'What's happening?' he asked Valecch.

'It is her vision of the future,' he replied in apparent wonderment. 'She sees in far greater detail than we are able, and analyses the visions to make sense of the possibilities.'

'So it's like a dream?'

'Yes and no. Dreams are mental analyses of past events. The

Destiny Mask engenders visions of the future. Sometimes we are able to predict what the Oracle will say as a result of seeing these visualisations, but in most cases the images that appear in the chamber are insufficiently distinct and we rely on her analysis of the metal images she sees.'

Delgado tried to ascertain what the distorted images in the air above Oracle Entuzo were. There seemed to be mountains, trees, large towers; but they flickered in rapid succession like sketches, to be immediately replaced by others. Other places began to appear, some of which seemed to have a resonance with Delgado even though he could not see them clearly. He narrowed his eyes, leaned forward a little. There were views of heavy seas, aircraft in flight. Then there was a crescent moon in a pale blue sky, and the towers returned. They looked distinctly like the habitats on Earth, only slightly distorted by the vision. Then, transposed over the towers, were strange shapes, like gigantic floral organisms or sea anemones, their tentacles moving in a current. Delgado recognised them immediately as Sinz vessels. If his analysis of this vision was correct, the Sinz appeared to be invading Earth.

Then, amid the confusion of images, a face began to form. At first it was impossible to see much detail, just the dark areas of the eye sockets, the nostrils and the mouth. But gradually the image cleared, gaining definition. It looked like a *vilume*, with short hair and an unusually rounded face. Suddenly the image sharpened, becoming clear only momentarily, but long enough to see that it was no *vilume*. Then it was gone.

Delgado looked at Ash. 'Did you see that?'

She looked shocked. 'Yeah. But I mean, that can't have been me, though. Can it?'

'I don't know. It sure as hell looked like you.'

'Nah.' She shook her head, but glanced at him, her uncertainty clear. 'It couldn't be. It was just a *vilume* that looks like me. Right?'

Delgado shook his head. 'It looked like you,' he said. 'It was you. And those towers? They were the habitat towers on Earth.'

'What about those round things? The things that looked like they had tentacles?'

'I don't know,' said Delgado grimly. 'They *looked* like Sinz ships. And it looked like they were attacking the habitats on Earth.' Delgado looked at Osephius, but the Structure officer did not seem to have recognised the significance of the images.

Gradually Oracle Entuzo calmed. Although some images were still visible above her, they were faint silhouettes that existed only briefly.

'So what happens now?' Delgado whispered to Lord Valecch.

'We wait for the Oracle to recover, and to give us her analysis of her visions.'

In the chamber below, Entuzo's senior attendant took the Oracle a glass of water. Entuzo sat up on the black leather couch and downed the drink gratefully in a single draught. When the glass was empty, Entuzo stood, walked forward a short distance, then looked up at those in the auditorium. Behind Delgado, Arbiter Messinat stood.

'What news have you, Oracle Entuzo?' the Arbiter asked. 'Did you see which of these two half-*mourst* is to be Monosiell? Can you guide us?'

There was a prolonged pause, during which Oracle Entuzo looked at the floor just in front of her. Whether she was struggling to find the words to describe what she had seen, or trying to analyse her visions, Delgado did not know.

Eventually the Oracle looked up. 'Unfortunately, Arbiter Messinat,' said Entuzo grimly, 'I am unable to say which is the rightful heir.'

There was a gasp, and a minor hubbub erupted in the auditorium.

'What do you mean, Oracle?' asked Messinat. The Arbiter did not seem to understand, as if all previous visualisations had been satisfactorily explained.

'I mean, Arbiter,' said Entuzo evenly, 'that I cannot say. They *are* both offspring of Vourniass Lycern, the former *conosq dis fer'n'at*. They were both fathered by the human male. But more than that, I am unable to establish.'

'Were the visions unclear?' Messinat seemed frustrated.

Oracle Entuzo briefly showed Entuzo the palms of her long hands, fingers splayed. 'There were clear images in which the two half-*mourst* appeared, Arbiter,' the *vilume* said, 'but I simply cannot ascertain which of them should be Monosiell.'

'Neither of them!' blustered a *mourst* at the rear of the auditorium. 'They are impure. Allowing one of them to become Monosiell is a preposterous suggestion.'

'Calm yourself Proctor Ulotz,' said Messinat. 'Oracle Entuzo has established that they are both born of *Conosq* Lycern. Whatever they may be, one of them *is* a future Monosiell.'

Another Arbiter spoke. 'As it is clear the Destiny Mask has not worked on this occasion, Arbiter Messinat, what options are open to us now?'

'It should be me,' shouted Michael boldly, standing up in the Chamber of Visions and turning to face those in the auditorium. 'I was the first-born. I should take the position.'

'Order of birth is unimportant,' said Messinat. 'We must decide who is *right* for the position. It is in just such matters that our Oracles are so frequently helpful, and it is frustrating that on this occasion our most experienced and perceptive Oracle is unable to guide us.'

'Where is your Saviour, Arbiter Messinat?' asked Proctor Coortien scornfully. 'Surely this is a time of most dire need.'

'The Saviour is among us, Proctor Coortien,' said Oracle Entuzo.

The Administrators muttered to each other.

'Where, Oracle?' demanded Coortien. 'Which among us is this Saviour?'

'I do not know,' the Oracle replied. 'And while I feel the Saviour's presence, I am also uncertain that this is the time when we are to be helped. Despite my hopes, I fear that having observed us the Saviour will not become manifest to us at this time. We are not yet sufficiently worthy.'

'This is absurd,' retorted Coortien. 'Let us delay no further. The issue of which of the half-*mourst* will become Monosiel must be decided through the rite of *di-fio nu'compria*. It is the only way.' Proctor Rümini, seated next to Coortien, voiced agreement, as did other *mourst* – and some of the *conosq* – in the auditorium.

Messinat paused briefly, then looked at Delgado and Osephius. 'This is one further option,' said the Arbiter. 'I had hoped to avoid *di-fio nu'compria* if possible, but it appears we have no choice.'

'Indeed,' said a *mourst* at the rear of the auditorium with apparent pleasure. '*Di-fio nu'compria* is the honourable course.'

'What's *di-fio nu'compria*?' asked Delgado, struggling to pronounce the Seriattic words.

'They must battle in the theatre,' replied Lord Valecch without emotion. 'The survivor will take the seat.'

'No! There has to be another way.'

'It is the ancient way,' said Messinat. She clasped her hands together and looked down. 'And in this instance I fear it is the only way.'

'You can't make them try to kill each other. I won't allow it. It's barbaric.'

'Barbaric? By your human standards, perhaps. It has long been recognised that humans feel they have the right to impose their ways on those whose traditions and beliefs are different to their own. The Arbiters and Proctors have studied Earth's history in an effort to understand you. Such imposition and interference between different races has plagued your world, and caused many wars.'

Delgado stood and began protesting vigorously, but he was

quickly restrained by the *mourst* enforcers and dragged from the auditorium. As the door closed he saw Michael smiling broadly while Osephius was staring intently at Ashala, a certain hunger in his eyes.

Nine

the king of thebes

When Delgado woke he found himself in a room that contained only the hard wooden bench on which he lay, and a latrine. He remembered putting up a fight with the enforcers as he was evicted from the auditorium, and receiving a blow to the head, but that was all.

He sat up, throwing off the coarse, thin blanket that covered him. He leaned forward, resting his elbows on his thighs and his forehead in his hands. The bright light strips in the ceiling reflected off the tiled floor. He felt as though he had slept for a long time – longer than he would have liked. His head ached dully and there was a heavy fug in his brain rather than a feeling of alertness. Whether this was due to his prolonged sleep or the blow to the head he was uncertain.

He tried to attain greater awareness of his surroundings and location by opening a nobic perception stream, but the traces were weak and inconclusive, and there was nothing upon which he would be prepared to rely as a basis for action. He sensed great excitement and fear, and a large number of Seriatts close by, however. Indeed, there were so many that the volume of streams was overwhelming. There was also the same sense of oppression he had felt in the corridors on the stretcher, as if the room were underground or deep within a large installation.

The gravity of the situation began to return to him. Soon,

he knew, Michael and Cascari would be set to face each other in combat. Cascari had proven himself to be a capable warrior in the air, but had limited experience of hand-to-hand combat. Michael had been raised as the son of General William Myson within Structure, and would almost certainly have been instructed in such matters.

But Delgado also realised that which of them was the better fighter, and thus the likely victor, was not the issue. Despite the importance of getting Cascari into the position of Monosiell on Seriatt to prevent Myson gaining any control, and particularly from getting his hands on the Seriatts' time portal, for Delgado the revelations regarding his relationship to Michael, and of Michael to Cascari, complicated matters considerably. Now Seriattic ritual and tradition were beginning to interfere, and with the possibility of Earth being attacked Delgado knew he had to act quickly. His feelings for Myson and all that he had done were unchanged, but Delgado could not allow his home world to be involved.

His primary objective in the short term, however, was to find Cascari and Michael, and prevent the battle they were soon to begin. Although he remained unsure of his feelings towards Michael, he could not allow either of them to die.

A rectangular panel two-thirds of the way up the cell's grey metal door suddenly slid open, and a pair of dark *mourst* eyes looked in at him.

'How do you do?' said Delgado grimly. 'Do come in, why don't you?'

The panel was promptly slammed shut, and another opened at the bottom of the door. A plate of food was pushed through, and the second panel was also slammed shut.

Delgado pushed himself off the bunk and walked over to the plate. Upon it were large slices of meat in a brown sauce. The meat looked gristly and raw, the sauce thin and pale. Despite the food's appearance, it stirred overwhelming hunger in

Delgado, and he began to eat as he carried the plate to sit down on the wooden bench.

As he chewed on the tough meat, a few dull thuds issued from the door as it was unlocked. It opened, a *mourst* peered in briefly before stepping back to allow a *vilume* to enter the cell. The creature – who looked distinctly male in human terms, in contrast to most other *vilume* Delgado had encountered – did not wear the usual *vilume* attire, but what was clearly a uniform of some kind: black trousers and a long, hooded cape with a bird embroidered on the chest. The garments seemed to be made from a smooth, nylon-like material, and rustled as the *vilume* walked.

Delgado put down the plate of food as the *vilume* strode across the room. The Seriatt removed his hood and raised Delgado's arm, pulled back his tunic sleeve and strapped something around his wrist with adhesive strips. It looked like a broad length of tough black fabric, into which a small flexiscreen was set. Apparently a medic, the *vilume* began to read the text that appeared on the screen.

The *vilume* placed his right hand on top of Delgado's head and pushed it back. Delgado studied the *vilume*'s delicate bone structure as the Seriatt leaned over him and examined his face intently, as if looking for a minute flaw on his human skin. The Seriatt then pulled a small device from a narrow belt around his waist and held it up in front of Delgado's forehead. The belt fell to the floor and the *vilume* stooped to pick it up. The small buckle appeared to be broken, and the *vilume* made husky coughing sounds as he tied the belt around his waist, securing it with a loose knot.

The Seriatt raised the device to Delgado's head again, and he felt a slight tingling sensation at the back of his skull. The *vilume* adjusted a small rotary control on the side of the instrument with his right thumb, and peered more closely at the display.

When the *vilume* took the device away from Delgado's head

and looked down at it, apparently making further adjustments, Delgado noticed that the cell door remained slightly ajar. Although the mass of relatively close Seriattic traces was very strong, he did not perceive any *mourst* guards immediately outside the cell.

The *vilume* mumbled to himself. Delgado cleared his throat. 'Where are my companions?' he asked in Counian.

The *vilume* did not look up, but continued to toy with the small device in his hand. 'They are to face each other in combat,' he said calmly, 'in the ancient rite of *di-fio nu'compria*. Although I am not aware of all the facts, the rumours are that both have a valid claim to become Seriatt's new Monosiell, and this is the only way to establish which of them it should be. They will also face other warriors, to provide entertainment to those watching, and to test their true skills. If they are to be *mourst* Monosiell, they must be worthy combatants.'

The *vilume* shook the small device he was holding, tapped it against the palm of his left hand, then looked at it closely. He thrust the object back into the belt, which almost came off again, then pulled the black strip from Delgado's wrist and shoved it into one of his pockets. 'You are well,' said the *vilume*. 'Eat your meals, sleep, and forget your counterparts. There is nothing you can do to help them now.'

As the medic stood, turned and walked back towards the door Delgado opened a short-term nobic stream – it was weak, but the strongest thread he could muster. When it had become effective he launched himself from the bunk and across the room. He hit the *vilume*'s back with a force that sent them both sprawling, then sliding across the smooth floor and crashing into the door frame.

As Delgado started to get to his feet the Seriatt kicked out. His foot made contact with Delgado's right shoulder with surprising force and caused him to slump forward, allowing the *vilume* to kick him in the face.

Delgado rolled to his right, but the Seriatt seemed to get up with remarkable speed, and before Delgado could counter it the medic had kicked him in the ribs. The contact was surprisingly good, and with his breath knocked from him, Delgado fell forward again. Somewhere at the back of his mind it occurred to him that he had underestimated this physically unimposing Seriatt.

The *vilume* kicked him again. Delgado grabbed the medic's leg and maintained his grip on the tough fabric of his trousers despite the Seriatt's attempts to shake him off. The Seriatt's loosely tied belt came undone and fell on to the floor in front of Delgado's face. Delgado managed to roll on to his side and grab the other leg. As the *vilume* tried to free himself, Delgado pulled the Seriatt's feet together, then wrapped his arms around them. As he felt the small amount of additional strength provided by his faltering nobics fading, Delgado gave a single, sharp heave, and the Seriatt toppled backwards.

Delgado jumped up and grabbed the belt. As the *vilume* tried to stand, Delgado kicked him to the ground and then knelt on the centre of his back, pinning the medic to the floor. Delgado passed the belt around the *vilume*'s neck and yanked it tight, pulling so hard on the narrow strip of material that the Seriatt's head was pulled away from the ground.

Delgado quickly twisted the belt, increasing the pressure on the back of the *vilume*'s neck with each turn. He could hear the Seriatt beginning to wheeze as he was able to draw less and less breath. The medic's beautiful, boyish face began to change colour, his eyes bulged and his lips and tongue swelled.

Delgado tightened the makeshift garrotte still further, his face red with the effort. The *vilume*'s increasingly shallow breaths were snatched and inconsistent. Grey drool trailed from one corner of his mouth to form a small viscous pool on the floor. The medic attempted to reach up and ease the pressure on his throat, but Delgado's weight prevented him from doing so. The Seriatt's eyes half closed. There were a couple of weak muscular spasms, but then Delgado felt the *vilume* relax completely.

Delgado tightened the belt once more, maintained his grip on it for another thirty seconds or so, then let the *vilume*'s heavy head drop heavily to the ground with a dull thud.

The pungent smell of the medic's opened bowels was thick at the back of Delgado's throat. He looked down at his right hand and massaged the broad red lines impressed in the flesh where he had tightened the ligature.

He stooped and gripped a handful of the medic's hair in his right hand and lifted the Seriatt's head. It seemed incredibly heavy. The creature's expression was an odd combination of euphoria and sorrow.

Delgado let the *vilume*'s head drop to the floor and moved to the door. He peered cautiously into the corridor beyond. There were no Seriatts in the immediate vicinity, but he could hear voices echoing through the narrow, tunnels.

He closed the door slightly and went back to the corpse. Delgado crouched and quickly unfastened the small metal clips that held the medic's cape closed, then unclipped the *vilume*'s trousers. He rolled the Seriatt over and managed to remove the outer clothing in a few moments. Beneath these garments the Seriatt wore a white, long-sleeved blouse and – now somewhat soiled – shorts, both fashioned from a silk-like material. Luckily the outer clothing remained clean.

He threw the outer garments into one corner of the cell and dragged the medic towards the bunk, the sheer fabric sliding easily across the smooth floor. It occurred to Delgado that a particular benefit of strangulation was its bloodless method, but the stink of excrement as he pulled the heavy body across the cell was foul indeed, and he wondered at the Seriatt's diet.

The bunk was slightly higher than a normal human bed, and this, coupled with the *vilume*'s dead weight, made manoeuvring the medic on to the flat wooden surface awkward. By the time the *vilume* was lying face down on the bunk, the front of Delgado's tunic was generously smeared with olive-green shit.

He rolled the *vilume* on to his side and picked the blanket from the floor, wiped as much of the muck from him as he could, then cast the blanket over the Seriatt. Delgado then bent the dead medic's legs at the knees and pushed the head and upper body forward to make it look as if it was himself, sleeping in a foetal position. He stepped across the room to the door, and turned to look back at the body. It was quite convincing.

He went to the clothes he had stripped from the Seriatt and quickly pulled on the dead *vilume*'s trousers and cape. He looked down at himself, then pulled up the hood. It was deep and dark and, he hoped, would hide his human features.

With time pressing, Delgado had no time to ponder strategies. He turned, checked that the corridor remained empty, then walked out of the cell.

Following the numerous traces he perceived, Delgado proceeded warily, thrusting his hands inside the opposite sleeve to conceal his comparatively soft human hands. After walking just a few metres he passed a table, behind which sat three *mourst* enforcers. They were playing a game of some kind which involved placing counters on sticks. One of them glanced at him and called something in Seriatt as he passed, but but Delgado continued to walk, and the *mourst* returned to his game without further challenge.

The maze of corridors was virtually deserted. He saw occasional Seriatts pass through others running perpendicular to the main tunnel he was in, but most were in pairs or small groups and engaged in conversation, or simply not close enough to become suspicious of him.

The sense of mass presence he felt was increasingly strong. It had to be the theatre where Cascari and Michael were to fight. He refocused his nobics, trying to gain awareness of his position in relation to the source. Despite their weakening state, he felt certain that the strength of presence was concentrated somewhere beyond the white walls to his left. This also tied in with the fact that all the Seriatts he had so far seen had been heading in this direction, as if going towards the same location.

The corridor floor began to slope upwards and became wider, and he felt as if he was entering a more important, more frequently used area. He heard voices, and when he reached the next corner he almost collided with a group of *mourst*. He began walking in the same direction as a group of maybe thirty of forty of them. Others were visible in the distance and, although he did not want to look, he sensed the presence of other groups behind him. There appeared to be a mix of *mourst*, *conosq* and *vilume*, all – with the exception of some of the *vilume* – talking and laughing in their uniquely Seriattic way, in a cacophony of *mourst* growls and more shrill *conosq* vocalisations. The sounds echoed off the hard walls and floor, their footfalls an irregular percussion.

Delgado looked up and saw that around two hundred metres ahead the corridor curved to the left, and that the quality of light on the right-hand wall indicated an exit leading into the open air not far ahead. The collective Seriattic traces were increasingly strong, and he realised he was getting closer to the crowd. He also began to distinguish traces whose origins he was unable to identify. While they seemed to be fundamentally *mourst*, they possessed a particularly raw, basal flavour.

As he walked around the curve in the corridor, it became brighter and wider. In the distance he could see lines of Seriatts queuing at black iron gates set into an arch, slowly filing through turnstiles. *Mourst* enforcers stood at either side of these gates, impassively observing those passing through. Light flooded into the tunnel from beyond the gates, the glare blurring away definition of shape and casting a diffused grid of shadow across the floor.

As he walked up the slope towards the gates, Delgado saw a

narrow arch in the wall to the left. He tried to make the most of his failing nobics but they were uncooperative, and he had to open several more streams before he was able to focus them as he wished. Even then they seemed unwilling to converge, reluctant to cooperate. When eventually they came to him, his head spinning slightly, the indications were strong, and when he reached the entry he walked into it with confidence.

The corridor was very narrow and seemed very old. As it sloped down towards a long flight of stone steps the noise from the wide corridor behind him faded rapidly, to the extent that Delgado could hear his own breathing as he walked. It was also much darker, illumination provided only by small lamps occasionally suspended by chains from the centre of the ceiling.

There was a damp, musty smell, and silver streaks of water and patches of lichen coated the walls. The steps were shallow and uneven. In the corners of some were small puddles and, with no handrail to steady him, Delgado almost slipped several times.

He paused and looked behind him as he reached a point at which his shoulders were level with the top step. Looking back, he could see Seriatts moving along the wider corridor outside. He was thankful to find that he was not being followed.

As he approached the bottom of the steps, Delgado sensed a strong *mourst* trace. He slowed down, creeping forward until he was just two or three steps from the bottom, then leaned forward to look around the corner.

He saw a small room approximately three metres square, divided by iron bars that stretched from wall to wall and floor to ceiling, with a gate at the centre of this partition. Beyond it were three dark, ancient-looking tunnels constructed from large square blocks of stone. A *mourst* guard sat on a stool in the right-hand corner near the railings; the Seriatt was leaning against the wall, asleep, legs crossed in front of him, hands together on his lap. As well as the mass presence he had so clearly distinguished since awakening, beyond the gate Delgado could also perceive Cascari and Michael, their emotional traces sharp enough to cut through the rest.

Delgado took another step, but his right foot slid forward on a small damp patch and he fell backwards, crying out as he hit the hard edge of one of the steps.

The *mourst* woke with a start and leaped to his feet. He appeared uncertain what to do for a few moments, as if momentarily unsure of his surroundings, and when he looked down at the sprawling Delgado he glanced at the tunnel behind the human, as if believing this to be some kind of prank played by colleagues.

Delgado saw an opportunity in the *mourst*'s uncertainty and, despite the pain in his back, he jumped to his feet. As Delgado rushed towards him the *mourst* took a step back, mouth slightly open, and reached out with one arm as if this alone would be enough to counter the human's advance. But Delgado was too quick and too determined. He grabbed the *mourst*'s wrist, spun the Seriatt around and pushed him hard against the wall. Delgado gripped the *mourst*'s coarse, wiry hair in his left fist while pressing the creature against the stone wall with his right hand. The *mourst* turned his head to one side as if trying to look back, but was unable to do so. The *mourst* began to speak, but the sentence was cut short as Delgado pounded the Seriatt's head against the stone wall.

Eventually, Delgado allowed the Seriatt's body to slide to the floor. He stooped, checked that the *mourst* was dead, then felt the corpse in search of a weapon. He found a small gun that looked similar to a short-stem rifle, but which was almost as compact as a sidearm. It seemed a simple enough device, and Delgado tucked it into his cape pocket before continuing to search the body. He found a suede pouch to which half a dozen large keys were attached by a metal hoop. He unclipped the keys, climbed a few steps to check again that no Seriatts were approaching along the tunnel, then walked over to the gate.

He muttered something to himself about it being typical when it was the last key on the fob that fitted, the oiled mechanism within the lock clicked precisely as he turned the key. The gate squeaked slightly as Delgado opened it. He stepped through, closed the gate and locked it again behind him.

He turned and looked at the three tunnels. The mass of Seriattic consciousness was all around him, almost overwhelming, and made it impossible to establish which might be the most appropriate route to take. He closed his eyes and took several deep breaths as he focused on the traces he perceived. A moment later he pulled the gun from his cape pocket, checked it was armed and ready, then pulled up the hood and proceeded into the cold darkness of the central tunnel.

The tunnel curved gently to the right, the walls glossy with the moisture that seeped between the large stone blocks. Delagado's feet crunched on the damp, gritty floor.

As he walked, he began to perceive an odd scent. He paused briefly and listened. He could hear voices ahead. Although he was unable to distinguish what they were saying or in which language, he recognised the tones as *mourst.*

He moved across to the right side of the tunnel and glanced in both directions. Deciding that unobstructed vision was likely to come in more useful than the slight element of surprise he might gain by wearing it, he pulled the hood from his head again and continued to walk stealthily.

The curve sharpened and Delgado proceeded more warily, edging sideways with the damp wall behind him, the gun held out to his right. He sensed both Cascari and Michael; not directly ahead, but somewhere close, somewhere behind him. He edged a little further around the bend and the tunnel straightened out, leading into a square chamber a hundred metres or so ahead. Constructed from the same large blocks of stone as the tunnels, it was much wider and higher, with a huge arch on each side, beyond which lay impenetrable shadow. Motes of dust drifted through four broad columns of sunlight passing through circular holes in the ceiling, highlighting areas of the chamber's cobbled floor.

Within the chamber were two *mourst*. They wore singlets and short skirts of brown, beaten leather that revealed much of their tough, dark skin. On their feet were open-toed leather sandals, while around their waists were broad fabric sashes from which hung numerous pouches of various sizes. Each also carried a short silver baton, the tips of which glowed faintly. Traditional leather whips were hung over their backsides like coiled serpents.

Delgado absorbed these details quickly, for the things that captured his attention most were the caged animals the *mourst* were tending. Made of thick iron bars, each cage was set on top of a wooden base with steps leading from the chamber's cobbled floor up to the wide gate in each cage. The animals within the cages bore a resemblance to *mourst* – but a resemblance was all.

Although a couple of the creatures were standing, they were hunched forward, their spines arched, yet each was still easily twice as tall as a human male. They were naked, the dark skin of these animals more scaly and visibly tougher than that of normal *mourst*. Their limbs and torsos were long and extremely muscular and their necks were also longer than normal, curving forward. Ridges of vertebrae were visible from the tail to the base of the skull. Their heads and faces were noticeably smaller than normal *mourst*, their ears set lower and their mouths tighter. The ridges of ligament at their necks were particularly broad. Three rows of short, pointed teeth were set close together in both the upper and lower gums. They were wild animals that seemed to represent the distilled, primeval characteristics of every modern *mourst*, or perhaps mutations of them.

One of the creatures turned in its cage, raised a short stubby tail and defecated on to a floor already covered with urine and faeces. It then sat on the pile of straw in the corner and began to gnaw on a raw thigh of some fresh carcass, which was attached by a thin sheet of misshapen skin. The meat flopped about as if still alive as the *mourst* manipulated its meal with its long, gnarled hands.

One of the *mourst* tending the creatures walked to another of the cages, within which one of the animals lay sleeping, curled foetus-like on piss-soaked straw. The *mourst* drew the baton from its belt, thrust it between the bars of the cage and thumbed a button on its haft. A vivid blue charge leaped from its tip and shocked the creature into consciousness. It jumped to its feet screaming and thrashing, kicking at the bars and rattling the cage with a ferocity that startled even Delgado. Its reaction stirred its brethren into similar activity.

After its initial outburst, the creature calmed a little and began to move, snarling and drooling, towards the *mourst* who had applied the charge. The Seriatt outside the cage remained steadfast as the wild creature approached and, when it was only half a metre or so away from him, he issued another bolt to its mouth, the power of which flung it against the opposite side of the cage. The other creatures became increasingly agitated, shrieking hoarsely and throwing themselves against the sides of their own cages, making the metal bars rattle.

Another *mourst* keeper stood on the opposite side of the cage to the first, whip and baton drawn. He stepped forward and unlocked the gate, tentatively pushed it open, then quickly took a few steps back. The animal moved warily towards the open gate on all fours, snarling and spitting as it eyed the two *mourst* awaiting it. Slowly the creature descended the steps and, when it reached the chamber floor, the *mourst* cracked their whips and discharged their batons, guiding it to the right and out of Delgado's line of vision. He heard numerous chains rattling, the sound of grinding metal and stone, and what he thought was a rich but slightly discordant fanfare from a chorus of brass-sounding instruments, and the sound of a cheering, jeering crowd. Delgado heard the grinding sound again, and the two *mourst* reappeared, coiling their whips as they returned to a table near the cages, where they began cutting a leg from a carcass with a cleaver with which to feed one of the other creatures.

Delgado extended his hyperconsciousness as far as he was able. He sensed both Cascari and Michael, and in close proximity to them the raw traces emanating from the basal creature the *mourst* had just released. There were others, too, but these he was unable to identify. Both of the young men's traces were strongly flavoured by heady combinations of fear, apprehension and arousal: they were classic combat indicators. For the first time he could also sense Ashala and Osephius. One of them was simultaneously fearful and angry, the other sensed approaching victory.

He would have to work quickly.

Delgado checked the gun in his hand once more, pulled up the cape's hood, and strode purposefully into the chamber.

The two *mourst* did not hear Delgado approaching as they enthusiastically butchered the carcass, watched by caged, salivating creatures. He was only around ten metres away when one of them turned towards the solid wooden table between the *mourst* and Delgado, upon which their various butchering implements lay, and saw him standing in one of the circles of light.

The *mourst*'s expression changed to one that Delgado thought represented surprise or puzzlement, but he did not have time for such analysis of Seriattic facial expression. He simply raised the gun and fired.

The weapon released a narrow stream of potent ammunition with minimal recoil. Delgado sprayed a wide area of the chamber, killing both *mourst* instantaneously and shredding the remains of the dead animal at which they had been hacking, the wooden table was virtually destroyed. When he stopped firing he looked at the small weapon and reflected calmly on its good balance and quality of construction. Unpredictable and bizarre they may be, but Seriatts were undoubtedly fine craftsmen.

The caged creatures stared at him, silent, wary and still. Above him a small bird fluttered from one dark corner of the chamber to another, briefly passing through one of the shafts of sunlight. The *mourst* corpses smoked thinly.

Delgado looked to his right. In the section of chamber wall previously obscured from view was a large iron gate. He walked across to it and peered through the bars.

The gate was set within a deep stone recess, beneath the spectator tiers, with high walls on either side and a section above. But immediately beyond was the flat, sand-covered expanse of a battle arena. The stone tiers of the amphitheatre surrounding the arena were packed with Seriatts, who were shaded from the sun by vast sheets of pale fabric suspended between huge stone columns. A commentator – it sounded like a *conosq* – was speaking excitedly about events to come. On the far side of the arena, Delgado could see a group of figures.

Screens strategically placed to offer the audience the best available view switched from showing advertisements for a beverage of some sort to close-ups of the combatants. There were five of them, watched over by a dozen *mourst* enforcers who were also standing in the arena. One of the combatants was a hulking beast the like of which Delgado had never seen before. Apparently female, it was incredibly muscular, around three metres tall with a heavy brow and considerable underbite that gave it a particularly menacing appearance. This was enhanced by the chainmail armour it wore and the huge club that was clutched in its right hand. It roared, large veins standing prominent in its thick neck, its biceps flexing as it tossed the club impatiently from one hand to the other.

The second warrior was a Lyugg male. He wore numerous gold chains around his neck, and the front of his leather tunic was encrusted with brooches that looked like metallic scabs. From a belt around his waist hung a number of ornately carved and jewel-encrusted daggers. Next to the Lyugg warrior was a small, swarthy-skinned humanoid wearing simple garments of leather and fabric, stockings and lightweight knee-high boots. Cradling a loaded crossbow, this creature looked proud and confident in his proficiency, prowess and athleticism, but to Delgado's eye he lacked the raw fighting potency of his counterparts. Agility and sleight of hand were not likely to help him here.

There were two other figures. They wore armoured suits of polished silver, matching helms and thick leather gauntlets with spiked knuckles. One clutched a mace that looked too large and heavy for him to use effectively, while the other rested his hands on the pommel of a broadsword, the tip of which was stuck in the sand. Although the eye slits of the helms were narrow and dark, Delgado knew who they were.

The animal the *mourst* had released was sprinting across the arena towards the waiting warriors, alternating between running on all fours and a bipedal motion, its footfalls creating small explosions of coarse sand. The screens around the arena switched from the creature's snarling face to the combatants awaiting it and back again. The enforcers walked away from the warriors and concealed themselves behind tall wooden screens in the arena wall. As the animal got closer, the warrior with the crossbow bent over, placed its tip against the floor and drew back the bowstring. He knelt and aimed carefully, but the first bolt he released missed its target by a wide margin. Trying to remain calm, he reached behind him and plucked another bolt from his quiver. Becoming more nervous as the wild creature bore down on him, he fumbled the reloading process, and before he could bring the weapon to bear a second time the animal was upon him, tearing at his throat.

The watching crowd cheered as a couple of the other warriors leaped forward and pounded and sliced at the beast, paying little heed to the needs of its victim, whose demise was hastened by the additional wounds they inflicted upon him. Weakened by blood loss as a result of the numerous deep wounds it had sustained, repeated blows broke the beast's limbs and shattered its skull. Within moments it was dead, its mutilated body slumped across that of its own victim.

The enforcers re-emerged from their shelter and herded the disparate group of warriors towards a platform in the arena, and bade them face an elaborate enclosure high above.

Delgado could not see clearly at first, but the display on the screen changed to show the figures sitting within the enclosure. It contained the Seriattic Administrators, Osephius and Ashala. All sat on huge, angular chairs, each of which seemed to be carved from a single block of dark, marble-like stone. Osephius kept looking at Ashala, his lascivious thoughts clear in his expression. Delgado only hoped he had not had an opportunity to assault her since his own eviction from the Chamber of Visions. Although, knowing Ash, she would not be an easy victim.

The display changed again to show the figures standing on the platform, then switched back to one of the *mourst* Proctors as he stood and began to address those within the amphitheatre, informing them of the forthcoming battle to decide the future Monosiell.

Delgado focused his hyperconsciousness directly on the two figures in the shining armoured suits, opening as many of the failing nobic streams as he dared. The mass consciousness of the watching crowd in the theatre blurred their definition, but he knew without doubt that the one holding the broadsword was Michael, while Cascari held the mace. As the *mourst* Administrator continued to speak, Delgado looked around at the sides of the gate that separated him from the arena. To one side was a metal wheel about a metre in diameter. It had thick spokes; halfway along one of these protruded a short handle. A chain around the lower half of the wheel's rim ran up to a series of smaller wheels high in the chamber, with more chains running through wheels across the top of the gate. He hurried to the large wheel, took the stubby handle in both hands and began to turn it quickly. After only half a turn anticlockwise it would move no more, and so he began to turn it clockwise. After taking up a small amount of slack the clattering chains became taut and the resistance increased. He redoubled his effort and the huge gate to the arena began to slide through the stone groove in the floor into which it was set.

When the gate was open, Delgado ran across the chamber to the two dead *mourst* and picked up their batons and one of the whips. He grabbed the key and went towards the cages. The *mourst*-like creatures within them hissed and spat as he approached. Delgado sensed a wariness within them towards the strange animal that had killed their captors. He checked himself and began to walk more slowly, stopping a metre or so from the nearest cage. The hunched animal it contained bared its innumerable, needle-like teeth as it eyed him, a line of thick grey saliva trailing from one corner of its slightly quivering mouth.

Delgado took a step forward and, although the creature hunkered slightly, he felt that somewhere at its core it was respectful of him, and knew that he meant it no harm. He noticed that the creature kept glancing towards the two batons in his left hand. In the arena the crowd cheered at something the *mourst* Administrator said, and then even more loudly. It seemed that more combat had begun. Delgado swore furiously: he could not remember when time had last been his friend.

He walked further around the cage towards its gate, the animal within it slowly turning its head as it watched him.

Clutching the whip firmly in his right hand, Delgado slowly crouched, then flung the two batons away on to a pile of straw heaped in one corner of the chamber. The animal looked at the implements where they lay for some seconds, then looked back to Delgado.

Delgado took a step towards the cage and, moving quickly and with confidence, reached out with one hand, inserted the key into the lock and turned it. A series of loud clicks echoed around the chamber as the mechanism worked, and Delgado pushed open the door of the cage.

The animal remained motionless, maintaining eye contact with Delgado. Then, still watching him, it began to move slowly forwards, then suddenly ran through the gate and down the steps. It stopped abruptly at the bottom, leaning forward as if about to get down on all fours, as if unnerved by its sudden release from captivity. It gazed warily at Delgado for a moment before glancing at the discarded batons lying on the nearby pile of hay. Attracted by another sudden surge in noise, it looked towards the arena. It seemed to sniff, and its long black tongue briefly lapped the air.

Suddenly the animal began to run, its pace far greater than its somewhat contorted appearance would have indicated possible. Delgado watched the creature as it passed through the open gate. It slowed for a moment, as if gauging its surroundings, then sprinted out of the shadowy recesses and into the sun, heading towards the figures on the other side of the arena. Delgado quickly ran to the other cages and released the other creatures, which followed the first without hesitation.

As Delgado tucked the gun into the back of the waistband of his trousers and picked up the two batons, he hoped his judgement was correct, and that the creatures would attack the easiest targets first. If he was right about the identities of Cascari and Michael – and he was sure he was – their armour should buy them some time. But whether it would be enough, he could not know.

★

Delgado began to run across the arena towards Michael and Cascari. As soon as he left the shadowy alcove the ferocity of the sun was breathtaking, and the heat of the sand burned through the soles of his boots.

After just half a minute Delgado began to feel short of breath, the sand in the arena seeming to suck at his feet, making every step an effort. His head began to throb dully, as if the blood in his veins had thickened. He tried to assign nobics to stamina, but they were unresponsive. Red-faced, sweating, gripping the batons in one hand and the whip in the other, he struggled on. Ahead of him, the animals he had just released had already reached their prey.

The three creatures acted as a pack instinctively, first targeting the huge warrior with the club: while she was the largest, she also wore the least armour. The warrior lashed out uselessly with her primitive weapon as, undeterred by her size, the creatures attacked, their sharp teeth easily piercing her thick flesh. Blood blossomed from numerous wounds as the creature roared and swung her primitive weapon wildly. At the same time as one of the *mourst*-like animals leaped on to the ogre's back, another went for her throat. As the warrior stood and took a few steps backwards, arms flailing, the third *mourst* hung from one of her thick, muscular arms, the creature's teeth sunk deep into her bicep.

Behind the Lyugg warrior, who held a long-bladed dagger in each hand and had adopted a fighting stance, Michael and Cascari faced each other, as if each was waiting for the other to begin the combat, ignoring the battle taking place next to them. Michael stood with his arms outstretched, broadsword pommel gripped in both hands with the tip of its wide blade pointing skywards. Opposite him, Cascari gripped the mace in readiness, but allowed the weapon's head to rest on the sand, as if it was simply too heavy for him to lift. Despite Michael's apparent confidence, Delgado sensed fear and uncertainty in both young men.

The frenzied creatures began to devour the now dead warrior as Delgado passed them. Cascari and Michael both turned their heads to look at him, their polished helms hiding their faces. Michael lowered the broadsword a little as Delgado placed one hand on his shoulder and turned him around so they were facing each other. Delgado then reached out and pulled Cascari towards him. He peered through the slits in their faceplates, trying to see their eyes, then thumped the side of each helm. 'Get these things off,' he growled. He glanced around the arena as the two men removed their leather gauntlets and unfastened the clips attaching their helms to the shoulder armour. When they were off Delgado could see that both of them were covered with sweat with a dark band across their grimy faces that matched the shape of the helms' eye-slits. Michael managed to maintain his defiant and proud air, despite obvious fatigue. Cascari looked dehydrated, but was determined to match his opponent.

'Don't do this,' Delgado pleaded. He looked from one to the other of them. 'You're brothers. You're my sons. We have to get out of here.'

Michael looked bitter. 'I'm no son of yours, Delgado,' he sneered. 'I'm the son of General William Myson, despite what some alien fortune teller might say.'

Delgado didn't reply but looked at each of them again. 'You can't do this. We *can* get out of here. Please.'

Michael laughed briefly and shook his head. 'Just how do you propose to do that, Delgado?' he asked. 'Look around you.' He indicated the huge amphitheatre, with its audience of thousands and the *mourst* enforcers standing nearby. 'You're surrounded by Seriatts. There is nowhere to go.' He adjusted his grip on his sword and looked at Cascari. 'Face it, Delgado. This is where one of us has to die.'

Delgado shook his head emphatically, gripping the hot metal of Michael's armour. 'No. This can't happen. I won't let you do this You have to see the stupidity of what you're suggesting.'

'But he's right,' said Cascari calmly, continuing to stare at Michael. 'There is nowhere to go. This is the end of the line. It's not about us, or what might or might not have happened in the past. It's about *mourst* honour. *Our* honour. They don't care about the human side of us.' He gestured towards the crowd with one hand. 'They just want another monarch, a figurehead to give them hope.'

Delgado shook his head. He felt his self-control slipping as he became increasingly desperate. 'You can't see it, can you?' he said to Michael. 'If you were Myson's son why would he put you in a position like this? You're here because no matter how much this place offers him, or how much he has at stake, you're *expendable*.'

Michael returned Cascari's gaze. 'You're not in Planetary Guidance now, Delgado,' he said. 'You're not even on the *Lex Talionis*. You're on Seriatt. You have no power here. Your opinions and values mean nothing. This is *our* territory.' He took a step back and lifted up his broadsword, ready to fight. 'Now, I suggest you take a step back and let us get on with what we have to do.'

Delgado took a step forward and positioned himself between the two young men, facing Michael. 'Look,' he said, 'I'm just not prepared to let you . . .' Delgado called out as a shadow reared up behind Michael. Michael ducked instinctively and the creature flew over him, colliding bodily with Cascari, knocking him to the arena floor. The *mourst* reared, hunched, opened its powerful jaws wider than seemed possible given the small size of its head, and bit deep into Cascari's abdomen just below the right side of his ribcage. Its strong jaw crushed his armour, its teeth penetrating the chainmail around his waist.

Delgado activated both batons and, despite the risk of their charges hitting Cascari, he unleashed a powerful bolt that hit the *mourst* and threw it ten or twelve metres into the air. When it came to rest on the hot sand there was tumult from the crowd. The animal jumped up quickly and turned towards Michael, crouching and snarling, revealing its sharp, discoloured teeth.

Then it pounced again.

Its lean and muscular form was defined in silhouette against the sun's glare. Delgado saw long claws extend from its hands and feet as it flew through the air, curved talons that glinted like metal.

Michael raised the broadsword and lunged, then staggered back several steps as the creature became impaled upon the weapon. The sword entered its body at the abdomen and emerged just above its stubby, vestigial tail, its weight and momentum carrying it halfway down the wide blade as it fell towards him. The creature emitted a thin, high-pitched cry and thrashed wildly for a moment, its thick blood filling the broadsword's runnel and flowing on to Michael's hands. Michael allowed the heavy animal to drop to the arena floor. By the time it hit the coarse sand it was dead.

As Michael placed one foot on the dead creature's chest and pulled his weapon from its body, Delgado turned towards the other creature. It was circling Cascari on all fours, prowling like a big cat. Its dark mouth salivated, its eyes were black pools. Delgado raised the batons to unleash another charge, but they slipped from his sweating palms into the sand. He cursed, fumbled with the whip, and when he looked up again he saw Michael running towards the creature.

The animal was focused on Cascari, sniffing at the blood, its body heaving as it hungrily lapped the air. Michael yelled as he raised the broadsword high over his left shoulder, then brought the blade slashing down. The animal cowered as a shard of sunlight glinted off the blood-stained metal, and with the gentlest of slicing sounds the weapon's honed edge cleanly separated its head from its body.

Delgado rushed over to Cascari and crouched next to him.

Gently, Delgado lifted the torn chainmail and fabric around the wound, and was relieved to see that it was less serious than he had feared. He looked at Cascari's face. He was regaining consciousness.

'Cascari. Cascari. Can you hear me?'

Cascari groaned, swore quietly, clutched his side and tried to look down at the wound.

'It's OK,' said Delgado. 'It's not as bad as you think.'

'Easy enough for you to say,' the young man replied weakly.

'Do you think you can stand?'

Cascari considered for a moment. 'Yeah, I think so. Might need a hand, though.' Delgado attempted to help the young man to his feet, but his pain was too great and he collapsed back on to the sand.

Delgado looked up at Michael who was now standing beside him, his face was lost in the glare of the sun above him. 'Come on,' he said. 'Help me get him up.'

'You don't get it, do you?' said Michael quietly, remaining motionless. 'Where do you think you can run? Look around you. There's nowhere to go. You think I killed that creature to save you?' He snorted. 'You're a fool.'

Delgado looked down at Cascari, who seemed to have slipped into unconsciousness once more. He was vaguely aware of a faint metallic scraping sound, and when he looked up he saw that Michael had pulled the blade of his broadsword from the sand. Sunlight highlighted the grime that now coated the wide blade. Michael's black outline changed shape as he raised the sword. Delgado yelled as the young man groaned throatily – a distinctly *mourst*-like utterance – then thrust the heavy weapon forward.

The wide sword entered Cascari's body at the waist, the weighty metal blade easily cutting through the soft tissues. Delgado cried out and Cascari groaned deeply, his back arching. Delgado heard Ashala's scream penetrate the overall tumult of the Seriattic crowd. As Michael took a step back, pulling the soiled blade from Cascari's body, the watching Seriatts yelled and cheered.

Delgado cried out and bent over Cascari, peering frantically into the young man's eyes. His face was already waxy and pale, so quickly his life seemed to be ebbing from him. Cascari rolled his head to one side and dark fluid trailed from the corner of his mouth on to the hot sand.

Overwhelmed with grief, trembling and sobbing, Delgado mumbled unintelligibly as he looked desperately for a way to help his son. But he knew that in reality the young man was beyond help. All he could hope to do was alleviate Cascari's suffering in his final moments.

Overcome with years of unexpressed emotion, Delgado cried, his entire body consumed by frustration, pain and love. His face was red, wet with tears, his body convulsing as he gasped and choked. His forehead ached. He coughed and snorted, spraying spit and snot as he was sucked into despair.

After a few moments, Delgado looked up at Michael. 'You've just killed your brother,' he said hoarsely, gasping for breath. 'How could you do that? Don't you feel anything? Don't you care that he's your own flesh and blood?' He looked down at Cascari again and shook his head. 'Why?'

'Because I had to,' replied Michael boldly. 'Because I want what's rightly mine and because the Seriatts expect it. Now I have given myself honour in their eyes, I will be their Monosiell. I've given *mourst* honour to both of us. He should thank me before he dies.'

Delgado bowed his head. A tear ran down his nose and hung absurdly from its tip. He felt Cascari move slightly and looked down at him. Clearly in great pain, Cascari was barely able to speak.

'Looks like this is it,' he murmured. 'Not quite the ending we had planned . . .' He gasped and closed his eyes in pain.

Delgado shook his head. 'It can't end like this. It just isn't right. All that we've done. All that we've fought for.'

'We knew the risks.' Cascari paused, gulping air. Colour was draining from him visibly, his blood merging with the sand in front of Delgado's knees. 'We gambled and lost,' whispered Cascari. 'No more than that. The odds were never in our . . .' He choked again and rolled his head to one side, spitting thick, dark phlegm.

Delgado looked up. Some of the *mourst* enforcers were gazing impassively at him from the side of the arena, while others were watching Michael, who had begun to parade before the Seriattic crowd. *Mourst* roared in congratulation of his victory, while *conosq* and *vilume* emitted shrill ululations of celebration.

Movement in the ornate enclosure suddenly attracted Delgado's attention. It was Ash, struggling with Osephius as she tried to extricate herself from his grip. He grasped her right forearm tightly, but was forced to release her when she bit his wrist. Once free, she immediately ran to the front of the enclosure, clambered over the wide stone parapet and jumped the three or four metres to the arena floor.

As she leaped to her feet and ran towards him, Delgado looked down at Cascari who was now unconscious. Ashala rushed up to Delgado, knelt and put her arms around him. She was crying, her face pink, her eyes swollen. Delgado clung to her as they looked down at Cascari, his wet cheek pressed against hers. Around them in the blood-soaked sand, lay slain creatures, mutilated bodies, discarded, soiled weapons. 'This can't be how it ends,' he choked. 'No man should have to watch his son die. It just isn't right.' *It's your own fault. You have done this*. 'No, no!'

Ashala shook her head. 'There was nothing you could do to stop it,' she said, fighting her grief. 'We've been working towards getting him here for so long, waiting for the right opportunity, the right time. This is just the way it was meant to be. He's half-Seriattic *mourst*, Delgado. It's ironic, but there's part of him that will want it this way.'

Delgado looked at Michael. He was absorbing the crowd's adoration as the commentator's words continued to echo around the theatre. Delgado felt for the gun, but it was no longer there. He looked back across the arena, following the path he had taken across the sand, but could not see the weapon. Instead he saw Cascari's mace lying only a few metres from him. He pushed Ashala away, stood, and walked slowly over to the cumbersome weapon. He picked it up and began to walk towards Michael, gauging its weight in his hands. The young man was facing away from him, waving to the adoring Seriatts.

Realising his intention, Ash jumped to her feet and chased after him. 'No, Delgado,' she cried out, wiping tears from her cheeks. 'That won't make things right.' She grasped him by the left elbow and tried to turn him around. 'You can't kill him, Delgado. *He's* your son too.'

Delgado tried to shake her off. The expression on his sweaty face was grim and determined. 'No,' he growled. 'I fathered him, but he's not my son. He's Myson's. He *killed* my son. And now he's killed Cascari there's nothing to stop Myson having an influence on Seriatt. We can't let that happen. We have to stop them. I've got nothing to lose now.'

Ash glanced back. She saw heavy *mourst* enforcers running across the arena towards them, struggling to make progress in the heavy sand. Behind them she saw Osephius jump down into the arena as she had done. She turned back to Delgado, becoming increasingly desperate. 'They'll kill you if you attack Michael now,' she said. 'But think about it for a minute, Delgado. You're his father. That will count for something with the Seriatts. You've lost one son already. Don't kill the one you've only just found.'

Ash looked back again, and saw that the *mourst* enforcers were quickly catching up with them, commanding them to stop, but the enforcers had been overtaken by Osephius, who was considerably lighter on his feet.

'You've lost, Delgado,' he shouted as he caught up with them. 'Accept it. If you kill Michael now you'll throw this planet into chaos. Probably the entire region. It could lead to all-out war. You want to be responsible for that? Michael's their best hope.'

Ashala tugged at Delgado's arm. 'Shit, Delgado, he's right,' she said. 'Listen to him. If you kill Michael you've lost everything. Sure, Myson might be able to get a grip on this place now, but as Michael's father you could negotiate with the Seriatts. You might still be able to have some influence over what happens here.'

Delgado stopped walking and turned. He stared at Cascari's body lying on the sand. Osephius stopped a few metres away from Delgado, careful to keep out of reach of the mace. The enforcers continued to lumber towards them.

'Face up to it, Delgado,' said Osephius, his mouth twisted in a conceited, victorious sneer. 'This is the end of the road. Give up now and retain some of your pride. If you have any.'

'Why would I want my pride when I've lost my son?' sneered Delgado huskily, his eyes red-rimmed. 'He's been the focus of my life; everything we've lived for has been centred on him.'

'Did you ever tell him that?'

'I didn't need to. He's always know how important he is.'

'That's what they all say, Delgado. All those fathers who think their kids just *know*, like they're all Seriattic Oracles. How much were you really there for him? Did you ever ask him what *he* wanted? You've got a choice now, Delgado. You can either try to heroically avenge Cascari's death, or we can make a deal. Who knows, we might work well together here. If you really are Michael's father, then that will carry considerable weight, like your pretty friend says.'

As Delgado opened his mouth to reply, shadows were suddenly erased and the temperature dropped as the sun was obscured by cloud. The Seriattic crowd seemed to fall eerily quiet, then a solitary *conosq* began to cry, a tremulous sound that was subtly different to both the recent celebrations and the expressions of grief he had heard at the racing facility. Other *conosq* began to make a similar noise. Delgado heard several *mourst* shout in what he recognised as fear and anger.

Something had changed.

Delgado saw many Seriatts looking up into the sky, and when he followed their gaze he saw that it was not cloud that had hidden the sun. Seeing the expression on Delgado's face change, Osephius turned to see what he was looking at, as did the *mourst* enforcers who were standing behind him.

In the sky were several huge, elongated vessel, from which long, broad tubes extended, writhing like serpents and changing colour in concert with the pulsating bodies of the craft. From the tips of these structures innumerable smaller vessels of a similar design emerged. These spread out in all directions, in turn releasing small alien figures, creatures with slender limbs and large heads, firing the weapons they carried as they descended slowly through the air. The larger craft extended thicker tentacles that spat dark spheres, which released intense shock waves just above the rooftops or exploded on impact with the ground.

Delgado knew immediately that it was the Sinz. As he watched he saw some of the smaller ships pass behind the towers from which the fabric shading the spectators was suspended and it was then that he realised the truth of Oracle Entuzo's earlier vision: the Sinz were not invading Earth, they were invading Seriatt.

Everyone in the theatre was looked towards the sky as thousands of Sinz craft descended through the Seriattic atmosphere. Many began hurrying towards exits, fleeing to their homes and families. Michael walked slowly past Delgado, his broadsword dropped in disbelief. Despite the implications of the situation, Delgado felt immense satisfaction when he saw the young man's incredulity. Given the reactions of Michael and Osephius, Myson wasn't instrumental in this invasion by the Sinz. Or if he was, then the two people closest to him had not been aware of the plans. It appeared that Michael himself may have been betrayed, and that his position on Seriatt was less secure than he had previously thought.

Delgado looked at Cascari's body again. Part of him wanted to be thankful that his son would be spared the horrors of the war that was undoubtedly coming to this world. Yet his death was something Delgado could not accept.

As those around him continued to stare at the invasion force, and although it pained him to leave his dead son's body behind, Delgado took Ashala's arm and pulled her close to him. 'Come with me,' he whispered. 'We might have a chance to do something yet.'

As they hurried through the Seriattic palace Delgado and Ash passed hundreds of Seriatts, who were running to see if the rumours of Seriatt's invasion were true. Consumed with fear, the Seriatts took little notice of the two humans going against the flow. Soon the place was deserted, with even the staunchest of *mourst* guards having deserted their posts to take up arms. Gunfire or explosions could occasionally be heard as Delgado and Ashala passed windows. Once they paused and looked outside. The sky was darkened by huge numbers of Sinz craft and swarms of descending Sinz troops. The invasion was under way in earnest.

When they reached the Chamber of Visions, Delgado smashed the door with the mace and hurried Ashala across the room, past the couch towards the time portal. They gazed at the object. It was beautiful, delicate, like a sculpture in drizzled gold. At such close range, the field within the frame could be heard fizzing gently as it shimmered, spirals of colour swirling upon it like oil on water.

'If we go through,' said Delgado quietly, 'we can escape.'

Ashala glanced at him. 'Are you serious? Even the Seriatts aren't sure this thing works. Instead of sending us someplace else it might just rip us to pieces.'

Delgado spoke grimly. 'I'm serious all right. It might give us a new start. Maybe even a chance to put things right.'

'Yeah. Or it could just kill us.'

'Well, that's a possibility. I'm not sure that would be such a bad thing anyway.'

Ash looked at him again. 'You don't mean that.'

Delgado shrugged. 'No? I'm not so sure. I'm tired of fighting, Ash. Tired of having to go against the odds. Tired of *losing*. Besides, if we stay here we're probably as good as dead anyway. I'm not sure what the Sinz want with this place but I don't think they'd be to interested in anything we might have to offer.'

There was a pause as they both considered the possibilities and options. Ash stared at the gate, then said, 'You really want to go through it?'

Delgado nodded, a single, curt movement. 'Yes.'

'Right. OK.' She took a deep breath. 'If that's what you think we should do, then I'm with you. All the way. We should test it first, though. See what happens.' She turned, looked around the chamber and took one of the small candles from its holder. 'Ready?' He nodded, and she tossed the candle towards the rippling field. It trembled briefly as the candle passed through it, a distortion appearing in its rippling surface for a moment, then it returned to its former state. They felt a brief breath of warm wind in the chamber. One of the candles on the wall flickered, another was extinguished.

'Not particularly conclusive,' she said with a sigh. 'Any idea where it might take us?'

Delgado shook his head. 'No. And it doesn't matter. Just as long as it's not here, not now.'

'Right. I guess we should go, then. Wherever.'

'Whenever.' Delgado reached out and took her small hand in his, then looked down at her. 'I love you,' he said gently.

Ashala's face reddened, highlighting freckles Delgado hadn't noticed before, and she looked back towards the sparkling portal before he saw the tears that welled.

They took a few moments to try to steel themselves for what might follow. Then, with no further words passing between them, they walked slowly towards the gate. A few seconds later a warm wind teased the flames of the candles in the Chamber of Visions, and Delgado and Ashala were gone.

Also by Martin Sketchley

THE AFFINITY TRAP

Vourniass Lycern – a conosq of the three-sex Seriattic race – holds the key to peace between Earth and Seriatt, and thus the continuation of the lucrative illegal arms trade conducted by General William Myson.

When Lycern decamps to the Affinity Group, Myson orders experienced Military Intelligence Officer Alexander Delgado to fetch her. Delgado, however, sees the mission as an opportunity to engender a much greater level of change.

But when he comes into contact with Lycern, Delgado faces his greatest ever challenge, the consequences of which have the ability to change his life – and potentially the future of Earth – forever.

ISBN 0 7434 6848 1
PRICE £6.99

CIRCULATING STOCK
PUBLIC LIBRARIES
BLOCK LOAN